BACKWARD-
FACING
MAN

An Imprint of HarperCollinsPublishers

BACKWARD-FACING MAN

a novel

Don Silver

This is a work of fiction. The characters and events in this book, with the exception of the extraordinary story of Patty Hearst and the SLA, are the products of imagination. I've taken the liberty of introducing theories about the U.S. government and some of the people whose stories connect up with the SLA, or who were on the periphery, theories that are not necessarily true or, at least, have not been proven.

BACKWARD-FACING MAN. Copyright © 2005 by Don Silver. All rights reserved. Printed in the United States of America. No part of this book may be used or reproduced in any manner whatsoever without written permission except in the case of brief quotations embodied in critical articles and reviews. For information, address HarperCollins Publishers, 10 East 53rd Street, New York, NY 10022.

HarperCollins books may be purchased for educational, business, or sales promotional use. For information, please write: Special Markets Department, HarperCollins Publishers, 10 East 53rd Street, New York, NY 10022.

FIRST EDITION

Designed by Cassandra J. Pappas
Photographs by Melanie Wellner

Library of Congress Cataloging-in-Publication Data

Silver, Don, 1956–
    Backward-facing man: a novel/Don Silver.
        p.   cm
    ISBN-10: 0-06-081928-6
    ISBN-13: 978-0-06-081928-6
        1. Loss (Psychology)–Fiction.   2. Betrayal–Fiction.   I. Title.

PS3619.I547B33   2005
813'.6—dc22   2005040883

05   06   07   08   09 WBC/BVG 10 9 8 7 6 5 4 3 2 1

For Reg and Rob,
who left early

PART I

Foreword

I first met Patricia Campbell Hearst at a summer camp for girls when we were fourteen. Our mothers had been sorority sisters in the late forties, although, technically, neither was in college at the time. Finishing school would be a more accurate term for it, yet it hardly matters to the story I'm about to tell.

Catherine Campbell was raised in the suburbs of Atlanta, a world of debutantes and huge colonial houses with Corinthian columns, part of a white aristocracy, which only two generations earlier had owned slaves. It was the middle of World War II, two years before Catherine met her husband, Randy, the youngest son of William Randolph Hearst. My own mother, Agnes Rittenhouse, had been sent away to boarding school by her parents in Philadelphia because of a persistent interest she'd taken in a roguish fellow named Edward Prescott, my dad.

Over the next forty years, the two maintained a long-distance friendship in hundreds of letters they wrote each other, recording the events of their lives, describing in longhand their courtships and marriages, the houses they decorated, gossip about their neighbors, and, later, the accomplishments of their children. In the letters, they held close their disappointments, their quiet struggles with depression and substance abuse, their husbands' occasional infidelities and their eventual divorces.

I remember the scent of her stationery on the antique rolltop in my mother's bedroom mingling with my own curiosity to discover how joyful or wretched a woman's life could become. That one summer, Patty and I talked about our parents and boys and sex and babies whenever we got a private moment: awake in our bunks; standing side by side in lineup; sitting in a canoe near boys' camp, the low rumble of the engine and the smell of diesel fuel wafting toward us in the early autumn breezes through the white pines, the scent and sally of manhood.

Though we would have bristled at the suggestion, we were miniature versions of our mothers, living in that impossibly dry heat of our parents' unlived lives. In that single season, fired up by adolescence—raw and incredulous—we shared every thought, every emotion, every perception we had about the world. All the while, dark hints of what would happen spread over us like the shadow of an angry giant—our fathers' departures, our mothers' illnesses, our siblings' infirmities, our ambivalence about success and love and fairy-tale endings, even Patty's monstrous ordeal.

At the end of the camp, we were wrenched apart—her to the suburbs of San Francisco and me to Center City, Philadelphia, and, within a few months, we completely lost touch. The next summer, I went to Ocean City, New Jersey, and advanced my study of boys, while Patty stayed home and took riding lessons with her sisters. After that, my life was so crowded with crushes and rumors and adventures with new best friends, I thought about Patty only once before the kidnapping.

It was Thanksgiving, 1973. I was a freshman, home from college. My mother had just received one of Aunt Catherine's letters. "Winnie, you remember Patricia Hearst, don't you, dear?" We were in the kitchen. "She's going to marry her math teacher." I was nineteen, the age when parental comparisons to others elicit only hostility. It was my first year away from home, away from my parents' anger and the burden of the stultifying reputation of my family as a pillar of Philadelphia society. I remember for the first time feeling free and hopeful about my future, as yet unburdened by the conditions of my trust fund and the knowledge that the road to addiction that my father, my brother, and I would each travel is a highway, with few places to stop, pull over, or get off until it dead ends.

Had my mother and I actually finished our conversation that night, I might have told her that math teachers and marriage were of no interest to me, that I wanted nothing to do with careers, husbands, or babies, that it was my first year in college and I was just discovering drugs and Hemingway, Lawrence, and Forster. "I am a writer," I would have snapped, had I cared enough to say anything at all.

Three months later, there wasn't an adult in the world who hadn't heard about Patty's abduction. In New York City, where I was in school, Patty's image as an urban guerrilla was everywhere—on newsstands and telephone poles, on huge screens in department store windows and in Times Square. She was the topic of conversation between parents and children, husbands and wives, colleagues at work in subways, and strangers in coffee shops. There were sightings and tips, news flashes and documentaries about her childhood, interviews with teachers and old friends, urgent pleas from her grief-stricken parents and Steve Weed, Patty's jilted fiancé. Over the next twenty months, the nation watched, fascinated as my one-time best friend converted to radicalism, robbed a bank, became a fugitive, and, a year later, was captured, put on trial, convicted, and sent away to prison.

It turned out that everything Catherine Hearst told my mother about Patty was false. She didn't love her math teacher, and she only studied art history because she was bored out of her skull listening to her fiancé talk about philosophy. Much later, I came to understand that until her kidnapping, Patty was struggling with many of the same issues I was struggling with, including how to escape from under the long shadow of a prominent family, into the far more alluring glow of the counterculture.

After college, I went to graduate school in Iowa and then moved back to Manhattan, settling in a studio apartment in the East Village. After her release from federal prison, Patty married her bodyguard, Bernard Shaw, moved east, and became something of a celebrity, acting in several of John Waters's movies. I drifted between writing poems, composing songs, performing in a punk rock band, and waitressing on Wall Street. That same year my mother developed emphysema, and my father ran off with his secretary, drinking and gambling away most of his considerable fortune in Atlantic City.

After a two-year affair with coke, my brother entered rehab in Florida. When he emerged, he married the woman who led his twelve-step group and took over an investment company that my uncle Jack had started. I did my own little dance with coke and weed, balancing the two perfectly for a while, before falling in love with speedballs and downers, burning out my metabolism, and most likely depleting my lifetime reserve of seratonin. Though my brother kept asking me to, returning to Philly would have been painful. The waters had long ago covered over the place where my childhood had been.

I sent poems and short stories to literary magazines and wrote lyrics for a punk rock band. I lived on fast food and stayed up all night at places like Max's Kansas City and CBGB, fancying myself to be part of the downtown scene. Mornings, with the garment district trucks rumbling by, I'd take a couple Valium or a phenobarbital, pull the shades down, and wait for sleep. The day I turned thirty, I got a call from a man at the Glendale Trust Company who told me if I could provide proof of full-time employment, annual payments from my trust fund would begin. "They're rather large," he said, sounding a bit uncomfortable. It was a turning point. By then, my dreams had fizzled. When I wasn't manic about a new song or a hot new band forming, I was strung out, overwrought, and sleep starved. I was tired of waitressing and biding my time until we, meaning whatever drug-addicted temperamental musician I was working with, got a record deal.

I found a job with a company that made precision ball bearings, whose founders hated each other so vehemently that every employee had to declare their devotion to one and then suffer banishment from the other. In between answering the phone, I wrote complex technical descriptions of products for their catalog—a tedious and unaesthetic compendium of line drawings and grainy photographs—but in keeping with his promise, the man from Glendale Trust wired me $500,000 two weeks later. In my drug-addled state, keeping normal hours was impossible. During my second month, the brother I had aligned myself with gave me an unpaid month off so I could go to the Betty Ford Clinic, and when I returned, I was clean. Against everyone's advice, I kept the same friends, went to the same shitty showcases and art openings, and lived *in the same squalid apartment, rationalizing that all this would inspire me to keep writing. Only it didn't.*

In April 1996 my mother died. I knew her health had deteriorated, but I kept putting off visiting until it was too late. By then, she'd moved in with my brother and sister-in-law, who orchestrated a rotation of nurses who fed and bathed her, answered the phone, sent letters until she was no longer able to dictate, preparing her for what was, by all accounts, a painful way to leave this world. By the time my brother called and told me, she was beyond my reach in a haze of medication, hooked up to a respirator and sleeping in an oxygen tent.

The day she died, I carried several cartons of my most outrageous clothes to a thrift store and gave away my foldout couch. I put a folder of rejection slips and my journals into a suitcase and lugged it to the curb, where I waited for my brother's black BMW to whisk me back to Philadelphia. As soon as we crossed over from Jersey, I felt an odd release. My father had disgraced himself. Now, with my mother gone, I could finally declare defeat and return from exile without shame. As soon as I got home, my brother told me that as far as he was concerned, I could stay in the Prescott cottage in Merion as long as I liked.

Much to my surprise, the day before the funeral the Hearsts arrived. There was Aunt Catherine, a brittle-looking wisp of a woman hanging on to Patty's husband's arm, and my old camp friend, fuller in the face and heavier. As they stood side by side, I could see the resemblance between mother and daughter—their small frames, smooth pale foreheads, mouths turned down, and shoulders hunched as if they'd spent their lives avoiding things that had been hurled at them from behind.

The Hearst-Shaws lived just outside one of Connecticut's toniest towns, a place with high-end retail stores and trendy restaurants where beautiful people of all ages hurry from Pilates to therapy. Patty described it as a place where people shopped like it was always Christmas. Like most suburbanites of my generation, Patty spent her life shuttling her kids around, except she did it in a van that had been fitted with bulletproof windows, a communications center, and a satellite tracking system.

Once everyone left, Patty got her mother settled in the sunroom with a glass of sherry and sent Bernard out to pick up Chinese. She confided that although her husband was steady and dependable, he was a far cry from the men we dreamed about thirty years ago. *The man who marries money works hard for every cent.* Bernie had come along when the Hearst family was vulnerable, putting aside his meager career aspirations to become Patty's husband. A few years after they were married, he was made head of security for the Hearst Corporation.

It's a strange thing when the parent you most struggle with dies. You look around and you realize that the one who resembled you most, genetically, physically, psychologically, and temperamentally is gone, and you're completely, existentially alone. If nothing else, you stop performing. You give up trying to prove things. You do things you might not have done before. That night, Patty was attentive and kind. She went out of her way to keep my spirits up. As I went through my mother's closet, she recited lines from the play I'd written at Camp Tidewater. She insisted I tell her the names of any magazine or chapbook where my poems or stories had appeared. We saw each other like we were fourteen years old.

It was obvious that I needed a change. I'd come to detest the bearing company and I'd outgrown my cynical Lower East Side self. It was painfully clear that I hadn't achieved a whit of recognition as a writer, and with a fellow trust fund friend, it was unnecessary to pretend that without a job I'd starve. I was forty-two, with no husband, no kid, no career, and no significant artistic output to show for myself. Patty declared it was time for me to do some serious writing.

The following morning, Catherine Hearst, Bernard Shaw, and my friend, the heiress turned actress, went directly from the Four Seasons Hotel to the funeral, dressed to the nines, and stood in the rain with the rest of us. Before leaving, Patty took my hand and told me that she'd already talked to her agent and that she wanted us to do a book together. In the cemetery parking lot, with Bernard behind the wheel of the van and her mother staring straight ahead, she pitched me like a Hollywood agent.

The plot was simple. Her grandfather, William Randolph Hearst—tycoon, flaneur, would-be politician, and the father of modern journalism—would reflect on meetings he'd had with world leaders on the eve of World War II. Patty believed we could reconstruct them, *along with bromides from his diary, and create a kind of faux journal, a series of observations and made-up conversations with his minions that could have taken place aboard an elegant ocean liner in the late 1930s. "You'll come to Connecticut," she said, rain streaming from her umbrella. "I'll get his journals. Permissions will be no problem." I must have looked less than enthusiastic. "Historical fiction," she said confidently, as if that would elevate her proposition to art. Bernie tapped the horn lightly, and Patty leaned forward, kissing me on the cheek.*

I remember watching the van disappear. There was nothing really to think about. Aside from a few punk demos and some pathetic short stories that a classmate of mine had published in a postgraduate chapbook, I'd been completely without success in my avocation. I accepted the next morning, calling in my resignation to the bearing company, watering the plants in my mother's cottage, and taking my old Corolla to an Audi dealership on the Main Line. By dinnertime, I was driving a cobalt blue coupe up the Merritt Parkway.

Patty's house was a huge, white stucco box with fake pillars and a circular drive that wove around two huge oaks, the only large trees on the lot that had been spared by the developer. The structure was as plain and unimaginative as San Simeon, the Hearst castle, was grand—symmetrical, boxy, out of no particular architectural heritage, with an indoor swimming pool, gym, and media center in a wing that was invisible from the front. Patty set me up in a guest bedroom with vaulted ceilings, huge windows, and elaborate motion detectors. The structure of her life and the sophistication of her security system were such that I couldn't tell whether I was being protected or trapped inside. As soon as I got there I was sucked like lint into the Shaw household. I was asked to run errands, drive her girls to and from their activities, even "invited" to plan a meal, while my host flitted between meetings and personal appointments.

On the third day, Patty produced the old man's diaries, which she'd borrowed from her cousin George. I excused myself and returned to my mother's cottage in Pennsylvania. A week later, I deposited my share of the publishing advance, committing myself to writing a fictionalized account of the life of William Randolph Hearst, a truly loathsome man about whom way too much had already been written. Six months later, after a solo trip to San Simeon, a structure Aldous Huxley called "a monument to a faulty pituitary," I delivered a nauseatingly detailed three-hundred-page manuscript to Meredith Hutchinson, Patty's agent in Manhattan.

What Mattered Most was released to universally bad reviews. "Self-conscious and contrived," one magazine said. "A superficial account of an obnoxious human being, too sloppy to be a history book, and too boring to be a good novel," wrote the Times. The only good news was that it disappeared from the bookshelves in weeks, although, unfortunately for Patty, bad press stuck to the more famous of its two authors. "As if she hasn't sullied her family's name enough," wrote Esquire, a Hearst Corporation publication, "Ms. Hearst has once again stepped onto center stage with absolutely nothing to say."

One curious side note connects all this to the book you are holding. As part of the brief promotional tour the publisher arranged, Patty and I appeared on the Today Show. Under impossibly bright lights, with technicians moving in wide arcs and assistants carrying steaming cups of coffee, we each answered prepared questions in the most superficial way. And though the appearance was not my finest moment (like a fool, I wasted my fifteen minutes of fame nodding while Patty waxed nostalgic about Camp Tidewater), it was, nevertheless, how Lorraine Nadia found me.

Friday, March 13, 2000

"Facing backwards on a moving train," said the man sitting across from her, "is the story of my life." He set his paper on the bench seat beside him and looked out the window. It was early Friday morning, and the first jags of sunlight struck the glass-and-metal office buildings in the distance. She stared glumly at the headlines, sorry to be sitting in those bench seats that faced one another, sorry to be vulnerable in this way at this particular time, but there was nobody nearby when she first boarded. Now, bone tired and barely awake, there was no easy resting place for her eyes.

The backward-facing man was wearing a wrinkled plaid suit jacket; a black sweater; gray, grass-stained sweatpants; and an old pair of running shoes. His hair, mostly gray and uneven, long in the back, bushy on one side, was stuffed inside a Seattle Mariner's cap, and his face was covered with stubble that reminded her of a hobo from the cover of one of her mother's old Woody Guthrie records. He'd taken the seat diagonally across from her under a poster that said WORKER BEES—FIND YOUR STINGER. A yellow-and-black-striped insect with a lurid smile called for pissed-off employees to report their companies for copying software. He was breathing heavily, struggling to catch his breath. When he sat down, he stuck his face forward and looked her up and down.

Any halfway-decent-looking girl who rides the train every weekday sooner or later gets hit on. And Stardust Nadia presented well—short skirt, nice legs, shoulder-length blonde hair cut stylishly, full lips, a small turned-up nose, and yellow-brown eyes that sparkled no matter how impassive her expression. When she first started this job, she actually listened to them—lawyers bragging how they'd saved their clients, corporate weenies with their schemes to dominate markets, rumpled college professors fetching for respect. In the beginning, it fascinated her how white-collar warriors puffed themselves up for battle and then dragged home their prey, how they licked their wounds, how they whispered and laughed into their cell phones and whined to one another about being misunderstood. But after a couple weeks, she stopped paying attention.

Most mornings, she sat like the Sphinx, arms by her sides, hands folded around her purse, head tilted slightly back, staring straight ahead, daydreaming about one thing or another. When somebody tried to chat her up, she let her eyes go distant and pursed her lips, draining them of color. In her mind, this lent a certain meanness to an otherwise pliant look. As the backward-facing man looked her up and down, she shut her eyes and exhaled.

Stardust was what Mr. Stretton, the HR manager, called a "membrane" between Drinker & Sledge, P.C., and their clients, the underbelly of society. It isn't *that* bad once you learn to play the game: transferring callers before they could start in with their tales of woe. Still she hated listening to people whine and bitch and lie about how wonderful their lives would be if only this or that had or hadn't happened. As if winning a lawsuit was going to make them happier. The job was a way of *doing time,* as her mother used to say.

As the backward-facing guy lifted his hands from his knees and started talking to her, she imagined herself slipping out of a tent in the mountains of Colorado, tying her hair back while her traveling companion filled his coffee mug and wrestled into a white ribbed undershirt, which reminded her of a commercial for men's underwear. Since her mother disappeared, Stardust had been leaving the TV on. That morning, she'd seen June Carter and Johnny Cash on the *Today Show,* and she had "Amazing Grace" in her head. Stardust imagined herself on a chain gang and let the thwacks underneath them, percussive and loud, tap out a rhythm she could sing to. She gave the little voice in her head some vibrato, a little old-time religion.

As the man leaned toward her, she hugged her handbag and let her eyelids flutter. "How much do you know about the past?" he said, sounding as though he was actually trying to start a serious conversation. She glanced at him sideways. If he was a drunk or homeless guy, his fall from grace was recent. He looked troubled and tired, but intelligent, and he smelled of a combination of cigarettes, soil, and booze. She wished she'd brought something to read, but it was Friday and she was traveling light.

"It's not just a random question." Tiny bits of spittle formed and then connected themselves to the corners of his mouth as he spoke. "I'm not some lunatic. I'm talking about Boston, 1968, just before you were born." His hands moved in little circles as he talked. He did seem more eccentric than dangerous.

Stardust made a little curtsy with her face, keeping her eyes focused out the window. The train rocked side to side, past cushionless couches pushed up against vacant buildings, jagged graffiti on the undersides of bridges, corrugated metal sheds, junk heaps, and skinny dogs. A few more stops and they'd be in Center City. "What I mean to say is . . . I mean . . . Jesus, you look just like her. . . ."

In a few minutes, she'd be taking the steps in Suburban Station two at a time with the urban professionals and their gym bags, their cell phones and their changes of shoes. Poor guy, she thought, fingering the latch on her bag. Jewelry, panties, toothbrush, and a flashlight. The jewelry and flashlight were for adventuring. The essentials. She'd been surprised how many after-hours clubs had no lights in the ladies' rooms. And there'd been more than a few occasions she needed to find her rings, her shoes, and sometimes even her wallet on the bedspread or the floor of a dark hotel room in the middle of the night. The panties and toothbrush were optional. Symbols of hope. Good-luck charms. Some Saturday morning, so the fantasy went, instead of sitting slumped against the window on an empty train, she'd wake up next to somebody she might actually want to have breakfast with. She'd brush her teeth, change her panties, borrow a shirt, and they'd go shopping for lingerie at one of those big downtown department stores. It happened last year to her friend Elizabeth, except she was living with her mom now, bouncing some stranger's baby on her knee, dark circles under her eyes.

"I'm not just some stranger . . ." he said next, interrupting her reverie.

She'd survived early adulthood without making any serious errors of judgment involving careers, husbands, babies, or tattoos. By some people's standards, this would have been her first real job, the only one with health insurance, even if it was a forty-hour-a-week endurance test. Lately though, weekends mainly, she'd been taking chances, visiting places paralegals and lawyers would never go. Monday to Thursday may have belonged to the firm, but Fridays after work were hers. To pursue adventures big enough to keep her stoked through the week.

"Your mother and I, we go way back," he said next.

"I think you're confusing me with someone else." She looked straight ahead.

For a few seconds, he sat back and looked at her and didn't say anything. The train seemed to slow, which caused him to bow forward and her to lean away. There was a long metallic shriek accompanied by the release of air. Out of the corner of her eye, she could see him nodding, taking her in. Since starting this job, she'd had plenty of losers size her up and offer some deep insight in exchange for her attention. But in the next moment, the backward-facing man said something that penetrated. "I loved her," his voice rising just above the din. As he said that, Stardust looked straight at him. An iron fence marking the beginning of the next station appeared over his left shoulder. The train slowed, and he said the name "Lorraine."

"Excuse me?" she said, mostly to give herself time to think. Since Christmas, when her mother had walked off into oblivion somewhere in the Swiss Alps, Stardust had avoided irritable groping for insight or company on her existential journey. It was true her mother had told her little, if anything, about her own origins and about Boston, 1968, although years ago, it had ceased to matter. Now, her eyes stung. What was Lorraine doing here, now? Stardust reminded herself that normal people don't listen to strangers on a train. She considered laughing, which must have shown, because his mouth turned up, and their eyes locked. There was another long, loud hiss, and the train came to a stop.

As the conductor pushed the door into the metal clasp, a man dragging an assortment of shopping bags walked past and a child somewhere behind them started crying. The backward-facing man stood up and moved to her side. "Come," he said, lifting her by the elbow and guiding her like a dance partner toward the door. "I want to give you something." Stardust didn't protest, pull away, or raise her voice. It was as though she was moving and watching herself move at the same time. Following him and watching herself follow him. Together, they stepped onto the platform.

There was a blast of hot air and the sound of steel scraping steel, and then the train lurched forward, dragging the drab faces in the windows until they blurred together and then disappeared. In its place, silence, a triptych of ads for high-speed Internet access, the local news at ten, and De Beers diamonds, almost completely covered with graffiti. The sun cleared the power lines and hit them square on their faces. The man's hands, small and delicate, moved inside his jacket. He pulled out a pack of cigarettes, Benson & Hedges 100's. He blinked several times as though unable to remember where he was, and then pulled a pair of sunglasses from his pocket. Stardust looked around. The rickety platform was deserted. There was the smell of industrial lubricant mingled with rotting wood, wet cardboard, and urine.

Stardust looked at him closely. The skin around his eyes sagged, and his cheeks twitched as if exhausted from sneering or maybe pouting. He could have been in his mid- to late fifties, maybe sixty, his face pale, a being diminished. There was something sad, almost clownlike, about him. As he crossed in front of her, Stardust smelled earth. Not mud exactly, more like potting soil, rich, black, fresh, and moist. The backward-facing man looked small, serious, hardly threatening at all. He touched the rim of his cap like a baseball player sending someone a signal.

She considered her options. She could cross over the tracks and wait for another train, or call for a taxi, but either way she would wind up spending even more time standing around. His cigarette smoke wafted toward her, and she felt a wave of nausea, even panic. Despite the promise of learning about her mother—perhaps even herself—she regretted getting off a train in the skankiest part of the ghetto at seven fifteen on a Friday morning. The man pulled his collar up around his neck and started walking. Barely suppressing panic, Stardust decided to follow him, at least for a while.

They passed deserted retail stores with boarded-up windows; buildings with old signs, hand-painted and covered with graffiti; schools lined with razor wire; and row homes with tiny porches enclosed in wrought iron. He moved with determination, like he knew the terrain, sidestepping trash and piles of junk on the sidewalk. From behind, his neck muscles strained and bulged, and his jaw moved up and down, tightening, then slackening, as if he was having a conversation with himself. They crossed a large street, passing a Dunkin' Donuts, a crowded bus stop, a couple of empty row houses. Stardust struggled to keep pace.

December 1999

It was Stardust's belief growing up that her mother paid too much attention to mundane things. Lorraine was meticulous about matching dry cleaning receipts to monthly invoices. She pored over the maintenance log to her Plymouth Duster, producing a spreadsheet that required updating every three thousand miles. She was as scrupulous about buying Stardust school supplies and a few new outfits each season, even if they were from a thrift store, as she was about telling her daughter to avoid people who claimed to know her. In Stardust's opinion, her mother experienced pleasure in one of two ways: planning or taking vacations.

As a loan officer, Lorraine got a week's paid vacation for every three years of service, and when she wasn't working, she fantasized, obsessed, researched, and eventually took great pleasure deciding whether to head to the tropics or visit museums, whether to accrue her time or take it as it came, whether to go alone, take Stardust, or wait until she met someone special. Over the years, she kept these romantic connections private. What Stardust knew, she learned from things her mother left around the house—movie ticket stubs, toll booth receipts, scribbled notes, and objects: garden tools, sheet music, a soprano recorder, a set of dead weights. On rare occasion, one of Lorraine's dates would show up at the door, but for the most part, Stardust met her mother's paramours in photos—grimacing on a burro in the Grand Canyon; sweating on the steps of Tulum; wincing from the spray at Niagara Falls—looking out from the album with impatience, as though the fun part of the trip was over and they could see the little girl staring at the pages of the album, eager to get her mother back. Lorraine would stand behind the couch, holding a gin and tonic in her slim fingers, giving them names like Big Foot, Fast Eddie, and Dimwit Dave, poking fun and purposefully playing down their importance to her only child.

When she was little, Stardust asked questions. "What was he like, my dad?" "Where is he now?" "Will I ever meet him?" Occasionally, she made reckless guesses, hoping to tease something out of her mother. "He was moody, just like me, right, Mom?" and "He wasn't very nice to you, was he?" after which Lorraine sighed, as if her time in Boston was just a silly lapse between Catholic school and this predictable and perfunctory life she now inhabited. Once, about a year after she got her period, Stardust became more aggressive. They were on their way home from a school dance and the air was redolent with wisteria. "Were there so many, you can't even narrow it down?" Stardust said, her face flush from making out with some boy. "I can assure you," Lorraine snapped, staring into the night, "it's of no consequence to either of us now." Thereafter, Stardust pretended not to care.

In her forties, Lorraine became interested in spirituality and the so-called New Age, whose products were popping up in health-food stores and in yoga studios, and for the first time, Stardust noticed her mother's sadness. It surfaced unexpectedly—as Lorraine was peering into the mirror, applying clay from the Dead Sea, looking up from her meditation as Stardust burst into the house, or as the two of them were driving somewhere and a long song by Procol Harem or The Doors came on the radio. There was just the briefest loss of composure, followed by an arching of her eyebrows, which Stardust interpreted as self-doubt and, in her judgment, made Lorraine more human and therefore more lovable. To the young woman who believed her mother tried to keep too tight a grip on things, the crystals and the cards with the affirmations and the workshops were a welcome change.

When Stardust graduated high school, Lorraine took the two of them to London, where they shared a tiny hotel room, drank Cosmopolitans, and saw shows, sometimes two in a day. They rode the double-decker buses from Carnaby Street, where the hippie boutiques first opened with their racy fashions, to the London Tower, where Anne Boleyn, the second wife of Henry VIII, awaited execution, and for a few days, the two of them giggled like boarding-school girls away together over winter break. One night, Lorraine told Stardust she was the most beautiful and talented daughter a mother could have asked for, but she said it with unexpected intimacy and with such fervor that she frightened her daughter. Once they got home, Lorraine returned with furious determination to her job at the bank and to housekeeping—having the curtains in the living room dry-cleaned and shoving their pictures into photo albums—her face tightening and her eyes gray and unfocused. It seemed to Stardust that the emotion Lorraine expressed overseas had been a fluke, or a breach in an otherwise impenetrable wall.

Instead of going to college with her classmates who graduated with honors, Stardust took a job as a waitress and then as a carpenter's assistant, an attendant on a psychic hotline, a mystery shopper, an aerobics teacher, a nanny, and a telemarketer. She read in long penitent jags that kept her up nights, wondering when, and then whether, her mother would insist she go to college. The following Christmas, Stardust vacationed in Jamaica with friends, and in the spring, she moved into her own apartment that, in the beginning, felt like an adventure with strange overnight guests, diet pills, and sprawling disorder. But it quickly soured. Stardust was feeling neither beautiful nor talented, and by the next fall, she'd moved back in with her mother. There were the same kinds of odd jobs. A year passed, then another, then another.

Lorraine continued to travel. She swam with dolphins in the Keys, she went to Whistler in British Columbia with the credit union ski club, and she took a bicycle trip in Spain. After getting a home computer, Lorraine began corresponding with people online; shortly thereafter, literature came in the mail describing the Great Barrier Reef, Mount

Fuji, the Galapagos Islands. One August, Lorraine attended a New Age workshop in Washington, D.C. The following spring, she drove to a yoga retreat in Massachusetts. Just before Christmas, 1998, Lorraine bought polypropylene long johns and wraparound sunglasses. She ordered an aluminum contraption with ski boots and ropes and channels that she wrestled with each night until she was sweaty. While Stardust called strangers at dinnertime extolling the virtues of cheap long-distance carriers, Lorraine read how to melt snow for water and avoid hypothermia.

In the spring, Lorraine began training more rigorously, stepping across their little patch of grass at dawn to stretch her calf and thigh muscles, adjusting her hair in the reflection of a car window, then jogging up the street with its matchbox row houses and their little squares of fenced-in yards. By then, Stardust had given up trying to make sense of her mother's life—running, working, dating her boss, and tapping out e-mails to strangers. She was busy extricating herself from a nowhere romance with her boyfriend, Mick, an occasional auto mechanic and self-declared clairvoyant she'd known from the neighborhood, and the two of them would have long arguments late into the night on the phone.

For a while, Stardust and Lorraine communicated in notes on little scraps of paper. "Mom. Does med. insurance cover b-control?" Stardust scribbled on the back of a ticket stub from a Prince concert. "Pls. pick up the dry cleaning before Friday," Lorraine scratched out on a direct-mail postcard about vitamin supplements and colon cleansers. But underneath the irritation was affinity—the kind of bond between mother and daughter so deep it can be ignored for long periods of time.

Over Thanksgiving, Lorraine's training intensified. Instead of turkey, she and Stardust had protein shakes. On Black Friday, Lorraine went to the Y, and when she got home, she kept flexing little plastic hand springs while watching TV. The next morning, Stardust read, "Am planning a trip to Switzerland. Went for ice crampons. Back in an hour." The following week, Stardust quit telemarketing and took a job selling memberships to a fitness club, working mostly nights and weekends on commission. Finally, after picking a fight with Mick, she decided not to see him again. In early December, Lorraine's and

Stardust's schedules became completely opposite. On the back of a catalogue advertising vocational schools, Stardust wrote, "Mom—Carmine's brother died. The funeral's tomorrow. Do you have anything black?" On the back of a home pregnancy kit, Stardust wrote, "Went to Elizabeth's for the weekend. Be back Monday."

Stardust found Lorraine's itinerary on the dining room table a week before she left. She'd known for months that her mother was going away, but details of the trip kept slipping her mind. There was a flight to Zurich and a small group with an enthusiastic leader. There was a sponsoring organization that had something to do with friends of the earth. It turned out Lorraine would be gone for almost three weeks over the holidays with a group of people she'd met online in a specially arranged cyber-event—a pair of empty-nesters from Arizona, a philatelist from Connecticut, an Indian doctor, a young graduate student, and two middle-aged men taking a break from their jobs as commodities traders. Each of them was drawn to the expedition by the desire to cross over into the new millennium in an exotic and exciting place. Stardust read an e-mail to her mother describing the interior of the ski lodge where they'd gather, check their gear, and acclimate to the altitude. Lorraine responded that the details seemed perfect. She was completely absorbed. "You realize that my trip ends after New Year's, which means I'll be away for Christmas," Lorraine told Stardust one Sunday night.

"It's all right, Mom," Stardust said. "It's not like we had plans." The Nadias had little extended family, and Lorraine had long given up visiting her cousins. In retrospect, Stardust was sorry she didn't question her mother's preoccupation with winter camping or her determination to get in shape, to hike and cross-country ski, or to sleep outside in the cold, but at the time, she had such a sad, heavy feeling about her own life—her stuckness, her peripatetic work history, her inability to cross into the realm of mature adulthood where accomplishments and careers and long-term alliances marked a person's progress toward achieving her dreams—that she almost preferred being alone.

Lorraine, who had never been waifish, was cut, buff, and lean as her trip approached. The week before she left, she said things to her daughter like "I feel like I'm finally in my body" and "I'm living my highest choice." The morning she left, mother and daughter met briefly in the hallway. Lorraine had just showered and was humming quietly. Her skin had developed a rosy sheen from the conditioning, and her face glowed in anticipation. A bluish mist enveloped her. Stardust stumbled sleepily toward the bathroom, smiling as she passed. Lorraine looked more like a spirit guide than her mother. A few minutes later, while Stardust hung between sleep and wakefulness, Lorraine sat down on her bed, smelling like patchouli oil and shampoo. She brushed her lips against her daughter's forehead and nuzzled her. "You *know* I love you, honey," she said softly. "Godspeed." That was her last word. *Godspeed.*

When Stardust woke, she set a radio on the sink and ran the shower hot, looking at herself until the mirror clouded over. There were tiny cracks in the skin in the corners of her mouth. In her eyes, which were deep brown, she could see little spears of yellow. Wisps of shoulder-length hair, streaked blonde, framed her face, which was round until it came to a soft point at her chin. She moved her lips, forming a seductive pout. The overall impression she gave was one of balance, proportion, and intelligence. Yet approaching thirty, she felt disconnected from the person she wanted to be. It was almost the end of the millennium, and she felt stuck in somebody else's life.

Exiting the house, she walked down Medley Street, past the reindeer statues, the frost-covered patches of lawn and the wrought-iron-fence outlines, the nativity scenes and mailboxes in the shape of barns, children on their way to parochial school. She followed Appleberry, past Atomic Tires, and across Street Road, where she entered the 7-Eleven, put a dollar on the counter, and took a paper from the stack. Back home, she made coffee and sat down with a fresh sheet of paper and a pen at the breakfast table until she'd made a list of her achievements; trying to make the last few jobs sound better than they were. Retail clerk became "senior merchandiser," taxi dispatcher became "logistics engineer," and psychic hotline operator became "customer satisfaction rep." It was not what anyone would consider a power résumé, but it was enough to justify quitting her job. She was good at quitting things.

That afternoon, with the help of a guy at the copy shop, she entered her achievements into a preset format and printed her résumé on fancy white bond. There were about a dozen administrative ads in the *Inquirer* with the words *Center City* buried in the copy. By the following Thursday, seven days after her mother had left for Switzerland, Stardust had submitted fourteen résumés, had received callbacks from four human resource managers, and had two invitations for interviews.

She dressed carefully in one of her mother's dark suits and took the train into town. The first was an insurance company near Independence Mall. The second was a radio station near Rittenhouse Square, in one of several high-rises that faced the park. On her way back to the train, a chiseled boy in a sentry uniform, white gloves, and a fitted maroon jacket in front of the Ritz-Carlton smiled and held open the door. The lobby was splendid—its understated opulence, its openness, the huge bouquets of fresh flowers set on marble tables. On a whim, she asked a desk clerk with an Australian accent whom she might talk to about employment and then took a seat in the atrium to fill in the application.

It was just a few days before Christmas, and the storefronts and sidewalks were jammed with men and women exuding that curious blend of holiday hope and distress. To celebrate her first *real* job interviews, Stardust ordered a drink. The sun had long ago set behind the skyscrapers, and the lights in the lobby had a warm glow. A middle-aged man in his forties wearing a dark suit and expensive loafers came over and sat down at a table next to hers. He arranged a leather pouch and cell phone in front of him and ordered a drink for himself. He asked how her holiday shopping was going. He explained that he was in Philadelphia helping a client complete a merger before the New Year. They agreed enthusiastically that the holidays could be dismal, and that there was little point in working so hard for money if one had no time or energy to spend it. They had another round. Stardust confessed to not having dinner plans. A couple hours later, she agreed to a nightcap in his room.

The following day and the day after that, she took the train into Center City for more interviews, and by late afternoon she had planted herself in the lobby of the Warwick or the Four Seasons with a slender black folder and a small purse. Stardust drew the attention of business travelers—articulate, well-groomed married men who wore after-shave lotion, held doors open, and invited her, albeit briefly, into their worlds. She understood the effect of fetching looks, clever banter, and sarcasm—of sighs, swallows, and looking up at just the right angle. It was extravagant, provocative, and fun—a wonderful contrast to hanging out at the garage with Mick or working retail—and a fitting finish to a day dropping off résumés, taking typing tests, and answering questions from people who weren't really listening.

As the evenings progressed, she came to understand how important undressing slowly was, how delicate the relationship between mystery and money, a man's nearness to orgasm and his moral weakening. Whether she had a good time or not was less about the men—most of whom were polite, boring, and self-centered—and more about what she was learning: how powerful men could feel so trapped in their lives as to risk everything for one honest moment, the quickening from the touching of fingers, the mysterious calculation between sips of wine and banter when they'd ask for the check, escort her to the elevators, and take the long, slow ride upstairs. She tingled with nervous energy as they straightened their rooms, closed their laptops, poured cocktails from the minibar, and whispered *Daddy loves you* into the bathroom phone. She experimented with back rubs, adoring looks, sharp words, and glancing blows, playing the predator, hungry for risk. By the end of her second week of job hunting, she was bored.

On Christmas Day, Stardust stayed home, made an omelet, and watched a parade on TV. On the kitchen table, she came across a brochure Lorraine had left behind. During their time in the Alps, it said, the group would spend only four days indoors. There were tips for staying warm and advice on clothing to bring—wool and polypropylene, not cotton. Stardust leafed through a book about ice climbing, which looked perilous and unforgiving. She marveled at her mother's nerve.

New Year's Eve day was unseasonably warm. Late in the afternoon, she put on a low-cut red-sequined top, black stockings, and a tight black skirt with a black belt around her waist. On her way to the door, she grabbed a lightweight leather jacket, which she carried to the train. Downtown, she passed the antique stores along Arch Street, the galleries on Second and Third, the Middle Eastern restaurant on Race. She spent a few minutes surveying the line in front of the Troc, but the crowd looked too Goth, so she walked a few blocks to one of the martini bars she'd read about.

The men there were local, a little older than Stardust, but for the most part polite, clean, and well off. Conversation, which was abbreviated on account of the loud music, was limited to acknowledgments—yes or no to certain predictable questions—amazing place, cool lighting, great night. After a few failed pickup attempts, Stardust joined a well-heeled man in a fancy suit at his table. It was just before midnight, and she was pleased to have settled with someone to her liking.

He wore a gray designer suit and a thin red tie that, when she let her eyes unfocus, looked like a gash of blood dripping down his chest. He put two cell phones and a pager on the table, all of which lit up right away. Covering the mouthpiece, he explained that he ran a transportation business from a nearby high-rise, complaining he was so busy he'd had little time for romance. He alternated between looking at her blouse and checking his watch. As Stardust drank, she relaxed, tossing her head back, laughing, happy to be engaged and socially comfortable on New Year's Eve—the millennium—such a momentous night. She let her second and third drinks run their course and smiled when the man in the gray suit asked her if she'd ever been laid in a limousine. She was curious, and he was very attractive.

He led her out of the bar toward a long white stretch limousine that was parked across the street. On her way, Stardust felt queasy, perhaps from the drinks, or maybe the boldness of his suggestion. Before she had a chance to change her mind, he opened the rear door of the car and pressed against her with his body. She fell across a fold-up table and onto a bench seat, bracing herself with her forearms.

Tiny lights illuminated the perimeter. Inside, on the seats facing her, were two men in their late fifties who smelled of cologne and high-quality weed. One of them lifted a carafe of champagne and poured her a glass. "Nice," he said to the man in the suit, who pulled the door shut. "Well, well," the other one said, holding his chin against his chest and arching his eyebrows as he inhaled. The limo accelerated.

"Hey, guys," Stardust said, suddenly sober. She understood that she had only a few seconds to establish an alternative agenda before she became their entertainment for the evening. "Can I have a hit?" she said, motioning to the reefer. One of the guys—heavyset, straight black hair, bushy mustache—laughed and extended the joint. She took it between her fingers and made a sucking sound. "How about we go someplace where we can get comfortable?" she said, letting her breath out in an exaggerated squeeze. The man in the suit pressed a button on the console as Stardust passed the joint to a wiry, nervous-looking man with bad skin. The limo headed south and then turned right onto Market. The man in the gray suit pressed another button, and Dean Martin began singing. Stardust dropped to her knees and swung her arms in time with the music to avoid being groped. When the reefer came around again, she turned to face the man in the gray suit who was whispering in his cell phone. Behind her, the men filled their glasses and passed the joint back and forth. One of them kept turning the music up. She continued her dance, trying to see whether the door handles were reachable. The smoke thickened, and one of the men behind her opened his pants while the other tried to help her out of her jacket. The man in the gray suit folded his cell phone shut and smiled. Something strange passed behind his eyes.

As they circled City Hall, Stardust felt a hand lift her shirt from behind. The heavyset man who'd opened his pants was pressing against her back. He gathered her hair in his fist and began turning her, forcing her around. As much to slow things down as to ease the pain, she took him in her hand. The limo made a sharper-than-expected turn, and she squeezed him hard as all three of them slid sideways. The others laughed as he yelped in pain. "Easy," the man in the suit called out to the driver. The car turned left and then stopped in the middle of a block. Knowing she was in deep trouble, Stardust leaned forward and whispered to the man who'd brought her here. "Let's go inside, where we can do this right."

The man nodded and unlocked the door, pushing it open with his foot. Stardust calculated. If she let him get out first, the three of them would overtake her, forcing her inside. At the very least, she'd be dragged upstairs, knocked around, and fucked, at least once, if not all night. She fought an impulse to beg for mercy and then, planting her right foot, pushed herself forward, giving the men behind her an eyeful of ass and kissing the man in the gray suit full on the mouth. As he yielded, she bit his lip as hard as she could and stuck her leg outside the car. The man in the gray suit covered his face. Stardust twisted her body around and swung her purse as hard as she could at him. As she stood, she found herself staring at a handgun. A long, whooping groan rose in her chest in volume and pitch until it became a scream and stayed there, while her mouth and her eyes froze open. A silver-haired man swung a large pistol around toward the men emerging from the limousine. What should have had a calming effect on Stardust, didn't. The pistol prevented any of the men from moving or doing anything else—good or bad—but stare.

"FBI," the silver-haired man finally said, flashing a badge. "Put your hands on the car."

The man in the gray suit was holding a white handkerchief to his lip. Stardust stumbled from the limo to the curb, where she vomited, then touched the hood of the taxi that was idling behind them, indicating to the driver to let her in. As they drove away, she watched the man with the silver hair pin the three men against the limo. It reminded her of something she'd seen on TV.

Back home, in the shower, Stardust wondered if the episode was a harbinger of the new year—or worse, the new millennium—and whether his bloody lip resulted in an exchange of fluids. Had she given anything to the man in the gray suit that was traceable—her name, her phone number? She stood for a long time under the hot water, which was probably why she didn't hear the phone ringing. When she got out, she ran the towel over her forearms, which were bruised where she'd banged the table, and examined her body in the light. There were red blotches on her neck, big circles under her eyes. She wrapped herself in her mother's robe.

In the kitchen, she opened the refrigerator and took out a lemon yogurt. She was thinking about the guy with the gun, wondering who he was and what he was doing beside the car, when she noticed the light on her answering machine. She put the yogurt down and pressed play. There were three messages. The first was from the human resource manager at the law firm where she'd interviewed a few weeks ago. Stardust copied the date they wanted her to come back onto a little scrap of paper. The next message was from Elizabeth. "And what are *you* doing New Year's Eve?" her friend sang in a suggestive tone. Since Elizabeth had her baby, anything besides watching television seemed scintillating to her. Stardust winced. So thick was the third caller's accent that Stardust almost deleted it as a prank call or a wrong number.

"Der haas bin a baad storm," the accented voice said, "unt vee had some concern veder she vas okay." Stardust listened all the way through once, and then halfway through again, before realizing the call had something to do with her mother. The voice recited a list of numbers. She scribbled them down. It was New Year's Day in Switzerland, the man on the phone was explaining. In the event she couldn't reach him, she shouldn't "vorry yet."

Stardust dialed and waited, cradling the phone between her shoulder and her ear. Her heart raced. She riffled through the papers her mother left behind. Why didn't anyone answer? She hung up and dialed again. Nothing. Shit. She pressed zero, and an operator told her to hang up and press zero twice for overseas. Finally, there was a far-off ring, strange and mechanical-sounding. For the second time in six hours, Stardust mumbled sounds a religious person might have confused for prayer. When the ringing stopped, there was fumbling on the other end of the line and, after that, a long silence. A woman came on, her voice heavily accented like the one on the machine.

"Hallow?"

Stardust said her name and explained why she was calling. There was a pause and then the same voice again. "Hallow?" The woman hadn't understood a word. Stardust repeated her mother's name. "Na-di-uh. It's urgent."

She could hear the receiver changing hands and then a man's voice, the one from the machine. "Ah, yes . . . yes, my dear," he said, "goot of you to call. Der is a terrible storm up der . . . missing from the rest of the party . . . vee been searching all day." Reflexively, Stardust shoveled a spoonful of yogurt into her mouth and then spit it into the sink. Her hands shook. What had her mother told her about this trip? What was she doing out there anyway? Stardust asked if there was anyone from the group she could speak to. Anyone who spoke English. "Please. Vee know nothing yet. Vee vill call you as soon as vee know something."

Out the kitchen window, behind her house, she could see a row of brick houses illuminated by the early-morning sun. Stardust held the receiver away from her ear as if that could prevent her from hearing bad news. The refrigerator buzz grew louder and every few seconds she had to remind herself to breathe. She thought of calling Mick, but what would *he* say? That he had a premonition? Either Lorraine was safe or she wasn't. Stardust hung up the phone and went over what she knew. There had been a bad storm. There'd been no contact with the expedition. Nobody knew anything yet. There was nothing she could do from here. She picked up the phone. "My mother is lost somewhere in a blizzard in the Alps," she said to the dial tone. Frantic, she picked up the brochures on the counter again.

Hope exists on a sliding scale, and Stardust drew it down over the next twenty-four hours the way a terminal patient uses morphine. She kept calling the number in Zurich, the proprietor of the lodge, throughout the afternoon on New Year's Day and into the evening. By midnight, after only three short conversations, she'd gotten few new details. Lorraine's survival, Stardust thought to herself, was now dependent on these muddy-thinking people, one of whom could barely string together enough words in English to form a sentence. The man on the phone told her that they'd lost radio contact, and that the group's exact location was unknown. He'd rattled off latitudes and longitudes, and talked about snowmobiles and avalanche beacons that he wished "all hikers vould vare." Of all the gear Lorraine bought, Stardust remembered, why hadn't she purchased one of them? Instead, she was out there in the freezing cold, with little or no visibility and a storm that showed no signs of letting up.

Stardust slept fitfully. She alternated between worst-case and best-case scenarios, trying to keep her own misadventure and the image of the silver-haired man with the gun out of her mind. By the following morning, she'd begun surfing the Internet, searching for news under "tourism," "Swiss," and "weather." This led her to avalanche warnings, which led to local ski patrol reports, which led to a listing of accidents. It appeared as a blue link on the left-hand side of an international weather site connected to a ski report. Under notices about an avalanche in northern Italy, a chair lift that got stuck in Colorado, and a pair of elderly German cross-country skiers who had been found eating chocolate from badly frostbitten fingers. The headline made her heart stop. "American Hiker Found Frozen."

Stardust double-clicked, and a grainy photo of Lorraine's group materialized. Everyone else was facing forward, smiling tentatively. Several were pointing to bits of clothing and gear, proudly. Lorraine was looking at the young man next to her. Underneath the photo, the caption read, "Clad in only long johns, a wool hat, and a miner's light, an American woman (third from left) was found facedown, 350 feet from her encampment." Why would Lorraine have ventured out alone in the middle of the night during a storm? Didn't they have guides or leaders to prevent these things? Stardust sat very still. It was only one day old, and the new millennium carried an impossibly heavy load. For her, an adventure gone bad, a narrow escape from rapists, a pistol aimed between her eyes, and her mother, Lorraine—first missing—now dead! Stardust closed her eyes and felt herself free-fall, no perch, no perspective, no solid ground underneath her feet. She sat hunched forward, breathless, as if she herself was buried under snow. Then she began to shake and then sob, before collapsing on the carpet.

The following week, Lorraine's trip mates invited Stardust to join their listserv in a discussion around understanding and accepting Lorraine's death. Stardust declined in a terse e-mail they discussed online for a week. She was determined to leave Lorraine's New Age mumbo-jumbo mysticism behind. A few days later, the graduate student from Lorraine's trip called to express his condolences. He'd been with her near the end. Stardust asked how her mother seemed—what she'd been thinking—but he didn't know. "She'd been reading Rumi," he said sheepishly. "In group circle the night before, she seemed kind of blissed out." That same day, a postcard arrived. "Stardust," Lorraine wrote in her meticulous block print, "I'm finally learning to let go. I love you. Mom."

She stared at the heels of his sneakers as they lifted and then touched the ground. Periodically he turned, dazed, as though he'd forgotten where he was, or that she was behind him, and then suddenly his stride would lengthen and Stardust had to struggle to keep pace. She became a scientist tracking a rare primate, a political refugee being led to a safe house, a pickpocket following her mark. She studied him—his shoulders slumped, chin forward, head tilted down, his urban skulk down one numbered street, across another, behind a row of blackened shells.

Although it was just after seven thirty in the morning, the streets were crawling with life. Young mothers pulled kids in ratty coats by their mittenless hands. An Asian man with aviator glasses called out to an Hispanic woman who nodded from behind a grocery store window advertising lottery tickets. Two black girls, their hair pulled into pigtails and their broad brown foreheads shining, played hopscotch parallel to a chain-link fence. A pay phone on the opposite corner was ringing. What compelled Stardust to stand up on the train and follow him receded in importance. Once committed, the adventurer must press on. The air was metallic and crisp. There was a smell like explosives. Winter. Poverty wearing itself like a scent.

When you're a receptionist at a busy downtown law firm and you're not going to show up for work, there's a certain protocol you must follow if you expect to keep your job. For starters, you have to call in ahead of time. And you need a pretty solid excuse. Under no circumstances do you just *not* show up. Stardust looked at a clock hanging in a grocery store window. It was seven fifty A.M. Work started at eight-thirty. If only she had a cell phone.

At Allegheny, they turned left and headed toward the river. Dark figures huddled around an oil drum facing a small fire. Suddenly, the backward-facing man reached into his pocket and Stardust froze, memorizing the moment, the sun glinting off parked-car roofs, a pickup truck filled with scrap metal pulling out into traffic. She imagined him pulling out a gun, lifting it to her temple, and firing; the headline: "Daughter of Frozen Skier Murdered in Ghetto." But the backward-facing man withdrew his hand and turned, slapping the parking meter next to him. He turned the dial and continued walking. Ten steps later, he repeated the motion. She didn't understand. A beat-looking, middle-aged guy dressed in a loopy outfit lures her off a commuter train promising information about her past—information she has waited a lifetime to hear—he walks twenty blocks in silence, then jams coins into some parking meters in front of empty spaces.

A few minutes later, they stopped at a twelve-foot fence surrounding a parking lot in front of several industrial buildings that were joined sloppily—brick to cinder block, cinder block to stucco—with nothing in common except their unredeemable ugliness. Off to one side was a large loading dock with heavy plastic strips hanging like sooty curtains. An old forklift gutted for parts sat in a truck well, and above it, along an iron girder, a row of pigeons looked as if they'd been feasting on Big Macs.

The backward-facing man raised a steel bar, swung open the gate, and walked across the yard. Stardust knew that if she followed him, her chances of getting to work at all would diminish significantly. Yet the possibility of hearing more about Lorraine and her life in Boston or something about her father drew her in. She looked around, first at the squat buildings and then back toward the street. There were rows of clapboard houses with tiny porches, well kept, nicely painted; no pay phones, no neighbors standing around, no cars passing. The only other commercial establishment, the Montana Beef Company, was shuttered. The backward-facing man seemed more confident now, like a kid near his clubhouse. As if sensing her dilemma, he turned and spoke to her for the first time since they got off the train. "C'mon in," he said. "Relax. Have some tea. I have a lot to tell you and not a lot of time."

Who could resist a fellow human being offering stories about her past? Stardust took a deep breath and followed him toward an archway that joined two of the buildings. She tried to memorize her surroundings, making note of something for later, an address, anything she could reference in case she needed to. They climbed the steps of an enclosed fire escape: him, stoop-shouldered, shuffling; her, light on her feet, tentative, uncertain. At the top of the landing, before a large red door, the backward-facing man flipped a cover up over a keypad, and his fingers tapped out numbers in a pattern. There was a high-pitched tone, and a small red light turned green. He pulled a round key from his pocket, inserted it, and turned it ninety degrees. The red door opened, and he stepped inside. Stardust took a deep breath and followed him.

The city has a thousand secret places. Stardust felt the soft whoosh of warm air and heard jazz playing softly in the background. A man, very slight, got up from a brown leather couch and walked toward them. Low ceilings, skylight, exposed ductwork, cantilevered lighting suspended from above that barely illuminated the floor, open kitchen, and beyond that, a large fish tank set off to one side. She had the feeling she was entering a kingdom inhabited by a separate species of people living strange lives in a make-believe place.

"Hey, Chuck," the wire-thin man with a knitted cap and small round glasses said to the backward-facing man. "And hello, dahling," he said, taking Stardust's hands. "My name is Rahim. Welcome to Fantasy Island." He smiled graciously. "Would you like some breakfast?" They were standing in the kitchen. The decor contrasted so radically with the exterior of the building that Stardust kept blinking, then looking from one visual anomaly to the next, unable to take it all in—the blighted exterior, the abandoned parking lot, the elaborate alarm system; and inside, the posh carpeting, the earth tones, the matte black kitchen appliances, the tropical-fish tank; and now this guy offering to make her breakfast.

"What am I doing here?" she said more to herself than to him. And then, considering he might be more talkative than the backward-facing man, "Where is *here* anyway? And where'd the other guy go?"

"Chuck has a big day Monday," Rahim said pleasantly. "Lots of preparing to do. I'm his assistant, the innkeeper, the beekeeper, the gatekeeper, the bookkeeper. I handle inquiries, enquiries, exquiries, investments, divestitures, one misstep at a time."

She looked at him carefully. On his hands and his face, the skin was translucent, and as he talked, she imagined she could see where his jaw met his skull. "You're probably famished," he said. "Let me fix you something." He spoke with a slight accent, reedy and effeminate. "A cup of tea, cappuccino, a Spanish omelet"—he moved his hand in a little circular gesture—"with egg whites . . . ?"

"No thanks."

He took her coat, and she looked down at her blouse for one of those plastic laminated badges visitors to the law firm are always forgetting to take off when they leave. "Can I use a phone?" she asked Rahim.

"You're in a no-phone zone."

"Seriously. I need to call work. I'm willing to go along with the game for a while, but I can't afford—"

"I'm serious, too. This is a no . . . phone . . . zone," he said slowly, pronouncing each word now with a heavy local accent, like he was sucking on a straw.

"Am I being kidnapped?" Stardust said.

Rahim looked at her, mock horrified. "No-oo-oo," he said in three syllables, putting his hands on his hips.

Stardust shuddered. "C'mon, I gotta make a call."

"How about a cup of tea?" Rahim said, smiling. He filled a pot with water and turned the heat up, then took two mugs out of a cabinet, set them on a counter, and walked across the kitchen. He was wearing a black turtleneck, black Levi's held up by a black belt with little silver studs, and black Adidas. His cheeks were concave and covered with some kind of rash. Under his knitted cap, his hair was jet black. Stardust caught herself staring at his diamond-stud earrings, which were larger than hers. She checked her watch. It was eight fifteen. Soon, the reception desk at Drinker and Sledge would be piled with unsorted mail. By eight thirty, somebody's secretary would call HR. By then, it would be too late.

"We're in a blackout zone," Rahim said, stepping into the living area. "No windows, no handhelds, no free-floating radio signals. The walls are lead-lined to prevent eavesdropping. The satellites see only a factory. We can't afford contact with the outer world. Our work may seem humdrum, irrelevant, benign even, but it's not. We antagonize the infrastructure. We're enemies of the status quo. We're the antidote to spin, the masters of spamnation, we're medication for the nation." Stardust stared at him. "The neighbors think we run a shelter, and in a few minutes you'll see why. The telephone is a weapon of oppression. It rings, and humans respond. It's autonomic, physiological. Have you ever tried to resist? It requires great strength. We're against knee-jerk re-actions, mechanical responses, mindless, thoughtless rote of any kind." He was working it very hard, like he was nervous or speeding, or trying hard to impress her.

"Listen, Ra . . . him," Stardust said. "You guys, this place . . ." She copied his little motion with her hands. "I mean, it all seems very in-teresting. It does." She made herself smile and then resumed. "The problem is that I have less than five minutes to call my boss and get someone to cover for me before I lose my job, and if I lose my job, well . . ." The water in the kettle started to boil. Rahim stepped lightly on the balls of his feet like a man walking on eggshells and poured. Louder, she continued. "I'll be fucked!"

Rahim leaned back on his heels, raised his eyebrows, and exhaled, shrugging his shoulders in an exaggerated way. There was something ef-feminate, theatrical, even comical, about his gestures. "I totally under-stand," Rahim said. "I really do."

"Why don't you show her the factory," Chuck said, interrupting. Through the fish tank, Stardust saw him standing at the end of a hall-way, a manila folder in his hand.

Rahim handed Stardust her mug with a teabag soaking in it and walked over to an elevator shaft with two sliding grids and a canvas strap attached to the top. He pressed a button on a junction box hanging from the wall and a noisy motor engaged. When it stopped, he slid the gate open, and Stardust breathed in cold air that smelled like metal and oil. Rahim held the door open and motioned for her to step inside. "Come, dear," he said gently. He smelled like antiseptic.

"This is fucked up," Stardust mumbled, stepping in.

"Indeed it is," Rahim said, closing the gate. "When you realize how easily the courts can be subverted by politicians to keep an innocent man locked away from his loved ones. It's fascism, really." Stardust felt the floor drop under her.

They descended into what appeared to be an old factory, now abandoned. Thirty-five-foot-high ceilings, fluorescent light fixtures hanging at odd angles, gas-fired heaters, epoxy-coated gray floors marred by forklift gashes and divots, chunks of plaster missing from walls where filing cabinets had been removed. It was as though Stardust was looking down into a dollhouse with the roof removed, except the dollhouse was decorated like a factory office—water-stained ceiling tiles, bare fluorescent fixtures, mismatched metal filing cabinets, a blackboard with little magnetic squares that might have represented production orders, long since canceled or filled—and as they descended, the old fixtures looked larger. The elevator settled into a small area sectioned off from the shop by drywall. Rahim used all his strength to open the gate and they stepped into a small, well-lit room.

On the wall was a photo of Chuck, in a dark business suit, wraparound sunglasses, and a tightly cropped goatee. He was smiling at the camera through clenched teeth, looking younger and meaner and more focused than he did now. Directly in front of them was a long table with four computers, each screen showing a different display. A young woman with short-cropped hair, long in the back and a row of bangs over her face, sat at one of the keyboards, reading something from a clipboard and then typing. When she finished, she turned around and smiled.

"Chuck would like us to show our guest what we do," Rahim said. Then he turned and disappeared into the elevator, shutting the doors with his spindly arms.

She looked to be in her late twenties, Latina, a little heavy in the haunches, with a line of studs around the outside of her left ear. She wore a gray sweatsuit and a button with a picture of a girl giving the photographer the finger. She had a strong chin and sleepy-looking eyes that were wary, but relaxed: a city girl, sultry, in a butch kind of way. "Ovella Rodriguez," the computer operator said, sticking out her hand.

"I have no idea what I'm doing here," Stardust said.

"Who does?" Ovella said, sympathetic. She moved to one of the screens and typed in a sequence of letters, which brought up a photograph of what looked like an industrial vacuum cleaner. "About a year ago, we started fencing stuff. Nothing hot, just stuff that didn't move in pawnshops—furs, rings, electronics, guns—stuff that was too expensive or maybe didn't appeal to people in the neighborhood."

Stardust must have looked uneasy.

"It's not illegal or anything. We just broker it. We're like an auction for pawnshops to put merchandise in front of people who wouldn't be caught dead in their stores. My brother set up the software, Chuck gets the pawnshops to list their shit with us, and we take orders. . . ."

Stardust still looked confused.

"I'll show you," Ovella said, pointing to the computer screen in front of her. "There's a guy in North Philly who has telecommunications equipment. We don't know where he gets it and we don't care, but he's selling and there's somebody out there who needs it. We type in descriptions, upload photos if there are any, and, boom, we're live." Ovella sounded like anybody doing any job. If she wasn't sitting in a windowless basement of an abandoned factory, she might have been a secretary or a paralegal having coffee and describing the intricacies of her job. There was something calming, chummy, even intimate, about her inflection, her cadence, the way she was explaining it.

"How many people work here?" Stardust asked.

"It's just me, Chuck, and my brother, Rahim, full-time. Occasionally, a couple of the guys from the factory pick things up or do repairs."

"I thought factories made things," Stardust said.

"The business may be shut down," she said, tilting her head toward a closed door, "but the bills keep on." As Ovella talked, Stardust grew more discouraged. Above Ovella's head, Stardust pictured an hourglass emptying. In the glass was her old life, the one with a routine, a good job, and the illusion of safety. The man she'd followed off the train may or may not have had information about her past, but she was beginning to think that he was some kind of a criminal. The computer beeped, and Ovella paused to type something. Stardust took a look at the clipboard and then the screen directly in front of her. There were three columns labeled QUANTITY, ITEM DESCRIPTION, and PRICE. Ovella appeared to be typing the names and descriptions of voice mail systems.

"What did you do before this?" Stardust asked.

"I'm a nurse. I used to work at Northeastern Hospital. Over on Allegheny."

Stardust looked at her watch. It was almost nine A.M. "You don't have phones here, do you?" she said.

"Only modems."

"You seem like you're pretty good at this." Stardust motioned toward the computers.

Ovella smiled.

"Can you make it look like I'm sending an e-mail from the hospital?"

Ovella brought up a browser and typed something in the address line. The screen refreshed once, then again, before flickering for a few seconds and coming up crimson. There was a picture of a large brick building with Doric columns. Ovella clicked twice on the menu bar, then clicked again. A list came up and then another empty field into which she typed something. A bunch of names and two columns of long numbers came up. "Which department?" Ovella said. A second later, Stardust was sitting at the terminal composing a message.

From: Emergency Medicine, Northeastern Hospital
Date: March 13, 2000, 9:01AM
To: astretton@drinkerandsledge.com
Re: Urgent

Mr. Stretton.
My train broke down this morning. A few of us got hurt. Nothing serious.
See you Monday.
S. Nadia.

Stardust hit SEND and sat back as the message disappeared. Below the desk, she heard the CPU crunching.

"Very clever," Rahim said from behind them, his eyes shining, his lips barely stretching over his teeth and gums. "I like that."

The first few days after Lorraine's death, Stardust wandered the house in a big flannel shirt and slippers, drinking tea and trying not to think. When she got hungry, she walked to the 7-Eleven and bought herself Hot Pockets and candy bars. She slept in Lorraine's bed with the TV on, not so much to follow the news or distract herself with shows as to keep herself company. On the third day, she filled a bucket of water with Pine-Sol and wiped down the walls and ceilings, dusted the baseboards, polished the furniture, and scrubbed the bathroom. The next morning, she started in on the closets. From the basement, she pulled out empty boxes that appliances had come in and filled them with Lorraine's sweaters, pantsuits, dresses, and underwear. Anything threadbare, shoes or clothing that her mother never wore, Stardust put in a large bag to give away. Jeans, socks, shorts, or T-shirts that Stardust liked, she carried into her own room.

Near the back of Lorraine's closet was a cardboard shelving unit with two of the three drawers missing. In the one that remained, Stardust found books of poetry, a hand-bound journal, empty except for a few drawings of wildflowers, a strand of mummy beads, a baby bracelet that said FERGUS in block letters, a priest's collar, and a mason jar with a bag of weed that smelled like hay. At the bottom was a photo album with pictures of what appeared to be Lorraine's grandparents: serious-looking immigrants posing in front of a variety store. Stardust sat on the floor and studied their broad Slavic faces, high cheekbones, and squat bodies. Near the back was a picture of Lorraine when she was nine or ten years old, dressed for parochial school—heavy-framed glasses, blonde hair held down with a barrette. Her older brother Nick stood beside her, his hair slicked down, his chest puffed out, and on his face, a big toothy grin. The space where the other two drawers should have been was empty.

In the crawl space above the bedrooms, Stardust found boxes with composition books filled with Lorraine's dream journals, matchbooks with the names of clubs and restaurants where she met friends with nicknames like Acid and Handjob, and a stack of yellowed magazines with psychedelic covers called *The Mission*. One was folded open to the following passage:

> To know yourself, forget everything you've learned. Forget throwing the Tarot, reading philosophy, and marching on Washington. Forget sitting at the feet of some Indian guru or some acidhead who says they've caught a glimpse of the ineffable. Forget blissing out on nature and helping the Negroes. Forget your lovers and your music and your drugs. The problem for most of you is that your trip isn't really *your* trip. You won't find yourself by faking humility, deprivation, or surrender. The only way to know yourself is through suffering. In the course of a lifetime, anybody who dares to live—anybody who dares to be real—betrays and is betrayed. The sooner you recognize this, the better for everyone. When it happens, be strong enough to admit it, look hard at who you fucked over and why—how you went about fixing or ignoring it—then you'll know who you are. When you give up trying to be perfect, then you can begin to let go.

Stardust tugged at the neck of her flannel shirt. She pictured her mother walking off into the snow, repeating the phrase *I am not perfect*. What a crock of shit. Notwithstanding her hippie pedigree and her more recent spiritual escapes, Lorraine was as incapable of suspending her earthly concerns, as neurotic and burdened by guilt and regret for her choices, as the next person. Stardust had seen her mother cling to every precious moment, no matter how miserable she was, always hopeful that her life would suddenly improve.

She lay down on Lorraine's comforter, which still smelled like her mother's body cream. Pulling the quilt up, Stardust tightened herself into a little ball. Whereas once she felt as though she'd been rocket-shot out of her life to impossible heights, now, miles above the earth, she orbited, disconnected, her mother's voice breaking up like a distant radio transmission, eventually disappearing into static; her own will to live, like the pull of gravity, slowly fading. There, on her mother's bed, strange, sad memorabilia all around her, Stardust felt only the absence of life.

Over the next few days, she lugged a pair of bridge tables from the basement and laid out all of her mother's stuff from her closets, the crawl space, and the basement. She worked methodically, like an archaeologist, unpacking one section of the house at a time, cleaning under beds and emptying boxes, studying the artifacts of her mother's fractured past. She found an old turntable, and, while she worked, she listened to her mother's albums—Buffalo Springfield, Jefferson Airplane, The Byrds. She discovered an all-festival camping pass from an Old-Time Fiddlers' Convention and buttons that said MCGOVERN FOR PRESIDENT and SCIENTOLOGY RULES; she read letters that chronicled Lorraine's brief career at Boston College, books her mother had read as a teenager, and poems written to her by a tubercular boy in sixth grade.

By the end of the week, Stardust was restless and angry. In the museum of her mother's old life, with relics from the past all around her, Stardust felt betrayed—like she'd jimmied a safe she'd been trying to open for years and found nothing. On Saturday, she called a local real estate agent whose name appeared on signs all over the neighborhood and made an appointment for him to come out. On Monday morning, Carl, Lorraine's boss, stopped by to tell Stardust how sorry he was and to let her know that she was the named beneficiary of her mother's retirement account, which had almost $20,000 in it. "Fully vested," he said, touching his lapel nervously. Stardust put the documents she was supposed to sign on a pile in the kitchen, which is when she saw it—a hardback written by Patricia Hearst and a woman named Winnie Prescott. Inside was the inscription: "To Stardust. Best of luck! Winnie Prescott." On Wednesday, Mr. Stretton, the human resource manager at Drinker & Sledge, called. The following Monday, Stardust Nadia started her new job.

Friday, March 13, 2000

Rahim led Stardust through a doorway into another small room. "This," he said proudly, throwing a spindly arm toward two very urban-looking men who were sitting at folding tables loaded with appliances and bric-a-brac, "is Softpawn." Stardust looked around at the cinder-block walls, stained linoleum floors, and low-hung fluorescent fixtures with tubes that flickered. Along the walls, shelving units supported boxes filled with extension cords, electronic gear, hand tools, and antique jewelry. The men at the table were in their forties or fifties, overweight, with frizzy gray hair. They were either very shy or completely absorbed in what appeared to be a couple of short-wave radios. Neither looked up.

Rahim rocked back and forth, hovering over one of the tables, his dark eyes open wide, his shoulders and upper torso moving like a boxer's, his head sticking out from his neck, birdlike, his mouth, like a sandpiper's, pecking in a tight pattern. Stardust noticed ripples of vertebrae underneath the shirt. He rolled his shoulders in an effort to get his neck to accommodate his head. Even though it was cold in the room, Rahim glistened with sweat. "This is where it all happens, baby . . . the repairs, the cataloguing, the freshening up of merchandise when required. . . ."

"Why are you showing me this?"

Rahim smiled. "The important thing is, you're here. Chuck wanted that more than anything." He said it with a dramatic flair. "There's so much you two have to talk about, but before you do, let me show you the factory." Rahim winked.

He took her mug and set it on a small lacquered table and then pushed a huge steel door open. Stardust felt a rush of cold air and smelled metal, paint thinner, and stale sweat. They were standing at a side entrance to a cavernous room—a bona fide factory—dark, damp, cold, and soundless except for the echo of their footsteps on the cement and the fluttering of a pigeon thirty feet above them. Stardust understood that the more time that passes in a bad situation, the more control you lose and the worse your chance of escaping. She had applied this theory with success in the limousine. You want to stay fresh and vigilant throughout an ordeal, to fight off your fatigue, to resist any tendency to show weakness or to identify with your captor, and, most important, to stay alert for an opportunity to get away.

On one side, dim light filtered into giant windows above scaffolding that ran alongside four huge steel vats. In the main area, huge cement columns six feet around were plastered with photos of women in bathing suits, diagrams of three-dimensional frames, and Polaroids of dark-skinned children. All around, the concrete floor was ripped up. At odd intervals, piles of concrete lay next to dark, round holes. It looked like a crew had stopped working midtask. Rahim led her to a wide-open area next to a large metal desk that was covered in dust.

"Assembly stations," he said, spreading his arms. "The Plexiglas came in on forklifts. We measured, cut, and assembled it right here." He pointed to three large scissors tables with hand tools attached to spiral hoses hanging from above. Stardust imagined the overhead lights on, machines whirring, men, sweaty with concentration, calling out to one another, hammering things until the buzzer buzzed or the whistle blew.

"At one time," Rahim narrated, "we worked here side by side— me, Chuck, Miguel, Big Lou, and our dads." Stardust looked above at the intersection of iron girders. Near the windows, a huge bridge crane with a gleaming steel hook dangled over the steel vats.

"How long ago?"

"They had a terrible time," Rahim said, ignoring her question. "The old man was a son of a bitch. Didn't cut anybody any slack. Especially Artie—he bore the brunt of it. 'Shit-for-brains,' the old man used to call him."

"What does this have to do—"

"Chuck was the outside guy. Helluva salesman. The old man's retirement plan. Worked like a dog."

Stardust cleared her throat. "I really have no clue—"

" 'Eagles may soar,' Charlie Puckman used to say, 'but weasels don't get sucked into jet engines.' If there was a way to make a buck—no matter how sleazy, a shortcut to take, a corner to cut—the old man found it. Your uncle Artie was loco you know. Probably retarded."

Stardust winced. "Did you say 'uncle'?"

"Not till I'm ready to give up," Rahim said, grinning. He had bad gums. "Artie was always looking for ways to bring his brother down." Rahim had stopped about twenty-five feet from the steel tanks. To their left was a loading dock. Behind that, offices and a dark void. It was only nine thirty in the morning, but Stardust was already exhausted. She wanted a drink. Finally, she asked Rahim flat out. "Who is it you *think* I am?" she asked.

Rahim looked at her as if she had amnesia. "Listen, honey, I've worked for this family since I was in high school. Before you were born. Before the accident. Before they shut us down." He motioned toward the tanks. "It could have been me that day."

"What accident?" Stardust asked, shaking her head.

Rahim looked at her closely. "He didn't tell you yet."

She stared back at him.

"Probably too ashamed. Over here." Rahim led her to tank number four. "We had no money to ventilate the welding area. Nobody denies that." Stardust felt a wave of panic. "So we limped along as best we could. Orders were way down, and our quality wasn't what it should have been. It was a Saturday. The kid was cleaning it out." Rahim pointed to the steel vats against the wall. "I dragged him out." Stardust thought of Gary Heidnick, the serial killer who dismembered young women in the basement of his Philadelphia row home. "The paramedics said it was too late. Even if he'd lived, he'd have been a vegetable. This is where he collapsed," Rahim said, pointing to an area about ten feet away. "Right here, in your father's arms."

Stardust stood absolutely still for a second, no longer listening to the thin man with the black hair and the little skullcap, no longer thinking about pawnshops or security guards or being late for work. Time slowed. She must have stopped breathing, because suddenly she felt as though she was choking. Did he say *father*? She needed air, so she took off, loping at first, then running, hoping to find an exit, some breach she could escape through. She remembered hearing her own footsteps and something flapping overhead. She remembered smelling metal or grease and felt herself moving through pockets of cold air, and she heard a far-away voice call after her, "Wait!" or "Watch out!" but all she could do was keep running until she heard a thwack and felt her legs crumble, and then there was nothing.

Saturday, January 23, 1999

It was a typical Saturday in the factory. A transistor radio hanging from a coat hanger blasted salsa music. Men in soiled work clothes stood at large tables cutting, then whacking, angle iron so it fit snugly into home-made welding fixtures; mitering corners, then tack-welding frames—tasks that bore little relationship to the gleaming Plexiglas security guards that sat stacked and crated near the entrance. Beneath the patter of the DJ, you could hear air hissing, the whir of a motor idling, the occasional report of a staple gun.

The man in the dip tank swooned. One of his fellow workers, hearing the scrub brush and the bucket fall, called out his name, "Gutierrez! Gutierrez!" When it became clear that the young man wasn't responding, two of them scrambled up the steps to a catwalk that ran alongside the tanks, their work shoes causing the scaffolding to shake and shudder, their bodies silhouetted against the giant windows. For a few seconds, everyone froze. Time stood still. Then abruptly, the factory transformed itself from calm to anxious, then hysterical.

Beneath the windows, four large tanks—eight feet long, eight feet high, and two feet wide, set close together, parallel and at a slight angle to the wall—were mounted on legs that straddled two large gas heaters that, in turn, were set above a pan that drained into a pipe that disappeared in the floor. The rig was homemade, and it looked to have been patched over the years with steel plates that formed a kind of pattern, quiltlike and mottled. Overhead, a heavy steel chain with a huge iron hook dangled from a pulley so that it took only one gloved hand to guide a 150-pound welded steel guard from the first tank to the last.

In the old days, before the environmentalists and the class-action lawyers, the Puckmans dipped every guard they built. In this way, rust and grease along with any imperfections were eaten away by acid that etched the metal, making it easier for paint to adhere. In the old days, you had to clean metal before painting it, whether it was for fireplace screens, radiator covers, outdoor furniture, or patio supports. It was the standard of quality. But gradually, with safety and removal requirements imposed by the alphabet agencies, only the premium product manufacturers could afford to keep doing it. Hazardous materials equaled expensive.

Until recently, the tanks had been empty. Years ago, to cut costs, Charlie Puckman Sr. decided to skip the process and spray-paint instead. He had the tanks drained of chemicals and cut off the heat and water supply, reducing payroll and putting an extra $30,000 a year in his pocket.

A few months ago, when their largest customer, Powerplex, started rejecting units because of shoddy workmanship, the brothers decided they had no choice but to strip and repaint the metal as they'd done before. In mid-November, as the first snow settled over the neighborhood and kids tossed snowballs at one another, a funky-looking flatbed with two fifty-gallon drums painted with skulls and crossbones pulled into the Puckman Security parking lot. The next day, while Chuck and his brother were busy in the office, workers poured caustic etch, water, and the chemical that arrived by truck, the same chemical that Ramon Gutierrez had been scrubbing from tank number four on this Saturday morning: TCE, trichloroethylene, a particularly noxious vapor degreaser.

One by one, workers shut off their machines and dropped their tools, drifting, then rushing, to the foreman's desk. Someone called 911. Somebody else ripped through the supply closet looking for a first-aid kit, or a gas mask, reading in accented English the medical instructions mounted inside the door. Rahim Rodriguez and the other worker who saw Gutierrez sprawled facedown on the bottom of the tank held their breath and lifted the young man under his bony arms and his chinos. The smell, acrid and intense, caused their eyes to burn. Together, they hoisted him up the steel ladder and carried him to an area near the foreman's desk. In the back of the shop, an older man wearing headphones piloted a forklift with a large wooden crate balanced precariously on its prongs, unaware that his son was losing consciousness. Toxic fumes had entered Ramon Gutierrez's lungs, and he was in spasm.

After what seemed like forever, an ambulance made its way down the narrow street into the factory parking lot. As the siren stopped, dispatchers barked coded commands from radios the paramedics wore strapped across their shoulders. They unfolded a stretcher and pushed it through the loading dock door, the wheels echoing on the concrete sounding like God's thunderous will. It was the second time in a little over a year that spinning red and white lights reflected off the Puckman windows.

Last Christmas morning, Charlie Puckman Sr., the founder and chairman of Puckman Security and the patriarch of the Puckman family, pulled his aquamarine Lincoln Town Car into the parking lot of his factory as he'd done every morning for forty years and fell forward, his grizzled face slumped against the steering wheel, smacking the wall directly in front of him, which detonated the air bag, which, in turn, depressed the car horn. The night before, after dinner with his girlfriend, a small blood clot broke loose from the wall of his heart and traveled through his arteries into the ever-narrowing vessels to the left side of his brain so that by the time the paramedics extracted him from his vehicle, he'd lost the ability to walk unassisted, to dress and bathe unaided, to understand, insult, endear himself to, and alienate himself from others.

The street in front of Puckman Security filled with neighbors. Because it was Saturday, those who would have been at work were home, and hearing the ambulance, they came outside in their bathrobes and sweatsuits, unshaven, ungroomed. They spoke in hushed tones reserved for the direst of circumstances. It was cold. Word spread quickly that one of the Gutierrez boys was down, barely breathing, and that another tragedy had befallen the little Puckman dynasty.

"They been here since the beginning of time, and nothing's ever happened," a woman in a housedress marveled.

"It's like the Kennedys," an old man with a hearing aid said.

"I didn't know they were Catholic."

"What do they make in there?" a girl mumbled from beneath a castle of hair.

"Security cages," the woman answered. "Like you see in them check-cashing places."

"Car armor, too," a teenage boy said. "Bulletproof. I saw them test one once."

"Hush," his mother said, as a man approached aiming a beat-up video camera at them.

Coleman Porter wasn't the brightest bulb in the chandelier, but because in this neighborhood he was usually first on the scene, he was something of an authority. Three years ago, he broke the Kensington cockfights. Last spring, he was the photographer who found a hooker's mangled corpse under I-95. He owed his good fortune to three things: a police scanner he kept under the seat of his pickup, a penchant for wandering and sticking his nose into other people's business, and a girlfriend whose apartment and Internet connection he persistently, and without permission, shared.

Immediately, people invoked the mannerisms of bystanders.

"Can someone tell me what happened?" Porter asked, angling his rig to get a shot of the factory in the background.

"I think somebody's hurt."

"These things come in threes."

"After Charlie's stroke, I knew something bad was gonna happen," the old man wheezed.

Porter turned his camera off and slid through the gate toward the front entrance. Red and white lights from the ambulance spun eerily across the factory walls, highlighting bare insulation, old tools, and boarded-up windows. A cluster of workers gathered around the boy, who was lying on the floor near the foreman's station. From the perimeter, Coleman watched them—short, chunky, dark-haired men, Hispanic and black, young and old, wearing chinos and sweatshirts, watching desperately as a gray-haired, middle-aged guy in stylish black slacks and a black turtleneck knelt over the collapsed worker.

Porter walked past some wooden crates that were pressed against one another. Completed, the security apparatuses looked like giant thick-framed glasses. Staying in the background, he climbed up on one and squinted to determine his best angle, his best light, and then zoomed in tight and let the tape roll. He was hoping he would catch the guy on the floor twitching involuntarily, gasping for air, writhing a little, anything that would improve the shot, but all he got was a crowd of people and the man in the turtleneck waving to the paramedics.

Dismayed, Porter turned the camera off again and looked around. In the back of the shop, next to the welding booth, was a wood-paneled office with large windows and fluorescent lights. Framed in the glass door was the silhouette of a man. Porter trained the camera on him and zoomed in. He was fat and bald, and the top of his head was slick with perspiration. Ridges were visible on his splotchy scalp, which from a distance resembled the surface of the moon. His lips were thick and rubbery, and he kept licking them, his tongue darting out like a little garden snake. He blinked repeatedly behind his thick-framed glasses, which resembled miniature versions of the Plexiglas guards being assembled in the shop. Porter could tell even through the viewfinder that the man's right eye wandered. The cameraman slid off the wooden crate and made his way toward the office in the center of the shop.

It was a curious little room. The outside walls were made of mismatched paneling, which terminated fifteen feet below the roof. There was an air conditioner that spewed moisture-laden air into a factory that must have already been intolerably hot in summer. Above the doorway was a wrought-iron sculpture of a man fishing. Coleman Porter stepped on a doormat that said PUCKMAN SECURITY. Behind him handsets crackled, and there was the generalized hum that seems to accompany disaster. The fat man was mumbling, oblivious to Porter, who tapped lightly on the glass. Getting no response, he turned the knob and pulled the door open so that the two men stood face-to-face.

"I c-c-can't believe th-th-this. I can't f-f-fucking believe this," he stuttered. "I can't believe this is h-h-happening." Porter looked down.

The man was making rhythmic little circles with one of his orthopedic shoes.

"Can you tell me what's going on?" Porter asked, flipping his camera on.

"I knew it," the fat man said. "I knew something bad was going to happen!" His nose was running, and under his glasses his eyes were red from being rubbed.

Porter put his hand on the man's shoulder, then walked around him so he could get footage of the paramedics lifting a stretcher with Gutierrez on it into the ambulance. "I'm Coleman Porter," he said, undaunted. "Independent photographer and freelance journalist. I'm from A and Erie. I was driving past when I heard the sirens." He took the fat man's limp hand in his and shook it.

The fat man groaned.

"Can I get your name, sir?" Porter asked.

"Ar-r-thur Puckman," the fat man stuttered.

"Who's hurt, Mr. Puckman?"

"G-Gutierrez," the fat man said as if he was holding his breath. "Ramon Gutierrez. Do you think he's going to d-d-die . . . ?"

"Can you tell me what happened?" Coleman held his camera at waist level, angling it up toward the man's face. For once, he was in the right place at the right time. Even better, nobody else would be allowed in once the police arrived.

"I don't really know."

"Is this your business?" Porter asked.

"It's my dad's," Arthur Puckman said, "but he's in a n-n-nursing home, so now it's just me and my b-b-brother, Chuck." Porter's shoulders sagged. Everything was perfect, except the stutter.

"What do you guys do?"

"We make custom defense barriers and security guards for taxicabs, police cruisers, check-cashing kiosks, and—"

The photographer feigned a short coughing fit to interrupt the fat man. It was strange to see a guy sobbing into his handkerchief one minute, then pitching his company's products the next.

"What do *you* do?" Coleman asked, looking for an angle.

"I'm the bookkeeper. Payables, receivables, and payroll . . ."

"How about out there?" Porter said, motioning with his free hand toward the factory.

Arthur Puckman followed Coleman Porter's hand to an area in the shop. "That's where we c-c-cut black iron. . . ."

"So tell me, Mr. Puck Man," Porter said, interrupting again. "If out there is where you cut iron, how come a guy looks like he's choking to death?" As many times as he'd been told by Philly news editors that he needed to have a lighter touch, Coleman Porter was not a tactful man. Shifting from one foot to the other, Arthur Puckman seemed alternately to panic and then to compose himself.

"Gutierrez should never have been in the t-t-t-tank," the fat man announced. "I told him we shouldn't even be using that stuff."

"What stuff?"

"The degreaser."

"Why's that?" Porter said.

"TCE is toxic," the fat man said, arching his eyebrows. "It's against the r-r-regs." Arthur Puckman wiped his face with the handkerchief.

"So who told him to do it?" Coleman asked warily.

"Same guy who makes all the d-d-decisions around here."

"Who's that?" Porter kept the camera trained on him.

"My b-b-brother."

Coleman Porter confirmed that the record light was still on, and he moved the camera to be sure the fat man was in the viewfinder. "You're saying your brother knew he was breaking the rules?" he asked.

"He didn't p-p-post MSDS sheets, or use respirators, or b-b-buy safety gloves," the fat man said, raising his voice now. "I kept t-t-telling him this kind of thing would happen someday." Arthur Puckman wiped his mouth with a handkerchief.

"Why didn't he do something about it?"

With weariness akin to remorse, Arthur Puckman answered into the camera. "He's the o-o-o-one who makes the decisions. He's the one who writes the checks—the b-b-big shot—the one who always h-has to be in charge, the one my father trusts. Over the years, I told him a l-l-lot of things. But he ignored me."

The fat man kept talking, dragging his brother down, blaming him for everything bad that happened, but by then, Coleman Porter had stopped listening. He'd gotten everything he needed for a scoop—a little local color from the neighbors, footage of the victim being carried on a stretcher, and this special bonus—one brother ratting out the other. This story would run locally, no question, but it might also get picked up. It would be worth a grand, easy, maybe two. It could even lead, which would bring him more work, possibly even reinstatement by the bureau chief who'd sworn never to put a press pass in the hands of Coleman Porter again. A moment later, the ambulance backed out of the plant, its lights flashing on the walls, its siren drowning out Arthur Puckman's words.

From the phone in his truck, Coleman called Billy Patrick. "You hear about the Puckman factory?"

"What about it?"

"One of the workers went down. They're taking him away in an ambulance."

"So what?" Patrick was on his way home, eating a pretzel with his free hand.

"He sucked in fumes."

"That's too bad, Porter."

"Yeah, very bad. The guy could be dead."

"What are you calling me for?" Patrick said, swallowing.

"I got a crooner," Coleman Porter told the cop.

"What are you talking about?" Patrick asked, taking another bite.

"I got a guy on video," Porter said, smiling, "saying it was his brother's fault."

"What do you want, a medal?"

Porter had expected a more favorable response than this. "I got the factory owner admitting safety violations," Porter said. "This is a fucking homicide, man."

"Is that your theory?" Patrick was sneering.

"You want to ignore it, fine. I'll take it to the media and tell them Philly cops aren't interested in protecting minority workers."

Billy Patrick had just worked a double shift, and he was only a couple miles from home. The notion of Coleman Porter telling the public anything was almost absurd. Now and then, the freelance photographer came up with something good, but most of the time, he was full of shit. He'd give you something that sounded interesting on the surface, but it almost always turned out to be bogus. You had to vet everything or risk making a fool out of yourself. "I've been on the street for twelve hours, and I'm heading home—"

"I'm giving you a fucking tip, man. That's what you pretend to pay me for, isn't it? If you're too tired to do your job, then go fuck yourself." Coleman Porter clicked off.

Patrick finished his pretzel. He was skeptical, but he decided to call it in anyway. Porter had a point. If you're gonna keep a snitch on the payroll, you might as well use him. "Ask the captain if he's heard anything about the Puckman factory," he said to the desk clerk. Ninety seconds later, his cell phone rang again.

"A kid named Ramon Gutierrez is at Northeastern Hospital, most likely brain dead. Whaddya got?"

"One of the factory owners is in a talking mood."

"Bring him in. Fernandez is here. He'll take the guy's statement."

Porter grabbed his bag from the backseat of his truck and took the stairs to his girlfriend's apartment two at a time. Inside, he turned on the computer, opened a Rolling Rock, and began arranging footage so that it opened with a pan of the factory exterior and finished with Arthur Puckman shaking his head. Three hours later, Porter compressed the file and sent it to all three local stations. At six, he finished the six-pack and turned on the TV. On two of the stations, he caught the anchors alluding to his story in that mock-serious tone. One of them opened with his shot of the Puckman Security sign hanging over the outside of the factory. As the police and fire trucks pulled up, a graphic with the words "Fumes in Fishtown" flashed across the screen. The newscaster, a light-skinned black woman with perfect teeth, commented that the security guard business was supposed to keep people safe, and then the video moved to the shot of Gutierrez being carried to the ambulance. Coleman flipped to the other stations. Either he missed it, or nobody else ran it. He'd find out soon enough. It was a $1,200 payday, with the possibility of syndication. "Bring me another beer, bitch," he called. His girlfriend, a leggy Puerto Rican girl, swatted his head from behind. "Get it your damn self."

At the precinct, Arthur Puckman was surrounded by telephones ringing, bright lights, harsh voices, radio static, buzzers bouncing off the cinder-block walls, and smells from a coffeemaker that had been on all day. The lighting alone was enough to make somebody feel guilty. Out of nervousness, he kept touching the cross hanging from his neck. He tucked his hands between his thighs and touched the vinyl chair.

"I kn-knew this would happen," he told the desk clerk, pushing his lips out until they looked like a pink volcano. The woman lifted her soda. Fernandez is gonna be thrilled to take this guy's statement, she thought.

"I jes need to get some information from you, and then you can 'splain it all to Detective Fernandez." Down the corridor, a door opened. Artie heard a man yelling. He felt his scrotum tighten.

"Where's my b-b-brother?" Arthur Puckman asked.

"Your last name?"

"G-G-G-Gutierrez?" Artie said. He hadn't stuttered so bad since his father's stroke.

The woman arched her eyebrows. "You don't look like a Gutierrez," she said, mocking him. Some babble; others clam up. It didn't matter to her. She lined up a form in her printer. "You want a soda?"

"H-h-how is he?" Artie asked.

"I'm sure they're doing everythin' they can," she said. She looked Artie up and down, his fleshy jowls, swollen mitts clutching a wool beanie. "Right now, I gotta finish this form." She looked at the clock on the wall. It had been her plan to have a couple of beers with her sister after work. Now, it looked as if she'd have to work late to type this guy's statement. "Your name and address?"

"Arthur Puckman, 916 South Tenth Street. I live with my mom. Since my d-d-dad left."

"Bet she's glad to have you around," the desk clerk said. The fat man listened for a trace of sarcasm. She seemed simple, asking her questions, lining up the forms, and tapping her keyboard. Simple women were usually kind to him, especially once they heard him stutter. She pointed to a small refrigerator behind her desk. "Help yourself."

Artie pictured Gutierrez lying on the cement, head tilted back, gasping for air. He felt his body clench, and he imagined himself being arrested, confined, thrown into a pen with hardened criminals. More than almost anything in the world, he didn't want to go to jail.

A buzzer sounded on her phone. "Detective Fernandez'll be right with you," the desk clerk said, pulling the paper out of the printer and sliding it into a folder.

To Artie, Fernandez seemed too young to be a detective. He wore his uniform tight, which gave him a pumped-up look, and he had a buzz cut that showed the veins in his temples when he swallowed. He was tall with an olive complexion and a bland expression. There was a revolver in a black leather holster under his arm, just like the guys on TV.

"Puckman," Fernandez announced, taking the folder. "Arthur Puckman." Artie set the soda under his chair and began a cycle of motions—inhaling deeply, shifting his weight forward, shuffling his shoes under the chair, and then leaning back. Thinking Artie was having trouble getting up on account of his weight, Fernandez reached out and took hold of the fat man's arm. Artie pulled away, kicking his soda over and splashing the detective's shoes.

"Goddamnit," Fernandez said, lifting his foot from the puddle. "What the fuck is wrong with you, man?" He pulled Artie like he was a farm animal, only the harder he pulled, the more Artie resisted, staring at him wide-eyed, his face quivering, his three chins and his bulbous cheeks and his fleshy arms shaking. The clerk leaned over her desk and handed Fernandez some paper towels and then turned away to avoid laughing. She wished others could see Fernandez tugging and swearing over a little splash on his hardtops. "Let's see if we can get you down the hall and into a room without takin' the fucking doors off," the detective said.

Artie wore dungaree jeans up high on his belly and a red-and-green button-down sweater. Short, bow-legged, with practically no butt, Artie wore orthopedic shoes that boosted his left instep and heel to balance

his height. "Can I have another soda?" he called to the clerk as he waddled down the hallway. Fernandez unlocked a door with a key from a
chain clipped to his belt and pushed the fat man into a small room.
Three of the walls were bare; the detective pointed toward a chair opposite the fourth, which was covered by a mirror. Turning sideways, Artie
shimmied along a table, then collapsed sideways into the chair.

Fernandez sat down and looked at the printed sheet in the file. Artie
removed his glasses. Fluorescent light bounced off the top of his head,
and the lazy eye made his face seem a couple centimeters off center. He
gave off a strange odor. Right away, Artie started talking. Normally,
you let a witness run, but the prospect of listening to a stutterer for
hours discouraged Fernandez.

"Excuse me, Mr., uh . . ." he said, looking again at the paper in the
folder, "Puck Man." He pronounced Artie's last name in two equally
weighted syllables.

"It's Puckman," Artie said.

"Puck Man," Fernandez said again, stressing the first syllable. He
smiled. Imagine, he thought, an imbecile teaching me how to talk.

Artie continued, oblivious. "The inspectors t-t-t-told us"—a sudden
rush of air escaped—"to stop cleaning metal in the dip tanks. . . ."
Artie sputtered and struggled, his voice thick and mangled, his words
several seconds behind his thoughts. "But Chuck said . . ." He gulped
for air, unable to catch his breath. His jaw dropped, forcing his bottom
lip to twist and quiver.

The detective rolled his eyes. He'd been working since early this
morning, and he was tired. "Whoa, whoa, whoa, whoa, whoa," he said,
sitting forward. "Let's start at the beginning." Fernandez was an imposing young man, with an ability to take charge of a situation when necessary. "How long have you worked for this, uh"—he looked at the
paper—"security business?"

"My dad started it after the war," Artie said, wiping spittle from
around the corners of his mouth. In a painstaking way, one syllable at a
time, Artie recounted the company's history, year by year since its in-
ception, how the market for security guards had developed, how the
business was a tough one, how Charlie Puckman, who'd practically in-
vented the industry, had persevered in difficult times. After a while, he

seemed to be enjoying himself, as though he was sitting with a new friend at a ball game or in a bar telling his life story. "The secret to staying in this b-b-business is keeping your costs down," he said at one point, conspiratorially.

"Which means what?" Fernandez interjected.

Artie seemed surprised by the question. "It means paying p-p-people as little and as late as you can get away with," he said proudly, as if his priority now was teaching the detective.

"How about you tell me exactly what happened today?" Fernandez said, tapping his pen against the paper.

"I don't know," Artie said, stuttering again. "I was in the office—"

"What was Gutierrez doing?" Fernandez said slowly.

"We have q-q-quality problems. Paint, mostly. That's why we w-w-worked Saturdays."

"What was he doing when he was overcome by fumes?"

"He was cleaning the tank. When you dip metal, you get r-r-residue. Dirt and grease and other impurities. Over time, the chemicals get weak. You gotta drain them and then c-c-clean the tank to get the s-s-sediment out."

"What kind of sediment?"

"I just told you—dirt and grease."

"What kind of chemicals?"

"1,1,1 trichloroethylene."

"What's that?"

"That's what it is."

"That's what what is?"

"The v-v-vapor degreaser."

"C'mon, man. I'm not a fucking scientist," Fernandez said. "How do the chemicals work?"

"If you take a penny in a p-p-pair of tongs and dip it in for a second, it'll come out in m-m-mint condition. It—"

"Okay, so it vaporizes dirt. What does it do to people?" Fernandez said.

"It's toxic," Artie said smugly. "Touch it, and it'll eat the s-s-skin off your fingers. Inhale it, and it'll r-r-ruin your lungs. Get it in your blood, and it'll affect your b-b-brain."

"So how you supposed to handle it?"

Arthur Puckman wiped his mouth on his sleeve. "I kept t-t-telling Chuck if you're gonna use this stuff, you gotta p-p-protect the workers. The tank has to be covered; you gotta f-f-flush the parts; you can't agitate it; you gotta g-g-give people respirators, aprons, rubber gloves, e-e-eye protection."

Fernandez stopped and looked toward the one-way mirror. It was exactly what Porter had told Patrick. Fernandez tapped his pen against the tabletop. He cocked his head to one side. Artie continued. "I was in the office when it h-h-happened. When I looked out, Gutierrez w-w-was laying on the floor."

Fernandez wanted to be methodical, to sort things out in a logical order. He reminded himself that crooners have their own agendas. "What about the regulations?" he asked, touching the pen to his lower lip.

"We've been getting notices f-f-from the DEP, the EPA, and OSHA since '96. There are federal regulations for halogenated solvents." The fat man knew his shit. "But my brother ignored them. I kept t-t-telling him, but he said . . . nothing b-b-bad would happen." Arthur Puckman rubbed his hands together.

"Maybe he doesn't know about chemicals."

"He went to MIT!" It was sounding too pat. There was something very calculated about this performance. Arthur Puckman was starting to really irritate Fernandez.

The detective leaned back in his chair and tried to summarize what he'd learned. There were workplace violations here, no doubt. And they'd be relatively easy to verify. There was negligence on the part of at least one, probably both, of the brothers. But it was unclear why Arthur Puckman was talking. Maybe he wanted to be in charge of the business. Maybe he just liked dissing his brother. Maybe he didn't realize that if he kept this up, both of them would be in big trouble; but if he shut up and called his lawyer, he'd walk away with a fine. The real loser was Gutierrez. The Puckmans would be making money again, and the world would stay the same. It didn't matter who you rooted for. A peculiar cooked-meal smell filled the tiny room. Fernandez had the feeling he was back working night shift in a mental hospital. A sharp knock on the door interrupted him. The detective slid his chair back and opened it a crack. "The captain wants to see you," the desk clerk said, poking her head in.

Artie was grateful for the detective's disappearance. He shifted his weight and released gas. He believed in his performance thus far, its rightness given the turn of events in the factory and in his family. He rolled his eyes up in his head and relaxed.

Fernandez took a seat in his boss's office beside a row of beat-up filing cabinets. Captain Murphy, a gap-toothed Irishman in his early sixties, veteran of more than his share of homicides, was talking on the phone and watching Arthur Puckman through the mirror. He leaned back in his chair, the phone up in the air over his mouth. "We got a kid in a coma," Murphy said, "and we got a business owner telling us he fucked up—no safety instructions, no equipment, no ventilation." From the sound of things, the person on the other end of the line was not responding the way the captain wanted him to. He was talking into the phone but looking right at Fernandez. "Can't you people get out here before Monday?" He put his hand over the mouthpiece. "Cocksuckers."

Fernandez smiled.

"Right," Murphy said, nodding. "Right. . . . Okay, okay." He hung up the phone. "OSHA can't respond till Monday," he said to Fernandez, throwing up his hands. The two of them watched Artie looking around the room, nibbling on Fernandez's pen. "What have you got, Detective?" "Same thing as Patrick's snitch. That and the history of the security guard business."

Fernandez said he believed the fat man was spinning things to serve himself, but that he was telling the truth. "Why don't we do an autopsy?" Fernandez said.

"Because the kid's not dead yet."

Fernandez bit his lip. "There's something fishy about this. Italian guys don't rat out their brothers this easy."

Murphy thought about it. "It's late. Get the guy's statement and take him home. Be nice to him. We might need him again." Fernandez stood up.

"And try to find out where they disposed of that shit, will you? If OSHA isn't interested, maybe the EPA will be."

"Yeah, boss," the detective said, turning to leave.

While Fernandez was out, the desk clerk returned to the interrogation room with a day-old box of doughnuts. Artie thought of Sister Theresa, the kindest of the nuns at St. Agnes. How grateful he was as a little boy to be tended to during those long afternoons while his tormentors—boys from the projects—waited outside. When he came back in, Fernandez told the fat man that he wanted to review what they'd discussed so far, so he could prepare Artie's statement and they could go home. But there was one more thing he wanted to know in order to understand the whole complicated process of cleaning metal. "I think you've given me an excellent education in how to clean metal, Mr. Puckman. But I wonder if you could tell me what you do with the chemicals when they don't work anymore."

"I told you that already. We drain them."

"Right. Yes," Fernandez said, pretending to make notes. "But where exactly?"

"We p-p-pull the p-p-plug," Artie said, his voice rising in pitch.

Fernandez nodded. "Of course. But where does it go?"

Arthur Puckman was silent.

"I mean the contents of the tank, the residue of those chemicals—1, 1, 1 TCE, whatever it's called." In his office, Murphy leaned toward the glass, listening intently.

"We s-s-spray it first t-t-to loosen it up," Artie said quietly.

"Uh-huh," Fernandez said. The detective flipped his paper cup into the trash can. "When the chemical loses its strength—when it doesn't clean metal anymore—you spray water in, to kind of loosen it up."

"Exactly," Artie said, nodding.

"And then you pull the plug and drain it."

"Yeah. Right."

Fernandez leaned forward. "So where does it go?" He was enjoying himself.

"Into the p-p-pipe . . ."

"Uh-huh." Fernandez tapped his pen against the table. "And the pipe leads where?"

"I d-d-don't know."

"Really? You seem to know so much."

Artie smiled nervously. "Not really."

"Into the sewer?"

More silence.

Fernandez leaned in again. "C'mon, Mr. Puckman, it has to go somewhere."

"I d-d-dunno."

In his office, Captain Murphy picked up the phone.

Artie folded his arms over his chest. His mouth hung open, his tongue pressed against his bottom teeth, and his eyes rolled up in his head. His brow was a deep shade of red, and there were beads of sweat on his upper lip and scalp. He was angry. These questions had caused him to lose his composure, which was a dangerous and familiar feeling. The detective had tricked him.

Fernandez would have kept going, but the captain interrupted. "It's a wrap," he said over the loudspeaker. He'd left a message with an Agent Keaton at the Environmental Protection Agency, Region Three.

Fernandez pushed his chair back from the table and studied the malodorous human being who sat before him. Artie's body posture had changed completely. While he'd never been at ease, the fat man had seemed comfortable enough before. Now, he was mumbling to himself and moving his hands around as if he were conducting several simultaneous conversations with invisible beings that encircled him.

Since he was a kid, Fernandez had heard about guys who rat out their friends out of loyalty to someone or something, either as a favor or to carry out a threat. Some trade what they have, and others tattle to extricate themselves from bad situations. There are those who plea-bargain, or buy what they think is their own safety, and there are crooners who say what they say and then regret it. There are religious nuts and those who just don't give a shit. The one thing they have in common is that you can't trust them. Every one of them is playing an angle. As a detective, you had to filter what you heard, examine the physical evidence, and then come back and ask questions. The faster you draw conclusions, the sooner you make mistakes. Even though the fat guy's story wasn't playing for him, Fernandez would write up the report, leave it with Murphy, and then head home for a few hours of rest.

"We're gonna break here," he said to Artie. "I'll have the girl type up what we've got," Fernandez said, looking at his watch. "You look it over, sign it, and I'll take you home. How's that sound?"

Artie nodded his head.

The statement Arthur Puckman finally signed contained three disclosures that Captain Murphy said would give the police, the EPA, and OSHA maximum leeway to investigate the Gutierrez accident. First was that the Puckman brothers knew about numerous safety violations that existed in the plant, including those involving the use of hazardous chemicals. Second, that Chuck Puckman specifically ordered Gutierrez to clean out the tank, knowing he'd have to climb inside, where he was likely to be overcome by fumes. And third, that either Arthur Puckman didn't know or, more likely, Puckman Security hadn't arranged for toxic liquid from the tank to be discharged legally.

In exchange for his cooperation, Arthur Puckman earned himself a ride in the back of a 1997 undercover police cruiser, driven by Detective Fernandez. This, in and of itself, was not unusual. It was rainy and cold, and Fernandez was exhausted. Sitting behind him, Artie closed his eyes. His mind was going a mile a minute. They were only a few blocks from the precinct when the fat man asked Fernandez if he could visit his father before being dropped off. "He'll go into shock if he hears about this from somebody else," Artie whined. Indeed he will, Fernandez thought, when he learns that his son has for some mysterious reason implicated all three of them.

Reluctantly, Fernandez took Frankford north a few miles into the Great Northeast, and then pulled the patrol car into the circular drive. Elysian Fields was a squat nursing home consisting of three brick rectangles, joined at odd angles to fit a footprint of land carved around the interstate. There was an odd slope to the parking lot. Had it been a putting green, Fernandez thought, getting to the glass front doors in a straight shot would have been a challenge. "Five minutes," Fernandez said, tapping his watch. Artie walked slowly, his head tilted at an absurd angle.

At the front desk, Artie announced his father's name. The receptionist typed something into the computer. Artie stared at the watercolors on the walls, amateurishly simple paintings of ducks, geese, and other waterfowl. They seemed perfectly useless, devoid of any cheer that might have been intended. "Orange. Second floor. Room 210." She motioned down a hallway to a bank of elevators. An acrid smell, a mixture of urine and disinfectant, wafted toward him.

Artie's father had been assigned to a floor for stroke victims who were frozen in a perpetual fluorescence that illuminated the physical world they were denied. There, men and women sat in wheelchairs along the corridor, their hands folded in their laps, their heads lolling from side to side, mouths suspended over wet bibs, looking sideways at each other. Behind the buzz of the lights, Artie heard canned laughter erupting from the TVs.

It had been a year since his father had been moved from Northeastern Hospital to Elysian Fields, and, in that time, the old man had lost most of his body mass. Each day, a therapist visited him, but the extent of his daily workout was using the fingers of his right hand to shoo her away. Charlie Puckman took his meals through a bag attached to his arm and breathed through a tube in his nose. He watched television all day and all night. He slept in jags. When he felt himself drifting off, he woke with a start. Mute, except for a little chalkboard that rested on his sunken chest, he had no choice on this night but to accept a visit from the son he despised.

Artie was not there out of compassion or curiosity. He had not come to reminisce about the childhood he wished he'd had, or to talk to his father about declining sales or problems with the bank, or to complain about Puckman Security since his brother, Chuck, had taken over. Every family business has its mysteries. Offspring wonder what they could have accomplished on their own, whether what they had was earned or given, whether after being mollycoddled and spoon-fed at the table of plenty, they could survive the trials and tribulations of the real world. Where there's a family business, there are brutal comparisons between siblings;

rivalries between cousins; animosity between spouses; that reflect slights, real and perceived, grudges, past and present, hatred and hurt, gnarly, emotional wounds exaggerated by secrecy.

For his part, over the years, Charlie Puckman had offered opinions and judgments to anyone who'd listen. He complained about his unreliable workers, his thieving bankers, his miserable customers, and his good-for-nothing sons. He sulked and loafed and paraded around, assigning shit jobs to those around him, sucking whatever cash and satisfaction he could as though he alone was entitled to it. And like many of his generation, he never planned for the fate of the business after he was gone. By avoiding this single task and refusing to delineate responsibilities beyond doing what needed to be done, and by hoarding shares of stock, he'd made it clear that there'd be nothing to inherit when he died. In his mind, this prevented his sons from wishing for his demise. So as Artie approached his father's room that night, he had a gleeful feeling seeing his father propped up in bed, thin as a rail.

"Can I help you?" a night-shift nurse holding a tray of medication asked.

"I'm Arthur. Ch-Ch-Charlie Puckman's son . . ."

"Your father is very agitated tonight," she said, pressing her lips together and arching her eyebrows.

The room was dark except for the flicker of the television. Artie stood in the doorway and looked at the shriveled form in the bed, which was jackknifed so the old man could see the television without moving his neck. There were two lumps under the blankets where knees would be. "Hello, Pop," Artie said, twisting his mouth.

Charlie Puckman Sr. stared straight ahead. If he was aware of his son in the room, he gave no indication. Artie moved a chair from against the wall and the two of them sat there in silence, watching commercials. A few minutes later, Artie heard the *Action News* theme, its staccato beat signaling something lurid and unimportant. A male newscaster appeared in a trench coat, live from Kensington. "Unsafe conditions and an industrial accident in Fishtown has left one worker in a coma and . . ."

Artie moved forward and turned the volume up. "That's us, Pop!" he said excitedly. They were showing Coleman Porter's footage now on all three networks. You could see the Puckman factory in muted daylight, the fence up, the garage like a gaping mouth. In the parking lot, off to one side, was Chuck's black Suburban. Charlie Puckman began to moan, soft and low. His head slumped forward, his eyes turned as far to the side as they could, and the fingers of his right hand pointed toward the television.

"The police are blaming Chuck . . ."

". . . in critical condition," the reporter said.

The old man blinked repeatedly and stared ahead. His cheeks were flush, in contrast with his neck and forehead, which had gone flabby since the stroke. His lips were grayish blue and they quivered, and he struggled to moisten them every few seconds.

"I know what you're thinking, Pop. None of this would have happened if only you'd been around. . . ." Artie paused. "But we have to face the facts now, Pop. Look at you." Charlie Puckman kept blinking, unable to focus on the television screen or his son. "Because you're not around anymore, I called Fat Eddie." Artie was improvising now. "He told me to get Chuck's bail." Last year, while pretending to nap at his desk, Artie watched his father emerge from the office bathroom, put down his newspaper, and kneel beside the small refrigerator in the pantry. Thinking he was not being observed, the old man slid open the panel in the wall and fidgeted with a dial. Something metallic clicked and there was a rustling of papers. Later that night, after everyone had gone home, with a flashlight and a penknife, Artie lifted the panel and found an old-fashioned safe built into the wall.

Artie moved his face up to his dad's. "You have to give me the combination to the safe," he whispered. Something akin to hatred passed between them—decades of mutual disdain—a pattern that began when Artie was an infant. "Write it down. I'll take it to Fat Eddie, and he'll take care of everything." Arthur Puckman picked up the little blackboard and a piece of chalk and held it under his father's hand. He'd waited a lifetime to be in this position. With Artie holding the chalkboard, it took the old man three passes to make it legible. "Don't worry about nothing, Pop," Artie said, transferring the numbers to a piece of paper. Then he rode the elevator down and ambled through the lobby. He was humming.

Fernandez ground his third cigarette out on the asphalt. A fine mist blew steadily toward them from the river. For thirty minutes, the detective had been playing with his radio and listening to fellow cops being dispatched to break up bar fights or domestic squabbles. "What took you so fucking long?" he said when Artie finally appeared.

"He was pretty upset," Artie said quietly.

"Where's your car?"

"At the factory," Artie said. It was near eleven, and Fernandez was eager to get home. Rain and the newly minted highway surface under the whitewalls made a sibilant sound as the Impala headed south on I-95 and then snaked through Kensington to the factory.

"This yours?" Fernandez said, as he pulled next to Chuck's Suburban, the only vehicle in the lot.

"Nah."

"Then where is it?"

"I don't dr-dr-dr-drive."

"Then what the fuck are we doing here?"

"I gotta pick something up," Artie said, opening the car door. Strange how the ones who need kindness the most are the ones who piss you off, Fernandez thought. Then he remembered the drains. "We're gonna spend no more than five minutes here," the detective said, "and then I'm leaving, with or without you." He intended to see where the tanks emptied so he could finish his report without coming back Monday. Pigeons roosting above the loading dock scattered as the two men approached. The flaps were closed, as was the overhead door. Artie fumbled with the keys.

"I'll just be a minute," he said to Fernandez.

"Switch on the lights, will you?" Fernandez said, pushing past him.

Artie wobbled past frames that were in various stages of assembly and opened the electrical panel. One at a time, rows of fluorescent lights flickered on throughout the shop, while the offices remained dark.

Fernandez looked at the assembly areas. Beat-up plywood tabletops mounted on scissor lifts, stacked parts, bins of hardware, electric drills suspended from hangers, posters of busty women wearing tool belts taped to columns, and partial assemblies gave the appearance of another world, one of organized mayhem in service to production. Fernandez made his way over to the dip tanks.

Artie hurried into the office. From his father's desk with the Plexiglas paperweight, the letter opener in a leather sheaf with his initials, and the Lucite ashtray with the fancy *P* insignia, he looked out across the factory as the old man used to, watching for the movement of workers, monitoring who was working on which projects, calculating how much material they'd scrapped, and who was dogging it. Artie saw Fernandez standing near the tanks. There was something eerie about an outsider in the factory unescorted. The old man would never have allowed it.

Artie crossed the office in darkness to a small alcove with a restroom, a microwave, and a refrigerator. The coffeemaker had been left on, and the same burnt smell from the precinct permeated this room. He opened the closet, took out a brown paper bag, and set it on the floor. Low down on the wall next to the refrigerator was the panel. Artie used his penknife to slide it up, revealing the front of the safe Charlie Puckman had built into the Sheetrock. It was too dark to see the paper, so he opened the refrigerator door and read the numbers to himself out loud, spinning the dial first to the left, then to the right, slowing after each turn. Twice he spun the tumbler to the end of the sequence. Both times, the door stayed locked. On the third try, the tumblers clicked, and the door opened.

Artie sat on the floor, out of breath, staring into the darkness. He reached in. There was a layer of grit on top of a thick stack of papers, and it smelled musty. It would have taken him too long to examine everything, so he pulled it out and stuffed it into the bag, one large handful after another, as quickly as he could. Some of it was cash. Several sheets had raised insignias. They were stiff and official-looking. He noticed familiar logos—General Electric, General Motors, Occidental Petroleum. The last stack appeared to be parchment with the U.S. Treasury seal embossed on top. Artie stuffed it all into his bag. At the very bottom of the safe was a leather pouch, the kind businesses used years ago to make bank deposits. Artie turned it upside down and more bills—twenties, fifties, and hundreds—spilled onto the floor. Behind him, he heard a click, a creaking sound, and then Detective Fernandez speaking to him from the doorway.

"Why is it so fucking dark in here?"

"I d-d-d-d-dunno," Artie said. "I think it's a circuit."

"What the fuck are you doing, anyway?"

Artie shut the door to the safe as quietly as he could and spun the dial. He slid the panel down and quietly closed the refrigerator. "I was just making sure the coffee machine was off," he said, folding over the top of the bag.

"How could the coffee machine be on if the circuit breaker's tripped?"

"I d-d-dunno," Artie said, sweating.

"Let's go," Fernandez said. He'd seen what he needed to see.

Outside, it had stopped raining, and the streets were slick. The two men rode in silence down Broad Street to Washington Avenue. Fernandez turned left on Eleventh and then stopped. Artie pulled the brown bag to his chest and opened the passenger door. Fernandez watched the fat man shuffle up the block, double back, and then turn into a doorway. Fernandez put the car in reverse and backed onto Washington Avenue, passing cars that were double-parked. He turned left on Ninth Street, passing the empty iron tables where the vendors set up and the trash cans that served as heaters in the Italian Market. He pulled over in front of a row of Asian storefronts, picked up the radio transmitter and called Murphy. "The dip tank drained into the floor," he told his boss. "These guys have been dumping methyl-ethyl-bad-shit into storm drains in the middle of Fishtown for God knows how many years."

"Take the rest of the day off, Freddy," Murphy said. "You done good."

Sunday, January 24, 1999

It was after midnight. Heavy clouds obscured the moon and stars. It had been raining steadily since Gutierrez had been whisked away and the employees of Puckman Security—those who'd been present when he went down and others who'd stayed home, all of them—gathered outside the hospital, whispering to one another in Spanish, smoking cigarettes and sipping coffee from plastic cups. After learning that the boy was comatose, with little if any electrical activity being generated in his brain, they felt a crushing sadness, not only for Ramon Gutierrez and his family, but for themselves—as if they realized their lives had been in service to something dangerous but trivial. Chuck Puckman stood among them for a while, shifting uneasily from side to side, trying to make eye contact with the doctors at first, then Johnny Gutierrez, even offering him a cigarette, which Ramon's father declined, before walking home, hands stuffed in his pockets, shivering, imagining the ambulance lights spinning in the quiet living rooms of the little houses that lined the streets. He kept his head down, measuring the approach of cars by the sound of tire treads and the hiss of spray, which made the street surfaces slick, like somebody had applied a layer of varnish. There was a make-believe quality to the night.

Arriving at the factory, soaked to his skin, Chuck entered the open gate and crossed the yard, passing the brick wall with the placard that reserved his parking space, then climbed the fire escape steps to the enclosed landing outside his red apartment door. Inside, he stripped, tossed his shirt and shoes onto the floor, limped down a short hallway in the dark, and collapsed on his waterbed. He made no attempt to organize his thoughts. Moments later, these images visited him: He was lying on a bed of cement, unable to move, twenty, maybe thirty stories below a high-rise apartment building. Filtering down from above, he could hear sounds from a cocktail party or reception he'd attended, along with a cross section of everyone he ever knew—his high school guidance counselor, the grizzled alcoholic barker from the vegetable stand at the corner of Washington and Ninth, his brother, Artie, his father, and several of his father's friends. Only moments ago, while Chuck had been having a drink, his father's mood had darkened and an argument erupted. With a crazed look on his face, Charlie Puckman was poking his son in the chest, berating him for ruining the business and squandering the family's fortune. Chuck defended himself as best he could, backing up so he was pressed up against the balcony, when, in a moment of clarity and courage, Chuck eased himself up over the railing and tumbled, feet over head, head over feet, until, unable to control his rate of descent or body position, he landed on his back with a thud. Minutes passed, maybe hours. He had to remind himself to breathe.

When he woke a few hours later, he made his way across the hallway into the bathroom, where he spilled three white pills into his palm and formed a cup with the other. He leaned down and swallowed them in one gulp, then shut the cabinet and stared in the mirror until his ashen face and sullen expression spooked him. He put the radio on and lay down on the couch, where he slept fitfully until dawn.

Sunday was clear and windy. After dressing, he went back down the fire escape steps and started walking. He passed a young man with a wispy beard who looked directly at him. "The heat is on, my brother," the man said, shaking his head. Chuck wrapped his arms around his body. The wind blew through him. A block ahead, the giant chain drug-store gleamed like a temple amid the blighted buildings under the El, which seemed to shrink in shame.

The store was laid out with the least important items in the front, forcing patrons to pass by acres of candy and snacks, expensive hair dye, greeting cards, nail clippers, wart cream, and adult diapers to get their prescriptions filled. A spinning display rack held security de-vices: Mace, whistles, flashlights. Chuck waited in line, surrounded by men and women of all sizes and types—the diabetics, the hyper-tense, the overweight, the overwrought with their baskets—all of them ex-posed to the mightiness of the health-care sector, the maw of modern medicine—until a pharmacist in training finally filled his prescrip-tion. On his way out, he saw it—or at least he perceived it in the way that an image comes before words and feelings, before thoughts. It was a photograph of the Puckman factory, shot at a wide angle from across the street—the faded sign, the hinged gate, the squat buildings, indifferent to the years, his Suburban parked at the same odd angle it had been yesterday. By instinct, his shoulders tensed, and he veered away from the stack of newspapers with the headline "Fumes Fell Worker in Fishtown." He lurched toward the automatic doors and took off across the parking lot, dropping the bag and the receipt and wrestling with the safety cap before spilling a little white pill into his hand and swallowing it dry. By the time he got home, the lorazepam had provided a buffer between the stunning reality of his life now, postaccident, and the past. In a daze, he lifted the phone and pressed the numbers of the foreman of Puckman Security, his only friend, Rahim Rodriguez.

Puckman Security

In the mid-1960s, Charlie Puckman was a sinewy little guy with close-cropped black hair and dark little eyes set close together. He was a coarse man with a short fuse and a propensity for swearing and also a way of charming people with what appeared to be plainspokenness. He had a vast store of patience, perseverance, and a salesman's tolerance for rejection. By the time he was thirty, he'd tried a dozen different schemes to get rich, one after another, including marrying a Sicilian girl for what he hoped would become blood ties to certain successful South Philly entrepreneurs.

Around the same time, with Cuba's Communist government in its infancy, Jose Rodriguez was a professor of engineering who made a risky move by petitioning Castro for an exit visa. After five years of harassment, a government official finally delivered it to him, giving the family four hours to pack up their belongings and leave. Two days later, Jose, his wife, and their two children—Rafael and Ovella—were huddling, exhausted, in a church off North Fifth Street in Philadelphia, listening to hymns in a language their father had dreamed about.

When Jose showed up at the factory, Charlie was two months into a venture he called the Puckman Security Company. He'd gotten the idea to make wrought-iron cages while driving by a pawnshop that was being robbed in broad daylight. In the mid-sixties, the need for security in urban areas was growing, and the economy was good, so Charlie Puckman was up to his ears in orders. He hired Jose on the spot, even though Jose barely spoke English and didn't have his own tools. Charlie Puckman pointed to the seven on his watch and then to the cement floor, and the two men had an understanding.

Charlie had won the building in a card game. During the Korean War, he and his friends invited young men—graduates of one of the Friends' schools who'd drawn deferments or were conscientious objectors—to play poker with them. Through a combination of distractions, deceptions, and an elaborate set of signals, Charlie and his buddies managed to win and win big, including one particular time when Charlie and a fellow from the Main Line squared off and the fellow made a foolish bet near the end of the evening for a pot worth almost $5,000. Rather than pay up, the loser convinced his father, an industrialist, to part with a cluster of run-down factories in Kensington.

Six months later, Puckman Security had enough orders to keep Jose and his friends from church employed full-time. Jose was a tireless worker and a fastidious organizer; however, his greatest talent was being able to build what Charlie sold, without drawings or specifications. From orders written on place mats, the backs of envelopes, and traffic tickets, Jose cut, welded, stripped, painted, built, and delivered completed units to pawnbrokers all over the city. He was the perfect foil for his boss: focused, humble, detail-oriented, and quiet. He worked fast, using no more materials than were necessary, and he generated little if any scrap. In less than a year, Puckman Security was shipping security guards to Atlantic City and Harrisburg, and Charlie was fielding inquiries from pawnbrokers in Trenton, Wilmington, even Baltimore. The only thing Jose Rodriguez couldn't do was answer the phone, which is in part why Charlie agreed to hire his oldest son, Arthur.

Arthur Puckman had been in and out of mental institutions at least a half dozen times by the time he was twenty. In between, he held a succession of short-lived, dead-end jobs, mooching off his mother in South Philly. By the late sixties, when Chuck suddenly and mysteriously quit college, Jose was running the shop, Charlie Puckman was on the road, and Artie was working in the office. Initially, Artie's job was to answer the phone, make out payroll checks for his father to sign, and source supplies. From the get-go, Artie developed sly methods of duping people—making out checks that were slightly less than they were supposed to be, and setting the clocks in the shop back so as to extract extra labor for free. Indeed, Arthur had a mean streak, and when Charlie was away, he directed it toward the trio of laborers making iron barriers and brackets for banks, taxicab companies, and pawnshops.

Although Jose's son, Rafael, was a bright kid, he'd had a rough paper route. Philadelphia was a difficult place to grow up in the late sixties, especially Kensington, where the Italians and the Irish watched angrily as Puerto Ricans, Colombians, Guatemalans, and blacks moved in. Being Cuban was the worst of all worlds, set apart not only from blacks and whites but, because of politics and their affinity and nostalgia for a burgeoning capitalist economy, from other Latinos, too. Rafael was a skinny kid with jet black hair, a beguiling smile, and a wicked wit. He was asthmatic and slight in stature, and therefore uninterested in fighting and sports. Fortunately, he was blessed with street smarts and a sharp sense of humor. He did impersonations of his teachers, talking in heavily accented English and joking his way out of fights.

A couple years after they arrived, Jose's wife, Rafael's mother, died, and Rafael changed his name to Rahim. He bought himself a pair of four-inch-high platform shoes and some eyeliner, and he started running with the pretty boys and the glam rockers under the El; once or twice, even climbing in cars with men on their way home from Center City for money. A few times, he fell in love—with a trash sculptor living in an abandoned warehouse, a PhD historian who worked nights in a hospital, and a mechanic who, for some reason, could perform only in his car. The relationships were exciting, and Rahim was always head over heels, but they didn't last. In the summer of 1974, after an especially rough breakup, Rahim lost interest in the scene and began playing chess with men in a nearby shelter, and building radios and TV sets with his father on weekends. Soon after, he started hanging around at the shop, where he befriended Chuck.

Long after the day's work was done—after the trash was emptied and the wooden skids were ripped apart and stored in bins, after the mail had been carried to the post office, the shop floors swept, and the bins of soaked rags and cigarette butts had been taken out back and burned—Chuck and Rahim got buzzed on hashish and swapped stories. Rahim made his father out to be a hero—part revolutionary, part Communist, part refugee. Chuck exaggerated his sexual escapades at MIT, telling stories about dangerous drug deals he'd done, demonstrations he'd led, deliberately confusing his past with that of others he admired. Sitting on the hill behind the railroad spur, with The Doors and Cream playing on Chuck's transistor radio, they absorbed each other's pasts.

Around the same time, Charlie Puckman found himself in a jam. The business was growing, which required his workers to be more productive. Tasks like taking trash to the Dumpsters, refilling the supply closets, sweeping up metal shavings, and filling out bills of lading weren't getting done. Meanwhile, Arthur Puckman, looking for areas of the company where he could wield influence, started interacting with workers. When he began taking meticulous interest in workers' arrival and departure times, their efficiency at their individual tasks, and even their grooming habits, several announced they were quitting. In response, Charlie hired Rahim to keep the shop going and assigned the more mundane tasks to Artie.

Charlie's younger son, Chuck, showed up at his father's factory in the middle of the first semester of his sophomore year of college, owing a New England rock band over $1,500 for a drug deal that went bad. When he first arrived, he carried himself like a man on the run—in trouble so deep, he couldn't hold his head up or meet someone's eye. With no money, no way of avoiding the draft, and no prospects for work, he took a position in his father's firm—something he swore he'd never do. In time, he proved an able salesman, and with Rahim's and Jose Rodriguez's help, he learned the ins and outs of the security guard business. Within a year, Chuck had himself a Datsun 240Z and a fancy apartment overlooking Rittenhouse Square. He learned to scuba dive at the YMCA and started traveling—to the Florida Keys, Mexico, Belize. An oral surgeon who lived in his building kept him supplied with Darvon and phenobarbital, which he used to take the edge off the black beauties he used during the week. Socially, he kept a low profile. His friends from high school had established themselves in marriages. Chuck preferred brief encounters and superficial affairs, ones he could make and break easily. In matters of the heart, he said he preferred leasing to making a purchase.

When Chuck turned thirty, he started dating one of his customer's daughters. Eileen Borowitz was a good-looking girl—tall, thin, well built, with a glossy made-up face and an impish smile that she used to deflect genuine conversation. She had a superficial notion of love, which revolved around using nicknames, purchasing trinkets, and reading rhyming poems on sentimental occasions like birthdays and odd anniversaries. She had a shrill, inappropriate laugh, which Chuck mistook for good nature, and she demonstrated an eagerness in bed that he confused with passion. In the fall of 1980, for the simple reason that he was tired of doing his own laundry, Chuck married her. A year later, before he could do anything to correct his mistake, they had Ivy.

For certain men, in certain phases of life, having a child can be a magnificent event, allowing them access to what is soft and vulnerable and nurturing inside them. The smell of an infant, the way she looks up at her parent, helpless, but without fear, often quiets the spirit of even the most troubled adult. Not so with Chuck Puckman. Ivy's arrival was an event that required massive changes to the way the two of them lived at a time when things at work were changing dramatically for the worse. For starters, Eileen decided that Chuck's apartment in Center City was completely inappropriate for a young family, and her constant badgering convinced him to buy an obscenely expensive center-hall Colonial in Villanova. And as if the mortgage wasn't big enough, Eileen racked up credit card charges and committed the couple to ongoing debt by furnishing the nursery, buying clothes, and making donations to private schools in which she expected their progeny to be enrolled. Finally, the baby's arrival seemed to mark the end of any genuine feeling Eileen had for her husband, and although Chuck tried, at least initially, to get to know Ivy, Eileen wouldn't let him near her.

Several years passed. Chuck went on the road, partly to expand the business and partly to get away from his wife. By day, he worked for his misanthropic father, selling a product for which he had no real interest, correcting his brother's mistakes, and enduring Arthur's not-so-subtle resentment. By night, Eileen harangued him for not earning enough to provide her with an adequate lifestyle. When he objected, she freaked, professing to be too sweet and accepting for his kind, a claim she'd make in the nastiest of ways, like a vicious little animal trapped in a cage. Over time, Chuck seemed to shrink in his own skin—coming to work, going home, disappearing with a drink onto the couch, and opting out of the franchise of fatherhood.

During this time, Rahim settled down, sharing an apartment with his sister, who worked across the street at Northeastern Hospital. At Chuck's urging, Charlie increased Rahim's responsibilities at Puckman Security, and, before long, he was creating a complicated build schedule every week and apportioning work to the various tradesmen and outside contractors, coordinating everything so that units could be shipped and billed to customers.

Early on, Charlie Puckman had told his boys that the security guard business would someday disappear and that the Puckman designs would become commodities, easily copied, imported for pennies from low-cost overseas suppliers. With three family members on the draw and a shop full of ancient equipment, he warned that no one would ever be interested in buying the business. Yet year after year, they kept cranking out product and meeting their obligations. By the early nineties, the old man was losing energy. He still swept cash from company accounts and drew a large salary, but he actually did very little. When Chuck petitioned his father for commissions on sales or an increase in salary, Artie threw a fit and demanded the same. When Chuck mentioned quitting, the old man reminded him that if he did, he would get nothing. They fought like dogs. Meanwhile, the business underperformed, drawing bank debt in excess of its asset value.

Chuck and Eileen's marriage died the long death of relationships that never should have been. By the time Ivy was in grade school, Eileen was a fastidious chronicler of Chuck's inadequacies, his self-absorption, his dalliances with drugs and alcohol, his bitterness, and his tendency to withdraw. They avoided each other in the house. They seldom ate together, and when they did, it was in silence. Sex, when it occurred, was perfunctory. Eileen blamed Chuck for every bad choice, every piece of bad luck, every mistake she had ever made; he froze inside at the sight and sound of her. There were glimmers of hope now and then—at home, after dinner in a fancy restaurant, or, when stoked with vodka, they danced for several hours at a black-tie affair. One night, Eileen professed to understand how badly Chuck needed to strike out on his own, to get away from his brother and father, how Puckman Security had become a toxic environment; but in the end, she refused to dial down her spending. "Anything that would lighten your load," she said curtly, "would by definition increase mine."

To the outside world, Chuck was distant, expressionless, and mysteriously unhappy, and when other people considered his situation, his station in life, they were baffled. He was the vice president of a successful business; he was married to an attractive woman; he was the father of an adorable preteen—an equestrian with trophies and pictures of herself standing next to beautiful horses and stern-looking instructors—yet something was dead and rotting inside him. One therapist guessed anhedonia, an inability to experience joy; and then acedia, an absence of feeling altogether. Chuck's mother recommended he suck it up and will himself to feel better. A marriage counselor suggested that Chuck and Eileen sign a contract, promising to date each other as if they were still courting. Reading a battery of tests he'd taken—a depression inventory, a suicide scale, a hopefulness index—a psychiatrist quietly nodded her head. The last summer they spent together as a family was made possible at least in large part by several vials full of mood enhancers and anxiety-reducing medication Chuck began taking. A biochemical orchestra in his brain began tuning up.

Meanwhile, the business teetered. Puckman Security, which had started by serving pawnshops and check-cashing stores, began losing orders to companies that furnished electronic surveillance. Cameras, motion detectors, heat sensors, and sophisticated recording devices replaced mechanical guards. Fat settlement checks from insurance companies made it easier for businesses to survive theft. Competition heated up. Sales flatlined, and costs kept rising. Chuck contributed articles to trade publications, spoke on panels, and made nauseatingly long pilgrimages into territories they'd never sold in before. Still, more often than not, he came home empty-handed. What they should have done was harvest the business, husband their cash, and put the thing up for sale. Instead, they hunkered down and waited. An investment banker could have told them that it was just a matter of time before the Puckman family was squeezed out by new companies—bigger ones with new equipment and better methods of manufacturing. It appeared to Chuck that he had worked his entire life in this miserable place on faith that someday he would be rewarded, and now, he had nothing to show for it.

Eileen dropped all pretense of being satisfied. She stopped cooking, keeping house, doing laundry, and, on occasion, even sleeping at home. In the mornings, while Chuck worked, she danced aerobically, played tennis, bought Ivy and herself new outfits, and lunched with friends. In the afternoons, she squired Ivy to violin, horseback riding, and acting lessons. That last winter, instead of making sales calls, Chuck spent entire afternoons in hotel rooms—drinking, smoking cigarettes, and watching TV.

One Thursday evening, Chuck borrowed Eileen's car to make an emergency service call. On the front seat was her appointment book, filled with the names and places of her activities and liaisons. It suddenly occurred to him: He might be stuck in a trap with his father, his brother, and his business, but there was no law forcing him to finance the excesses of a woman he despised. The following morning, he packed as if he were leaving for a business trip—passport, fancy watch, toothbrush, shaving kit, and a couple of suits—and checked into the Radnor Hotel. The next day, he moved himself into the apartment above the factory and, with Rahim's help, bought some secondhand furniture and a dozen tropical fish for the big tank his father had bought years ago. Two days later, Chuck received a petition for divorce demanding full custody of Ivy. When he called Eileen to make a financial settlement, she hung up on him.

At about the same time, Rahim had some trouble of his own—fever, swollen glands, diarrhea, and strange purple splotches appearing on his skin and then disappearing. In the fall, he developed a cough, and by Christmas, he'd started spitting blood and losing weight. One night, Ovella practically had to carry him into the emergency room, where he was diagnosed with *Pneumocystis carinii* pneumonia. A day later, a somber-looking resident told him he'd tested positive for HIV.

At the factory, Chuck tolerated Rahim's latenesses and assigned him easy tasks. He made sure Artie didn't let Rahim's insurance lapse. When Rahim was well enough to return to work, Chuck withdrew enough cash from the business for Rahim to sign up for computer classes in the event he had to work from home. Rahim threw himself into this new field, exploring search engines, Web design, and information technology strategies. He studied computer architecture, read books that detailed assembly and machine language, and helped Ovella apply for and get a better position at the hospital.

Each time Rahim's symptoms returned and he was forced to stay home and rest, Chuck settled into a pattern of postponing his business trips and working long hours in the shop. When Rahim felt well and the business had a good month, Chuck allowed himself a few days off. Meanwhile, Eileen's lawyer mounted an impressive offensive, demanding half the value of the business in cash, the house less any mortgage or home equity loans, and alimony for life.

Chuck awoke startled on the morning of the third day to the sound of rain, percussive and steady over the tiny apartment, particularly the bedroom, where the metal roof was uninsulated. He went into the kitchen and took a package of Benson & Hedges out of a bag under the sink. Then he splashed some water on his face. Slowly, it came back to him. In the living room, he gathered the empty beer bottles into which he'd dropped cigarette butts. The apartment had a dank, bitter odor, like old coffee grounds. It was hard to believe that only forty-eight hours ago, his biggest problem had been repairing and returning security partitions for a bank in Bristol. The clock on the VCR said seven A.M. The jazz station had switched to classical, its daytime format. By now, the shop would be open, a pot of coffee already brewed, and his brother, Artie, would be sitting at his desk reading the *Daily News*. Across town, a young man was fighting for his life. He put on some slacks, a pair of socks, shoes, a button-down shirt. At seven thirty, Chuck Puckman opened the front door, stepped out on the fire escape landing, and looked down through a small opening in the brick wall.

As unsettled as he was by the day's arrival, he was wholly unprepared for what he saw. The rain had stopped, at least temporarily, though the sky was opaque. Instead of a parking lot full of beat-up old cars and a cluster of workers surrounding the breakfast truck, smoking and talking to one another, it was empty and quiet. There was no life, no sign that the shop was open, no indication even that a business had ever operated there. Chuck raced down the steps and faced the loading dock, cupping his hand around his eyes and peering in the tiny windows. It was pitch black inside.

As he strained to see, a man called to him from behind. "Charles Puckman Jr.?" he said stiffly. Chuck turned and squinted. A tall man with a ruddy complexion hauling a large black case reached into his suit jacket and shook open a single sheet of paper, holding it chest high for Chuck to read. "I'm Agent Keaton with the Environmental Protection Agency, Region Three, Criminal Investigation Division. This is a search warrant for the factory and offices of Puckman Security." As he spoke, he waved to the first of three vans that were idling in front of the gate. "By order of the U.S. Attorney's Office, these offices and its contents belong to us. Until our investigation is complete, remove nothing. No files, computer or paper, no raw materials, no work in process, no computers, faxes, office objects, equipment, tools, loose pieces of paper, written notations of any kind. Do you understand?"

A half dozen men in what looked like moon suits emerged from the vans and began unloading equipment—coolers, toolboxes, and devices that looked like fishing spears, robotic arms for lifting things. "Unit One," Keaton said, making a bullhorn with his hands. "Take the rear; Unit Two, the southern side; Unit Three, the tanks, including groundwater; Unit Four, soil; Unit Five, office and records. Mr. Puckman," he said, still yelling, "I'd appreciate it if you'd accompany me." He lowered his voice. "We've got a lot of work to do, and I could use your help." Keaton's teams dispersed to the different sections of the plant. As instructed, three men in suits went to the back of the factory and into the yard. Others with cameras, sketch pads, and tool kits headed toward the paint-spray booth, taking photographs from different angles, studying the flow of air to and from it, and scraping paint samples from the sides and the floor. Two of the men took yellow tape and cordoned off an area so that another, more heavily outfitted, could climb inside the dip tank—the one that Gutierrez went down in—depositing samples into a large yellow container, which he carried outside. For the better part of an hour, there were flashes of light every few seconds as the men took pictures of every conceivable object from every conceivable angle, particularly the drainage areas under the tanks.

Inside the office, Keaton and two assistants held up items for Chuck to identify while an assistant scribbled answers on yellow Post-its until every filing cabinet, drawer, computer, and loose piece of paperwork was labeled. By noon, they'd loaded everything in the office, including computers, into large anvil cases, which they wheeled across the floor, through the overhead doors, and outside into one of the vans. They took no more than ten minutes—the HAZMAT teams and photographers— to eat lunches from little coolers they'd brought, leaving the guy in the lunch truck shaking his head, wondering what he was going to do with the sandwiches he and his wife had made the night before.

While they ate, Chuck went upstairs and left a message for his insurance broker asking about his business interruption policy. He called the hospital to check on Gutierrez, who was unchanged, and then left a voice mail for Fat Eddie Palmieri, Charlie Puckman's old friend and the family lawyer. After a few minutes pacing his apartment, he took ibuprofen and some more antianxiety medication and went back downstairs.

There wasn't much for Chuck to do for the rest of the afternoon. Periodically, he walked outside or paced the shop floor, but wherever he went, the strange swaddled figures poked their heads up or raised their respirators and rattled off measurements or regulation numbers, requests for authorization to use special equipment, and estimates of the time required to complete what they called subtasks. Frequently, Keaton would walk by, nodding or shaking his head. By three P.M., the teams had dusted, pried open, sampled, photographed, and diagrammed every piece of equipment as well as disassembled the tank-drainage system, piece by piece. The office was eerily neat—empty of accounting records, purchase orders, invoices, shop drawings, and supplies. By four o'clock, the men in the moon suits had siphoned chemical samples from drums, paint from cans, soil from the yard, concrete from under the dip tanks, and handwriting samples from the brothers' desk blotters. Before leaving, Keaton presented Chuck with a list of what his men had taken.

"When do I get my business back?" Chuck asked.

"It depends," Keaton said casually. "We intend to talk to some of your workers." They stood in the parking lot. The wind had picked up, and Keaton held a thick manila folder against his chest. "It would be a bad idea for you to do or say anything that would impede our investigation." Keaton opened the folder and thumbed through it. "You have a brother, Arthur, don't you?" The sun was setting over the portion of the factory where Chuck lived. Chuck squinted. The men in the white suits had loaded their trucks and were milling around. Ghostbusters, he thought. A white Ford pulled up alongside the gate. "We're gonna want to talk to him."

Chuck shrugged. "Suit yourselves," he said, and then smiled. Funny thing to tell a HAZMAT guy.

"There may be an opportunity for you to cooperate with our investigation," Keaton said, staring at an area just above Chuck's head. "I have two suggestions for you. First, if and when that opportunity arises, take advantage of it." He paused, putting the folder in his briefcase. Chuck had his hands in his pockets and was shifting his weight from one foot to the other. "In the meantime, get yourself a good lawyer." As he spoke, a burly guy in a leather coat and shiny black shoes got out of the sedan and headed across the yard.

"Friend of yours?" Chuck asked.

"He'll be watching the building tonight," Keaton said matter-of-factly. "Nobody goes in—nobody comes out." He looked Chuck up and down. "It's against the law to remove or tamper with anything inside. Am I making myself clear?" The guard appeared to be in his early sixties, built like a fireplug, with a bulbous nose and a handlebar mustache. He set a small lunchbox next to a little stool he'd brought and sat down. Keaton got into one of the white vans, which pulled out of the parking lot and crept down the street. Several of the neighbors watched the procession from their porches.

For Chuck, as far back as he could remember, dusk was an inhospitable time of day. He would sit in his bedroom by a window as the sun set, familiar objects fading, their lines losing definition, becoming grainy until they disappeared. It was suddenly impossible for him to stand where he stood or to go upstairs. Ignoring his neighbors, Chuck walked across the yard, turned right outside the gate, and started walking south. As he walked, he felt the gravity of his situation, like sand in his pockets.

It took him a little over an hour to get downtown to the mid-rise at Thirteenth and Juniper. In the vestibule, he pressed a column of buttons until someone buzzed him in, and then he made his way to the cluttered waiting room that Eddie Palmieri shared with two other retired lawyers. It was close to six, which meant Fat Eddie might already be at the Union League, but Chuck rapped on the door anyway. From inside he heard the old man. "Yeah?" Eddie wheezed. Chuck opened the door.

The office looked as though its owner had stopped working and started an elaborate project stacking files until they were perilously close to spilling over. "You look like shit, you know that?" Fat Eddie said. "You want a drink?"

Chuck nodded.

"So you've got the EPA looking up your ass," Eddie said, referring to the phone message Chuck had left earlier. Fat Eddie had only recently retired his rust-colored toupee, long after the hair on the sides of his head went gray; his neck looked a lot thicker than it needed to be to support his head. Fat Eddie Palmieri had never been very successful practicing law. Now, in retirement, he lived off his wife's teaching pension. He came to work only to get away from his own stink.

"Maybe this is just a routine investigation . . ." Chuck said, his voice cracking. For some reason, he felt even worse in front of Eddie than he had looking at the newspaper headlines yesterday. He reached inside his pocket for the vial.

"If this kid dies, Chuckie," Eddie said, blowing air out, "they're gonna be after you for workplace safety, environmental shit, who knows what else? What's Arthur doing? He must be shitting himself."

"He didn't come in today."

Fat Eddie pushed his chair back so he could open a drawer, a set of motions that left him out of breath. "I'd handle it myself for you, of course, but I don't do this kind of work anymore. Too complicated." He pulled out a beat-up black book with business cards sticking out of it.

"I don't have the staff, the computers, the support, know what I mean? You're gonna need a lawyer who knows how these pricks work. . . ."

"There's another problem, Eddie," Chuck said.

"What's that?"

"I'm broke."

"Take a draw. What's the big deal?"

"There's nothing to draw from."

"What the fuck are you talking about?"

"We didn't ship enough this week. We barely made payroll."

Eddie put a cigar stub in his mouth and struck a match. He squinted at his old friend's son and remembered how he and Charlie Puckman had worked a Ponzi scheme on members of the Philadelphia Athletic Club back in the fifties. How Charlie had taken the rap so Eddie could still practice law.

"Listen to me, you dumb fuck," he said, exhaling. "Your father may be pissing in a diaper, but he's got a chit from me, you understand?" Fat Eddie set the cigar in an ashtray and stood up. He put his hands on his hips and turned his body toward several quick-fold cardboard file boxes, one stacked on top of the other. "Besides, he has a stash—a safe loaded with cash, securities, bonds, maybe some gold." Leaning over, he read the labels on the sides of the boxes. "Gimme that one," he said, pointing to one in the corner.

Chuck lifted one of the boxes and set it on a radiator next to the window and then handed Eddie a stack of papers that he sorted, one by one, letting several fall to the floor, until he found what he was looking for. "We'll get you one of them hot shit lawyers who's connected." Fat Eddie took a separate sheet of paper out of his desk drawer and scribbled a series of numbers. "There's a safe in your dad's offfice beside the refrigerator. Put whatever's in there in a briefcase and meet me tomorrow night at the Union League."

Flush with hope, Chuck treated himself to a taxi. He entered the fire escape from the side and climbed the steps quietly, peering from the missing brick at the guard, who hadn't moved. In the kitchen, he took a bottle of vodka from the freezer. The key to functioning under this kind of pressure was substance management. With the radio playing, he looked in the kitchen drawer for his master keys. Soon, everything would be fine. His faith in his father was restored. He was sorry for every ugly thing he'd wished, every mean thing he'd ever said. It was a damn shame about Gutierrez, but with the money, he would hire Artie and himself a fancy lawyer with connections. They'd get on with their lives. He'd buy inventory and start selling again with renewed vigor, hit the road again, even give Rahim a pool next Christmas from which to dole out bonuses. Who knows—maybe he'd upgrade his father to a suite at the nursing home. When Chuck could barely feel his fingertips, he got a flashlight out of the hall closet and took the elevator downstairs.

It had been more than two decades since anyone had used the inside entrance to the shop. Years ago, when Chuck was a kid, Charlie Puckman used to let himself into the factory this way in the dead of winter. A blast of cold air gripped him. Chuck kept the flashlight off. A yellowish haze—streetlights—leaked through the windows above the dip tanks. When Chuck could see the outline of rivet guns and tack-welding machines, he began making his way, one step at a time, toward the center of the factory.

In the early sixties, Charlie Puckman had built the little office on weekends out of mismatched wood paneling nailed to angle iron stolen from construction sites. Above the frosted glass door was a small bracket with a wrought-iron man fishing, and at the end of the pole was a steelhead twisting in the air. The roof wasn't a roof at all, but ceiling tiles laid between more angle iron welded together. Chuck let himself in and turned the flashlight on, keeping it pointed at the ground. Artie's desk, which was usually stacked with paper, Post-it notes, paper clips, pens, pencils, and extra supplies, was almost clear. He picked up a piece of paper. An old to-do list Artie had made. Except for their handwriting, beaten into them by nuns, the two of them were so different it was hard to believe they were brothers. Chuck walked to his father's desk and fingered the objects on the blotter—letter opener, ashtray, and paperweights Charlie had collected. Chuck looked up at a sailfish his father had mounted, taken as payment from a customer. He hadn't even caught the thing himself.

The safe Fat Eddie told him about was well hidden behind what looked like a circuit-breaker panel. Aiming the flashlight down, Chuck pulled out the card with the combination. Maybe his relationship with the old man could be salvaged. Who cared why his father hadn't told him about it before? The family business was a crypt, full of necessary secrets. Chuck sat on the speckled linoleum floor and ran his hand along the wall, the smell of stale coffee and cleanser around him. It took him a few seconds to locate the tiny notch in the panel, which he pressed and turned with his fingernail, sliding the panel up. Holding the flashlight under his chin, he spun the tumbler. The safe itself was vintage, a relic of ancient industrial Philadelphia. At first, it didn't open. He tried the sequence a second time. Again, nothing. His heart pounded in his chest. His palms and neck tingled with perspiration.

It opened on the third try. Directing his flashlight into the small rectangular opening, Chuck felt a glow—the nearness to his needs being met—similar to what he felt moments before orgasm, or smelling an exquisite meal as it was about to be served. His movements slowed. Chuck reached in. Finally, he would see a payday from this wretched business. He leaned down to examine his cache.

Panic began in his sternum and spread to the inside edges of his skin, the back of his neck, and his temples, as though his blood pressure was rising. Another wave of nausea overcame him as if he had actually fallen from the balcony in his dream. Kneeling forward, he vomited an acidic mix of vodka and mucus. He held himself in that position for what seemed like a long time, his right hand dangling over the small sink, his face contorted. Steadying himself, he looked down in horror, clawing the emptiness.

Saturday, March 14, 2000

By the late nineties, the FBI had picked up virtually every fugitive from the sixties with the exception of the Volcano Bomber. It was the case that Special Agent John Russell cut his teeth on and one of the last vestiges of Weatherfug—a thirty-year-plus FBI Special that for all intents and purposes had drawn to a close—that dogged him for his entire career. "This much we do know," the older agent said, angling a toothpick between his incisors. "The whole frickin' thing was a fluke." It was the witching hour inside the Stinger Lounge, just after four A.M., when the shift changed and the clean-up crew, such as it was, began its half-hearted workout, mopping down and scraping the grime and grizzle of Friday night off the brown-stained floors. The two agents sat down just as the last suburbanites, pleased to have dipped their sticks into real life, even if only for one night, even if only through a prescription drug and alcohol haze, turned their BMWs with the online rescue systems toward babysitters asleep in sprawling Tudors with rhododendron hedges and meticulous lawns. A thin man whistling a gospel tune swept the stinking shrimp husks into piles outside the kitchen. A depressing shade of gray pressed up against the little rectangular windows where streetlights illuminated leftover Lotto cards and Burger King bags and

Septa transfers that blew across Broad Street. As they made their way toward the back of the bar, John Russell III remembered what his ASAC had told him about the younger man.

Eric Dodson was a plebe, one of a half dozen new agents the Bureau had hired in an attempt to upgrade their computer capabilities. He was young, sturdy, and handsome, with fullback features and a neck the size of an ordinary man's thigh. He wore Clark Kent glasses, which only intensified his good looks by conveying a technical proficiency that was well beyond most people's. But Eric Dodson was more than a computer jock. He was a dot-commer with no college degree and lots of money. And though he'd spent less than a year at the Bureau, he was the one who'd been assigned the case John Russell had wrestled for over thirty years.

The older agent led them to a booth in the back—past a woman in her late fifties wearing a slinky black dress and a huge necklace that dripped into her cleavage. She was smoking a thin brown cigarette and talking to a bartender drying shot glasses. If Dodson was uncomfortable here, in the heart of the ghetto, that'd be just fine with Russell; the veteran was pleased whenever young agents called for his advice. Nobody was going to solve this case without help from him. John Russell called for a couple of bourbon and waters.

It was Russell's idea to surveil the girl after the HR manager from Drinker & Sledge called Friday and told Russell she'd called in—or e-mailed at the very last minute—saying she'd been in a commuter train accident. Russell checked with Septa. There'd been no accident. When the ASAC approved the tail, he'd told him to take the new kid and bring him up to speed.

"We're not sure how he'll do," the assistant special agent in charge had told Russell when Dodson first came to Philly. "But he impressed the hell out of them at Quantico, and not just with computer stuff. Con law, personal safety, defensive tactics, even firearms. He was off the charts. Only problem is he's green. No field experience. No sense of history." Russell winced. It was a brittle bone he was being tossed, and Russell knew it. How could a kid who wasn't even born then manage a case that originated in the sixties? The future of the Bureau was sitting across from him in a blue blazer, an open Oxford shirt, fresh-pressed

Dockers, and Cole Haans, while in six months, everything—his case-load, the contents of his desk, all his clearances, and his institutional memories—would be gone and his career with the FBI would be over.

"Anybody who's connected to a fugitive goes missing," Russell had said as they left Center City, "you pay attention." He'd been following the mother and daughter for years, waiting for Keane to make contact, asking a few of her neighbors and each of her employers to call him with anything out of the ordinary. The woman in the black dress pretended to swat something aside. "Not on your life," she told the bartender, shaking her finger and laughing. The two agents sat across from each other in silence, Dodson's hands on the table, his back to the entrance.

"What brought you to law enforcement?" Russell asked him in the car.

"I never pictured myself doing this," Dodson said, as if he was talking to his uncle at a cocktail party. "I spent my early twenties traveling, you know, various projects and assignments. One summer, I came home to visit and wound up at my dad's country club in a foursome with a retired G-man. At the end of the round, he took my number, and, I don't know, maybe a year later, I got a phone call." He turned his hands up and shrugged. "Next thing you know, I'm at Quantico." How nice, Russell thought. No waiting for the mail, no agonizing interviews, no torturous psych evals. A fucking phone call. Russell didn't like a single thing about the new, improved Bureau with its casual Fridays and its emphasis on computer programmers and hot shits. He knew, even if *they* didn't, that of all the problems the Bureau faced, it was lack of discipline that would hobble them.

Dodson's FBI career thus far consisted of three months doing lab work in D.C. before being shipped out to Denver, where he spent his first year tailing a special agent and playing intramural softball. As they drove up Broad Street, Dodson went on about how easily he made friends on account of him being an extrovert and how happy he was for the opportunity to move east. "The day I got here, I found this awesome sublet. I can actually walk to work." All his other cases had something to do with cyber-crime.

Russell disliked Dodson from the moment they met. What pissed him off most was not how easily things had come to Eric Dodson or how little the young man knew about the sixties or even how Russell, who'd tracked the Volcano Bomber unsuccessfully for thirty years, was now supposed to tell this kid everything he knew about the sixties' most elusive radical. What got under his skin was how untroubled the kid was, how trusting and confident he looked sitting across the table, waiting to be briefed. Even here now, at four in the morning in the heart of North Philly, with an old whore and a junkie bartender and a washed-up special agent with no manners, Eric Dodson had faith. And why shouldn't he? Had Dodson been more articulate, he would have said his life was like a time-lapse photograph of a bouquet of flowers opening, a series of fortuitous coincidences, strung together like chemical reactions, resulting in his being secure in whatever moment he was in, assured that the ground he stepped on would support him, that those around him who could, would help him when he needed it.

The two men sat in silence nursing their drinks. Russell flicked his toothpick onto the floor. Dodson rubbed the bridge of his nose. Dodson held the older agent's gaze as long as he could and then took his glasses off and spoke. "So what was he like?"

"Never start an interview like that," Russell said immediately. "Unless you want to be bullshitted, you don't ask something outright before establishing rapport." Dodson nodded. If he was insulted, he didn't show it. "Since we're both professionals, why don't you try out an idea of your own," Russell said, sipping his drink. "That is, if you have one." Dodson smiled but said nothing. After another long, uncomfortable silence, Russell looked toward the ceiling and said, "I can see you're gonna need my help." He opened his napkin and wiped the table in front of him.

"What did you mean, the whole thing was a fluke?" the young agent said quietly. His hair, spiked with gel, appeared in silhouette against the window.

Russell finished his drink and folded his arms across his chest, feeling the familiar bulge under his arm. He would miss a lot of things about this job. Wearing the badge, carrying a weapon, maintaining that practiced vigilance even when he wasn't on a case, especially the long hours in surveillance, with nobody breathing down his neck. Everything but the red tape and the bullshit approvals you needed before you could get anything done. Without answering, Russell stood up and walked toward the bathroom. He let himself into the small closet, un- buckled his pants, and then turned his head away.

Despite his recent health problems, John Russell had aged well. His hair was silvery white and thick enough on top to hold its form all day. Without much effort, he'd stayed trim enough to be asked to pose in an ad for a retirement community. Even up close, the mirage held. His teeth were good; the skin on his hands and face, tan, tight, and supple; and his features, thin and sculpted, patrician-like. Except now, after sixty-two years without as much as the flu, he was pissing blood.

John Russell didn't see himself as an aging G-man with malignant cells and incontinence. In his mind, he was the kid from Cleveland who busted his ass for an appointment letter from J. Edgar Hoover and six months later, a badge, a regulation Smith & Wesson Model 10 revolver, and a $12,500-a-year salary. Back in the days before there was an academy—before the Hoover Building, before Efrem Zimbalist Jr. put a face on the FBI—Russell and thirty other guys went rushing downstairs in the DOJ Building, stripped down, butt to butt, for defensive training. They sat together in their starched white shirts and laced wing tips in academics and ate cheeseburgers at the Globe and Laurel, hurrying back by curfew to sleep on cots, twelve to a room. This was before there were voices in his head other than his supervisor's and doubts in his mind about good and evil, and which he was destined to become. At twenty-five, Jack Russell became Special Agent John Russell III, Es- quire, smart and fit, ambitious and handsome.

At first, he came across as a guy with charm, ambition, and intelli- gence. With a law degree, no wife or girlfriend, and no kids to tie him down, he had none of the attachments that distracted the younger agents and, in many cases, limited their careers. During his first few months, his supervisors thought he'd be promoted fast. But that was in the beginning, when he mastered his assignments and managed to show up consistently in the right place at the right time.

After his training, Russell was sent to the Boston office, where he was attached to Special Agent Lou D'Mitri. From the get-go, he was commended for following procedure, being quick on his feet, and read- ing between the lines. One day that summer—it was 1968—he picked up an Airtel from Chicago. A very unusual kind of incendiary device had gone off in Oneonta, New York, killing a kid and severely burning three others. That same day, Selective Service Headquarters in D.C. got one of those letters composed of cutout newsprint that read, "Peace Erupts Now." No signature. No attribution. No rumors from informants. The bomb data center drew blanks, but the Chicago office suspected Weather Underground. By luck, Russell remembered a strange incident at Fenway Park involving the same type of explosion. It was the beginning of his involvement in a case that would stretch forward some thirty years.

John Russell was transferred from Boston to Chicago, then Denver, then Philadelphia, where he became an expert on the Weather Underground. In 1972, he played a key role leading to the apprehension of Mark Henry and Diana Applegate. In the mid-seventies, Russell solved some cases involving the Mob and counterfeiters, but his career languished. In the late seventies, he was transferred again. While his peers showed their talent for training new agents and handling paperwork, John Russell was a one-trick pony—an extraordinary hunter—capable of devoting himself to a single task like the pursuit of fugitives without distraction. The problem was what to do between stakeouts. He became easily bored and irritated; he drank too much and spent too much time at the track. Unless he was in pursuit, he was hot-tempered and unpredictable.

Shortly after he arrived in Philadelphia, people at work learned to keep their distance. John Russell seemed a bit cardboard, his personality contrived, as if something sinister was fighting his manners for control. He was erratic. He was obstinate with his superiors. Some days, he was like a ghost, a vaporized version of a real person, or a person who hadn't fully formed. In the late eighties, after an interview and a Minnesota Multiphasic, he overheard the shrink at the Bureau tell his ASAC that he thought John Russell might be dissembling. By the mid-nineties, Russell understood deep down that although as an agent he might have been viable, as a human being he was failing.

In recent years, he had moved himself and his mother into a spacious twin in East Falls, and for the first time in his life, he opened and read his retirement account statements. Nights after work, leaving her in front of the TV, he'd walk to McCabe's and order the prime rib, then sit there watching television and drinking himself into a stupor. Once in a while, for exercise, he'd hit on one of the neighbor girls, somebody's recently separated wife, the single woman who lived next door. Other nights, he preferred to lease company for a few hours, though never at the house.

Russell returned from the bathroom and ordered himself another bourbon. He'd doused himself with cologne from a bottle he carried and slicked back his silvery hair. Like an old gumshoe, it was his way of welcoming the new day. "It was a cool night in September," Russell began. "No rain. No humidity." It took Dodson a second to realize that Special Agent John Russell was going to tell him the story of the Volcano Bomber from the very beginning.

PART II

Lorraine Nadia was an attractive woman and as she stood in line at Borders in Center City, people's heads turned. She wore a light blue skirt, a white blouse, and a purple-and-black scarf that accented her eyes, which were big pools of blue, set wide apart. Her hair, streaked blonde, framed an open face that glowed with a mix of moisture, melanin, and optimism. I guessed correctly that she was fifty, although she could have passed for at least five years younger. When it came her turn, Lorraine looked directly at me as if she and I were the only two people in the room and she, not I, was the one signing books. "Inscribe it to Stardust," she said, as I opened the front cover. Then she leaned forward and whispered in a voice that was private, almost flirtatious, that she had something important to tell me about my friend Patty Hearst and her time underground.

I'd first noticed Lorraine hanging in the back of the store, watching me read and then answer questions. Apparently, she'd waited until the line had dwindled to ask me if I'd join her for a cup of tea. I was exhausted from the attention and eager to relax. "The whole SLA thing was a government setup," she said as soon as we were alone, her eyebrows arching with intrigue. There was something intimate, almost physical, about the way she engaged me. "I want you to tell the world a very different story."

I held the cup under my nose and inhaled deeply. "I'm sorry," I said as politely as I could. "I'm a poet. This project with Patty was a fluke. Just a way to pay the bills. I'm not really into conspiracy stuff, or even journalism, for that matter." I remember thinking that the Hearst family was going to dog me for the rest of my life.

"You don't understand," she said. "This isn't UFOs or Watergate. I'm talking about history and the human condition."

I told her I had the feeling that I'd been born too late to get all lathered up about the sixties and that I was more a weed than a flower child. When a clerk approached and asked me what to do with the extra copies of my book, I thanked Lorraine for coming and said I had to be going. She followed me downstairs, past the registers, and out onto Walnut Street. When we got to my car, I stuck my hand out. "It's been nice meeting you."

"The next time you talk to Patty," Lorraine said, "ask her if she knows somebody named Frederick." Then she handed me a piece of paper with her phone number on it and walked back toward the bookstore, her bag bouncing against her hip.

I did a few more book signings and some local TV, including a cable show about people who'd once been famous; and then, mercifully, the book disappeared. If I hadn't heard from Patty almost a year later, I doubt I would have ever remembered that conversation with Lorraine.

It was late in the afternoon, and one of the neighbor kids was setting up the computer in my mother's cottage. I'd joined the Y, found a local twelve-step group, and had pretty much forgotten about What Mattered Most *and William Randolph Hearst when Patty called, distraught.*

At first I thought it was the reviews. I hadn't spent much time in the limelight, and, honestly, I was surprised at how ferocious the critics had been. But it wasn't the press; it wasn't even about the book. That morning, UPS delivered a package to her house in Connecticut. "It was a box . . . cardboard . . . heavy . . . wrapped in brown paper, about the size of a laptop," she said. "Hand-addressed, not like Lands' End or L.L. Bean." Using instincts honed during her time with revolutionaries, she called the police. No sooner had she hung up than another van came screeching into the driveway. "Winnie, you have no idea what these people will do," she whispered into the phone. The last thing she heard before collapsing was muffled conversation on a two-way radio. When she awoke, she was sprawled on the front steps, the cordless phone in pieces, watching three people in jumpsuits huddled by the van talking into a handset. Then her voice softened, and she spoke in the same monotone I would later recognize from audiotapes of her kidnapping. "I knew I was in Connecticut," she said, "but it felt like Berkeley. I knew it was 1999, but it felt like 1974. I knew I was forty-five, but I felt like I was nineteen again."

I pictured Patty, her platinum blonde hair pulled back in a pony-tail, her famous profile, without makeup, having lost the sharpness of the extreme upper class. I felt sad that with all the money and fame, she was still traumatized by the past, whether real or imagined.

"When I came to," Patty said, "the back of the van was open. A man in a suit was kneeling, and I could see that the guys in the jump-suits had DEA printed on their backs. The three agents talked to one another for a few minutes, and then one of them came over and told me that the package contained narcotics and that I was damned lucky I hadn't taken it inside. Just like that, Winnie. Like they intended to bust me."

I must confess to being quite skeptical. I was also surprised that of all the people in her Rolodex, she'd have picked up the phone and called me to tell me about it. "What do you think it was all about?" I asked her.

"Somebody set me up, Winnie. To blow my chances for a presiden-tial pardon." She paused to sip something. I struggled to think of some-thing to say, and then for some reason, I remembered what Lorraine had told me.

"Have you ever heard of a guy named Frederick?"

Patty sucked her breath. "Oh God, Winnie," she mumbled. And the line went dead.

It took me several hours to get through again, and when I did, Bernie answered. "Patty's sleeping," he said brusquely. "She's all shook up. Had to take a pill." Bernie told me Patty would call me when she awoke, but she didn't—not that night or the next—or on any of the following days, despite many messages I left on her machine. When I fi-nally reached Bernie in his office a week later, he told me that Patty was all right, and that those who hadn't lived through what she had couldn't understand. He said it was important for us not to keep pushing the past back in her face, or something to that effect. That it'd be best if I didn't call again for a while.

I felt compelled to tell him what I'd heard. "Somebody approached me at one of the book signings and said Patty's kidnapping was some kind of government plot," I said, half expecting him to laugh out loud. Bernie sighed. He sounded weary, perhaps because this single episode of Patty's past had become the major theme of their entire adult lives.

"A lot of people say a lot of things, Winnie. You're gonna have to sort them out yourself. Meantime, cut us all a little slack, will you?" Until then, I hadn't really understood what a burden the kidnapping was on Patty, her husband, her children, her family, even her friends. The wall had gone up. What an odd little footnote to our reunion, to our little project together, I thought as I hung up.

People don't realize it, but too much time on your hands, too much money in the bank, and no idea what you want to do with your life is a dangerous combination for a recovering addict. I wrote bad poetry and went out to dinner a lot with my brother and his wife. I went to AA and joined a health club, where I tried to make new friends. I read books I found in the cottage—mostly mysteries. I went to Target a lot and bought household items. One morning, I called Meredith Hutchinson, Patty's agent, to see if she'd heard anything about the UPS incident. She hadn't. Then, more out of boredom than anything else, I took out the little card with Lorraine's phone number.

We met at an Irish bar on the corner of Second and South. She was wearing jeans and a sweater, and when she took off her coat, she seemed thinner and more muscular than when we'd first met. She hoisted her handbag, a colorful knit sack that looked like it was imported from Central America, on the table between us. For a few seconds, she just smiled—there was no awkwardness or impatience in her demeanor— and I remember thinking how, sitting there with her hands folded, she looked beatific. I told her about the UPS incident and Patty's theory about somebody wanting to ruin her chances for a pardon. I had the feeling she already knew what I was going to say. "Why would Patty freeze up when I mentioned Frederick?" I asked.

"Good question," Lorraine said.

"Who cares whether or not Patty Hearst gets pardoned?"

"A lot of people, Winnie. The noose is tightening around the surviving SLA members. The Feds finally caught Kathy Soliah, the soccer mom from Minnesota, and a bunch of people who've been living free for twenty years are going to trial for murdering a woman during one of the bank robberies. Patty was the only eyewitness." Lorraine tilted her head.

"I don't get it." It was becoming clear that although I may have been Patty's childhood friend and coauthor, Lorraine was the real expert on Patty Hearst.

"Clinton leaves office in two months," Lorraine said. "For twenty years, Patty and her lawyers have been lobbying to have her name cleared. If she's busted now, it would fuck up her chances and discredit her testimony." Lorraine spoke with authority. "That would be very good for certain people."

We looked at each other as if to decide whether to take the next step. "How do you know all this?" I asked her.

"That's what I want to tell you," Lorraine said, waving the waitress over.

Saturday, March 14, 2000

Stardust took a deep breath and moved her hand to an area above her left eye. There was a raised bump, a little track of scabbing, and a generalized swelling that hurt to touch. Her head throbbed and she had a bad taste in her mouth. Her determination to continue sleeping seemed to push her toward wakefulness. Then she remembered the train, the walk through the ghetto, and the abandoned factory, where she'd smacked into something low and hard. She touched her legs, which were bare. Beneath her, she felt a tight rubberized surface, like a trampoline. She had to pee. Down and to the left, a narrow rectangle of light under the doorjamb shone on linoleum. From another room, she could hear music, jazz maybe, kind of old-fashioned. Within a few moments, she was able to make out the out-lines of the wall opposite the door, the edges of the bed she lay on, a small table beside it. The digital clock read twelve thirty; in the bluish glow were a pair of nail clippers, an ashtray, and a photograph. She picked up the frame and examined it. It was an old print, creased in sev-eral places. On one side was a man with long hair, a mustache, freckles, and glasses. He had his arm around a smaller man, also thin, with dark kinky hair and a full beard. On one side of the picture was a couch, and on the other, a young woman with dirty blonde hair who seemed to be moving out of the frame.

Somewhere outside the room, Stardust heard someone laugh and then the music shut off. There was muffled conversation, more laughter, and then footsteps heading toward her, before the knob turned and the door opened slightly. "You got a nasty bump there, honey," Ovella said, seeing she was awake. Ovella extended a small towel with ice. "I fixed you something to eat."

"Bathroom," Stardust said weakly. Ovella helped her into her skirt, which had been laid neatly at the base of the bed. Then she pointed to a door across the hallway and stepped out of the way.

"Who undressed me?" Stardust asked.

"You knocked your head. We carried you upstairs. You slept a long time." Ovella helped her to the bathroom. Afterward, the two made their way slowly down the hallway and into the kitchen, where Ovella poured coffee and then pointed to a wrought-iron chair next to the table. She held a skillet and spooned out a generous portion of eggs, rice, and beans. Midway through the meal—her first in a long time—Stardust noticed the backward-facing man standing by the aquarium with his hand on his chin, watching.

Without looking directly at him, she observed what she could. His face was pale, his olive complexion sun-starved, his hands stained yellow from cigarettes. In this light, and in her condition, he looked like someone who had only partially materialized before the transporter malfunctioned. She ran her hands through her hair and took a deep breath. She felt hungover. She might have slept three hours or fifteen. Cautiously, she studied his features—the shape of his face and lips, his bone structure and posture, his body type—in the event she was finally meeting someone of significance to her mother, a mysteriously close friend or a person with important information about the past, perhaps even her father.

With her vision still hazy, Stardust made comparisons. Chuck was taut, tightly wound, bony, wiry even. She was big boned, Rubenesque, prone to being overweight if she let herself. He seemed shorter than she remembered from the train; his shoulders sloped as though he was backpacking and his head angled slightly forward from his neck. She considered herself average height and her posture good, perhaps thanks to constant reminders from her mother. Instead of laying flat and soft like hers, his hair—salt and pepper, now—extended from his head like bristles on a wire brush. All told, it was difficult to come to any conclusion.

Taking another tack, Stardust tried to assess whether he was her mother's type. Lorraine liked confident, lackadaisical, easygoing guys: the divorced dad who coached her softball team; the general contractor who was always doing projects in their neighborhood; Carl, her boss from the bank. Chuck seemed cautious and restrained, inhibited, impatient in an aggressive way, like someone continually bracing himself for bad news. He lacked authority. It seemed unlikely that he could have run a business that employed people, even less likely that he'd ever had a family. If this man and Lorraine had once been lovers, it would have had to have been a long time ago and under some pretty strange circumstances. She felt relief and disappointment.

Along the wall of the kitchen were sleek, brushed aluminum cabinets with concealed handles. Underneath them, a microwave blinked SET CLOCK and next to that, a Plexiglas pot sat on a matte black coffeemaker. The refrigerator had a couple small photographs and three eleven-by-fourteen papers attached by magnets. Stardust squinted. "Notice of Preliminary Hearing." "Federal Indictment." "Request to Appear Before Grand Jury." There was a picture of a young girl wearing an equestrian helmet, her face in shadow.

Across a yellowed Formica counter that curled around the edges was a small sitting area with a beat-up leather couch. For a second, it seemed as though the backward-facing man was walking toward her, then he turned and headed down the hallway. A gray upholstered recliner backed up against the aquarium he had been standing beside. Stardust could see a sleek barracuda-shaped minnow with mottled skin, and a little school of silver fish with paste-on eyes darting through the bubbles. Before they were renovated, the complex of rooms they were in might have been offices. She imagined metal desks, filing cabinets, typewriters, and women with piled-on hairdos answering phones and drinking coffee; faded circles where posters or calendars once covered the paneling, absorbing smoke and tired exhalations. Somehow, it seemed even uglier now, like a hideout. There were no plants, no artwork, no decorations on the walls—nothing ornamental save a giant fish that was stuffed and mounted over a tiny bronze plaque whose inscription she couldn't read. An absurdly bright shade of turquoise, it was stuck in a frozen leap over paneling where a window once had been.

Stardust felt better after drinking coffee. A toilet flushed down the hall, and she felt the pressure change, the way it does when a door opens somewhere in an air-conditioned building. From the bedroom, there was the sound of drawers opening, then footsteps. Chuck had changed into jeans and a flannel shirt. He made his way back into the living room, around piles of books, his eyes downcast, then he took a seat under a Plexiglas skylight, which was black either because it was evening or from paint or soot that had accumulated over time. He made a motion for Stardust to come sit beside him on the couch, which she pretended not to see. Her head throbbed, and she was still very shaky.

He opened a pack of Benson & Hedges and set an ashtray on his lap. Stardust finished her meal and pushed away the plate, deciding for now at least to reserve judgment, and to project apathy. Memorize him, she told herself—his nuances and quirks. Try to match whatever he says against some measure of authenticity. Light from the lamp spread itself over the carpeting and then diffused, stirring and igniting dust particles around him. Elbow on the armrest, chin in one hand, he was staring at the floor not seeing, his knees bouncing rhythmically, like Rodin's *Thinker* between a shit and a sweat. Occasionally, he shrugged his shoulders. The skin on his face was stretched thin, fixed in a kind of grimace, as though relaxing might lead him to say things he would regret. Finally, after what seemed like forever, he spoke.

Spring 1968

It was a sunny Saturday morning. A sooty mixture of car exhaust and litter fossilized against the curb of Memorial Drive, and the trees along the stone retaining wall stretched toward the sky like starving prisoners. On a thin sliver of lawn between MIT and the river, dozens of students walked or sat, in singles, pairs, and clusters—freaks in turtlenecks and bell-bottoms, engineers in tight Farah slacks, young Republicans in white, buttoned-down oxfords—smoking cigarettes, sipping from plastic cups, moving their hands in conversation. A long-haired kid made a strumming motion across a guitar. Music wafted across the quadrangle from speakers propped in windows.

Chuck leaned against the cinder block wall in the hallway of his dormitory, the pay telephone pressed to his ear; in the background, Tony Bennett, the sound of slippers shuffling across linoleum, and the achingly familiar rat-a-tat cadence of his mother's raspy cough. Even though she could hardly afford a lengthy long-distance call, Regina Puckman wanted her son to know she was offended by his being away, even though he was in college, learning a profession, avoiding a certain fate in the draft lottery. After a minute or two, he heard footsteps, fumbling, and then his mother's voice. "Do you know where your brother is?"

Arthur Puckman was a problem child almost from birth. In Chuck's earliest memories, his brother's face was swollen and red from holding his breath, or wiggling to get out from under furniture, getting stung, burned, pinched, or squished, having hurt himself for the sympathy it evoked from their mother, who ran after him with a towel or Band-Aid in her hand and a look of concern across her face. She dressed the boy in heavy fabrics, even in summer—wool pants, tentlike shirts, heavy sweaters—that accentuated his girth and inhibited his clumsy movements. He wore thick-framed glasses in a failed attempt to correct a lazy eye and breathed heavily from his mouth, which he held open in a kind of stupor, or half pout. It seemed to Chuck that his mother ran her mouth at Arthur nonstop, cautioning or admonishing him for everything he did, while praising him excessively for ordinary things like eating dinner and taking a crap. To Chuck, his mother's entire existence seemed committed to reinforcing Arthur's incompetence and dependence.

In the years the boys lived together, there was perpetual trouble. In third grade, Artie started a fire in a trash can in the plaza outside school. The following year, he made up variants of Bible stories with deviant acts and twisted outcomes and told them emphatically to his younger brother, who repeated them in school. Arthur wasn't just ostracized, he was ridiculed—at home by his father, at school, and in the neighborhood, where he was like a pin cushion, a magnet for derision, a receptacle for trash talk. His last name became an insult heaped by one kid on another. And the worse it was for Artie, the more he antagonized Chuck. When the brothers were nine and twelve, Pasquale De Vita heard screams behind a shed at Southport Metal. De Vita found Chuck facedown on the ground, with Artie sitting on him, cutting into the younger boy's butt cheek with a nine-inch piece of angle iron. In a move that surprised no one, Charlie Puckman came by one afternoon and spirited his younger son away.

Unlike many fathers, who soften at the sight of their firstborn, Charlie Puckman bristled with enmity toward Arthur from the very beginning, even before the little boy manifested his grossness and his emotional dependence on his mother. The old man mimicked him when he whined. He teased and yelled at Artie when he cried, and he hit his son, hard, every chance he got. The more Charlie humiliated Artie, the more Artie tortured Chuck. Nobody understood why Charlie Puckman took even a momentary break from philandering to marry Regina Puckman, much less sire a son. They were of two different worlds: Regina, long-suffering and bitter, even at twenty-one, resigned to a life of disappointment, and fast-talking Charlie Puckman, the opportunist always looking for a scam. To their friends and family in South Philly, Charlie's disdain for his oldest boy seemed inversely proportional to Regina's love for him; everything about the boy was an example of Regina's damaged bloodline. Before they separated, the neighbors heard Charlie screaming every night. The next day, Regina would emerge, her eyes red-rimmed, a handkerchief in her fist, casting about for sympathy. Three years later, in a move that mystified everyone, Charlie and Regina reunited to produce a second son.

On this particular Saturday morning in 1968, Regina Puckman was upset, not only because she'd been robbed, but because her house, her only asset, the single repository of her life's dreams and an extension of her psychological being, had been thoroughly ransacked. "Animals," she told Chuck on the phone, coughing. "They took my cash, my silver, my jewelry. They emptied the cupboards and ruined the furniture. They defecated on my photo albums!" Chuck rolled his eyes. He knew what was coming next. "If they didn't kill Arthur, they probably scared him to death. You must help me find him, Charles. Please."

Theirs was a volatile family, even by South Philly standards, and the consensus was that given his temperament, his father, and the way he was treated by everyone, Arthur would someday explode. That he would rip off his mother and deface his own home was, in some ways, mild compared to expectation. Still, Regina Puckman was in a bind. If she called the cops, they'd announce to the world what everyone but she acknowledged.

After the incident behind Southport Metal, Charlie converted the offices above his factory into an apartment and enrolled Chuck in private school, where he thrived. Chuck Puckman was a sturdy little kid, hardened by his brother's provocations and indifferent to his mother's histrionics. In this industrial neighborhood, a curious kid could explore the barren lots between factories and the abandoned railroad spurs as long as he kept a low profile or curried favor with the neighborhood toughs. Chuck spent his weekends downstairs in his father's shop, wiring buzzers and alarm systems and putting together stereo systems. Weeknights, he did his homework in the little apartment and steered clear of his father and his girlfriends. In junior high, Chuck did well in school, particularly in math and science. He won second prize in a statewide science competition by building a radio that operated on a cell that stored static electricity. When he was fifteen, he got a job taking inventory in a pharmacy, where he learned the concept of shrinkage by siphoning pharmaceutical cocaine, quaaludes, and Benadryl for making speed. Chuck finished Central with high enough grades to earn automatic admission to MIT. With the war in Vietnam escalating, the summer of 1967 seemed a particularly good time to go to college. It was also an especially good year for the security business, and Chuck Puckman was one of the few students to pay tuition in cash.

That Saturday morning, the phone conversation between Chuck Puckman and his mother was brief. Chuck was fuzzy from having smoked a particularly strong chunk of hashish the night before, and he had no interest in or idea where his brother was. Like he'd seen his father do many times before, he held the receiver a foot away from his ear and waited for his mother to exhaust herself, then told her he was busy with exams and hung up. Regina Puckman savored her suffering, he told himself as he put the phone back in its cradle; she compressed it into its purest form, crushing it like a diamond. " 'Bye, Mom," he said into the air.

Along the path, buds were still tight on the bushes and traffic along Memorial Drive was sparse. Sharp sunlight cast strange shadows of the Latin letters carved along the tops and sides of old classrooms and bounced off the brand-new office buildings across the Charles River on the Boston side. Chuck was walking north along a row of bushes when he first saw her bare arms reaching up like someone climbing an imaginary rope. They were white and fleshy and they swayed from side to side like a belly dancer's. He pulled aside the branches and leaned in, admiring the nape of her neck from behind, blonde hair, soft shoulders, bare back. When she turned, the sun was in her eyes, which picked up specks of sky and ambient light. Her lips pressed together in a combination of concentration and pleasure. Without planning or forethought, Chuck Puckman pushed aside the bushes and entered the clearing. As he did, the young woman burst into laughter and collapsed onto a blanket beside a scruffy-looking guy who, until then, had been obscured by foliage. The young man touched the neck of his beer that rested against his belly.

"You're not gonna bust me for drinking in public, are you?" He was stretched out on his side, his shaggy head propped up on his hand, his face full of freckles, wire-frame glasses, mustache, a tiny tuft of reddish hair growing under his lower lip.

"I was on my way . . . I mean, I didn't see you. . . ."

"It's okay," the woman said, smoothing the blanket. Her ankles jutted out from underneath her dress so that he could see the inside of her calf, pale and smooth. There was a stack of books between them. "Have a seat."

"Really, I oughta just keep going. . . ."

"Hey, you're here," the man on the blanket said. He had a thick Boston accent. "What are you studying?"

"Uh, pre-med," Chuck said. It was a strange thing to say. He had no interest in medicine, or in any of his freshman courses for that matter. "How about you?"

"Lorraine is studying God," the young man said. "Her mission is to find a man who rides a motorcycle, reads scripture, and doesn't worship his mother. She wants to become enlightened through fucking. Satori. Religious ecstacy. Spiritual orgasm."

Lorraine made a motion like objecting.

"Maybe this here's your guy," the man said. "What's your name, sailor?"

"Chuck."

"Maybe Chuck's your God-fearing man, Lorraine, your saint in denim vestments. That is, if he's a believer. Are you a believer, Charles?" he said in a southern preacher's voice. Chuck looked at the books. Sylvia Plath. Richard Brautigan. Herbert Marcuse. He felt as if he'd walked into a scripted drama.

"Maybe Chuck's relationship to God is none of your business."

"Religion is a crutch. And Chuck here's probably no different from the rest of humanity." The guy on the blanket took a swig of beer and wiped his mouth on his sleeve. "Afraid of freedom, afraid of death, ready to devote himself to anyone with a beard in priestly robes who promises salvation!"

"And you," Lorraine shot back, "Mr. Independent—"

"Atheism is the only true expression of inner freedom. When it's chaos inside, we seek order; we pledge allegiance to the flags of corporations, the military, the university." His lip curled into a sneer.

"So, what're you studying?" Chuck asked. A squirrel scurried across the lawn. Chuck had a feeling something akin to fear, as if these people were bored with civility and would have enjoyed any distraction.

"Frederick let his scholarship lapse," Lorraine answered. "He's gonna help spread atheism to the rice paddies of Vietnam. . . ."

"Chemistry, until recently," Frederick said. Chuck felt a point of contact—vials of pills and powder from the pharmacy he'd worked in, the periodic table, symbols and abbreviations, combining atoms into globs—structure and predictability that had always appealed to him about science.

"He was here at MIT," Lorraine said, "but he quit." Her voice was flat, uninflected. She arched her eyebrows.

"I got tired of repeating experiments people have been doing for a hundred years, and I refuse to help people in the military-industrial complex, the trustees and the corporate sponsors, get richer. The world is fucked-up enough. . . ."

"You could be effective working from the inside," Lorraine said in what sounded like a long-running feud.

"Only if I was looking for spoils," he said. "When the revolution's over, you're not going to find me making napalm for Dow Chemical or developing germ strains for Pfizer."

"What about the draft?" Chuck asked. If you were of age in 1968 and you dropped out of college, either you had connections or you went to Vietnam.

Frederick pointed to himself with his thumbs. "You're looking at the future commander in chief of the People's Army. In the meantime,

I'm gonna stay fucked-up." He tilted his beer toward her like he was making a toast. With this gesture, Frederick released them from the requirement for serious discourse.

Chuck withdrew a stone pipe from his knapsack. Lorraine stood up and began stretching again, facing the river. Back then, getting stoned in public was a way of bonding with someone, an act of daring, an expression of solidarity and of civil disobedience. In certain circles in Cambridge, taking the right drugs in the right quantities was like having school spirit. Frederick and Chuck took turns inhaling and holding their breath. Lorraine watched a sailboat motor toward open water. The wind picked up a little, and it was starting to get cold. For Chuck, the world narrowed to a small piece of land slightly larger than the blanket. Clouds moved across the sky like a time-lapse photograph, and a cold breeze came in off the river. After a little while, Lorraine started loading books into her pouch. Sensing their imminent departure, Chuck asked where they lived, hoping for two different answers.

"In the country," Frederick said, rolling off the blanket.

"Near BC," Lorraine answered, motioning across the river.

Chuck followed them through the quadrangle, past the stone buildings. Frederick talked nonstop about the movement and Abbie Hoffman, a kid from Worcester who'd graduated from Brandeis a few years earlier. Hoffman founded his own political party, the Yippies, which had become famous for its subversive goofiness, organizing freaks to levitate the Pentagon, sticking flowers in National Guardsmen's bayonets, and hosting large gatherings of pot-smoking hippies called be-ins that attracted widespread media attention. For this and for being from Frederick's hometown, Hoffman had earned the former chemistry student's deep and abiding respect.

Chuck looked from Frederick to Lorraine and then back at Frederick again, and he wondered what kind of relationship they had—casual and temporary, loving, or contentious. They were standing in front of a row of retail stores while Frederick described a stunt Hoffman had just pulled off. In Manhattan, a dozen freaks signed up for a tour of the New York Stock Exchange and tossed dollar bills over the balcony, causing the ticker to stop and all the brokers on the floor to scramble and cheer. With the major networks' news teams filming, and everyone dancing with joy, Hoffman declared the end of money. As Frederick spoke, his eyes narrowed behind his glasses and he tilted his head back as if he, too, aspired to a stunt this brilliant. "A bunch of acidhead Communist freaks made national news for under a hundred dollars!" Frederick said. "Is that fucking brilliant?"

Traffic whizzed by. Neither Lorraine nor Chuck said anything for a minute, and then Lorraine spoke. "That's the stupidest thing I've ever heard."

Frederick stumbled backward, acting stunned. "Do you have any idea how many kids in Iowa who never considered burning their draft cards will join the movement because of this?" The sky was cloudy now and the wind made a sound like the ocean. The light changed and Frederick stepped down off the curb. Behind him a guy dragged a heavy satchel into the Laundromat.

Lorraine stood still, her arms across her chest. "You think regular people are going to turn themselves into revolutionaries?" she asked calmly. Chuck had heard about people burning their draft cards, but he'd never much thought about it. He wasn't only receiving new information about politics and civil disobedience, he was observing up close how a cutting-edge radical couple behaved.

"Absolutely," Frederick said. "Once they get our message, it's just a matter of time." He spoke as if he, too, was a Yippie. The light changed again from green to yellow. "Confuse the symbol with the thing," Frederick said, "and you change people's minds. The map may not be the territory, but it gets you close."

"The stunt completely obscures the message," Lorraine said, taking Frederick by the arm. "Yippies are confusing civil disobedience with theater of the absurd. It's too far-fetched. Normal people don't see something like this on the news and just forget about their mortgages." She pointed to a Chinese restaurant across the street and said, "I'm hungry." The wind blew a piece of trash up against Frederick's leg.

"What do you think?" Frederick asked Chuck.

He felt as if he'd been caught daydreaming in class. The truth was he had no opinion. He was along for the ride, hoping to get close to this girl whose arm was hooked around Frederick's. He considered the question. Whether the stunt would have an effect on people was so fundamentally different from a mathematical proof, he had no idea how to approach it. He tried calculating how many people might be watching when the prank was shown. That was the denominator. Of those, how many would it actually mean something to? There was no numerator, no way to know, which made him slightly nauseous, the same way he felt walking around Cambridge, which was full of radicals and freaks, intellectuals and professors, jocks and stoners.

"What exactly is the message?" Chuck said, hoping to buy time.

Frederick looked at him as if he was kidding.

"Well, I guess if you want to show people that money is the root of all evil," Chuck stammered, restating what he thought was Frederick's argument. "Maybe they'd have better luck with kids." There was silence. Lorraine and Frederick were both staring at him now. In the background, traffic passed indifferently. "Maybe they oughta set up at 4H fairs or sponsor Little League teams. You know, teach kids how to resolve conflict peaceably. . . ."

Lorraine moved her arm in front of Frederick, who began to laugh, long and low, making a sound like horns honking. "Maybe you oughta be a babysitter, man," he said loudly, waving his hands above his head and sticking his face forward. "In between wiping kids' asses you could draw pictures of Vietnamese children playing with cluster bombs and napalm." The whole scene—Chuck's answer and Frederick's response—struck Lorraine as funny, and she, too, started laughing. This was unfortunate. It was the first time Chuck had really taken a position on something political, even though he'd done so primarily to align himself with a girl, and this little exchange forged a permanent place in his memory. "That's got to be the lamest thing I've ever heard," Frederick said in a falsetto, taking Lorraine's hand and crossing the street.

Chuck had to shake his head to think clearly. For a moment, he considered throwing himself into traffic. The embarrassment of saying something stupid combined with the wind whipping around the buildings made his face redden. He stood on the curb watching as Frederick and Lorraine crossed the street. Before entering the restaurant, Lorraine turned and looked back with what Chuck imagined later might have been a sympathetic nod.

A week later, Chuck found himself in the back of a dormitory lounge with a couple dozen students watching TV. It was just after dinner and the volume on the little black-and-white was jacked way up, blasting the canned music that precedes a news bulletin. "The Reverend Martin Luther King Jr. was assassinated today on the balcony of his motel room in Memphis," Walter Cronkite said, in a voice reserved for tragedy, "just months before he was to lead a huge march on Washington." The camera cut to a crowd of blacks outside the motel, looking angry and dazed. Dr. King had been seen by many as a symbol of hope, Cronkite lamented.

In the lounge, the talk turned quickly to conspiracy. A frizzy-haired student from Brooklyn said that J. Edgar Hoover and the FBI were behind it. Within hours, riots broke out in cities all over the country. Instead of peaceful marches and a boycott that Dr. King had planned, angry blacks picked up rocks and sticks and began fighting with their hands.

Over the next several weeks, Chuck watched the news on TV every night. The networks showed blacks being rounded up, fire hosed, shot at, billy clubbed, and attacked by dogs. To describe the mayhem one night, a reporter let slip the word *revolution*. "The revolution is coming, man," Frederick had promised a few weeks ago on the lawn. "In a system like ours, ordinary people are fed up. If you can't see that, you're blind."

April in Boston is a dicey proposition and soon the weather turned nasty again. People swaddled themselves in their winter gear and went about their routines—eating in restaurants, attending classes, going to work, getting high—yet nobody could put Dr. King's death far out of mind. The reaction in black and liberal communities around the country went from bereft to outraged, and soon, blacks in U.S. cities took to the streets, marching and chanting and, in some parts of Boston, hurling bricks through storefronts. Students organized teach-ins, which often erupted in violence. Chuck pictured Frederick being interrogated under bright lights, burning his draft card, having his eyelids pinned open or his fingernails pried off, while Lorraine huddled next to Chuck, her face buried in his chest. Since their encounter at MIT, nothing in Chuck's life had changed, yet everything around him seemed different. He was restless, uncertain, excited.

Most mornings, Chuck slept late. By the time he showered and dressed, his classes had already started; for breakfast he wandered to a nearby shelter populated by homeless people, paranoid schizophrenics, runaways, and religious nuts. He spent his afternoons, stoned, in Boston and Cambridge, wandering into foreign film screenings, bookstores, hospital waiting rooms, pawnshops, public gatherings, marches, and be-ins, especially in parks, listening to music, Hare Krishnas chanting, and soapbox orators bemoaning the war. He lived in distraction and denial, deploying powerful drugs in their service.

Earlier in the year, Chuck met a guy in a club on Mass Avenue who dreamed of playing percussion with the rock band the Inter Galactic Messengers. Augie Pearson was a roadie, part of a two-man sound crew that worked for the band's manager, who sold dope to pay for the band's thunderous sound system. Through the fall and winter, depending on road conditions and the most recent Mexican harvest, Chuck drove a borrowed van down the Mass Pike to the band's rented house in Connecticut, his knapsack full of cash, returning with a shopping bag full of buds and shake, which he broke up and sold out of his dorm.

By spring, unable to get Lorraine out of his mind, Chuck showed up for a chemistry lab and waited outside to talk to the teaching assistant. "How would somebody go about getting a scholarship to MIT?" he asked, after the other students had filed out. The graduate student squinted, trying to place the impish young man.

"You could start by getting a passing grade," he said.

Chuck followed the instructor into the hall. "Did you know a scholarship student who dropped out last year? Reddish brown hair, glasses, a big talker, weird ideas about politics, a radical?"

"What's it to *you*?" the TA replied.

"The other night, I ran into a guy who was bragging about getting a free ride," Chuck said.

"So?"

"He said he quit because he outgrew the people in the department. . . ."

The graduate student laughed. "He outgrew us, huh?" They made their way down the marble stairs.

"He made it sound like he was some kind of a genius—"

"The guy was an asshole," the graduate student said. "Some kind of Communist. He refused to do the labs. After he was expelled, we found a bunch of lab equipment had disappeared."

"He was expelled?" Chuck said, smiling.

The graduate student pushed open the door and stepped into the cold. Chuck pulled his parka up and followed him down the steps. "This place doesn't graduate lunatics."

By May, the world—once as comprehensible as a quadratic equation—seemed dangerous and strange. Unable to sleep, Chuck spent many nights watching the Krishnas and the Fantasy Jugglers near the all-night newsstand in Harvard Square. As the sun rose, he read about arrests and curfews in Detroit and Los Angeles and the aftermath of the Tet Offensive in Vietnam, picturing boys he'd known—kids from the old neighborhood—in hospitals or body bags.

One morning, he caught the first bus of the day to Kenmore Square, where he changed to the T and rode it to the end of the line. Directly across from where the trolley stopped was a huge stone archway with BOSTON COLLEGE carved in it. Chuck followed students up a long driveway and a steep set of stairs, which led to the main campus, passing old buildings arranged in quadrangles, imperial structures linked by paved pathways, where he stood outside lecture halls that held courses with names like "The Symbolic Presence of Redemptive Mysteries of Christ" and "Religious Currents in the Third Century."

Not that morning, but on his third visit to BC, he found Lorraine, her blonde hair pulled back in a bandanna. She was standing in the back of a line of students who looked to be out of a Clearasil commercial. She was wearing a suede Davy Crockett jacket, her arm hooked around a tall brunette's, her hand moving now and then to adjust a piece of hair that kept falling in her face. Chuck followed her to Commonwealth Avenue and the trolley terminus, where the taller woman boarded. Chuck watched as Lorraine kissed the woman full on the mouth and then hiked up the hill and down a small street in Brighton to a small ramshackle duplex. Unable to think of what to do next, he took the Green Line home.

Two days later, he had a plan. He returned at sunset and took the steps to the front porch, which was cluttered with a sofa and a couple of old bicycles. A calico cat sat motionless on the windowsill. Inside, Jefferson Airplane was playing. Chuck took a deep breath and knocked. "Petition," he said through the screen door. When it opened a crack, Chuck smelled food cooking—a soup or stew—stale tobacco, moisture from a recent shower. A young man with long stringy hair wearing a Jimi Hendrix T-shirt looked him up and down. "I'm collecting signatures to keep ROTC off campus."

The young man held up his index finger and then shut the door in Chuck's face so he could remove the chain. "Right on, brother," the man said, taking the pen. He wore a pair of tight-fitting jeans and large tinted aviator glasses. Chuck looked inside. In the living room was a beat-up couch and a large coffee table covered with magazines, newspapers, record albums, and a bong. A sleeping bag and some blankets were balled up against a wall. Both the television and the stereo were on and Chuck could hear people talking in other rooms. He asked the guy with the glasses if anyone else in the house might be willing to sign. "Jerry, Lorrie, Mark!" he called over his shoulder.

A man in his mid-twenties with a buzz cut walked out of the kitchen carrying a spatula and turned the record over. "What's up?" he said, looking bored. Lorraine had four roommates that spring—all guys.

"The ROTC is an instrument of American foreign policy," said the one who'd answered the door.

She stepped into the living room with a towel wrapped around her torso, her shoulders bare, her hair dripping onto the floor, took the clipboard without looking up, and read the first few paragraphs Chuck had typed calling for the withdrawal of the Reserve Officers' Training Corps from campuses in the Boston area. With all three of them staring at her shoulders, she thumbed through the attached pages, which were blank. "Haven't gotten very far, have you?" Lorraine said to Chuck matter-of-factly. Then she motioned for the pen. "Colleges shouldn't teach people to kill," Lorraine said simply. She signed her name, passed the clipboard back to him, and turned around.

"Do you think anybody else would want . . . ?"

She turned around and considered the question. "You could try—" Then she stopped, squinted. "Hey, aren't you the guy?" She cocked her head. "MIT man," she said, smiling. "Whatever happened to you that day?"

A Sousa march started up in his head, which started bobbing up and down. "I had to go."

"Come," she said, pulling his hand. "Have tea with me."

The kitchen was a narrow, linoleum-tiled box with no windows. They sat at a table covered with mail, matches, wads of keys, cigarettes, bags of candy and nuts, all tossed in piles. The guys Lorraine shared the house with were a hodgepodge of students, drifters, and passersby, most of whom were flying below the radar, avoiding parents, academic advisers, and the selective service, and for those reasons avoided registering for utilities and answering the phone. The first thing Lorraine said to Chuck was that she liked his idea of teaching kids conflict resolution. It was something she'd have liked to do back where she grew up. After discovering they were from the same place, they commended themselves for leaving Philadelphia and compared notes about Boston: the more liberal atmosphere, the prior winter, and the insanity of drivers. But most exciting to Chuck, besides the object of his desire sitting nearly naked across from him for fifteen minutes, was that Lorraine wrote her phone number on one of the pages of the petition. "Call me," she said coquettishly. And call her he did.

As the weather turned, Chuck stood in his bare feet by the pay telephone in his dorm at all hours of the day and night, waiting for someone to answer. Failing that, he started riding the bus to Kenmore Square, switching to the Green Line, and walking three blocks to Lorraine's house. He did it rain or shine, weekday or weekend, whether he found her home or not, almost every day, until suddenly, his world seemed manageable, his fellow students less intimidating, even his professors and their review sessions for finals easier to abide.

When Lorraine was home, they sat together in the living room, got stoned, and listened to music, talking, while Lorraine's roommates passed through with beers and young women they hoped to befriend. Lorraine talked about the nature of being, transcendence, the church, and her disillusionment and grief over the early death of her parents. Chuck listened. For the first time in his adult life, someone was being honest with him.

"You're a scientist, right?" she asked him one day.

"More of a math person, actually."

"So what do you think? Is there a God?"

Chuck let some time pass. Many times in conversation, Lorraine would let the outside of her leg brush against his, and he found this both energizing and distracting. He knit his brow. "I believe what I can see," he said. Like his mother's love for Arthur or his father's self-interest. He was skilled at avoiding arguments about things he couldn't quantify. "I mean, if you're talking about some guy in a tuxedo with a baton"—she put her hand on his knee—"or some cosmic scorekeeper on the side of good," he said, encouraged, "I don't think so."

Lorraine nodded. "So you think everything is random? Arbitrary? Accidental?" The question seemed to make her sad.

"Not everything," he said quickly. "I mean, you boil something and the molecules move. . . ."

"I'm not talking about cause and effect," she said. There was a sizzling sound and then a cloud of smoke drifting up from the stove. Chuck was at a loss. Although the conversation was about ideas—science and religion—he felt it in his genitals. Struggling, he reached for her hand. "Some kind of organizing principle, I guess," he said, sound rushing in his ears.

"So you think everything happens for a reason?"

"I guess."

"Like us meeting?"

"Uh-huh." That sounded good.

She smiled. "Bad things, too?"

"I suppose," he said quickly. He would remember this moment, infused with sexual energy. It wasn't so much he doubted the role of fate or destiny; even as a scientist, he attributed a certain illogical good fortune to having escaped his brother and South Philly, evading a hellish apprenticeship with his father, and finding himself sitting across from Lorraine. He would remember this conversation thirty years later for the chance Lorraine had given him, but he had forsaken, and how little of his life he'd spent reflecting, instead, blithely accepting the proposition that what a human being winds up with as his destiny, he either deserves or forfeits by virtue or lack thereof. Lorraine hopped up and walked into the kitchen. "Jerry!" she yelled. "Your pasta's burning!" Then to Chuck, as if his concession had earned him this: "You wanna get a beer?"

The Phoenix Room was a neighborhood bar and Mexican restaurant with a loud jukebox and sawdust on the floor. They found a table near the back and took seats across from each other, Chuck leaning forward, his elbows on the table and Lorraine pulling her legs to her chest. A waitress approached. "Draft," Lorraine said, tapping the table in front of her. Chuck lifted a finger. "Me, too." Someone turned the music up and a drunken couple started to dance.

I was going to be a nun," Lorraine said unexpectedly, laughing. "Until I discovered sex." Chuck took out a cigarette and lit it. "In my senior year, I ran with a tough crowd," she continued. "I got interested in guys late." As she said this, she smiled wistfully. "I mean, I love rippling muscles, the way you talk to each other, even your musky smell. . . ." She looked at him directly, forcefully, as if daring him to turn away, but he didn't. "When my parents died, I stopped believing in heaven and hell. Underneath, I guess I was angry," she said. When the waitress returned, they ordered shots of tequila and beers to chase them. In addition to her frankness, Chuck was becoming accustomed to long pauses, during which Lorraine looked implacably into his face. After a while, the conversation idled, Lorraine's eyelids fluttered and got heavy, and she invited him back to her place.

Theirs had the manic illogic and fiery intensity of all brief affairs, with a few bizarre twists. Had he been thinking clearly, Chuck might have considered each one a data point, making note of them at least, and then linking them together in a way that might have presaged the betrayal and confusion that came at the end. For one thing, Lorraine seemed very connected to other men who approached her—on the street or in bars—guys who came by the house in Brighton, with half smiles and hooded eyes, as if they were in the midst of an enchanted conversation or an extraordinary encounter. For another, as persistently as Chuck showed up at the house in Brighton or waited for her outside of class, Lorraine surprised and disappointed him, resulting in Chuck's being stood up or waiting hours at designated areas only to have Lorraine deny they'd planned to meet. She was alternatively flirtatious and distant, giving herself over the first few times they had sex (she was as comfortable with her naked body as Chuck was inhibited). Yet she dismissed any attempt to categorize their relationship, and she was extremely evasive about the future.

Still, nothing was more confusing and ambiguous to Chuck than Lorraine's feelings for Frederick, a man Lorraine talked about a lot, yet who seemed never to be around. She recounted conversations with him verbatim, describing his positions on politics, economics, and sports—sometimes with reverence and affection, sometimes with cynicism and resentment. Some days, she seemed paralyzed by his absence; other times, she acted like he didn't exist. In the early days, to make it easier for himself, Chuck imagined Frederick as Lorraine's older brother, which cleared his conscience somewhat and allowed him to indulge his romantic fantasies with little reservation.

One night after finals, Chuck arrived at the house in Brighton. The house was dark. An old Yamaha motorcycle was leaning against the outer stairway. He hesitated and then took the steps two at a time, thinking that most likely nobody was home. For the first time, Frederick answered the door, looking thinner than Chuck had remembered him from the lawn at MIT. He was bare-chested, with tufts of reddish brown hair and freckles covering his sinewy arms. "Yeah?" he said, opening the door. Inside, it reeked of cigarettes, sweat, and sex.

"Lorraine home?" Chuck asked, screwing up his courage. Frederick shook his head as if Chuck's question wasn't registering. For a few seconds, Chuck stood in the doorway staring at his shoes, trying to decide whether to leave. The memory of his humiliation at MIT was still fresh.

After a few seconds, Lorraine came out of her bedroom wearing a blue terry-cloth bathrobe, squinting.

"MIT man," she said. And then, to Frederick, "You remember Chuck." She seemed happy to see him. "The guy we talked to that day?" Frederick turned and walked into the kitchen. Lorraine invited Chuck to sit down, as if his showing up at this moment was something she expected. Chuck imagined her beneath the robe—her curves, the dark patch at the intersection of her legs, her smell. Frederick came back into the room with a beer and fiddled with the record player. Lorraine motioned for Chuck to take a seat on a stuffed chair, while she sat on the couch, her bare legs curled under her. There was an awkward silence, and then music started up—something hard-edged—Iron Butterfly or Blind Faith. Chuck stared into his hands.

Frederick lit a cigarette and sat down. He let the smoke linger around his mouth, as if the curling cloud was fortunate to spend a few extra seconds near his face. "What's up, Doc?" Frederick said, remembering Chuck's reference to being pre-med.

"That's funny," Lorraine said, laughing. "What's up, Doc?" She ran her hand along Frederick's thigh, and Chuck's heart sank. If it hadn't been before, it was obvious to Chuck now that Lorraine Nadia—the object of his fantasies for the past two months, the first woman who'd shared intimately the details of her own past, who'd confessed to having sexual urges like a man's, who drank with him and then walked up the hill, her arm locked in his before pushing him up against the front door of her house, yanking off his shirt, and unbuckling his pants as though he and his body were a meal and she hadn't eaten anything in days—belonged to Frederick and that he, Chuck, was the interloper.

Out of nervousness, Chuck pulled a leather pouch out of his knapsack and extracted a package of rolling papers. He rolled and sealed a joint with buds from a special envelope—black gooey sinsemillia that he mixed with whatever he was peddling at the time to ensure his customers got good and fucked-up before they bought. Then he handed the joint to Lorraine, who looked at him without even a hint of awkwardness. He lit a match and let her take his hand, which he tried not to let tremble as he brought it to her face.

Frederick returned from the kitchen with a couple of beers and launched into a story about how he'd been asked by an old buddy to help rebuild a school bus for a commune in North Cambridge in time for the Democratic National Convention. "You haven't really worked under a car until a girl comes over, straddles you, and asks if you're ready for lunch." He grinned lasciviously and slapped his knee, and the three of them began to laugh. The conversation turned from communes to the Red Sox, whom Frederick adored, to a speech Frederick said he would be making to one of several radical groups he claimed membership in. When he disappeared into the bedroom to work on it, Lorraine told Chuck she wouldn't mind getting together again sometime soon. "You know," she said, brushing the hair from her face, "to get stoned and fuck."

At five fifty A.M. Tuesday, the chunky Puerto Rican with dreadlocks pulled his red tow truck up to the gate of Puckman Security. He sat in his truck, eating a sandwich, until the security guard ambled over. "Can I help you?" the guard said.

The driver wiped his mouth with a paper towel. He motioned to the black Suburban parked at an angle. "Got orders to tow it," he said, holding up a clipboard.

The guard shook his head. "No can do," he said. "The place is sealed. Nothing comes in, nothing goes out."

"Not a problem, buddy," the driver said cheerfully. He held the clipboard out the window. As he raised his left arm, a devil with a pitchfork came to life on his bicep. "Just let me have your signature for City Hall." The guard grimaced. "This guy's got over five grand in parking violations," he said, pointing to the Suburban. "Fuckers think they can hide forever." The guard shrugged. "I need your name, your badge number, and the name of your company."

"I'm off duty," the guard said. "This is just part-time—"

The driver interrupted him. "When the fines get this high, they'll wake up the judge."

The guard looked the driver up and down and then checked his watch. He was two years from retirement and didn't need anything to call attention to him. He told the driver to wait a minute and walked over to the Suburban. The front seat was littered with coffee cups, copies of customer orders, and paper bags; the back was empty. Keaton had said to watch the building. He hadn't said anything about the car. It took the tow truck less than a minute to hook up and tow the Suburban four blocks east to Aramingo. The driver called Rahim Rodriguez from his cell phone. "You're all set, buddy."

As the sun crept up over Jersey, Rahim drove the Suburban around to the back of the Super Fresh on Aramingo, gathered a half-dozen empty boxes, and then returned to the factory, parking near the fire escape steps. Inside Chuck's apartment, they gathered items of value— a coffee grinder, an espresso maker, a teak humidor that had long been emptied of cigars, a crystal wine decanter, a Nikon SLR, a selection of lenses in a leather bag, and a set of porcelain teacups that Regina Puckman had asked Chuck to keep away from Artie. From the bedroom, Chuck pulled a dozen fancy Italian suits and two dozen monogrammed shirts and stuffed them in a garbage bag. Rahim unhooked signed photographs of sixties luminaries Chuck had bought from a pawnshop customer. By the light of the aquarium, he unplugged a Tiffany lamp—the only item he'd managed to keep from his marriage. When it came time to disconnect the television, VCR, and stereo, Chuck hesitated, a pained look on his face. "Leave it," Rahim said.

While the security guard sat on his little stool in the parking lot, waiting for Keaton and the EPA goons to arrive, Rahim and Chuck quietly carried the bulk of Chuck's material possessions down the fire escape steps and out the side entrance. On his last trip, Chuck touched the Rolex on his wrist, purchased after closing a large order with a chain of retail pawnshops almost ten years ago. He took it off and turned it over in his hand, held it away from his body, then tossed it in a box. By seven A.M., they were barreling down I-95 South, past trucks carrying steel girders and chemotherapeutic waste, listening to Howard Stern.

When Harvey Slutzky pulled his Mercedes-Benz SL500 into the parking lot of his pawnshop, he saw two figures sitting in a black Suburban. It was only seven thirty in the morning when he left Moorestown, New Jersey, but it looked as if it was going to be one of those dazzling days in January when you say fuck it to the cold and walk to the Italian Market for lunch. Suddenly, he wasn't thinking about weather, or business, or the girl in the Asian market he'd been banging. He swung the vehicle around so that, if necessary, he'd have two ways to exit. With the engine running, he took his Glock .357 semiautomatic from under the seat and set it in his lap. Harvey checked his mirrors. There was nobody else around.

Herb Slutzky opened a small pawnshop on the waterfront in the late forties. Today, his son Harvey owned five of these concrete pavilions, two pawnshops in Philly and three in South Jersey, one of which was attached to a metal building that housed an all-night strip joint featuring X-rated videos, sex toys, and topless dancers behind Plexiglas partitions. When Harvey saw the trench coat, the Nikes, and the three-day-old beard, he almost laughed out loud. It had been a long time since he'd been shaken down by a wino, which is what his old friend Chuck Puckman looked like, squinting in the morning light. "Jesus Christ, Puckman! What the fuck happened to you?" Harvey said, wedging the Glock between the seats.

"I need a favor," Chuck said. Harvey opened the door and swung his legs out. He was a large man with a full head of hair dyed black, big bushy eyebrows, and bulbous lips, which had a cigar permanently attached to them. The inside of his car smelled like aftershave. As they walked toward the building, Rahim backed the Suburban up till it was only a few feet away from the door. "I'm in a jam," Chuck said, rubbing his face.

"I heard," Harvey said, disabling the building alarm and unlocking the door. "You talk to Palmieri?" he asked. In the neighborhood, Fat Eddie was the go-to guy for problems.

"This is big," Chuck said.

Rahim opened the back of the truck. Harvey took the cigar out of his mouth and held the door open. Inside, he filled the coffeemaker. Rahim carried in boxes.

"Your mother okay, Chuckie?" Harvey asked, relighting his cigar.

"The normal aches and pains, I guess."

Rahim set the boxes with Chuck's belongings around Harvey's desk.

Like most pawnbrokers, Harvey was practiced at surveying people's belongings quickly and without reaction. He separated the Nikon and the lenses, the kitchen appliances, the china, and the photographs from the clothing and other knickknacks. "The suits are nice, but not for me. The people who come here have taste up their ass." Harvey reached into the box with the Rolex. He put a magnifying lens in his eye and held the watch under the light. He hadn't expected his day to start out this way. "You want I give you a note for this shit for when things settle down? I hate like hell to see you this way." Chuck waved his hand. Harvey sounded like a little kid winning too easily. "The most I could give you for the lot is forty-two, maybe forty-five hundred. And that's 'cause you're family."

"What about the truck?" Rahim asked.

"Take it to the Automall," he said. "Talk to Mario." Chuck looked around the office. He moved his hand and touched his mouth as if he was going to say something, but changed his mind. Harvey didn't know exactly what was going on, but he felt really bad. Forty-five hundred bucks wasn't gonna get a guy very far. "What's with Artie?" Harvey asked. "Anybody hear from him yet?"

Rahim cleared his throat and looked away.

"What are you talking about?" Chuck said.

Harvey looked at him with a sad expression. "Nothing," he said, turning away. "Call me if you need anything, man."

Owing to the ease of video duplication and Coleman Porter's ego, the interview of Arthur Puckman implicating his brother for the near-fatal injury of Ramon Gutierrez had already appeared a dozen times in at least three bars in Kensington. By Sunday, AP and Reuters had picked up the story, and pictures of EPA trucks and men in moon suits were plastered all over the Internet. A couple of environmental groups focused on the incident and issued statements critical of American business for ruining the environment.

Chuck hadn't heard any of this yet, but Harvey asking about his brother worried him. Chuck knew Artie would construe the Gutierrez accident as a disaster, which might easily cause him to do something stupid. Leaving Big Harvey's, Chuck wanted to find Artie right away, warn him about the investigation, tell him to keep his mouth shut, and assure him that they would find a good lawyer soon who would make the mess disappear. He had Rahim park the Suburban on Washington Avenue and walk up Tenth Street with him to the tiny row house where, more than fifty years ago, the brothers had been born.

Regina Puckman cracked open the door and glared at them. She had deep creases in her face and dark circles around her eyes. "Finally," she said, when she recognized her son. "Where the fuck have you been?" Rahim and Chuck followed her up the staircase into an apartment that smelled as if a window hadn't been opened in years. Regina took a seat in the kitchen. Steam evaporated from some kind of bubbling concoction. A fluorescent light flickered overhead. The radio was so loud the only evidence that the old woman was talking was that her lips were moving. Chuck stood in the doorway. Mother and son didn't smile, didn't touch, didn't look each other in the eye. After a few seconds, Rahim slid his hand across the counter and turned the radio down.

"Hanging around with Puerto Ricans now, are you?" the old woman said, reaching for a teabag.

"Where is he?" Chuck asked, his voice shaking. It was the same question his mother had been asking him about Artie all his life.

"If you'd been here Saturday when he came home, maybe he wouldn't be missing now."

"What do you mean missing? Since when?"

"He came in late Saturday night with some rough-looking character who looked like a longshoreman. Big guy—red hair, freckles, a beard, glasses. Arthur fixed me my drink and then the two of them went into his bedroom. When I woke up Sunday, he was gone."

"Has he called?" Chuck asked.

"If you'd have treated him better, maybe he'd be there with you, helping you outta this mess you're in—"

"It's important, Ma. It's not just me. Artie might be in trouble."

"Of course he's in trouble. The pressure he was under. And your father paid him nothing!"

Chuck left Rahim and his mother in the kitchen. In the hallway were pen-and-ink drawings of old Italy and photographs of Regina's family that had hung there so long the images had faded or had been covered with dust. Artie's twin bed had a wooden headboard and a navy blue quilt with yellow muskets. There were matching lamps with soldiers at attention on a wooden night table, a brown dresser with big yellow knobs, and a small writing desk that looked as if it'd been lifted from an elementary school. The only items in plain view were a Bible and a porcelain serpent curling up from a dish, which held paper clips, cuff links, and a ring containing Artie's office keys.

Chuck opened the night-table drawer. There was a checkbook with detailed entries ending last week: $16.47 to a stamp collector Artie had been buying from for thirty years, $42.95 to Bell Atlantic, $10 to a coffee shop on the corner, and $50 to a company called Culver City Costumes. The dresser was empty, except for the top drawer, which had receipts going back at least a few years, and beneath them, Artie's address book and copies of utility bills. There were no plane tickets, no scribbled notes with telephone or flight numbers. Chuck got down on his hands and knees and looked under the bed. No suitcase either. And the closet was empty except for two long-sleeved shirts, a pair of overalls, and a thermal undershirt. No underwear. No socks.

"Charles!" he heard his mother call from the kitchen.

In the medicine chest were prescription bottles, tweezers, cotton swabs, and a couple of Fleet enemas. Chuck tapped a few Valium into his palm, shoved them in his pocket, and turned off the light. "Charles," she said again as he returned to the kitchen. She touched a large brooch hanging around her neck and looked up at him sadly. "If he calls, tell him to come home," she pleaded. There was a tiny tic in her shoulder, a shred of disingenuousness that, at the time, Chuck attributed to anger—toward him, toward his father, toward all of mankind.

Rahim parked the Suburban on a side street. Chuck stuffed the cash in the front of his pants, put on his sunglasses, and walked to the side entrance of the factory. At the top of the stairs, he surveyed the yard. Pigeons lined the eaves. Generations of birds bred for arrogance roosted on the property. Many times, he'd imagined shooting them with a .22, then listening as their little bodies landed with thuds on the asphalt. The white vans were back, and the maroon LTD was parked next to a white Ford. Quietly, he let himself in. In the time it took him to open the freezer, empty some ice cubes into a glass, and fix himself a drink, there was a knock on the door.

Chuck shut the freezer and leaned his forehead against a color Xerox of his daughter, Ivy, on horseback. The knocks came again. "Mr. Puckman," a voice said. "Mr. Puckman, we know you're in there." Chuck thought about his fish. It had been more than twenty-four hours since he'd fed them. "We'd like to ask you a few questions," a voice said.

Chuck tiptoed to the tank and stared at the bubbles from the aerator. Soon, it would be time to add water. He picked up the bottles one by one—dried worm casings, flecks of plankton, and dried algae—tapping them against the glass. Each one drew different fish in a specific order. It amazed him that they recognized their food from the tapping of the bottles. Chuck laid food on the surface in three separate areas. The knocking continued. He crossed the living room, took the envelope of cash from his pants, and slipped it into a corner of the elevator shaft. Then he opened the red door.

Standing there was a smallish older man, with white hair, large glasses, and a neatly trimmed mustache. "Cyril Deacon," he said, sticking out his hand, "regional inspector, Occupational Safety and Health." He wore a rumpled gray suit and a crimson bow tie. Behind him was Keaton with his arms crossed. "Can we come in?"

"No." It was a simple expression of will.

"We just need a few minutes of your time." It was Keaton behind him, trying to sound collegial.

"I don't think so." Chuck moved to close the door.

"If you'd be more comfortable, we'll wait for you downstairs," Deacon said.

According to Fat Eddie and every bit of legal advice Chuck had ever received, it was best to avoid talking to your adversaries without a lawyer. This particular day, however, Chuck felt it would be helpful to smoke out the government's position as early as he could. Provided he was cagey enough, it could save him legal fees. Besides, OSHA inspectors were bureaucrats, not prosecutors. He told them he'd think about it and shut the door.

"Take your time," Deacon said from outside.

From his jacket pocket, Chuck took two Valium and washed them down with his drink. Ten minutes later, he made his way slowly downstairs.

The factory floor was cluttered with the remnants of jobs in process: cut angle iron and sheets of Plexiglas. The men in the moon suits had again made a huge mess, clearing a two-foot-wide strip from the tanks to the back of the plant. Overhead, lights and gas-fired heaters were full on, something neither Charlie nor Artie would have tolerated. It was a strange feeling for Chuck to walk through the shop and feel warmth in the winter. The EPA man stood in the doorway of the office watching him approach. "Last I heard," Chuck said as he entered, "there was this thing called private property."

"You want to see the search warrant?" Keaton said evenly.

"I just want to run my business. . . ."

The bathroom door opened, and the older man stepped into the office area. He wiped his hands on a paper towel and extended a box of doughnuts to Chuck, who declined. Cyril Deacon lifted the coffeepot and began pouring. "The floor here is rather sticky," he said to no one in particular. Chuck was glad they weren't upstairs, sitting knee to knee in his living room. Tropical fish had subtle sensory capabilities—they could detect changes in a room—temperature, nervous energy, a vibe. They knew when something was awry. An angelfish had died one night when a woman Chuck brought home flipped out. Besides, he didn't need these guys poking around his prescription pill bottles and his ashtrays with little reefer stubs.

Cyril Deacon pulled a couple of chairs from behind the desks and arranged them so that he was sitting with his back to the shop. He smiled as he did this, an old man observing some kind of etiquette that nobody practiced anymore. Then he laid a paper towel across his lap. Keaton pulled his chair a little bit back and away. The older man smiled sheepishly again and looked admiringly at his doughnut. "I'd like to start things off by saying that this is just a friendly talk, a couple of professionals trying to get to the bottom of things." He took a bite and chewed slowly. "We look at this as an opportunity for you to help us, although you're under no obligation to do so. All we're asking you to do is answer our questions truthfully. The sooner you do, well, the sooner you can get back to your business." He opened the folder in his lap and smacked his lips, as if the two men had shown up at a parent-teacher conference. "This stuff, 1,1,1 trichloroethylene. What can you tell us about it?"

Chuck shrugged. "Nothing."

"1,1,1 TCE," Deacon repeated, as if Chuck hadn't heard him the first time.

"I've never heard of it. Sorry," Chuck said, shrugging.

Keaton shifted in his chair. "Tell me about cleaning metal, Mr. Puckman," Deacon said cheerfully.

"Tell you what?"

"Why is it necessary, how do you go about doing it, that kind of thing." Deacon folded his arms, as if he was really pleased to be having this conversation.

"You have to clean it before you paint it," Chuck said, pretty sure Deacon knew exactly what was involved. "Otherwise, you get bubbles under the surface, and it looks like shit."

"How do you do it?"

Chuck leaned back in his chair. Keaton had obviously briefed the OSHA inspector on the tanks and Puckman's methods.

"You could sandblast, etch, or dip it. Shit, you probably know better than I do, Mr., uh . . ."

"Deacon," the inspector said. "Cyril Deacon." He pulled a business card from his front pocket.

"Look, I'm just the sales guy," Chuck told them. Cyril Deacon smiled again. Keaton stood up and poured himself a cup of coffee. He opened the refrigerator next to the safe, looking for milk.

"I understand you're primarily involved in sales," Deacon continued. "But perhaps you know more than you realize."

"We used to hang the sub-assemblies from hooks on a track that lined up over the tanks. You'd press a button and the pieces dipped. . . ." Chuck made a gesture with his hands.

"Into the tanks," Deacon said.

"But we don't do that anymore."

"No?"

"No."

"So what do you do?"

"We use chemicals."

"Can you tell us what kind of chemical was in tank number four?"

"Some kind of caustic etch. Water. Alkaline. Honestly, I don't know."

"What exactly is your role here at Puckman Security?"

"Like I said, sales, pretty much." Chuck looked around the room as Cyril Deacon shuffled his papers.

"Who's in charge of production?"

"We don't have fancy titles, if that's what you're asking."

"Who tells your workers what to make when?" It was Keaton again, aggressive.

"Our guys have been with us a long time. They kind of figure things out," Chuck said, smiling. The questions were easy. Even though he was tired, with the vodka and the Valium in him, Chuck was able to relax. He was confident he would be able to see trouble coming one or two questions ahead. "How long is this going to take, anyway? I've got a meeting with my lawyer." Keaton looked up from his coffee.

"Just a few more questions, Mr. Puckman," Deacon said. "Can you tell us who built the tanks?" He sounded like a guy admiring his neighbor's shed.

Chuck laughed. "Sorry. Way before my time."

"Whose design are they?"

Chuck laughed again. "They look designed to you?"

"I mean, who decided how big to make them," Deacon asked,

"where to place them, what kinds of chemicals to put in, where to put the heating elements?"

"You'd have to ask my dad that," Chuck said, thinking how much fun that would be—these two guys sitting on the old man's bed watching him drool. Deacon smiled, too, now. It was a regular smile fest. Chuck's face was beginning to hurt.

"Yes, yes," Deacon said, clearing his throat. "At a certain point," he tried again, "you stopped using the tanks."

Chuck stared at him, waiting for the question, but none came. "Like I said, you'd have to ask my father." Then, thinking about what motivated Charlie Puckman Sr., he said, "It probably had to do with cost."

"To save money?"

"I guess."

"Did it work?"

Chuck shrugged his shoulders. "Business continued. Nobody complained."

"So," Keaton said, "how come in, uh . . . mid-November, you guys refilled tank four and started using it again?"

"I told you, I don't know anything about it," Chuck said, folding his arms.

Deacon wrote something down again. "Whose idea was it?" he asked.

"Whaddya mean, whose idea?"

"To begin cleaning . . ."

"The power goes out in your house. Who decides to light candles? You just do it."

For the first time, Cyril Deacon frowned, as if Chuck, by losing his patience, was being unsporting. Keaton spoke next in a voice that was barely above a whisper. "Somebody had to pick a chemical, Mr. Puckman. Somebody had to place an order. Somebody had to fill the tank." They were both staring at him now. "Was that somebody you?" Any semblance of casualness that Cyril Deacon had tried to invoke was gone.

"No," he said, looking away.

"Are you saying no to making the decision, or no to picking the chemical, or no to placing the order?" Keaton asked. Chuck had the impression that Cyril Deacon liked pretending he was a slightly senile paper pusher with no clout, and that Keaton, despite his officious manner, endless inspections, reports, and citations, was determined to trap him.

"Anything you could tell us would be extremely helpful," Deacon reminded him, his voice slightly higher now.

Chuck folded his arms. "I don't remember."

"If you didn't order it, who did?"

"I'm not going there, guys." The old man was out of reach, but he wasn't about to betray his own brother, especially not this early in the inquiry.

Cyril Deacon put his hands out in front of him and leaned back. "In most businesses, purchases have to be accepted. Somebody signs a packing slip. Sometimes there's an invoice. In your company, who was in charge of receiving?"

"My dad."

"And who decided where to put supplies?"

"What's to decide? You put them where there's room."

"So how did this particular degreaser wind up in tank four?" Cyril Deacon was smiling again.

"I don't know."

Keaton riffled through a stack of papers until he found the one he wanted. "Is this your handwriting, Mr. Puckman?" Chuck squinted at the letters on the page. The word *received* was written—misspelled—in cursive; the date 11/18/98, underneath.

"Nope."

Keaton thrust another piece of paper at Chuck, obscuring the top and presenting only a scrawl at the bottom. "How about this?" he asked Chuck.

It was one of Artie's to-do lists with the words *prep tank* highlighted. Chuck shook his head no. It could have been that the word *prep* was the first part of a compound word, a noun, or a verb.

"It's not my writing."

"Well, whoever's it is, we'd like to talk to them," Deacon said calmly.

Deacon leaned forward in his chair, hovering over the paper. Keaton's breath was sour and the veins in his neck were pulsing. Chuck could tell that the agents were pissed, but by then, the businessman had clammed up.

Since they'd been little boys, Chuck had come to an accommodation with his older brother. As often as he sat on the sidelines, watching Artie self-destruct, Chuck assiduously avoided actually causing or facilitating it. This was, for the early part of his life anyway, his experience of love; no matter how irritated or disdainful of someone you were, family members never practiced anything worse than benign indifference. Even now, with his own ass in a sling, Chuck was unable to be the agent of his brother's demise.

"I gotta go," Chuck said, standing.

Cyril Deacon raised the index finger on his right hand. "You're the president of Puckman Security, right?" the older man said.

A regular Lieutenant Columbo, Chuck thought. "This is a family business," Chuck said. "You don't apply. You don't get elected. You wind up here when you're the only member of the lucky sperm club who can think straight." Chuck felt a tingle and then a wave of heat rise up the back of his neck. For a moment, his face regained its color. For the first time since the accident, he felt like his old self. He intended to find Artie and tell him that he'd better keep his mouth shut, that he was going to have to stand up to some pretty intense questioning.

At Broad and Sansom, there is a magisterial stone building whose hallways are lined with bronze plaques and portraits of Philadelphians who fought in the Civil War. The Union League is a meeting and dining club—oddly anachronistic, with a barber in the men's room and austere bedrooms upstairs for guests and inebriated members—a home away from home for the stiff and corpulent, the haves and the enfranchised, the status seekers and the protectors of the status quo. There are a few blacks and women and a mix of upwardly mobile Asians, Italians, and Jews, but overall, it is not a place people go to admit their mistakes.

Just before five o'clock Tuesday night, Chuck Puckman appeared at the front desk in his soiled trench coat, sneakers, and four-day-old beard, identifying himself as a guest of Edward Palmieri. In the locker room, he wet and combed his hair, shaved, and then spent a few minutes with the *Wall Street Journal* before going up to the bar, where an attendant lent him a black suit jacket and a red tie with little roosters on it. He ordered a scotch and soda, which he drank quickly. At a quarter to six, Fat Eddie put his hand on Chuck's shoulder. Eddie looked shorter and rounder than Chuck remembered. They took a small table off to one side. "It was empty, Eddie," Chuck said, as soon as the maître d' disappeared.

"What?"

"The safe. There was nothing in it but some old envelopes." Chuck put his napkin up to his face. He watched his father's friend closely. "No money. No nothing."

"Impossible. Your father had his stock certificates in there, all his cash, some gold coins."

"You sure he didn't give it to somebody for safekeeping?" Chuck said, narrowing his gaze.

"Jesus Christ, Chuckie, you can put that out of your head right now, all right?" Eddie took a big gulp of his drink and wiped his brow. "I talked to him before his stroke. There's no way he would have taken anything out." They were quiet for a moment. "Where's your brother, anyway?"

"Missing," Chuck said flatly.

"What the fuck are you talking about?" Eddie said nervously. Around them, glasses clinked and people's mouths moved. A buzzing sound started up in Chuck's head. The rooster tie was tight around his neck. Chuck's eyes focused on Eddie's bouncing eyebrows. Entertaining the possibility that Artie had access to Charlie's fortune, Chuck retreated into himself, sinking lower and lower until that very thing began to make sense. Chuck touched his forehead. He was nauseous and hungry at the same time.

Fat Eddie balled up his napkin and laid it on the table. "You all right?" he said.

Chuck nodded. The more he thought about it, the worse things looked. The business was finished, which meant the work Chuck had done his entire adult life—all the clunky knowledge he'd accumulated, all the time he'd spent and the random ass-kissing he'd done—was useless.

He had no way to support himself, finish paying off Eileen, or keep his father at Elysian Fields. On top of this, it looked as if he was going to have to fund his own defense against government bureaucrats like Keaton and Cyril Deacon.

Under the table, Chuck spilled another Valium into his palm and knocked it back with his scotch. "I'm sure we'll hear from him," Fat Eddie was saying. "Artie never makes it on his own for long."

"I gotta go," Chuck said, stumbling past tables full of boisterous businessmen onto Broad Street.

Back home, unable to sleep, Chuck paced the living room, swigging vodka and popping lorazapam and Valium. At one point, he got the idea to call Eileen and explain his predicament, but he couldn't find the phone. Later, he decided to confront his father about the safe, but he couldn't find the keys to his Suburban. As the white vans arrived for the third morning in a row, Chuck poured himself another drink, falling into a deep sleep, the first since Gutierrez went down almost four days ago.

When he woke, it was late afternoon. He swallowed a couple of ibuprofin and stood in the shower until the water turned cold. He called the hospital to check on Gutierrez, who was still in intensive care. Then he listened to his messages—the electric company, a credit card company, and Rahim, who said that a couple of Puckman employees had been offered immunity if they talked to the EPA. The last call was from Fat Eddie, who read off the name and number of another lawyer. Chuck toweled himself off and put on a sweatsuit. He poured himself a glass of water, unlocked the red door, and peered through the opening in the bricks. Keaton's white Ford was gone, and there was no sign of the night guard. To be safe, Chuck took the inside elevator downstairs.

A lot had changed since yesterday. For one thing, the factory was a lot neater. The sub-assemblies and wooden crates that had lined the entrance before had either been removed or piled off to one side so that a trench could be cut near the dip tanks. Tank four was turned on its side like a beached whale, revealing a patchwork of repairs. Chuck stared at the bottom. It appeared that years ago, the drain plug had been removed and replaced with a pipe that disappeared into a trench that extended to the back of the shop. There was a white stain along the trench into the yard, which is where whatever was in tank four disappeared into the ground.

Considering the implications of dumping chemicals nasty enough to almost kill a man into the public water supply, Chuck bent down and let his head drop. His torso felt like a metal shell with corrugated walls that flexed and shook each time he inhaled. All the years he'd buried his disdain for his family's business but didn't stand up and resist no longer mattered. Chuck was the last guy standing and, as such, was going to have to answer for all their actions. For thirty years, he'd wished for the demise of this wretched business. He was getting his wish.

On Thursday, a team of geologists gathered in the parking lot and circled the factory, while another van full of white-jacketed EPA men wearing rubber gloves moved through the plant with little beakers. On Friday, a letter was hand-delivered to each domicile in a four-block radius. "The EPA is investigating reports that trace elements of metals and unsafe amounts of certain chemicals have been released into the water supply. It is recommended that residents evacuate until further notice. Those who choose to stay should use only bottled water rather than drink what remains in the pipes." Over the next two weeks, Chuck walked around the property in a daze, usually fucked-up on booze or pills, watching the Geoprobe, a bony-looking pneumatic drill mounted on the back of a conversion van, boring a series of one-inch-diameter holes thirty feet into the earth.

He drew down his remaining cash slowly, paying the utility bills to keep the building open. He bought snacks, coffee, and booze to stoke his metabolism and to keep himself from spinning completely out of control. He slept fitfully and awoke in a panic. He lost weight and developed a hacking cough from smoking too much. Poor now, and facing the wrath of the law, even days he began clear and determined ended with him in a losing battle with medication. It was pharmaceuticals—Xanax, Klonopin, Ativan, Valium, and booze—that kept him going.

Over the next weekend, Fat Eddie called, his voice pinched. "The

U.S. attorney convened a grand jury to decide whether to charge you with violating the Clean Water Act, and OSHA's investigating you for workplace safety violations."

"What's that mean?"

"It isn't good."

"Worst case?"

"Bad."

Chuck was pacing, "What do you mean bad?" His voice got higher in pitch. He became frantic. "We were loose with some regulations, Eddie! It was a paperwork thing. A mistake."

Eddie paused. "There's more."

"What?"

"It seems that before he disappeared," Fat Eddie said slowly, choosing his words carefully, "Artie wiped his boot heels on your doorstep."

Silence.

"The prosecutor says Artie talked to the police. He pretty much said it was all your fault. . . ."

"Are you fucking kidding me?"

"Don't get your panties in a bunch. As long as he's missing, Artie's statement can't be admitted in court . . . and if they find him, he'll be easy to discredit. Nobody's going to believe your brother on the stand—"

"Listen to me, Eddie. You gotta help me make this thing go away. I can't deal with this!"

"You listen to me, Chuckie. You got yourself in a real mess, ya hear? You need another kind of guy. You gotta call that lawyer, Harry Hammond. From what I hear, he's got pull. What you need now is a heavy hitter."

Chuck hung up the phone and collapsed on the couch. For a long time, he held his breath, waiting . . . waiting . . . for what, he didn't know.

The reception area was huge but empty, except for several small Art Deco chairs arranged along the perimeter and a kidney-shaped coffee table. When Chuck arrived, in the middle of the afternoon, there were no employees visible and no sounds, save the switchboard trill that preceded a little greeting uttered by a tiny gray-haired woman wearing a headset, each time with exactly the same inflection. "Thank you for calling Spitz, Crandall, Wilson, Haroldson, and Hammond, this is Jean speaking, how may I direct your call?" Chuck picked up the only piece of reading material in the room, a stiff-stocked, glossy, four-color brochure that extolled the virtues of the law firm.

Based on the photographs, Spitz Crandall could easily have been a talent or modeling agency. Chuck thumbed to the section on "Partner Profiles" and looked up C. Harris Hammond. He found a youthful-looking frat boy with bushy eyebrows, pudgy cheeks, and a full head of brown hair. Mr. Hammond, it said in a hard-edged font, had graduated from Princeton and Case Western Universities with honors, made law review, and was leading the firm's growing practice in "the vigorous defense of the expression of corporate environmental rights."

Twenty minutes later, a man in a herringbone suit appeared from behind a partition, his right arm outstretched. "Charles Puckman?" There was a clipped quality to his voice, a certainty or determination not to waste time that both reassured and intimidated Chuck. He selected one of four halls that emanated from reception and started walking. "I spoke to Mr. Palmieri yesterday, m'k, and I had an associate do a little research. I'm already more than a little familiar with your case."

Mr. Hammond's office was at the very end of a wide, well-lit corridor that also was devoid of people, desks, or office sounds. The lawyer took off his jacket and directed Chuck to a low, plush chair. On each of the four walls were very large framed degrees, each one inscribed in Latin, gilded, and pressed smartly under glass. Off to one side was a long table with stacks of papers, easily a foot high. Out the window, Chuck could see a section of City Hall surrounded by scaffolding. Harry Hammond stood with his backside against his desk and his hands folded over his crotch. "Can I get you something to drink?" Chuck noticed his monogrammed shirtsleeves and the gold chain that dangled from his vest pocket.

"No, thanks."

"Well, then, let's get down to business. I spoke with Mike Merrill, the assistant U.S. prosecutor, who's a good friend of mine, m'k." He held up a manicured finger. "Not to worry, I spoke in strictly hypothetical terms, as I haven't yet been retained by you. Anyhow, based on his reaction and what one of our environmental specialists confirmed, the essence of what I believe the charges will be, and I tell you this in confidence . . ." Hammond spoke as though he believed that most people understood only a small percentage of what he said, and therefore tried to put as much out there as possible. The only indication that he was the slightest bit self-conscious of his dominating conversational style was his verbal tic, m'k, which seemed to be a variation of the expression okay. "If he hasn't already, which I would be surprised to hear, I believe Mr. Merrill intends to convene a grand jury." Hammond paused to catch his breath. "He has to," he said, and then waited for Chuck to ask why. "You've got a life-threatening injury, coma, perhaps death; you've got the media and, hence, voter awareness. And I wouldn't be surprised if we heard from all the workers' rights people and the environmentalists." Hammond clicked his pen in time with the points he was trying to emphasize. "Right or wrong," he continued, "publicity drives these environmental cases, Charles, that's a fact, m'k? And this one here," he said, driving his finger in a yellow legal pad, "this one's a doozy. We were talking about it this morning—my associates and I. First, you've got the class tension, m'k—a wealthy business owner against a poor blue-collar worker. Then you've got racial and ethnic overtones. Plus, you've got the brother-against-brother thing going— something I know a little bit about from personal experience," he said, winking. Outside, it had begun to rain and the little droplets beaded up on the window, catching streetlights that were starting to come on. "I don't know what Merrill will do if the grand jury decides to indict, but I have some ideas, which is, after all, why you pay me the big money." He smiled broadly.

"Let me try to paint a picture for you here, Charles." Chuck sank down in his upholstered chair. "If I was Merrill, I'd be looking for someone besides your brother who was willing to talk. It could be anybody— a current or former employee, a supplier, you tell me, Charles—who's got something on you to trade to the government?" Chuck looked up at the ceiling. Was this rhetorical? Did the lawyer expect him to answer? "Look it, Charles," Harry Hammond said, putting his hands in front of him. "Your business is shut down. Your records, seized. Your shop has been videotaped and sampled, the computers confiscated, the chemicals taken for testing. They're going to find violations. How could they not, m'k?" Chuck was slumped in his seat, huge circles of sweat forming under his trench coat. The lawyer with the pink face and the helmet hairdo droned on while Chuck tried to fathom the depth of his dilemma. "The way I see it," Hammond said, leaning back, "we have three battles to win, m'k? First, the Feds are going to try to nail you under the Clean Water Act. Second, the attorney general has asked a grand jury to determine if you're responsible for creating a situation that led to a man being seriously injured. . . ."

"What do I do?" Chuck croaked.

Hammond lifted a bottle of spring water to his lips. "Excuse me?" he said, as if surprised there was someone else in the room.

"What . . . do . . . I . . . do?" Chuck said, much louder than he'd intended.

"You guys *all* want to know the same thing," Hammond said tersely. "Am I going to jail and, if so, for how long?"

"I didn't ask that," Chuck said. "I want to know what you would do if I hired you."

"Believe me, Charles, I understand. You're concerned about your family; you're wondering how much this is going to involve them; you want to know when you can have your business back." Harry Hammond grinned, opening and closing his hands. "The first thing I do, m'k, is meet with your employees. I tell them that I represent the company—not them, not the government"—he looked at his papers again—"Puckman Security. I tell them to go home, watch some television, play with their kids, run some errands. There isn't going to be any work today, probably not tomorrow, maybe not all week. You probably don't want them quitting, but your legal team doesn't want them hanging around. Then I explain—"

"This happened three weeks ago," Chuck said. "My guys have already been contacted. I've already been questioned by the EPA and OSHA. . . ."

"That's not good," Hammond said, pacing. "I'm surprised Palmieri would let that happen. . . ." The lawyer paused and put his wrist under his chin. He wore a large gold ring with a ruby on it, indicating he'd once been associated with a fraternity or a football squad.

"How much?" Chuck asked. "How much would you charge? I have limited funds right now. . . ."

"Sometimes you fight, and sometimes you cooperate, you know, cut your losses."

"How much?"

"You want an expert to advise when to come out shooting," he said, making his hands into pistols and dipping his shoulder, "and when to hunker down."

"How much do you charge?"

"It depends on the case," he said finally. "You've got investigations, interviews, company records to examine, other cases to study, and, of course, negotiations with the prosecutor. If it goes to indictment, there'll be motions and then trial prep, which means experts, investigators, and that's before you even try it."

Chuck focused on the rain, which was coming down in sheets.

"For example, if we go to trial, m'k, we've got prep, two lawyers in court every day with a few in the office doing research and writing memos as issues arise. That's five people working twelve, fifteen, sixteen hours a day for six, maybe eight weeks." He scribbled something on a yellow pad beside him. "I can get a team of junior lawyers for one seventy-five an hour each." There was another long silence. He looked up and blinked. "Something like this could cost as much as two hundred fifty, maybe three hundred grand." Chuck tried to stand, but he felt wobbly. "I'll need a retainer, of course," Hammond said, craning his neck. "Say, fifty thousand, which you could work down . . ."

The lawyer didn't finish his sentence. His prospective client stumbled through the doorway and dry-heaved in front of a watercooler across the hall. Other than Hammond, who stood watching with disgust from his doorway, there was not a soul around to help Chuck Puckman stand up, brush himself off, or find the elevators.

In early spring, when the EPA finally announced that the plume of trichloroethylene around Puckman Security extended no farther than the property lines, and the yellow police tape came down, Chuck's neighbors, who were encouraged to return to their homes, were jubilant. The U.S. prosecutor told the media that while the Puckmans might still be cited for violations of the federal Clean Water Act, their manufacturing operations appeared not to have introduced any more toxins into the groundwater than what was already there. It was the first piece of good news in over a month, and it caught Chuck off guard.

By then, the urgency and, in a way, the excitement had died down. The phones had stopped ringing; the old employees had stopped coming around; even the kids selling toner and copier paper, industrial coffee, and insurance had stopped showing up with their catalogues and their demonstration kits. Chuck seldom left the apartment, except to get his prescriptions refilled, to buy groceries, or to visit Rahim. A few times, he visited his dad at the nursing home, but Charlie Puckman was almost always either asleep or nonresponsive.

During the day, Chuck slept in the recliner, listening to jazz. At night, he watched TV and got high. In the beginning, he tried to sort out his thoughts. He started letters to old friends, which ended crumpled up in a corner of the kitchen. He shaved his head, and when his hair grew back, it was white around his ears. Neighbors noticed him—gaunt, hollow-cheeked, ashen—sweeping out the truck well and pasting handmade signs on the walls directing delivery trucks to nonexistent entrances. One weekend, he repainted lines for parking spaces. The next week, he laid duct tape across the shop floor as if he was rearranging workflow. He tried to remember a time in his life when he looked forward to something, but his memories were of empty gestures that would excite and then bore him—a new car or rivet machine, a fancy suit or a new TV, the closing of a big account—temporarily fulfilling, yet ultimately disappointing. As it got warmer outside, he took to walking until his feet hurt, noticing the neighborhood for the first time since he was a kid—its brutal plainness, its broken fields and dead-end alleys, its hidden commerce—muted transactions between generations of immigrants.

In May, Rahim got a fever that wouldn't go away, and his body erupted in sores. Ovella took as much time off from work as she could to take care of him. One bitter-cold night after bathing him and getting him settled in bed, she walked ten blocks to Chuck's apartment, climbed the fire escape steps, and took a deep breath. After a few minutes of pounding, Chuck opened the door and stood there blinking, huddled beneath a blanket. Ovella stared at him and shook her head. "You wanna come in?" he said, slurring.

"We need to talk," Ovella said, stepping into the kitchen.

"Drink?"

She shook her head.

"I've been thinking, Ovella," Chuck said. "Maybe you and Rahim oughta come live here. I got this big place, and you guys live in that shhhhhithole." He made a flourishing gesture with his hands. "You can take the rooms downstairs—"

"You oughta think before you go running your mouth off. You made a fine mess out of your own life; now you oughta be more careful with other people's."

"What?" He turned his hands upside down.

"Come on, Chuck. A man in the kind of trouble you're in has no business inviting people to join him." Chuck walked into the living room and let himself fall onto the couch. "I got a brother who's sick as a dog and a sixty-three-year-old father with no job and no savings."

"Sorry," he said, looking away.

Ovella stared down at him. "I don't need you to be polite to me," she said. "What I need is money for health insurance. Without that, Rahim can't get the drugs he needs to keep his immune system functioning. And if he gets pneumonia, he's fucked."

Chuck winced.

"We need you to figure out a way we can make money."

Chuck ran his hands over the top of his head and stared into the fish tank. "Let me ask you something, Ovella." She rolled her eyes. "Do you think this whole thing is my fault? Do *you* think I'm responsible for Gutierrez, for everything being so fucked-up?"

She narrowed her eyes. "You feeling sorry for yourself, Chuck? You on some kind of guilt trip now? Of all people, you oughta realize how this happened doesn't matter—Gutierrez isn't gonna suddenly wake up and go home to his kids, and the factory isn't gonna reopen to business as usual—no matter how much penance you do." She took a deep breath. "But there's a half dozen others who don't have the wits or the strength or the smarts to figure out what to do for a paycheck, for health insurance, for hope."

In the glow of the fish tank, with jazz low on the radio and the aerator bubbling and the refrigerator humming, Chuck felt an almost overwhelming affection toward his old friend's sister, standing here in the middle of the night talking straight to him. "Do something, Charles," she said with her hand on the door. "Do something." Then she pulled the door shut, leaving him blinking in the dim light.

As the afternoons got longer, Chuck watched kids playing soccer, trucks rumbling down Aramingo toward I-95, and women in housedresses hauling trash to the curbs. Toward the train station and back, along Allegheny Avenue, past the Polish cafeterias, past the hospital where Gutierrez lay, beside the hotels and the bodegas and back up to Frankford, stopping for a drink in one of the few remaining Irish bars,

Chuck walked the neighborhood, slapping nickels into empty parking meters intent on redeeming himself any way he could. Without his tinted windshield, he began to see life differently. Billboards with earnest Latino faces and blazing white teeth promoting American products seemed hypocritical, and the razor wire that surrounded nearby factories seemed as much a warning for those inside as it was for intruders. The litter-strewn field off Castor Avenue, where kids might have played ball but for a locked gate and an eight-foot-high fence; little girls, standing on their stoops, experimenting with provocative poses, makeup, and cigarettes; a shelter for homeless people with broken windows and cops patrolling nearby; a graveyard for abandoned cars; empty storefronts and failed businesses; old people whose faces he might have known once a long time ago, now shrunken and softer in the eyes—all of it produced in him a deeper sadness than he'd ever known.

Shortly after his talk with Ovella, Chuck drove his Suburban to the car dealer near the airport and traded it for five grand and a 1985 Ford Escort. The same day, he drove it into Center City, parked near a porn shop, walked up to the cashier's window at the Blue Cross headquarters, and paid Rahim's insurance premiums for the next three months. The next morning, he picked up his friend and took him to breakfast.

"How you feeling?" Chuck asked Rahim.

"You know, most people have less than they want, but more than they need," Rahim said, eating a piece of toast. He'd put on a few pounds over the past few weeks and was feeling strong enough to start rebuilding computers that he found in the trash or at shelters. "Take poor people, for example. We have no money, no land, no education, and no power, but we got kids, relatives, time, body fat, acres of decrepit property, and abandoned places to hang out. . . ." Rahim had designed a Web site for his landlord, a Polish guy, who wanted to become a specialty-food importer. "We buy these computers with bazillions of megabytes of hard-drive storage. Do we need it? Fuck no! It's like a meal somebody serves you when you're not hungry. It just sits there until you scrape it off your plate and throw it away."

"We need a lot less than we think," Chuck agreed.

"What if we could redistribute it?" Rahim said, waving to the waitress. "Another glass of juice please, love . . ."

"You sound like Castro."

"We could set up a system to collect excess computing power and make it available cheap to poor people." He turned his place mat over and drew little boxes connected by wires.

"Like they do with electricity?" Chuck said. He hadn't had a conversation like this since his college days.

"Exactly," Rahim said. The wires on his drawing extended to a box he labeled Puckman Security. "Think what the average person could do if they had the computing power of a corporation."

"I give up."

"Analyze stocks. Send tips to poor people. Collect news stories. Deliver information to voters." Rahim smiled broadly, showing his gums.

"So you wanna change the world now?"

Rahim pushed the place mat with his scribbling to Chuck's side of the table and looked at him. "In Cuba, my father was a professor. My mother was a nurse. They came here thirty years ago for opportunity, and still we have nothing." The two of them sat there, the smell of burnt coffee and cigarettes all around them. Something stirred inside Chuck, a connection between this moment and another, long ago. "I don't know how much time I have left," Rahim said, "but I want to do something that matters."

After breakfast, they picked up some old CPUs, screens, keyboards, and computer parts from shelters and thrift stores in the neighborhood; later that day, they started cleaning the offices under Chuck's apartment. Rahim directed Chuck, who pushed old filing cabinets against the walls, swept metal shavings and dust balls into piles, and took a stab at some basic rewiring, running a cable down the elevator shaft, tapping into the T1 line. The following morning, Rahim brought over a Zenith laptop and set it up as a server on the second floor. "We're live," he declared an hour later, logging his laptop onto the Internet.

Before attempting to distribute processing power free to the ghetto, Chuck suggested they load the last backup disks of Puckman Security's computer system so as to print accounts receivable—invoices that hadn't been paid. It turned out that back in January, when Puckman Security was shut down, they were owed almost $12,000 from thirty-five different customers. The largest, $4,400, was from Powerplex, which they would never see. But of the remaining $7,500, Chuck guessed about five grand was collectible. He picked up the phone and struck up the old refrain. Meanwhile, Rahim hit up the search engines for details of convictions and prison sentences meted out to business owners convicted of EPA or OSHA violations. For the next several days, while Chuck drove around town in his Escort, picking up checks, Rahim played legal researcher.

"Last January, a guy who recruited homeless men to strip asbestos pipes without wetting the material was convicted of manslaughter."

"Why is it the more somebody else has, the less we feel we have by comparison?" Chuck wondered.

"Some guy got five years on twenty counts of pesticide misuse and violation of the federal Insecticide, Fungicide, and Rodenticide Acts."

"Everything from public policy to people's fates is decided on the goddamned TV," Chuck noticed. "Who needs judges and juries? The army's in the airwaves."

"In Alaska, a CEO got a suspended sentence for the release of hazardous substances in connection with the outer rim of oil wells on Endicott Island."

"Most human beings think in terms of abundance and shortage," Chuck declared, returning to the factory late one afternoon.

"Indeed," Rahim said, his face buried in printouts.

Chuck's collection efforts yielded almost four grand. It'd been a long time since he felt the rush of making money that had once been fundamental to his existence. Now, he was hard-pressed to spend it on anything other than food, health insurance premiums, and the fund he'd set up for the Gutierrez family. Rahim asked Chuck if there was anything else on the old computer that might have value to them.

"I don't know," Chuck said. "There's the order history, backlog, production schedules, designs, payables, suppliers, customer lists."

"Customer lists?"

"Yeah, every pawnbroker, taxicab company, and bank in the mid-Atlantic states," Chuck said with pride.

Rahim stroked his chin. "Can't we sell the old customers something beside guards?"

"Like what? They already have safes, cash registers, electronics, lottery tickets."

"If you were a pawnshop owner, what would you want?"

"A clean conscience."

"You got that right."

"And cash flow."

"What do you mean?" Rahim asked.

"Some guy leaves his old lady. She waits a weekend, maybe two, then gets her son to help her load his big-screen TV and his hunting rifle into her sister's car, which she double-parks in front of Big Harvey's. Harvey charges her for storage, cleaning, ticketing, and interest, and then gives her cash, which she says she'll pay back as soon as the guy comes to his senses. She waits for her man to come back, gets her hair done, buys a new dress, flowers, maybe a bottle of perfume to make herself feel better. A month later, the boyfriend's still gone, so Harvey puts the big-screen TV in the window with a sale sign on it. He's got the merchandise, but he's out the cash."

"So?"

"So all this stuff is sitting in a store nobody with money is going to set foot in. Harvey can't lend against it 'cause of banking regulations, and he can't advertise it 'cause it's mostly hot."

"If it's such a shitty business Harvey's in," Rahim said, "how come he's driving a Mercedes-Benz and we're eating diner food worrying about paying rent?"

"I'm not saying it's a shitty business—just that all these years we've been focusing on security, maybe we could be doing something about cash flow."

Rahim wasn't biting. "Help Harvey steal from the poor and sell to the rich?"

"It isn't that simple," Chuck said. "People run into trouble and decide to sell their shit for cash. Harvey isn't the cause of their trouble."

"How did *you* feel selling your Rolex?"

"Maybe we could bring in the suburbanites—the Main Line housewives, the Center City professionals, Big Harvey's neighbors, rich kids—people who wouldn't be caught dead in a pawnshop."

"We're still supporting a system that exploits people," Rahim said.

Chuck thought about this for a while. The last time he felt good about what he did for money was when he was dealing weed in college. "This may not be the purest logic," he started, "but everybody needs cash to stay afloat in this system—a living wage for food and shelter and health care. We'd be expanding the market so poor people can get more money for their unwanted possessions. We'd make enough money to keep the lights on in here, to pay for health insurance, and maybe to hire back a few of our guys. A rising tide floats all boats." Sure it was a con, but he was tired of being broke.

I held the door open for Lorraine, who carried her handbag against her chest like it contained treasure. It was a cold night, so I started the fireplace, one of those gas-fired rigs my mother put in the cottage in Merion before she got sick. Lorraine set the bag on the edge of the table, reached in and extracted a sheaf of papers bound with a rubber strap, a cassette recorder, and a blank tape whose seal she scored with her fingernail. I went to get cheese and crackers. When I returned, Lorraine was standing under one of the spider plants touching her toes. She was wearing black tights, and she was really buff. "I'll be honest with you, Winnie," she said. "I'm not really interested in Patty or in William Randolph Hearst. I read your book—well, I skimmed it, actually—just to see how your mind works. I realize I don't know you other than what you said on the Today Show, *but I feel like I can trust you. I want you to listen to what I say with an open heart, and if it moves you, tell it in your own words."*

She said this as if she'd been planning it for a long time, using certain gestures that I wish I had on videotape. When Lorraine knew something sounded unlikely, she arched her eyebrows as though beseeching me to be rigorous in my research, but to accept it if it turned out to be true. And when she asserted something really strange, she let the end of her sentence trail up, as though by sounding skeptical, she would be more credible. The more controversial or unlikely things were that she told me, the more placid her expression and measured her delivery.

Lorraine talked almost the entire time we were together. It was important, she told me, to create a record of everything she said, hence the tape recorder; she looked me in the eye the whole time and periodically touched my forearm or leaned toward me for emphasis. I didn't interrupt much, except when I couldn't hear her or I didn't understand something she'd said. And for reasons that will become evident, I have written much of what she told me exactly as she described it.

"In the early seventies," she said, pressing RECORD, *"even though the war in Vietnam was winding down, the people in power in this country felt threatened. They believed that draft resistance and the civil rights movement with all the media coverage had stirred the pot so much that, unless steps were taken, revolution was possible, even likely." She stopped the tape to make sure it was recording and then resumed. "At the time, San Francisco was home to dozens of radical groups—United Farm Workers, the Chino Defense Fund, Venceremos, the Nuestra Familia, the SDS, the Weather Underground, Black Panthers, Yippies, Diggers, Motherfuckers. It was also a haven for runaways and radicals and the place where the black liberation movement began." As she talked, she moved her hand gently across the upholstery of the couch. It was soothing to listen to her voice, and several times, I had to force myself to concentrate on what she was saying.*

"In early 1972, the CIA came up with a plan they called Operation Chaos. Sounds like something out of a James Bond movie, doesn't it? The goal was to portray counterculture radicals as violent and dangerous people who most Americans wouldn't mind being wiped out." She asked me how much I knew about the black militant movement.

"Not much," I said.

"In the late fifties, an eighteen-year-old black man named George Jackson got busted in L.A. for robbing a gas station. He was sentenced to life in prison." She paused to let the significance of that sink in. "He wrote a book speculating that the reason blacks break the law is that white America is an oppressive and racist place for them to be." Lorraine arched her eyebrows and put a cracker in her mouth. "The

book became very popular." She took a minute to chew. "Jackson was a very good-looking man. Charismatic, too. An inspiration to people, especially blacks. So when he was killed by guards, his message spread like wildfire. A month later, the largest prison riot in U.S. history happened in Attica, New York. It was exactly what President Nixon feared and what the CIA had been waiting for." Lorraine raised her eyebrows.

"Are you saying the government was behind all this?" I asked.

"Not exactly, but it gave them an excuse to act," Lorraine said. "By the early seventies, the FBI had infiltrated the radical underground. And the CIA started a program for prisoners in California called the Black Cultural Association, which they wanted people to believe was about black convicts venting their anger so they could begin to heal." She said this in a way that was skeptical but serious. "They hired a professor who lectured about black history and literature and held meetings where the participants chanted African songs. But the real purpose of the BCA was for undercover agents and informants to see and hear what the militant radicals were planning."

"How do you know all this?" I asked, more than a bit skeptical.

Lorraine put her hand on mine and smiled. "I know you're going to research this, Winnie, and I welcome that. I absolutely do. A lot of this is in the public record. Some stuff you can get under Freedom of Information. Some of it, you'll have to dig for." She leaned toward the tape recorder. "Look up Vacaville Psychiatric Prison. By all means. It's where they had meetings. And the guy who ran the Black Cultural Association was named Westbrook, Colston Westbrook. To make sure the prisoners kept coming, Westbrook invited young, middle-class whites, girls mostly—students and hippies with long hair and large breasts." She laughed.

"It sounds like a farm team for revolutionaries," I said.

"It was like throwing a lit match on a pile of dry kindling." Lorraine got up and walked to the fireplace, where she stretched her calves. "Enter Donald DeFreeze," she said. "Thirty years old, grew up in Cleveland, the oldest of eight, fatherless, with a fourth-grade education. By the time he was sixteen, DeFreeze had been arrested twenty times. Shoplifting, vandalism, dealing drugs, and fighting. In the mid-sixties, he turned up in L.A., where he was arrested again."

Lorraine sat down. "It was 1967 and the cops made him an informant. For the next two years, DeFreeze led police to guys who were dealing weapons and to gang leaders. But when he got arrested again, this time for bank robbery, the police cut him loose. The judge sent him to Vacaville Psychiatric Hospital near San Francisco for evaluation, which is where he came in contact with the Black Cultural Association." At this point, you can hear me clearing my throat on the tape. "None of this in and of itself might sound suspicious, but bear with me," Lorraine continued. "After less than a year in prison, DeFreeze up and walked out of prison and disappeared in Berkeley. It turned out he went to live with a couple of white women from the BCA. He changed his name to Cinque M'Tume, after the slave who led the Amistad mutiny, and over the next eight months, he convinced eight college-educated, middle-class whites, all of whom attended those same meetings, to start killing, kidnapping, robbing banks, and bombing buildings in the name of this ideological trash heap called the Symbionese Liberation Army."

Symbionese. A made-up word based on that condition in nature where people or things exist dependent on one another—dissimilar organisms thrust together—moss on oak trees, lichens on rocks. Liberation armies were a dime a dozen back then. Part Maoism, part Marxism, and part Monty Python with a heavy dose of racial guilt.

I was confused, and I told her so. "How did the FBI get some guy with a fourth-grade education to discredit the black and youth movements of the sixties?"

"Mind control," she said, without skipping a beat. "Techniques perfected during the Korean War and practiced on American soldiers under the supervision of American psychiatrists in the fifties." Lorraine was dead serious. "This is all documented, Winnie," she said, sensing my cynicism. "Colston Westbrook was in covert operations in Korea." She touched the papers she'd taken out of her bag. At the time, I was thinking how many times I'd made friends with someone who seemed perfectly intelligent and friendly and then something—it could be anything—came out of left field and ruined it.

"You're saying these middle-class white kids followed DeFreeze because the FBI used mind control on them?"

"No," Lorraine said patiently. "DeFreeze was converted by the CIA, and then he brainwashed the others."

"Why DeFreeze?" It sounded like one of those theories that gets customized to fit an otherwise inscrutable set of facts.

"I'm not really sure," Lorraine confessed. "But I have two hypotheses. First, since he'd been an informant, he'd already crossed the line. Ideology is interchangeable. After the first betrayal, the snitch loses his sense of self. Whoever feeds him, owns him. If there are any two organisms in society that are symbiotic, it's police and informants." On this subject, she seemed very confident. "Second, convicts—especially tough black guys with nothing to lose—were celebrities back then. By activating DeFreeze, the Feds were creating the very problem they wanted permission to solve."

"What do you mean?"

"In the fall of 1973, the SLA completed their first mission—the murder of Marcus Foster, superintendent of schools in Oakland, California. A black man."

"Why?"

"No one's really sure. The official story was he wanted to introduce ID cards for students to keep the riffraff out, which reminded DeFreeze too much of prison. But think about it, Winnie," Lorraine said. "The SLA commits a murder so heinous that everybody—even black Americans—is horrified. This only makes sense if the SLA was created to discredit itself."

"What happened?"

"When Cinque heard that the police had stopped a van with two SLA members in it, he and his followers torched the apartment they were living in and went underground, where they could do their real work." Lorraine stopped talking while she turned the cassette tape over. "What the SLA lacked in ideology, they more than made up for in literary output. The FBI recovered several cartons of half-burned papers with notes—long drafts attempting to outline a political ideology, revolutionary logos, shopping lists, obscene doodles, and a spiral notebook with a list of future kidnap victims—including your old friend Patty Hearst."

"Are you saying Patty was in on her own kidnapping?"

Lorraine laughed. "You knew Patty back then. Do you think she'd

have signed up for that? Besides, the FBI never showed the list to anybody."

"How come?"

Lorraine made a face that indicated she didn't expect me to understand things yet. "Because they hadn't accomplished their mission."

What happened to Patty has been talked about, written about, recorded
in legal files and transcripts, described to television audiences, and
made into TV movies and documentaries. On Friday, February 4, 1974,
three weeks before her twentieth birthday, while she was making dinner
for her fiancé, Patty heard the doorbell ring. It was a weeknight. They'd
been watching TV. She was wearing panties and a robe. Slippers. From
the kitchen, she heard a woman say she was having car trouble and
then ask if she could use their phone. A few seconds later, two men
waving automatic weapons broke down the front door. They beat up
her fiancé and rushed into the kitchen. Patty was thinking, If this is a
robbery, how come I'm being blindfolded, bound, gagged, and dragged
outside. She felt the cool night air on her legs and around her waist. She
remembered a neighbor calling out and then bursts of automatic gun-
fire. Somebody threw a blanket over her head and pushed her into the
trunk of a car that sped away.

Lorraine told me things about the abduction I hadn't heard, or, if I
had heard, I didn't remember. How Patty was held in a tiny closet that
reeked of mildew and body odor for fifty-seven days. How she was
raped and threatened with automatic weapons, woken in the middle of
the night, harangued by her captors, deprived of food and privacy, and
ridiculed in front of the others for her naïveté about people's suffering.
Sitting in my mother's cottage, hearing about Patty's kidnapping, I was
ashamed by how little I knew, how I'd viewed Patty's experience as a
cultural phenomenon rather than a personal tragedy that a friend had
suffered.

"Over the course of a year, the SLA delivered seven audiotapes to
Bay Area radio stations." Lorraine reached into her handbag and pulled
out a ninety-minute cassette that was marked "FOIA: Freedom of Information Act, January 1983." "I believe this is the fourth, or maybe

fifth." She stopped the recorder and put the tape in. An unexpectedly steady voice came through the tinny speaker.

"Greetings to the People! All sisters and brothers behind the walls and in the streets! Greetings to the Black Liberation Army, the Weather Underground, and the Black Guerrilla Family, and all combat forces of the community! This is General Field Marshall Cinque M'Tume speaking." Between phrases, I could hear the sounds of lips moistening, static crackling, and the microphone being handled. "Combat Operation: April 15, 1974, the Year of the Children. Action: appropriation. Supplies liberated: one .38 Smith & Wesson revolver, condition good . . . five rounds of 158-grain, .38-caliber ammo. Cash: $10,660.02 . . . Casualties: People's Forces—none. Enemy Forces—none. Civilians—two." He spoke in monotone. "Reasons," the voice continued, "subject one, male—ordered to lay on the floor, facedown. Subject refused order and jumped out the front door of the bank. Therefore, subject was shot." The words and syntax were of another time, too self-conscious and serious to be a bluff or a toss-off, too far-fetched to be real. Field Marshall M'Tume continued. "We again warn the public: Any attempt to aid, to inform, or assist the enemy . . . will be shot without hesitation. There is no middle ground in war. . . . I am the bringer of the children of the oppressed and the children of the oppressor together. . . . I am bringing the truth to the children and opening their eyes to the real enemy of mankind. . . ."

There was a fumbling sound, the microphone changing hands, and then a different voice, also a man's. "Bill Harris," Lorraine said. "Cinque's second in command." Harris spoke in the manner of a white man trying to sound black, a prissy, educated guy trying to be streetwise. "If white people in fascist America don't think they are enslaved, they only prove their own foolishness . . . the thing the pigs have feared the most is happening . . . a People's Army of irate niggers of all races, including whites—not talkers anymore, but fighters. The enemy recognizes that the People are on the brink of revolution. . . . Death to the fascist insect that preys upon the life of the People!"

Lorraine turned off the tape. "You have to understand. These were the days of law and order. Richard Nixon was president. The sixties had flamed out. It was the beginning of everyone being afraid. Before the SLA could even state their demands for Patty's release, Governor

Reagan announced there'd be no deals. Patty's father donated two million dollars in food to California supermarkets, while Ronald Reagan told reporters he hoped the poor people eating it would get botulism and learn their lesson about handouts."

I asked what was happening to Patty all that time.

Lorraine was calm and relaxed as she spoke. "Patty stayed in the closet, except to bathe or relieve herself. After a while, she lost muscle mass in her legs. She couldn't walk. She stopped menstruating. When she balked at sharing the group's toothbrush, she was teased for her bourgeois tendencies. When she tried to be sympathetic, she was called a rich bitch who would never understand. They broke her down."

I would learn later that the formal name for this is the Stockholm syndrome, after a bank robbery in Sweden, where a female hostage was so thankful that her life had been spared that she fell in love with one of the robbers, had sex with him on the floor of the vault, even pleaded with police to spare him when he surrendered. Any person held prisoner or hostage, traumatized long enough, will go from defiant to dependent to sympathetic.

Lorraine put the blank tape back in and pressed RECORD. "Of course, what the SLA became most famous for was convincing your friend Patty to renounce her parents and her privileged upbringing and become Tania, the gun-toting urban guerrilla who participated in a string of SLA robberies until the spring of 1975, when six of the nine SLA members, including Cinque, were incinerated in a small house in Los Angeles." Lorraine produced another thick folder and handed me a photograph of cops surrounding a small house in Los Angeles that was billowing smoke. The caption read: "9,000 bullets, 125 tear-gas canisters, 320 police cars, 400 siege officers, 2 helicopters, and an array of media, and SLA is history. Media heiress Patty Hearst feared dead."

I shook my head, trying to imagine my little friend from Camp Tidewater at the center of such a strange drama. "It was the first live cremation—right up there in television history with Jack Ruby shooting Lee Harvey Oswald. Patty watched her comrades go up in flames on TV from a motel in Disneyland. By the time the inferno was over, she and the Harrises were in a car heading back up to San Francisco, listening to their own eulogies on the radio."

"You think letting Patty escape was part of the government's plan?"

"In the world of double agents and brainwashing, once a handler turns his back on an operative, they're finished. Keeping somebody you've tried to kill around is generally a bad thing." I was surprised how knowledgeable Lorraine seemed about all this. "To stay sane," she said, utterly convincingly, "operatives imprint to their handlers. After Cinque broke her down, Patty thought of him as a father figure. When the FBI killed him, Patty probably felt like she'd been orphaned. Despite the fact that she'd be unpredictable, the government would have needed her to denounce the SLA, which, after she was captured, is exactly what she did."

"The three of them—Bill and Emily Harris and Patty—scrambled, avoiding the Feds, evading police, and dodging roadblocks for another year. They traveled across the country and back—staying briefly in Manhattan, upstate New York, and near the Pocono Mountains in a house in Honesdale, Pennsylvania, which is where I hooked up with them." Lorraine paused to look at her watch. "I'm exhausted. I need to get some rest. We can get together once more . . . before I leave. Can you give me a lift home?"

Although the government conspiracy theories and the details of Patty's brainwashing fascinated me, I was much more interested in hearing about Lorraine's and Patty's meeting in the mid-seventies. I had the feeling that something really important had happened, not just for the two of them, but for me as well. "I'll leave the bag with you," she said, standing.

Outside, it was very cold. The sun had set and the moon was a tiny sliver along the horizon. Most of the lights in nearby houses were off. A little over an hour later, when I got home, I ate some leftovers and cleared a space on what had been my mother's dining room table. I took a stack of sixties memorabilia and SLA clippings from Lorraine's tote bag and began reading. It was an astonishing archive of this particular era within an era. There were articles about race riots, break-ins at Selective Service offices, pictures of nuns in soup kitchens and priests in field hospitals, eyewitness accounts of bombs that went off in basements and behind statues. There were pamphlets and position papers by all kinds of revolutionary groups, photographs of long-haired men and women blurred by time or an unsteady camera, group shots and individuals, hippies and flower children collapsing with laughter, standing with signs against the war, flashing the peace sign and smiling. In several of them, I recognized Lorraine: young, beautiful, full of life. One showed her sitting with a man against a tree, their eyes closed, sunlight from directly above settling around their hair like a halo. In another, the same young man with long, tangled reddish brown hair, a turned-up nose, and freckles was looking earnestly into the lens. Underneath, it said: "Frederick Keane: Wanted, Armed and Dangerous."

In a box marked "SLA," I found an eight-by-eleven print. Eight young people held automatic weapons in front of a seven-headed snake. Someone had drawn an arrow pointing to Patty, who was wearing a kerchief, crouching, and smiling timidly, just as she had in the Camp Tidewater play a few summers earlier. She was dressed in brown fatigues, her shirt open midway down her chest, her small hands supporting a machine gun, staring blankly ahead. A newspaper account speculated that an army of revolutionaries had descended upon the Bay Area as in a science-fiction movie.

Before falling asleep, I found individual pages torn from a child's coloring book. On the back of each page, in crayon, was what looked like the Hearst family history, written in cursive handwriting as though it was a fairy tale.

After finals, Chuck Puckman found a cheap room on the Boston side, about a mile down the road from Lorraine, between Boston College and Boston University. By walking up and down Harvard Avenue, nodding at the freaks and holding a cigarette ambiguously, he attracted new customers for weed, hashish, and hash oil, which he began buying in larger quantities from the road manager of the band in Connecticut. For the summer, Lorraine got a job selling life insurance door to door. Everyone teased her about it, but she had a way with regular people, especially when it came to talking about what matters. She was successful from the start, earning sometimes as much as $1,000 in commissions, to be paid out over the life of the policies.

Consistent with the belief that after the revolution, professional sports would replace war, satisfying man's craving for aggression, Frederick applied for a job with the Red Sox organization. By mid-May, he'd joined the ground crew at Fenway Park, tamping, sweeping, digging, piling, and preparing the field for play. When the Red Sox were at home, he worked from early in the morning until midday, and then sat in the bleachers for free. When the Sox went on the road, Frederick did, too, traveling to Providence, New York, and New Haven to meet other radicals planning demonstrations against the war.

While Frederick was away, Chuck helped Lorraine with laundry or paperwork on the life insurance policies she'd written; other days, they'd go to teach-ins or rallies to distribute flyers. Lorraine made no effort to hide their relationship from Frederick. Several times, Frederick came home from a trip shortly after Lorraine and Chuck had been intimate and started one of his rants, oblivious to the messy bed and their flushed cheeks. "Revolution and baseball," he would say. "The perfect combination." And it was. The nexus of his two loves.

One sweltering afternoon in July, Chuck let himself into the house in Brighton before Lorraine got home from work. Her bedroom was stuffy, the sheets on her bed damp with humidity. He opened a window. On a small desk were newly printed broadsides against the war and the guts of a black box Frederick was building that enabled a user to make free long-distance calls. Chuck laid a couple pinches of weed on one side of a double album and let the seeds roll into the center. He put a pillow against the wall, propped himself up on the bed, and lit a joint. Despite evidence of Frederick all around him, he felt lucky to be in Lorraine's world. Shortly thereafter, she came home. "What are you *doing*?" she asked, irritated.

"Waiting for you," Chuck said.

Lorraine tossed her bag on the floor and her keys on the bed and walked into the kitchen. "You just show up in someone's house whenever you feel like it?"

"I thought maybe you'd want some company after work," he said, sitting up. "You know, with Frederick always running around . . ."

Lorraine walked back in with a glass of water and sat down. "Listen, Charles," she said. "Frederick's working for something he believes in. He doesn't have a cushy job with his daddy waiting for him." Chuck watched her open a bottle of aspirin and shake a couple into her hand. "When it comes right down to it . . ." She held her tongue.

"What?"

"Nothing."

"What is it?"

"You'll never know what it's like, Charles," Lorraine said matter-of-factly, "to be out there on your own."

Chuck collected his stash from her desk and stood, his head bobbing up and down, his eyes filling up like they had when he was a kid and his brother would set him up to take his mother's wrath. Lorraine slipped out of her shoes and her shirt without even looking at him.

After winning the California primary, Robert Kennedy was shot at point-blank range in the kitchen pantry of the Ambassador Hotel in Los Angeles in June 1968, leaving liberals in a gloom. Two radical groups—Students for a Democratic Society and the Mobe, the National Mobilization Committee to End the War in Vietnam—pushed for nonviolent demonstrations at the Democratic National Convention in Chicago. They filed petitions for permits that would allow freaks and demonstrators to sleep in the park, picket the convention hotels, and march in the rallies.

The Weather Underground, the Panthers, and the Yippies, all groups with whom Frederick claimed high-level connections, wanted their efforts to be coordinated, confrontational, and flagrant. They envisioned a half million people occupying downtown Chicago, disrupting the proceedings, and drawing worldwide media coverage. In preparation, they planned marches through the commercial districts, all-night gatherings in Lincoln Park, and missions to spike the water supply with LSD, launch a flotilla of naked people in Lake Michigan, even send young radical girls dressed as prostitutes to seduce delegates. It was to be the culmination of years of civil disobedience and protest—the chance for young people to influence politics on the presidential level. Frederick said the antiwar movement was at a critical juncture and it was time for decisive action.

But by early August, Mayor Daley denied the permits and told young people to stay away. He also told the Chicago police that if kids got unruly, they had his permission to shoot to kill. Naturally, this caused much consternation among radical leaders. Factions splintered off and formed new groups; intellectuals and leftists who'd supported civil disobedience started talking revolution.

"You can't just destroy things," Lorraine argued one night. "You need a vision for what comes next."

"Fuck vision. Fuck values," Frederick said. "It doesn't matter what you believe, what you stand for. Either you do something to stop the war or you don't. It's time for action. The Vietcong attacked Hue, Saigon, Khe Sanh. American casualties are heavy. We've got to do something, now." The three of them were in the Phoenix Room, two tables from where Chuck and Lorraine had first gotten drunk together months earlier. Once Frederick got started, it was impossible to get a word in edgewise. "The SDS manifesto and the Port Huron statement are too tame." Frederick took a copy of Mao's Little Red Book out of his knapsack and pounded it for emphasis. "The revolution is at hand!" Chuck pictured him in fatigues and a beret, standing on the table waving a machete. Sometimes, his enthusiasm was exciting and contagious, but just as often, it was too intense, toxic. Frederick had started using speed—black beauties and crystal meth, cooked up in makeshift labs outside of town—which had the effect of making him sound desperate, windmilling around topics, his voice scratchy and thin. "The Vietcong are fighting for their fucking lives. We should be, too."

"They're being attacked," Lorraine said. "They have no alternative."

"Yeah, it's kill or be killed," Chuck said, siding with Frederick.

"Killing is wrong," Lorraine said.

"Right and wrong is subjective," Frederick said. "Even a sniper acts consistent with his values."

"So assassination's okay?"

"Like floods and plague," he said, shrugging. "Part of the plan."

"What plan?" Chuck asked.

"What plan?" Frederick repeated, sending bursts of cigarette smoke toward the ceiling. A television in the background blared. "In all your time together, Lorraine hasn't explained the plan to you?" Chuck looked at Lorraine, who looked down at her hands. "How is it you talk about everybody's destiny except his?" Frederick said, sneering at Chuck.

"Frederick . . ." Lorraine said, pressing his arm.

"How we live in service to it or we run away," Frederick continued, his eyes glowing behind his glasses. It seemed to Chuck that Frederick was referring to something specific. Frederick lit a cigarette with the stub of an old one. "Of course, we all know my destiny," Frederick said. "Leading the revolution!" He raised his beer.

"And Lorraine here, she wants to be around for the great spiritual awakening, right, Lorraine?" She was shaking her head. "So what about you, my friend?" Frederick said. Chuck kept looking at Lorraine, who was looking at the television. Frederick's face was within inches of Chuck's. "Seems to me you came to college to avoid the draft. And you deal dope because you have the capital."

"Frederick . . ." Lorraine said.

He lifted his beer as though he was going to sip from it again. "There's nothing wrong with that," he said. "Somebody's got to keep us high. What I want to know is what you're hanging around us for?"

"Frederick!" Lorraine had both hands on the table. Frederick shrugged his shoulders.

"Be cool, Lorrie," Frederick said, staring hard at Chuck. "Are you in search of your destiny?" Frederick twirled the base of the beer in circles, his fingernails blackened, the areas under his eyes gray and wrinkled from lack of sleep. "You looking to get your hip card punched?"

Chuck drained his beer, stood up, walked out of the bar, and lit a cigarette. The moon was midway up the sky, clearing the apartment buildings across the street, casting a bluish pall over Commonwealth Avenue. A trolley car rumbled toward him from up the hill, its steel hull shaking like a nocturnal beast. Above, a streetlight flickered, but failed to ignite. Chuck leaned against the stucco, trying to decide whether to leave when he heard her. "Chuck," she said, touching his shoulder and back, sending shivers through his entire body.

"C'mon, buddy," Frederick said, softer now. "Let's go hear some music."

With Frederick and Lorraine on either side of him, Chuck headed down the hill, past a clothing store with a mannequin wearing bell-bottom jeans and paisley shirts. On Harvard Avenue, beneath a rotating sign in a second-floor real estate office, they wandered into a smoky bar that advertised twenty-five-cent beers and R&B covers.

Frederick was magnificent that night. He introduced himself to a gaggle of girls from a nearby secretarial school and struck up a conversation with a table of electric company techs still wearing their tool belts. He ordered a round of shots for the band—Jose Cuervo—and persuaded Chuck to open a stick of gooey black primo hashish he'd been saving. As the two of them huddled together in a stall in the men's room, smoking, Frederick insisted they share some crusty yellow powder from a little vial. When they returned to the bar, their hearts pounding, the keyboard player was articulating the opening figure in The Doors' "Light My Fire." By then, the club was filled with BU students chasing shots of Jack Daniel's with cheap drafts. Before long, everyone was on the dance floor, a tangle of arms moving up and down, hair plastered with sweat, eyes glazed over.

Fueled by meth and booze, Chuck pressed against Lorraine, while Frederick worked the crowd—disappearing for a while with one of the secretaries or a couple of locals resentful that out-of-town students with money were wandering back into Boston, changing the vibe from loose and summery to uptight fall. The band worked its way through "Whiter Shade of Pale" and, drunk and fucked-up on meth and hash, Chuck forgot all about being challenged in the Phoenix Room. He imagined himself, too, a warrior in the great revolutionary struggle and felt sublime pleasure being near Lorraine and Frederick. At that moment, he felt he had a right to his naïveté and plenty of time to develop political views and a sense of his own purpose in life. On some level, he forgave Frederick for the line of questioning and understood how his innocence could be an irritant to someone as world weary and wise as Frederick. Sweaty, dancing, and feeling surges of energy flooding through his veins, it didn't matter that Chuck wasn't Lorraine's main man. He was grateful to have a place—any place—in their near-perfect lives. As the set ended, the lead singer announced last call.

The three of them made their way, singing and laughing, up Comm Avenue toward Lorraine's. Frederick suggested they smoke some more hash, but Chuck couldn't find the pipe. When they got to the house in Brighton, Lorraine put her hands out to each of them, leading them up the steps, stumbling in, past the bare furnishings in the living room, until they collapsed in a heap on Lorraine's bed, a tangle of legs and limbs, clothing and hair.

Chuck's senses softened and then blazed. Every sound, every movement, every smell, was magnified. He felt a limb move under his leg and tried to orient himself on the bed, to visualize his own body in relation to the others. He smelled booze and hair—thick, moist, and smoky. The room swirled. Sometime later, Chuck became conscious of the quiet, the rhythm of his own breathing, and the two of them—Frederick and Lorraine—nearby. He tried focusing on the clock ticking above his head. He played a little game, anticipating sounds, using them to try to sober himself up by calibrating his mind to his surroundings and the passage of time, but the ticking seemed to surge and then fade away, speeding up and then slowing down. Someone belched and Chuck smelled beer, which nauseated him. He felt his own consciousness drift to the very top back portion of his head. There was a thicket of rustling, and all their weight shifted. Whoever was nearest the wall rolled toward him so that their mouth was close to his ear and their body was pressed up against his. A hand moved against his thigh. He felt hot breath on his neck, sour, relaxed. The hand on his leg moved higher, up across his stomach and then underneath his shirt, touching the tuft below his navel. He inhaled and held still. It flattened and then pressed itself, a rough palm against his skin. He reminded himself to breathe.

Minutes passed this way, and Chuck alternated between trying to figure out who was where and what exactly was happening. The body that was pressed against his side held still, the breath on his neck became steady, the flattened palm on his abdomen was motionless. Then it moved. He timed his own breaths to every third or fourth tick of the clock. After what seemed like a long time, he felt his belt unbuckling, a wave of excitement, and then fear. There was an exquisite pause in which he felt the bed dropping out from underneath him as the hand slid down, down, down.

Chuck woke sweating, the sun beating down on the bed. There was a clattering in the kitchen, and when he opened his eyes and focused, he saw Lorraine, stretching, her back to him. He pushed the covers away and watched her extend her arms toward the ceiling, exposing the sides of her breasts, her shoulders and neck, the smooth line of skin that ended at her panties. Chuck watched her step into a white Danskin leotard and a short black skirt before leaving the room. His own shirt and pants were balled up at the bottom of the bed, and his underwear was sticky. In the bathroom, he splashed water on his face and rummaged through the medicine cabinet for some aspirin. He could hear Frederick talking in the kitchen, though he couldn't make out what he was saying. A teapot screamed and then subsided, and Chuck pictured them drinking instant coffee. He made his way through the living room and onto the porch. Outside, the sun rose over the brownstones, beating down on the asphalt, making the air over the street ripple. He lit a cigarette. After a little while, Lorraine came outside with her little portfolio and purse and kissed him on the cheek before heading off to work. A few minutes later, Frederick came out and sat down beside him. "Some evil shit we smoked," he said, opening a beer.

In their first forays into friendship, Chuck felt a self-conscious mixture of pride and shame; he was cuckolding someone famous, whose attention both flattered and intimidated him. Uncertain, and often hesitant to speak, Chuck alternated between feeling as if they were developing a legitimate friendship and feeling that Frederick was all coiled up and ready to spring at the slightest provocation. Gradually, instead of haranguing him with revolutionary ideology or heated discourse, Frederick was becoming conspiratorial, even gracious. On the Fourth of July, the three of them drove to Worcester, where Frederick and a few of his high school buddies launched Hail Marys, Fat Boys, cherry bombs, and thumpers to the accompaniment of Jimi Hendrix, blasting from speakers mounted on the back of a van. As the fireworks exploded, Frederick leaned back and smiled, invoking combat noises from war movies or giggling like a kid. A week later, when Robert McNamara, President Johnson's secretary of defense, arrived in Harvard Square, a dozen radicals, including Frederick, were arrested for surrounding and rocking his limo. The next day, after his mother posted bail, Frederick rushed into Lorraine's apartment, waving a copy of the *Boston Globe,* hardly even noticing Lorraine, saying to Chuck, "We did it, man! We made the news!"

By late July, Chuck's relationship with Lorraine had changed. For one thing, he no longer skulked around her house, pining for her exclusive affections. He and Lorraine had a routine, which seemed acceptable to everyone. When Frederick was involved in revolutionary actions, Chuck and Lorraine were a couple. When Frederick returned, Chuck kept busy on his own or became Frederick's confidant, sidekick, and friend. Some nights, after Lorraine fell asleep, Chuck and Frederick went out listening to music, getting stoned, and talking about the revolution. It was in this context late one night that Frederick asked Chuck where he got his dope.

It took a few weeks to arrange, There were logistical issues. The band was playing an outdoor concert—a wedding in Vermont—and Augie Pearson, the percussionist who'd cultivated Chuck as a Boston distributor, didn't call him back for nearly a week. The family, as they called themselves, would be partying in the mountains until late July. Chuck had misgivings about introducing Frederick to his dealers, a premonition that these two forces in his life—his passion or at least his proxy for passion and his bread and butter—should not come too close in contact, but it wasn't strong enough to cancel the trip.

Frederick showed up at Chuck's apartment early one Saturday morning, his hands chapped, his nails bitten down, and the pores of his skin unusually dilated, causing his freckles to stand out like moles. He was chain-smoking Marlboros and talking nonstop about nothing and everything. Together they rode Frederick's bike out the Mass Pike to East Windsor, a little suburb of Connecticut, with maple saplings and sidewalks with hopscotch grids, little kids' tricycles, and mailboxes with names like "The Martins" and "The Howes" stenciled on them.

The house that served as worldwide headquarters for the Inter Galactic Messengers was a fading split-level in need of paint and landscaping. In the driveway, a half dozen black shiny orbs with grills featuring a lightning bolt logo and the words "Audio Adventures Inc."

emblazoned across them were sitting side by side. The orbs, Chuck explained to Frederick, were gigantic fiberglass speakers.

They let themselves in the yard and entered through the back door. A stereo played live rock music—badly mixed audiotapes of the band—and the house smelled like cigarettes, stale beer, bong juice, and body odor. A couple lay sleeping on a beat-up couch. Chuck led Frederick through the dining room, past a couple of guys wearing black leather, and into the kitchen, where a small man with curly hair—the band's manager—sat on a stool sorting through receipts. Three or four sleepy-looking young women in flowing skirts and skimpy T-shirts sat around him staring at a pile of burnt French toast. Chuck said hello to everyone and told Frederick to wait there while he went looking for Augie.

In one of the bedrooms, two guys were splayed on the floor holding guitars. In another, boxes of microphones and light fixtures and a huge mixing console were stacked almost to the ceiling. Circles of black cable lay coiled on the floor. The third bedroom was pitch-black. Augie wasn't around, despite his promises to be there. Chuck was thinking he and Frederick might go somewhere for breakfast, but when he walked back into the kitchen, Frederick and the band manager were having a serious conversation.

"I don't see why not," Frederick was saying.

"You don't understand," the curly-haired man said. "They belong to the band." The young women were leaning back in their chairs as if Frederick and the guy were spraying each other with hot liquid.

"*You* don't understand, man," Frederick sneered. "Two hundred thousand kids—some of whom may even have the poor taste to be your fans—are fighting for their lives in the jungles of Vietnam right now. To get the politicians to pay attention we're gonna need a good PA system in Chicago. We'll take good care of it. I promise, we'll return it so you guys can get rich." It appeared to Chuck that Frederick was in the process of shaking down his dealer.

"No fucking way, man. This equipment is worth twenty thousand bucks."

Frederick lowered his voice. "You can't just turn your back on your brothers and sisters." The women in the room were listening intently now. Several had shifted so that their bodies were facing Frederick.

"Oh, yes, I can. The guys are rehearsing new material. They're this close to a record deal." He held his thumb and his forefinger a quarter inch apart.

"I'm talking about bombs going off and people losing limbs," Frederick said. The only sign that he was upset was his jaw working up and down under his cheek. "And you're worrying about some stupid rock-and-roll band. . . ."

"I started working with this band when they were playing open mics and jamming in clubs in Wallingford and East Hartford." The manager made it sound like a holy mission. "Now that they have a chance to make it, I'm not gonna let some speed freak fuck it up." He made a sweeping motion with his arms. "Who the fuck is this guy anyway?" he said to Chuck. "Get him the fuck out of here, will you?"

By the time they got to the front door, the roadies were standing on the stairs and in the foyer, hitching up their pants. In the driveway, Frederick kick-started the bike and turned it around. "Pussies," he called out beneath the engine noise. Then he flipped them the bird just like Dennis Hopper in *Easy Rider* and away they went.

In the summer of 1967, the Red Sox went 92 and 70, making it all the way to the World Series before losing to the Cards. The following winter, there was a lot of excitement in the air until Lonborg, their star pitcher, got hurt in a skiing accident. By the time Frederick and Chuck got to be friends, the Sox had already squandered their season and were, as was their habit, doing abysmally bad.

In early August, Frederick and Chuck started going to the Scoreboard Tavern, and, if Frederick was able to weasel a free pair of tickets, they'd see a game. Together, they sat in the narrow wooden seats in Fenway Park, history all around them, while Frederick talked about the coming revolution or the inevitable collapse of capitalism. In between, he ruminated on the shameful sale that sent the Babe to the Yankees and bizarre tales of Tom Yawkey, the mining magnate from South Carolina who bought the team in the thirties and slowly rebuilt it, bringing Ted Williams and, later, Carl Yastrzemski to town, while refusing to let black players like Jackie Robinson and Willie Mays even try out.

Listening to the radio from the time he was little, Frederick was an avid fan and a Red Sox expert, memorizing the team roster, the sponsors' slogans, players' averages, stats on attendance, and trivia about the ballpark; for example, how the plate steel and concrete wall that was rebuilt and painted green in the forties came to be called the Green Monster. From bus trips to the park, he came to know the stadium on game day, pristine and symmetrical, foul lines etched in lime, the pitcher's mound sculpted in red clay, the peanut and the beer guys' caw, the cigar and paper wrappers that lofted in ballpark breezes that changed mysteriously under the violet sky, joined during those few hours with thousands of others by hope that something beautiful might actually happen, something that could deliver them from their lives. Sitting in the bleachers, looking out at the CITGO sign that towered over the left-field fence, Frederick waxed poetic about the sport itself. "In baseball, nobody gets bashed or exploited. There's no thrusting, no penetration, no violence," he told Chuck. "Every at bat, every inning, every game, is a chance for redemption. A man can step up to the plate, no matter what he did his last time out, and have another chance. He can defy his stats, begin again, even win back the hearts of the people who booed him off the field." And the ball, Frederick believed, soaring out into the bleachers, was a little agent of consciousness.

By early August, like all Red Sox fans, Frederick had given up hope that his team would make it to the World Series. His work as a groundskeeper had become tedious and repetitive and Frederick was using crystal meth more and more—staying up two, three, four days in a row. To anyone who'd listen, he bragged about getting stoned with other radicals and how he'd been asked to draw up plans to disrupt the Democratic National Convention later that summer. The idea for the Fenway hack probably came to him in late July.

For at least a hundred years, MIT students have advanced the state of the art of practical jokes. Hacks, as they're called, are a blend of ingenuity and courage, the personal statements of people who don't easily and ordinarily express themselves—kids who didn't write or sing or dance or paint. They're the marriage of electrical engineering, mechanical mastery, social satire, and elegant pranksterism, and they usually require intense preparation, creativity, steely nerves, and split-second timing. In prior years, students have implanted transistor radios in telephone receivers, hoisted a police cruiser onto a campus rooftop, and set up a dormitory room in the middle of the Charles River when it was frozen. At MIT, hacks are a part of life—a way for the geeks and brainiacs to triumph over the more well-rounded Harvard boys. And so it was one day in August 1968, with man coolers blowing hot air across their faces, Frederick told Chuck his idea.

"How'd you like to help me hack one of the oldest franchises in baseball?" Frederick said. Chuck had just fired up a joint and was cupping it in his hands. "Picture a volcano erupting in the middle of Fenway Park during a game. All you'd see is lava—a steaming mass of multicolored goo that curdles up and starts smoking on the field."

Chuck laughed.

"The coaches and the managers and field umpires running out, scratching their heads, and the players gathering round, holding their noses, and the fans having no fucking idea what's going on. Then, in the center-field bleachers, a banner unfurling that says, 'Stop the War,' or 'Bring Our Boys Home.' "

"It's ballsy," Chuck said. He thought for sure his friend was kidding. He'd seen it a dozen times before: Frederick getting all fired up about something he never actually intended to do.

Frederick took out a composition book filled with equations, chemical reactions, drawings, even the names of companies that made or sold chemicals that could simulate a volcano erupting. He'd already thought a lot about it.

Chuck played along. "It's not without its challenges," he said.

The other groundskeepers at Fenway whose job it was to bring out the crushed brick, clay, and Kentucky Bluegrass were a mixture of college boys with connections to the front office, Puerto Ricans and Mexicans working illegally, and a couple of career mechanics all laboring under a grizzled old full-time landscaper named John Touey. In

Frederick's opinion, none had the right political leanings or could be trusted to help. His regular posse, the people he claimed to operate with, were, as he explained it, engaged out of theater.

For a hack like this to work, Frederick said they would need strong support, extensive setup, outside resources, and, depending on how well it went off, the ability to disappear afterward for a while. With clouds passing over the bleachers and the white noise of traffic coming off the Mass Pike, Chuck heard himself egging Frederick on—telling him it had all the elements of a Hall of Fame hack, mischievous with a message, a combination of science, technology, and social commentary. He told his friend he was intrigued by the idea. He spoke in glowing terms about how amazing it would be to pull off. By the time the two of them got up to leave, stoned out of their gourds, Chuck told Frederick that he was on board.

New Year's Eve Day, 1999

John Russell was pleased when his pager went off. As a favor to his old
friends at the Bureau, former special agent Ken Ford, who'd retired to a
desk job with Interpol, had agreed to keep an eye on the next of kin of
fugitives like Fergus Keane. "I dunno know if this means anything to
you, Jack," Ken said, "but the Volcano Bomber's old lady just went
missing in Switzerland." It was Friday—the day of the dreaded millen-
nial shift, Y2K—one of the few times you'd find right-wing survivalists
and New Age crystal gazers side by side, joking in the aisles of Wal-
Mart. Most other guys Russell's age were barbecuing ribs in the
Poconos or snuggling their honeys in the suburbs. Whoever was assigned the Volcano Bomber case had probably long since stopped working it, except to make out paperwork each month.

Russell took the turns to Lorraine's house without thinking. He
hadn't given up. Many a night since he'd arrived in Philadelphia, he'd sat
outside their house, watching the Nadia women on the unlikely chance
that Fergus, aka Frederick, might try to see his daughter. It was that way
with fugitives. He knew this. Some—like Abbie Hoffman—have a face-
lift, get married, and become activists all over again, only to circle back
and turn themselves in. Some walk away, but just as many, or more,
awakened by age or infirmity, return to see an old lover or a child on

holidays, anniversaries, or in times of trouble. He realized this was a long shot. Even if Keane was still alive, somebody would have had to tip him off to Lorraine's disappearance, which would have been unlikely. The radical underground had pretty much dried up.

Being honest with himself—a habit he fell into now for reasons he didn't much understand—it wasn't just the fantasy of catching Keane in the twilight of his career. The week between Christmas and New Year's is a tough time in law enforcement. Everyone's heard about holidays and depression. Russell had experienced firsthand how this time of year leaves a man with too much time on his hands. Nowadays, his peers did woodworking in their basements, traveled, coached Little League, bought boats, and babysat their grandkids. Russell read a little—mostly mysteries—and he still went to the track, but for the most part, his only hobby, the thing John Russell liked most, was work.

He parked on Medley Street about three hundred feet from the Nadia house and slid his seat back. Satisfied he could see the front door clearly, he took a newspaper out and stuck it in the visor. Then he memorized his surroundings—the lights that were on, window treatments and whether they were up or down, the position of vehicles on the street, the young man in a military jacket, the middle-aged woman at her doorstep looking for her cat, the heavyset guy with the hood of his car up, a couple of teenage girls sharing a cigarette. Twice, he emptied his bladder into a Nalgene. He read the paper and ate a Mars Bar. Less than an hour later, Stardust Nadia appeared in her doorway, dressed to the nines.

The girl looked more like her mother now. She was a little fuller in the face, and curvaceous. There was confidence in her gait, coolness in the way she shook her head to keep the hair out of her face. She was wearing a tight-fitting red shirt with sequins and carrying a leather jacket. Her blonde hair, short skirt, black tights, and pumps would make a lovely New Year's Eve package for whomever she was planning to meet.

Russell put the car in gear. He'd been present at key moments in the girl's life—outside the hospital waiting room the night she was born, at her christening, school plays and graduations, her confirmation, a

Christmas pageant or Halloween parade here and there. From behind the wheel, behind a newspaper, or from the back of a crowd, Special Agent John Russell understood things about Stardust Nadia that most agents didn't know about their own kids. He knew, for example, that she was bright, left-handed, had a pretty bad sense of direction, and was forgetful, inclined to lock her keys in her car and leave her credit card in stores. Yet if someone had pointed him out to Stardust, she'd have pegged him as a neighborhood guy, somebody's dad, a familiar face in a photograph. It was Russell's belief that Stardust knew nothing of the Volcano Bomber or Fergus Keane. The very idea that the Feds thought her father was the prime suspect in a federal criminal case—a fugitive from justice for thirty years—would have amused her.

Russell followed her to the end of the street and turned left, riding the brake. At Appleberry, she turned left again and waited at the intersection. Russell parked and followed her up onto the train platform. Downtown, Stardust Nadia walked from Market Square to Third Street and turned right. On South Street, she bought a falafel and then headed up west to Eleventh. By ten thirty, she was standing at the end of a line of urban hipsters in spiked leather and long black coats, before deciding to move on. At eleven, she entered a martini bar on Arch Street called Rox.

It took Russell a few minutes to find her. At the bar, she exchanged polite smiles with men who said things that either she ignored or that made her laugh politely, and then drifted away. It was so loud Russell's rib cage shook. At eleven thirty, somebody gave up a stool next to her, and a sharp-dressed man sat down. Russell put him in his late thirties—fancy suit, slicked-back dyed hair. After a short conversation, the man in the gray suit pointed to a table, stepped back, and made a little motion for Stardust to sit down. He was too young, too slick, and too flashy to be directly connected to the radical underground, though he could easily have been the messenger.

Stardust opened her purse and pulled out a compact and lip gloss. They ordered drinks. The guy laid an array of electronic devices on the table—a pager and two cell phones, which lit up, one after the other. John Russell moved in an arc around them. From a little alcove near the bathroom, he watched her toss one back, then another. Just after one A.M., they headed toward the door.

According to John Russell, a woman who's decided to go home with a man walks tall in her heels. She lets her hips sway and sticks her chest out. If you look closely, her head sits back on her shoulders and her eyes dilate, which, in his opinion, accounts for a lot of bad choices. A man who thinks he's about to get some swaggers. If he's insecure, he'll stretch his neck, looking around to make sure he's being noticed. The guy in the gray suit who led Stardust through the crowd looked like he didn't want to be recognized, as if he was embarrassed or hiding something. He practically pushed her into the limousine. Russell was suspicious. He flagged a cab and followed them down Arch to Fifth, then west on Market.

Both cars proceeded around City Hall to Eighteenth Street. Russell could have called in the plates, but that would have alerted the office he was working on New Year's Eve, something he wanted to avoid. When the limo stopped in front of Quick Copy Center, Russell gave the taxi driver a twenty and told him to wait. He stood in the shadows near a door that said ORIENTAL MASSAGE, SECOND FLOOR. It seemed odd. The limo driver didn't get out. The lights didn't go on. The doors remained shut. John Russell drew his weapon—a 9-millimeter Sig-Sauer.

When the back door finally did open, a man's shoe touched the ground at the same time a woman's stockinged foot kicked, then retracted. There was a struggle, then an embrace. As Russell stepped forward, Stardust twisted loose, her midriff bare, her skirt hiked up around her waist, revealing her ass, divided by a black string. She swung her purse around, almost hitting Russell, who was standing with his feet planted, his pistol aimed at the man's temple. The man in the gray suit was bleeding from the mouth. Stardust screamed, which caused them both to freeze.

The first few names they came up with for the new venture—pawnshop
.com, pawnbroker.com, pawn.com—were taken. These were the heady
days of the Internet when opportunists would squat on desirable do-
main names for years, waiting for big businesses to buy them out.
Rahim found a server farm near Temple University and a software company in Minneapolis that offered a catalogue system in modules for up-
loading, viewing, and purchasing online. They registered the URL to a
shell corporation that was registered to another shell corporation,
which was owned by an offshore Bahamian company that Charlie Puckman had set up in the seventies. Fat Eddie told Chuck to put the stock in
somebody else's name, somebody who couldn't be linked to him, which
would protect any money they earned from a civil suit, should one occur. Chuck thought of it late one night, while surfing porn sites stoned.
In less than a month, Softpawn.com was up and running.

Chuck's former customers were a motley crew—street toughs,
loan sharks, money launderers, petty thieves, scammers—most of
them guys like Charlie Puckman Sr. They got their starts dealing
drugs or fencing stolen goods, made only vague encoded notes about
transactions, watched one another's backs, kept their business to
themselves, and never forgot a favor. Chuck's first few sales calls felt

awkward. His business suits—once tailored and pressed—were wrin-kled and too big on him now, and his hair was wiry and unkempt. One guy asked if Chuck was feeling better since his surgery. Another wondered if Chuck was another Puckman brother, returned to salvage what he could of the family fortune. But Chuck's unsteadi-ness came across as credible, and he was more successful than he'd expected.

Big Harvey agreed to let Chuck catalogue his high-end inventory. So did two North Philly accounts provided Softpawn.com agreed to take title. To those engaged in illicit trading and hot property, commitment and consignment mean nothing. Physical possession rules. Whoever holds an item, owns it. "I have a civil suit pending," Chuck stammered, uncertain about the effect. "You can't afford your merch to be seized." Miraculously, everyone agreed. By the end of their first week, four pawnbrokers had furnished Softpawn.com a list of items that hadn't moved in months for Chuck to post on his Web site.

Rahim visited the dealers and took pictures of furs, jewelry, and electronic equipment. Within days, he'd uploaded the photos and arranged them by category along with a two- or three-line description, written by Ovella. Chuck hadn't said much about his marketing plan, alluding to kiosk displays in malls, students going door to door, church sales, and the like. In truth, pawnshop owners couldn't care less what Chuck and his friends did as long as they got paid.

Finding customers wasn't as easy, particularly because it involved Chuck calling people he'd known in his old life—the guy in charge of the softball team Puckman Security sponsored, the head of the Eques-trian Academy where Chuck's daughter, Ivy, had ridden, and a handful of ex-neighbors and business club members with whom he'd played tennis. His worst fear—that he would be regarded as a pariah—never materialized. People remembered him. They'd even heard about his dif-ficulties. But they just weren't very interested. He called his daughter's friends' parents, former suppliers he'd favored with large orders, even a couple of Eileen's uncles with whom he felt some rapport. Nobody was

the slightest bit interested until he got through to Sharon Gladstein—
customer zero—as Rahim called her.

Ms. Gladstein was a waxy-faced, hook-nosed gossip and shopa-
holic, too homely to breed. In the early eighties, through the nuances of
divorce law, Sharon turned a short ill-fated marriage to a low-level environmental lawyer into a lifelong pension and thereafter devoted herself to becoming a human Rolodex. She was also the best friend of
Chuck's ex-wife, Eileen. "Nu?" Sharon said, as if she'd run into him at
a bar mitzvah.

"You've probably heard," Chuck began, "the security business is in
the crapper."

"Anybody could see *that* from Eileen's settlement," Sharon said.

"Actually, I'm into this new thing where I got really top-shelf stuff
from pawnshops and put it on the Internet where people can buy it at a
fraction of its retail cost."

"Say more," she said, taking an earring off and pressing the phone
against the side of her head.

"It's really simple," Chuck said. "The pawnshops get really upscale
stuff, but nobody with taste wants to drive into their neighborhoods. I
put it on the Internet at ridiculously low prices, which is probably why
this thing is taking off. . . ." He let his voice trail off. "I should have done
this a few years ago."

"So how does a girl get in on this?"

"You got a pen?" he asked, smiling.

Over the next few weeks, Chuck solicited dozens of pawnshop owners
from Newark, Delaware, to Trenton, New Jersey, and west to Harrisburg, sending Ovella with a digital camera to take pictures of the booty.
Back in the factory, Rahim and Ovella's girlfriend, Gloria, uploaded the
photos and typed in detailed descriptions, pricing merchandise between
20 and 40 percent over what the pawnshop owners told them they
wanted. As Chuck hoped she would, Sharon Gladstein told everyone
she knew, including former decorator clients, bridge and mah-jongg
partners, women she played tennis with, and her girlfriends from the

club. The first weekend online, there were eight purchases, ranging from a fourteen-inch color television for $25 to a twenty-four-piece set of cutlery for $80. Over the next few weeks, there were eight hundred hits and fifty-five sales, including a moped, a high-definition color television, a his-and-hers pistol set, a snowblower, and a trunkful of Elvis memorabilia. In the first month of business, they filled orders for more than a hundred items, with revenues to Softpawn.com of $3,700. When Chuck took ad space in a few upscale shopping mall circulars, sales increased another 50 percent. After paying quarterly real estate and payroll taxes, utility bills, and a couple weeks' wages to Jose, Ovella, Gloria, and Big Lou, Chuck put $1,200 into an account for Gutierrez. By June, Chuck told his pawnbrokers they could ship directly to customers and be guaranteed payment while remaining anonymous. It reminded Chuck of dealing dope in college—or a hack some brainy student might have conceived as a joke—a novelty that started blossoming into something much bigger—something with upside, commercial appeal that could make something out of nothing. Rahim became more adept at writing computer code and developing the Web site. Almost by accident, he figured out how to hack into Web sites, tap into databases, even send and receive messages from e-mail addresses that weren't theirs.

"Give me the name of some mail-order catalogue your ex-wife got, someplace you remember from the credit card bills," Rahim said to Chuck one morning.

"What for?"

"Just give me one."

"Lattie's Under Covers." Chuck was standing behind Rahim, reading a spreadsheet that summarized the prior week's sales. A moment later, they were looking at a photograph of a teenage girl with thick lips and heavy eye shadow wearing a dark lace bra. Rahim went back to his desktop and clicked on an icon with a skull and crossbones.

"Perfect," he said, a minute later. "Port Eighty's open. Let's see if we can get into the FTP." He minimized that screen and opened up a new one that was blank except for a blinking cursor and a blank space into which he typed a string of characters. "Bingo. Port Twenty-two is open."

Rahim typed a long string of numbers and codes—passwords, screen IDs, alphabetical and numeric iterations. When the CPU stopped crunching, the screen displayed a list of names, addresses, phone numbers, dress sizes, e-mail addresses, birth dates, marital statuses, and purchase histories. Next to one record was: "cashmere sweater with diamond studs." Beside another: "two pairs of bathing suits—1 thong, 1 with skirt." Next to a third: "tennis outfit." "From behind the curtain, I can do anything," Rahim said, sitting back and smiling.

"Do they know we're doing this?" Chuck asked.

Rahim shook his head. "It'll take me a few minutes to copy their customer list. I'll merge it with our database offline. They'll have no idea." It took Rahim less than an hour to configure and merge it into the Softpawn.com customer database. Somewhere on the Internet, he'd found a program that let him send e-mail messages that were untraceable. "An IP address is like a fingerprint," he said. "You want to leave it in as few places as possible," he told Chuck as he typed. "While I'm doing this, you should come up with an e-mail we can send to Lattie's customers."

"Profit from Misfortune!" he wrote in the subject line. "Furs, Jewels, Electronics, Clothing, Valuables, and More. It's your lucky day. Click here now." For Chuck, selling had been an instinct inherited from his father, sanctioned by everyone around him. To have misgivings about it now seemed strange, silly, yet something about this was distasteful to him. For some reason, he pictured himself thirty years earlier, standing in Lorraine's doorway in Boston holding his fake petition, her shoulders wet from the shower, her big eyes looking up at him, and something passed across his consciousness that felt fraudulent and bad.

Over the next five days, Rahim sent that e-mail to tens of thousands of individual addresses he'd surreptitiously acquired from unsophisticated online retailers. By the following weekend, they had over a thousand hits, which resulted in orders for almost $6,000 worth of merchandise. By July, word of their success had spread among pawn dealers, art and antique brokers, and money launderers. Chuck began getting calls from liquidators—people with excess inventory that hadn't moved—which is when Fat Eddie asked him down to the Union League.

———

"Wilkie Crackford," the man said, sticking out a meaty hand and winking. He was an affable fellow in his mid-forties with an ample belly, a handlebar mustache, and blue eyes that twinkled behind wire-frame glasses. "Wilkie, on account I'm from Wilkes Barre. Crackford because I'm a crack litigator." Despite his disheveled demeanor and humble origins, Crackford graduated at the top of his class at Temple. He had an easy way about him and a voice that sounded like tiny bubble wrap crackling. Over vodka tonics, Fat Eddie made a ceremony out of telling them he would put up Crackford's initial retainer so he could represent Chuck against any residual claims that arose against him. It was a pleasant meeting, not unlike many Chuck had taken over the course of his career. From a combination of success with Softpawn.com and the right dosages of alcohol and antianxiety medication, Chuck felt better than he had in months. They shook hands on the steps, agreeing to meet again after Crackford had a chance to get familiar with the file.

Chuck bought more computer equipment, food, nonprescription drugs, a couple of Thelonius Monk CDs, and some good weed. By the end of August, he'd put five grand in an account for Gutierrez and split another ten grand with Rahim. By the end of the summer, Softpawn.com was generating enough revenue for Ovella to quit her job. With a solid source of supply and a reliable schedule of online auctions now, Rahim put his cyber-capabilities in full service to Chuck's case.

"What should we be looking for?" Rahim e-mailed Wilkie Crackford, once he'd been retained.

"Violations of the Clean Water Act, old trial transcripts, legislation, prior case law covering white-collar crime, even research and development by the chemical companies that make 1,1,1 TCE," Crackford wrote back. Late at night, Rahim sat at the keyboard hacking into the search engines, downloading summaries of environmental law and reckless endangerment in the workplace, while Chuck paced behind him, a glass of vodka in his hand. Rahim ran his data through a statistical program someone had given him, entering the number of charges Chuck would likely be found guilty of against the average penalties, and e-mailed Crackford with the results. He did this with a determination that bordered on obsession. To Rahim, Chuck wasn't just a friend in trouble. The factory that housed Softpawn, employing four people almost full-time, risen from the ashes of Puckman Security, was Rahim's mission.

Meanwhile, Chuck grew more and more restive, spending his time surfing the Internet, drinking, getting stoned, listening to the steady drone of the Spanish-speaking radio stations, watching his fish, and waiting.

Throughout the spring and summer, the bedside vigil continued, with visitors and members of the Gutierrez family sharing meals from plastic containers and watching daytime television while Ramon—or what was left of Ramon—stared into the abyss, connected by wires and tubes to all kinds of equipment, his body stiff and atrophying under the sheets. Every few days, Alverez Gutierrez, matriarch of the Gutierrez clan, would make a scene, declaring that if God wanted her son to live, He would enable the boy to breathe on his own, until finally, with the support of their priest, she convinced a doctor that the family really did want Ramon taken off the respirator. A day or two later, the doctor conferred with the hospital administrator, who notified the U.S. attorney in Allentown of the family's decision.

On September 9, the very day Ramon Gutierrez was permitted to expire, a federal grand jury returned an indictment, charging Arthur and Charles Puckman Jr. with multiple violations of the federal Clean Water Act. Chuck was booked, fingerprinted, and then released on his own recognizance, while Arthur's mug shot was printed and distributed across cyberspace and a warrant was issued for his arrest.

America loves to watch someone's life disintegrate. There was a blurb on the *Inquirer*'s Society Page, identifying Chuck and Eileen

Puckman as former sponsors of equestrian and floral shows, and a long article in the Business Section about various business practices that could result in his criminal prosecution. Chuck's name was dropped from a few civic and art organizations he'd been a part of, and he was quietly removed from the online directory of Philly CEOs, a social organization made up of big cheeses looking to share tips about making money and living the good life. By fall, the accident at the Puckman factory had become a kind of socioeconomic parable and a topic on various radio call-in shows.

Then it seemed to fizzle. For one thing, the prosecution was unable to locate Arthur Puckman. In the nine months since he'd disappeared, there'd been no phone calls to his mother; no wire transfers; no sightings at airports, train stations, or bus depots—despite a material witness warrant and a search by a clerk at the FBI whose job it was to check ocean liner and airplane manifests, hotel registries, and Interpol. "The prosecution can't introduce Arthur Puckman's statement unless we have the opportunity to cross-examine him," Crackford argued in a letter to the judge. "We see his flight as evidence of guilt." More distressing to the Feds was that, even after drilling, sampling, collating, computer modeling, and analyzing soil samples around the factory, the EPA came up with nothing in the groundwater more toxic than heating oil and lead. So while Puckman Security had most certainly violated the Clean Water Act, the consequences simply didn't amount to enough to warrant locking the owner up. On top of all this, Agent Keaton's thoroughness had rendered Puckman Security defunct, with nothing in the way of assets for the government to seize. It was beginning to look as if Chuck would wind up with nothing more than a slap on the wrist, when the media started in again, making a mockery of the government's ineffectiveness. Reluctantly, a week after Chuck's arraignment, the U.S. attorney notified Wilkie Crackford that the government was going to drop the case.

Surprisingly, Chuck became despondent. Without the pressure of prosecution, his own aimlessness, his vulnerability, and his anxiety lay naked and exposed. In front of his bathroom mirror, he tried to feign jubilation, which seemed altogether inappropriate, given the fate of Gutierrez and his family's role in all this. He made an expression of relief, sighing deeply and releasing the tension from his shoulders, but he didn't feel it. Without the prospect of financial ruin, even jail time, he felt a strange surge of pressure, the phrase "Now what?" bouncing around in his head.

Three weeks later, after Wilkie Crackford and Fat Eddie Palmieri toasted Chuck's good fortune, two policemen climbed the fire escape steps and banged on Chuck's red door. Once again, he was handcuffed, pushed into a squad car, and taken to the Roundhouse, where he was fingerprinted and photographed. This time, he wasn't released so fast. "The U.S. attorney turned his files over to a state grand jury who decided to indict you and your brother for murder in the second degree," Crackford explained to Chuck over the phone.

"Which means what?" Chuck asked, irritated.

"Criminal homicide constitutes murder in the second degree when it's committed while the defendant is a principal or accomplice in the perpetration of a felony. The arcane term is 'depraved indifference,' if somebody were to drop a brick from the Empire State Building—"

"What the fuck are you talking about?" Chuck said. He had swallowed twenty milligrams of lorazepam on his way out the door.

"Since they couldn't nail you for a Clean Water Act violation, the Feds leaned on the state prosecutor to do something." Crackford sounded concerned. "It's politics, Chuck. We can probably plead it down to man three."

"Where's that leave me?"

Wilkie Crackford made a clicking sound with his tongue as if searching for an appropriate answer. "I'm not sure," he said nervously. "Technically, no more than twenty years."

Chuck's lips moved, but no sound came out.

"I'm gonna try to get you a bail hearing tonight," the lawyer told him, "but we're gonna need ten grand. Try to hang in there," Crackford said.

A heavy caseload kept Chuck from being arraigned until Monday midday. Over the weekend, Chuck saw a guy get beat up for not giving up a cigarette. Twice he was hassled until he gave up his seat on a bench. All night Saturday, he was regaled by ex-cons and junkies with stories about tattoos and hair dye and being somebody's fuck-boy in the slammer. On Monday afternoon, after Crackford showed up with a gym bag full of cash from Fat Eddie, photographers caught Chuck looking up at the sky and covering his eyes, an expression of horror pasted on his face. Crackford told him to take a few days, get some sleep, and try to clear his head. He had to decide whether to go to trial or make a deal.

That same day, Chuck visited his father at Elysian Fields. There was a single fluorescent light over Charlie's bed, and Chuck was surprised to see his father's upper arm, once thick and muscular, looking like his own wrist. A TV flickered at the base of his bed, and his eyes, which were glassy, seemed to have difficulty staying open. When Chuck came in, the old man looked in his direction.

"It's me, Pop."

The old man nodded.

"How you feeling?"

Charlie Puckman closed his eyes and took a deep breath, then coughed a feeble, phlegmy little gasp.

The room had a rank, putrid smell. If only his father was strong enough, stand-up enough to take the heat, to call Crackford and serve himself up to the D.A. "Has Artie been to see you yet?" Chuck said. Silence hung between them like a sheet of glass. There was a general announcement over the little intercom that hung over the bedrail. Charlie Puckman didn't move. "How about Fat Eddie? Has he been here?" Nothing.

"They're gonna put me away, Pop," Chuck said. The old man closed his eyes. They'd removed his dentures since Chuck had last been to see him, and he looked as if he'd swallowed part of his face. "They wanna nail me for what we used to do." Chuck could hear the clock ticking over the bed, the steady flow of oxygen from the tank pressing into his father's body. "I need a hundred grand. Minimum. Maybe more. I got thirty in retirement, and Fat Eddie says he'll give me twenty, maybe twenty-five. Of course, the building is mortgaged." All his adult life, Chuck had been in this position with his dad—on bended knee, a grown man beholden to his father. "You got anything hidden anywhere, now would be the time to tell me." Charlie Puckman, who couldn't have spoken if he wanted to, dismissed his boy with an almost imperceptible wave of his index finger.

It was the last time they saw each other. The old man died in his sleep a couple of weeks later, leaving no assets, no cash, no life insurance, and no will—only creditors: a furniture dealer on Frankford Avenue, a Visa bill in the mid-four figures, and a bridge loan on a piece of real estate Charlie had long ago traded for cash.

"Unless you plead guilty," Wilkie said to Chuck six weeks later, "this trial's going to be a disaster. We have no money for resources and no time to prepare." Chuck was standing at a pay phone near Aramingo Avenue, trucks on their way to and from the steel distributor rumbling by. "As it stands now, we can't really mount an adequate defense, and the prosecutor is going for the maximum penalty."

"Which is what?" Chuck said feebly.

Crackford ignored him. "I tried for a delay, but the judge denied it. I was hoping as the trial got closer, the prosecutor would offer up a deal."

Chuck reached in his pocket for a pint of Seagram's and took a nip. "Maybe Rahim can gather the research and you can just read it."

"It's not like I want to get rich off this case, Chuck," Crackford said patiently. "But without money, I can't get any help, I can't prepare arguments of law, rules of evidence."

"I just don't have it," Chuck said.

"I know you don't. I just don't want to go to trial and lose," Crackford said. A bus rolled by, its transmission obliterating part of what Crackford said next. ". . . in exchange for a lesser sentence."

"I'm a dead man," Chuck said thickly.

"I'm just saying—"

"Enter the plea."

"I want to be sure you understand the implications."

"I give up."

"The sentencing guidelines are clear. If the judge wants to stick it to you, it's between nine and twenty—"

"What happens to Artie?"

Crackford paused. "He's a wanted man. If he shows his face, he's looking at the same thing."

"If I plead guilty, will they let him off?"

Wilkie Crackford said nothing. He'd seen Porter's tape on the Internet. He'd heard all about the family from Fat Eddie. "You want me to ask?"

"Might as well," Chuck said.

"If we go ahead with the plea, there'll be a sentencing hearing in about a month. It'll be very important for you to line up what we call character witnesses. Credible people who'll say something good about you—an ailing relative, a dependent child, a key business employee— even better, somebody who could plead hardship as a result of your prolonged absence." Chuck didn't say anything. "Think about it," Crackford said.

Thursday, March 12, 2000

In addition to being his best friend and confidante, after the accident, Rahim Rodriguez became Chuck Puckman's shithouse lawyer, financial manager, and public relations agent; he helped Chuck manage cash flow, keep creditors and tax authorities at bay; he got Coleman Porter to send the *Daily News* pictures of Chuck in a playground surrounded by Latino kids. He even talked the Gutierrez family out of filing civil charges against him, citing, as evidence of Chuck's intention to do right, monthly statements of the trust account he'd suggested his friend set up for the benefit of the widow and her kids. When Rahim heard Crackford's suggestion to get character witnesses to testify on Chuck's behalf, Rahim began a series of inquiries that resulted in his locating Chuck's daughter, Ivy. The Thursday before the sentencing hearing, he presented Chuck with a hand-drawn map with her address on it.

"But I haven't talked to her in seven years," Chuck said, running his hands through his hair.

"She's a human being, and she's your daughter."

"She's her mother's daughter. I'm not sure about the human being part."

"She has nothing to lose."

"She has nothing to gain."

Nonetheless, the next afternoon, Chuck put on a sweater, a pair of sweatpants, and sneakers, and left the factory with Rahim's map wedged in his back pocket. He walked four long blocks east, past a yard with giant spools of wire crated and stacked for shipment, past a strip mall with a thrift shop, a dollar store, and an upscale Italian restaurant, where he'd made deals with pawnshop owners and suppliers, surviving the silent assessments and the big lies they told each other over rich meals—people he didn't like and who didn't like him, alternately sucking up and then slinking down in their seats, knowing none of them would deliver what they were promising.

Along Aramingo Avenue, a bus rumbled by, spraying pebbles and diesel fumes over his shoes. He imagined God as a cameraman, recording every move, monitoring his thoughts. What makes a human defective is in his soul. Not cell phone radiation, not chemicals in his carpeting or vapors from his air-conditioning system, not nicotine or a lifetime of bad habits. As he walked, Chuck counted cars, slid coins from his pocket into parking meters, and avoided stepping on cracks, little rituals of contrition—rhythmic, soothing, nervous gestures— tonic for a lifetime of betrayals.

Crossing the street, he climbed a steel staircase and stood next to shift workers, women on their way home from work, and high school students wearing headphones and feigning nonchalance while checking out one another's clothes and piercings. He shoved his hands in his pockets. The membrane separating Chuck's most private self from the world was stretched so thin that every ding, every noise, every slight, every violation of his nature, was transmitted to his brain as an out-and-out assault. He knew when he stopped medicating, all his misdeeds, his secret life, his entire past, would lay raw and open before him. He faced the hearing Monday with dread, but also with relief. Deep down, he believed that no penance, no humiliation, and no authority could punish him adequately for the sin of living a false life.

When the El terminated at Frankford Avenue, he transferred to a bus. A trio of teenage boys in cargo pants and long black coats walked past him toward the back. A large black man with a huge belly moved down the aisle, grabbing the seat backs to steady himself. The bus lurched forward, passing newsstands, Laundromats, convenience stores, bowling alleys, and pedestrians standing in intersections governed by complex traffic light sequences that were impossible to anticipate. He ran his tongue over his front teeth, fingered the little bottle in his pocket—Xanax, the palindrome that calms—then swallowed a pill dry. He looked at his watch. How would he ever survive without medication?

In the seat next to him, a bookish man with a wooly comb-over was reading the obituaries. Miniature characters from Chuck's past dangled from an imaginary mobile—corporate weenies and cheek squeezers in pin-striped suits, union men with braided arm muscles and angry eyes, the aging secretary prattling around the office with her bruised feelings and her fallow womb. Since the arraignment, Chuck had stayed in a sixteen-square-block area that occasionally extended down to the Union League, focusing on simple tasks—buying food and booze, picking up his prescription refills. It was a shock to his system to be out, passing Holmesburg with its guard towers and imposing brick walls—the place where, years ago, doctors had inflicted harrowing medical procedures on hapless cons. Chuck closed his eyes and pictured a bare cell with a small window high up, vans with metal cages, porcelain bowls in the middle of dank cells. He imagined himself in lineup or in the yard, being forced to the ground. He had no illusions about his past. What was happening to him now had been set in motion a long time ago. He checked the map and moved toward the aisle, passing a woman holding a brown bag, squeezing out a small gesture of arrogance.

Once, a long time ago when he was a kid, he fantasized that he was Mighty Mouse, the cartoon hero who puffed out his little chest and flew into harm's way to save the world. Human beings begin life too hopeful, he thought. A man carrying a large Panasonic carton maneuvered his way down the aisle. You're born, and, almost immediately, you start making concessions. All his life, Chuck had guessed what kind of person he needed to be to get by or to get over on others. Obligations, possessions, and promises piled up in a museum of detritus and debris. Over the course of fifty-five years, his life had become a catalogue of betrayals, large and small.

———

It was getting cold. Dusk settled over the Great Northeast like gray soot. Across the street was a hotel—a Sheraton or a Doubletree with a glass rotunda over a swimming pool that nobody used. Roosevelt Boulevard was eight lanes across, impossible to cross in a single cycle. Standing on the median strip, waiting for the light to change, Chuck felt a momentary kinship with humanity. How exquisite to be among regular people—not exactly free—but not in prison either. He crossed the lobby with its worn carpets, bad art, and signs welcoming forensic accountants and small-aircraft pilots.

The bar was an alcove—not even a separate room—with a television suspended over a cash register. A sullen woman sat at a small table in the corner, smoking. On a television, tiny hockey players slid back and forth across a white surface. A couple of guys in suits called out the names of microbrews, none of which the bartender seemed to recognize. Chuck ordered a double shot of vodka, knocked it back with another Xanax, and slid off the stool.

At the front desk, he asked the clerk if they maintained a lost and found. From a large cardboard box, Chuck pulled a plaid jacket and carried it into the men's room. He looked himself up and down in the mirror. His hair was matted like a toupee. Earlier in the week, he'd cut it himself in short uneven clumps. He had dark creases around his eyes, and the jacket made his shoulders look even thinner. It was at least one size too small. He walked back through the lobby, past a man in a suit who was arguing about a room upgrade. Chuck imagined himself suspended in liquid—petroleum jelly—heavy, translucent, vague, inchoate.

Crossing back over the boulevard, he entered a maze of streets with names like Robin's Way, Carole Circle, and Steven Drive, after the sons and daughters of developers who'd gambled fifty years ago that someday this farmland would become commuter territory. He tried to orient himself to the map. The houses, with their aluminum siding, bay windows, lawn ornaments, minivans, and fences were identical. Occasionally, headlights forced him to cower on the sidewalk. He followed a street to the end, then turned, when, from out of nowhere, a blur of fur tore across a little patch of lawn yapping at his ankles, coming within inches before it miraculously stopped, its hind legs lifting, its torso spinning, as it reached the end of its tether. He lit a cigarette and looked up at the sign. Sharon Court. Ivy's street. Squinting at the curb, he steadied himself: 13658, 13644. 13630.

Chuck paused to catch his breath and let his eyes adjust. Smoke curled from a line of chimneys. An electric garage door engaged and then shut off. The house next to Ivy's was dark, and Chuck tiptoed down the driveway and into the backyard before crouching behind a doghouse set next to a clump of bushes. Behind Ivy's house, a spotlight shone on the back patio, giving the air a bluish tint. Someone drew the shades. After a few minutes, a light clicked on behind the second-floor window. Chuck crawled over to the fence and stood up. The metal felt cold. A swing set for a toddler trembled in the breeze. He put both hands on the fence that separated the yards, swung one leg up, and put his face next to the rail. His brain conducted a series of calculations. Then he put his weight on one leg and swung the other up, lifting his torso until it was on top of the fence, parallel to the ground. As he rolled, his pant leg snared. At that moment, the bushes and the doghouse flipped skyward. When Chuck opened his eyes, he was looking up at the stars. An alarm sounded in the distance. The little terrier started barking again.

For what seemed like a very long time, he lay on the ground, unable to breathe. For a split second or perhaps an hour, he had the cognition, beautiful and clear, that unless he forced himself to inhale, he would die. In that moment, Chuck experienced a complete release from anxiety. Just before the Soviet Union collapsed, U.S. immigration eased up, and this part of Philadelphia had flooded with Russians. Ethnic supermarkets replaced the record shops in strip malls; PhD electrical engineers took jobs as janitors; doctors operated cash registers in all-night markets; and symphony violinists became data-entry clerks. Seconds passed. He considered what it would be like to disappear into another country, to start over as a laborer, inarticulate, oddly dressed—a worker in a factory. He groped at the dirt with his fingers, indifferent to outcome. Then he was aware of the ground beneath his head—cold and hard—and the sound of his own blood pulsing. He thought about Ivy, the equestrian; Ivy, the yellow-haired girl; his little girl, Ivy, once so clear and pure and defenseless and guileless.

The last time he saw her was the week his marriage ended. He'd gone home after work to pick up his clothing, papers, photographs, antique wooden jewelry box, and audio equipment, all of which Eileen had seen fit to toss out of the second-story window. After loading what he could into his truck, he stopped for a drink at a nearby hotel. At around eight, the bartender told him about an outdoor concert being held at the township municipal complex, a half mile from his old house. By the time he arrived, the music had already started, and he was righteously buzzed.

He followed a manicured pathway through a playground with intricately assembled equipment toward the stage. A paunchy guitarist, an accordion player, and a stand-up bass player struggled through a cheesy arrangement of a Jim Croce song. In the distance, a small covered bridge extended over a man-made pond with a huge, extravagantly lit fountain. To this misappropriation of tax dollars, Chuck ascribed everything that was wrong with the suburbs—a furious falseness, vainglorious and virtueless—the ceaseless march from Norman Rockwell to the Toll brothers.

Soon, it was intermission and a balding emcee with a scraggly ponytail dispatched a dozen boys and girls in green Day-Glo shirts with buckets to canvass the crowd for donations to the township soccer program. One hundred thousand dollars for stadium lights was all they needed. People started reaching in their pockets. Chuck took a swig from a pint bottle of vodka and lit another cigarette, one of several delicious vices he could fully indulge now that he and Eileen were through. All around him, people stared. Yes, I have been drinking, he thought, and, no, I will not be buying a raffle ticket. He was rehearsing his tirade—lamenting the fact that for all the money he paid in taxes, the ground was too muddy to sit on—when a fat man in a green shirt approached him.

"There's no smoking near the crowd, sir," the man said calmly. Chuck looked around. They were outside. There was a nice breeze coming from the gazebo, where an elderly couple slow-danced in the declining light. Chuck took a long drag and exhaled into the man's face. He felt a little tingle rising up his neck. The man recoiled, then recovered. "Excuse me, sir, would you mind leaving the concert grounds"—he paused—"to smoke."

"As a matter of fact," Chuck said slowly, staring at the man in the green shirt, "I would mind. We're standing in the open air. The last time I checked, the township ordinances *require* me to smoke outside. So how about you leave if it's bothering you." The man in the green shirt disappeared. Chuck was pleased. It had been a stressful week. He'd lost an account to a competitor; he'd ended his marriage; and, only hours ago, he'd picked up pieces of an old Gibson hollow-body from his former front lawn. He continued smoking, and, with each inhalation, the cells in his body rejoiced. Early in every confrontation, his anger energized him.

A minute or two later, the guy in the green shirt returned. This time, he brought the emcee with the ponytail, a walkie-talkie clipped to his belt. "Enter the King of Prussia," Chuck said, bowing. A small crowd gathered now. A second later, a uniformed cop who had been standing off to the side approached and said something about not wanting any trouble.

"Then go hassle the geezers on the fucking gazebo."

"Sir," the emcee said, putting his hands out in front of him, "this is a family concert." He seemed mildly disappointed, as if he were talking to a child. "We don't think it's such a big deal to let the kids breathe clean air."

Around them, people had turned in their lawn chairs. Why were people always invoking the health and moral purity of their kids? "I think it is," Chuck said defiantly. "I pay my taxes. Show me the law I'm violating." The man with the ponytail gave him a doleful look. A boy and a girl in identical green shirts approached them with their buckets, but they were shooed away by the emcee. The speakers played a smarmy melody over a polka beat. "All my life assholes like you have been telling me how to live," Chuck said, much louder now. The emcee's walkie-talkie emitted a frothy static. Chuck reached in his jacket pocket for another cigarette. It was the principle of the thing.

The officer lunged forward, thinking Chuck was going for a weapon. Chuck put his fists out preparing to fight, but two concertgoers dropped their sodas and grabbed him from behind. There was a gasp from the crowd, heaving sounds, and then a brief struggle among four over-weight middle-aged men.

At the same time, a group of teenage girls, barefoot, wearing long skirts and halter tops, their navels pierced with silver studs, gathered around one of their own, who appeared to be in severe pain, her tail of auburn hair in one hand, bent over like she was vomiting, or, at the very least, severely cramping. "Stop it!" she screamed. "Please, Dad, stop it!" Chuck didn't recognize her until well after he'd been carried off by his shoulders, his legs kicking the air. That was it. Thirteen years of parenthood—whatever good he'd done, however loving and generous he'd been—down the toilet over one twenty-minute encounter.

Ivy refused to take his calls. She returned his letters, unopened. It was the event Eileen was waiting for so she could banish him from their lives forever.

With a pop, his throat opened, and he took a gulp of cold air, and then another. Soon, his chest was heaving up and down, and his daughter's house was as distant and unapproachable as the moon above.

PART III

Belize City, 2000

The heavyset man with thick glasses and olive-colored skin made his way through this once-upon-a-shanty-town toward the docks. On his way, he crossed and recrossed the crowded streets, avoiding pushcarts, bicycles, barefoot children, and stray animals looking for food; he paused in the shade of a store awning and again under a scrawny palm tree. In this part of town, the streets are narrow and oriented toward or away from the water. From almost anywhere, you can feel the pull of the river with its marshes and mangroves, mosquito bogs, canoes and log rafts, and you can sense the presence of the ocean, which has pounded this peninsula since before the British came with their quinine and their man-made reefs. Scowling, he removed a misshapen fedora and pressed a stained handkerchief to his face. Although it was only nine thirty in the morning, the rayon shirt he'd bought in one of the shops that cater to the cruise lines was ringed with perspiration. In front of the Bank of Belize, he paused beside a fruit stand, where he bought a container full of papaya slices. He closed his eyes and sucked the pieces down as the sun rose over the squat buildings, juice dripping onto his chest.

A month earlier, the man had gotten off the plane from Havana, walked into the small airport, gathered his beat-up suitcases, and presented himself to Belizean immigration as Alejandro Preston, a businessman from Cuba. He'd written "vacation" as his reason for entering the country and scribbled the words *Hotel Mopan,* just as Jim, the strange man who'd suddenly appeared on his doorstep in South Philly, had instructed him to. Outside, he stood facing an old British airplane mounted on the grass, bag in hand. With his Coke-bottle glasses, his wide girth, and his short stature, he looked like an ugly, overgrown child. A few minutes later, for thirty dollars U.S., he hired a taxi to take him downtown to the part of Belize City where tourists, reaching around their big bellies and into their bulging pockets, wandered among the natives and the young hustlers.

After finishing the papaya, he spit on his hands and rubbed them together. Despite Jim's advice to keep a low profile, the fat man spent two full days interviewing banks and solicitors, inquiring how he might go about cashing a large bundle of securities and bonds. On the morning of the third day, he established a weekday routine from which he had rarely deviated over the past four months.

The first thing he did when he woke was let his hand drop to his side and feel for his money belt underneath the mattress. Once he confirmed the outline of the key that opened the safe deposit box that held his fortune in cash, gold, bearer bonds, and securities, he opened his eyes and looked around. Slivers of light entered the wooden slats and exploded on the floor at the base of his bed. In time, he'd reach for his glasses and look over at the chair propped up against the door, the fresh towels on the rattan chair under the window, and then up at a satellite map of the world he imagined in the imperfections of the stucco ceiling, picturing Belize, his adopted home, a little crook in the elbow of Central America.

After dressing, he descended four flights, grabbed the English-language paper, had coffee and some bread, and then shuffled down to the bank. After conducting his business, he walked to the ocean where the seawater lapped at a concrete retaining wall that rimmed the city, bringing scum and residue from fishing skiffs, cruise lines, and smugglers' boats. "Belize City is a hub of illicit activity," Jim had told him when the fat man said he wanted to disappear to a place where nobody asked questions. "You'll fit right in," Jim assured him. "There's no such thing as a foreigner without a past in Belize."

On the street, the man with the chickens passed on his bicycle. The truck that delivered baked goods arrived at one of the hotels. There was a release of greasy fuel from the one postal service truck that took mail to and from the airport. Behind the window, Beulah Johnson, the smartly dressed officer, stood next to the security guard as he opened the doors to the Bank of Belize, Belize City branch. Slowly, the guard removed the two padlocks, disengaged the electronic alarm, and then unbolted the top and bottom locks. Every day, they opened five minutes late. You could set your watch to it.

The fat man watched from across the street, his bald head up in the air. He might have been hungry again, impatient, weary, or preoccupied with some story in the paper about corruption or electrical blackouts or delays in opening a toll road. According to Lydia O'Rourke, the owner of the Mopan, Belizeans were neither punctual nor competent, which is partially why he liked being the bank's first customer. There was less time for them to fuck up, for things to go wrong, less chance of a long line or frustrating delays. Besides, what else did he have to do? By seven A.M., he'd already spent almost an hour lying on his bed, watching the ceiling fan spin, measuring the time of day against spears of sunlight that jutted through the broken wooden window slats, estimating the number of gulls in the print over his bed—a harbor impossibly crowded with pleasure boats—or counting the clicks of the windup clock he'd bought on his first day in Belize, his own watch, a Timex, having failed somewhere on the long journey—perhaps on the long bus ride to Miami, or when he was lifting his luggage out of the plane to Cancun, or on the bouncing boat ride to Havana, or in the little propeller plane to Belize. In the distance, stray dogs barked, roosters crowed, reggae music blasted, doors slammed shut then open again. He breathed in car fumes, the smell of meat cooking, wood burning. On this particular day, he had with him his alligator-skin suitcase, which appeared to swing easily from his hand.

Since his first night on the run, the fat man had slept fast and deep. There had been no close calls, no regrets, no bad dreams, and no nagging urge to call home. And he had an even higher degree of confidence in his safety, thanks to Jim, an old college acquaintance of his brother's—now estranged—a man so well connected, so familiar seeming, and so knowledgeable about the ways of the world, especially travel, that on the night of the accident, after only a few drinks, the fat man told him not only about his desire to leave Philadelphia, but about the money, too. In less than six hours, Jim had arranged everything—passports, contacts, even flights—asking only 10 percent for his trouble.

The building that housed the bank was old, with stone walls, narrow windows, and wooden floors, as if, over the years, hurricanes and heavy humidity had caused it to swell and then return to its original dimensions so many times that it was now bent and wrinkled like an old person. From across the street, the fat man waited as the guard turned on the lights and a young woman set the numbers in the window that advertised today's exchange rates. He crossed, approaching windows with travel posters advertising the Cayes and the Mayan ruins just as the guard pressed a button that started the fans spinning overhead.

Beulah Johnson had a handsome, well-tended brown face. She wore a gold cross over her blouse and her skin was smooth and uncreased. She asked him the same questions every day, in her British English. "Is the weather agreeing with you, Mr. Preston?" "Have you sampled some of our fine cooking?" Her manner was professional and polite, neither interested in nor bored by his presence or his routine. In her opinion, she was as kind and as pleasant as God intended her to be to a stranger, a fine representative of the Bank of Belize, and a good Christian.

Together Mrs. Johnson and Mr. Preston walked a dozen steps to a wooden card catalogue, withdrew his card, and then filed into a small room. In the center of the room was a table and a little stool. She accepted his key and inserted the one that hung around her neck into the locks. His eyes fluttered. As she opened the little door, he lifted slightly off his heels and moistened his lips. Mrs. Johnson hoisted the safe deposit box onto a small wooden table. The fat man's odor filled the room.

When the banker left, and he was alone with his stink, he spent as much time as necessary to conduct his ritual—to feel the presence of his fortune, to count and calculate, to calibrate and make himself feel secure. Underneath a photocopy of his passport was a stack of papers loosely bound—bearer bonds uncashed, all negotiable. He touched the pile, feeling the raised ink and, underneath that, the starchy surface of hard currency: hundred-dollar bills, both Belizean and U.S. Toward the back was another stack of dollars—U.S. currency, thousand-dollar bills. In total, well over half a million. He peeled off a hundred-dollar bill and slid it into his jacket pocket. He deposited $22 that he hadn't spent yesterday in a cloth bag, then he lifted a tiny ledger from underneath the bills, and scribbled what he'd done, adjusting his balance—plus $22, minus $100. He drew a line underneath and made the calculation: $615,914, including the bearer's bonds and negotiable paper. From that he subtracted 10 percent of the total, the amount he'd agreed to give Jim for arranging his getaway. $61,591. Pursing his lips, he exhaled. It suddenly seemed like a lot for advice.

The fat man sat for a moment, his hat in his hand, his head leaning back against the wall listening to the usual sounds outside—someone tapping a calculator, muffled voices, someone talking into a phone. Now that he was in Belize safely, he could afford to make a counteroffer. What choice would Jim have but to accept less?

If Beulah Johnson was surprised that Mr. Preston, the English-speaking retiree from Cuba, was converting approximately $30,000 in U.S. securities to cash, she didn't show it. Theirs was a relationship of nods and curtsies, of discreet banking gestures that reflected the assumption that at least while Mr. Preston was a customer of the bank, all transactions would be confidential. The fat man handed her his alligator-skin suitcase. It took nearly an hour for the securities to be logged, valued, stacked, and the cash presented. While the tellers worked, the fat man sat on a wicker chair with his hat on his belly and his eyes closed. At one point, Beulah Johnson asked if he would be going away for the holiday.

"I thought that a man in your position, sir, would be spending the holiday out of town." He accepted the suitcase, which was now loaded with mostly small bills. "Friday is Baron Bliss Day," she said, smiling. "Why don't you ride the bus out to San Ignacio. Spend a few days there. I know a couple of people who can take you to church with them."

"Th-Th-Thank you," the fat man said, grimacing. This country has too many fucking holidays, he thought, stepping outside. Handsome black-skinned men and women in dress shirts and tight-fitting slacks and skirts pushed past him, carrying parcels. Laborers in casual clothes lifted boxes into trucks, carried packages into stores, and pressed against each other. His eyes moved from the hand-painted signs that advertised attorneys, customs houses, and insurance companies to the Arab standing outside the electronics store, his arms folded, a brown cigarette burning down, his dark eyes watching traffic. The temperature had risen at least ten degrees. The buildings in this city seemed to lean inward, trapping heat and fumes from cars that made their way, inch by inch, honking steadily. Anywhere there was metal or asphalt was too hot to walk, even at this hour.

Alejandro Preston crossed to the shadier side and waddled up Main Street, past modern buildings and squalid shacks, past jackhammers in buildings that were under construction one day and abandoned the next, only to be swarmed over by work crews the following weekend. This was a city unaccustomed to steady schedules, reliable electricity, and safe travel after dark. A man with an apricot-colored kerchief sitting on the balcony of a partially built apartment building drinking coffee watched impassively. Nobody does an honest day's work around here, he imagined his father saying. He missed the old man.

A young African man without a shirt or shoes started walking beside him. He remembered Jim's advice from when he first got here. Stay home after dark. Stay in a crowd. Don't wander. "Gimme a cigarette, man," the African said. The fat man gripped the suitcase handle tighter. Ever since he'd arrived, he wanted to get himself a gun. The African pressed. "C'mon, man, gimme one, gimme one." He'd asked Jim once he'd settled into his routine, but Jim said a gun was a bad idea. Although the fat man hated being told what to do, he was out of his element here. Besides, everything Jim had told him so far had turned out to be right. Eventually, the African drifted away.

Alejandro Preston took the steps to his hotel slowly. "Why Belize?" he'd asked Jim the morning after the accident. "You wanted a place you can disappear. In Belize, you can drink the water. There's no banking reciprocity. And everybody speaks English." And so far at least, no detectives had tailed him, no bounty hunters or federal agents had shown up at his door. The bus ride to Miami, the flight to Cancun, the cruise ship to Havana, the Cuban passport—Jim knew what he was doing. And for that, he was entitled to a fee. Not the full 10 percent—that was just his asking price—but some amount that two fair-minded people could agree was reasonable.

Alejandro Preston's shoes made a clunky sound on the wooden steps. He removed his hat and wiped his brow. He didn't like being sweaty or winded when Maria, the pretty young desk clerk, presented him with his key.

"Will you be having lunch with us today, Mr. Alex?" Maria asked.

"Yes, me and a guest," he managed to say. "Mr. Jim." He moved his face in close to hers, forcing her to look down.

"You asked me to tell you. The young man who checked in last night, Mr. Alex. He's from Colombia. A student, I think."

He nodded and slid a coin across the counter. "Thank you, my d-d-dear." As she reached for it, he put his hand over hers. She leaned away, but he held it there—her fist trapped like a small bird.

"Thank you, Mr. Alex," she said, tugging slightly.

"Would you like to visit with Javier tonight?" he asked.

Maria nodded. "Thank you, Mr. Alex."

The fat man released her hand and ambled toward the stairwell, climbing slowly, pausing on each landing to catch his breath. In this new place, in this new phase of life, without a television, without his mother to talk to, he was lonely, his contact limited to the people who ran the hotel. He walked the length of his balcony to the very end and leaned over. Here in Belize, detached as he was, he couldn't afford to make mistakes or act out in the ways he had back home. He inserted his room key and let the door open a crack, till it touched the chair. "Arthur Puckman," he said softly, as if looking for his old self.

Safely inside, he leaned back against the door and surveyed his room. When he was satisfied that no one had entered while he was gone, he moved to the edge of the bed and removed his shoes, his jacket, his shirt. He slid the money belt from around his waist and wedged it under the mattress. Although he knew the Bank of Belize would not allow anyone without identification access to his box, he treated the key with great care. Losing or misplacing it would surely result in limited access for some period, which would frustrate and frighten him unnecessarily. He finished undressing and lay down on the bed, this time invoking the image of Maria—her soft lips, her unguarded smile, her desire to please—undressing Javier as he entered the room.

He thought about traveling for the holiday, perhaps to the place Beulah Johnson had suggested, but he would miss his routines and the familiar characters with whom he'd established rapport—Mrs. Johnson at the bank, Maria downstairs, Lydia O'Rourke, the widow who inherited this hotel. He put on a fresh shirt, his second of the day, then lifted the alligator suitcase, hesitated, and opened his door. He pulled the chair to within a few inches of the door, and pulled it shut. On the other hand, it would be a relief to be away from the street urchins, the noise, and the offensive smells.

Jim was waiting for him on the veranda. He wore a wide-brimmed straw hat that cast a shadow over his face, which was covered in a mixture of reddish freckles and gray stubble. His arms were thin, muscular, and dark in contrast with his face. They stuck out of an old American-style T-shirt that had a picture of an R. Crumb character eating an ice-cream cone and the words WHY NOT? underneath. Behind his aviator glasses, Jim's eyes danced from the front desk to the faces at the bar and back to the front desk again. As always, he seemed distracted.

A light-skinned woman was serving beers to a table full of German tourists, all talking at the same time. The fat man motioned to a table nearby and set the alligator-skin suitcase with half of Jim's fee in it between them on the floor. "You want a sandwich?" the fat man asked, sticking his paw into a jar of oyster crackers. Jim ignored the question. He was watching one of the German tourists, playing with a digital video camera.

"I've been thinking," Artie said, taking a sip of water. "Mayb-b-be it's time for me to see a little bit of the country. Not that I mind it here at all," he said, backpedaling. "I think I need a lit-t-tle break." He was careful not to mention San Ignacio.

"You don't need my permission," Jim said. "Is the money all here?"

Arthur Puckman believed that Jim, like all businessmen, was mistrustful, yet there was no way he would open the suitcase here. "Yeah, sure," he said. "Go ahead and count it."

Jim's head was turned so that he was looking over his left shoulder. "There's a guy named Manny," he said. "He and his brother drive a taxi. They can take you wherever you want to go. You can trust them." Artie followed Jim's eyes to the German tourist with the camera.

"How do I find them?" Artie asked.

"Manny fishes off the pier near the InterContinental." Suddenly, Jim grabbed the suitcase and jerked himself up, twisting his body so that his face was turned away from the table of tourists. As he lurched toward the street, he knocked his bar stool, which collided with a table, causing a couple of drinks to topple over and soak an elderly man studying a map. By then, the Germans had assembled on one side of their table, arms around one another, grinning at a man holding a camera. Before Artie realized what had happened, he was caught staring straight ahead into the flash. His first reaction was relief. Jim wouldn't realize that the suitcase was light by thirty grand until he got home and opened it. It didn't occur to him until it was too late that a photograph, even a random snapshot by a tourist, could find its way to the FBI.

After a long nap, Artie stood in the shower for the second time that day, as much to wash away any residual doubts he had about his new plan as to cool himself down. His main concerns about traveling were his money and his safety. He began to catalogue the things he would need in a new home—a well-appointed room, privacy, of course, a clean bathroom, laundry and meal service, and a place from which he could observe people without being conspicuous. Belize City made him nervous. And Jim's reaction to the German tourists reminded him of how careful he needed to be. The fat man straightened his bed. He checked himself in the mirror and then turned to inspect the room. Neat enough for young lovers, he decided. He opened the wooden slats directly across from the bed so that they faced up.

At the front desk, Maria was straightening a shelf full of brochures.

"Tonight," he whispered. "Between seven and seven fifteen." He pointed to his watch.

"Thank you, Mr. Alex," she said, blushing.

Artie had dinner near the bay at a restaurant run by a large, middle-aged woman and her daughter. He sat on the concrete porch that was attached to a cinder block enclosure, which surrounded a barbecue pit. Judging by the number of motorcycles and pickup trucks that pulled up and then sped off, food was only one of many things being sold from the property. The waitress was a heavy, slow-moving girl in her twenties, and she wore dresses and shoes that looked as if someone else even heavier, perhaps her mother, had broken them in. Night after night, she watched Artie lather himself up with mosquito repellent and then wipe his hands with antibacterial cream. After seeing him spill hot sauce on his shirt, she'd taken the liberty of tying a bib around his neck.

"Chicken wing appetizer, and t-t-two plates of fried chicken," Artie said, sitting down. To celebrate his decision to leave Belize City, he had two beers. When he finished, he pushed his rice and vegetables into neat piles for the girl to scrape off and give the dogs.

On his way back to the hotel, Artie bought himself a bottle of schnapps and a cigar. On the front desk was a little folded paper tent that said "Back in ten minutes," which meant Maria was already upstairs. Lydia was watching satellite TV, which meant *she* was into her third or fourth whiskey. Angie, her daughter-in-law, was serving drinks and keeping an eye on reception. If a guest were to show up to check in or ask for their key, Angie would attend to them, the goal being to make sure Lydia didn't know Maria was gone. Artie checked the clock over the front desk.

Javier was a soccer player and could make it up four flights of steps faster than Artie could get out of the way, so he took the steps as quickly as a man his size could, then he tiptoed around to the end of the balcony and around the corner, sidling up to the window with the wooden slats. Quieting his breathing, he pulled in close. He heard a zipper open, a gasp, then Maria making a purring sound. Through the slats, Artie saw Javier on his back, up on his elbows, his head off the edge of the bed while Maria leaned over him, her dark hair spilling over his body. While she ran her hands over his chest, Javier rose and then fell, his torso arching up toward the ceiling and then sinking into the bed. Artie took a swig of schnapps. Javier lifted Maria and turned her over, sliding down and then moistening her between her legs, before climbing on top. Against the back wall, Artie watched their silhouettes become one person, together as in a tango. When at last Javier collapsed, Artie slid to the floor of the balcony with a soft thud. *"Cuál era ése?"* Maria whispered, looking at the wall. A moment later, he heard bedding being pushed aside, whispering voices, and fabric sliding across skin as the two of them dressed and then slipped out the door. When Artie entered his room, he knelt down before the bed as if praying, moving his hand to feel the warmth. In a few moments, he would pour himself a shot of schnapps and light a cigar, but not until the scent and the imprint of their ardor had disappeared.

The next morning at the bank, Artie pulled out of his front pocket several brochures he'd selected from a rack at the hotel—Ambergris Caye, Placencia, Honduras, and Costa Rica—while Mrs. Johnson watched, smiling. Beulah Johnson considered it her civic duty to sell foreigners on the merits and the beauty of Belize. Over the past month, she'd regaled Alejandro Preston with stories of her country's liberation from Britain some thirty years ago, its easy commerce and, unlike Guatemala, its friendly ways. "I want to see Central America before I g-go back to Cuba," he told her before entering the safe-deposit room.

"You really shouldn't leave Belize before seeing the jungle," she said politely.

Actually, San Ignacio sounded perfect to him. It was inland, surrounded by river and jungle, yet far enough from the Guatemalan border that it would be difficult for thieves to cross back and forth. According to the literature, it had a friendly integrated community made up of Africans, Spaniards, Mayans, and whites, including Mennonites, who Mrs. Johnson told him were very good at business. The other day, Beulah Johnson had assured him that San Ignacio had several major international banks, including a branch of the Bank of Belize, to which she would be happy to phone ahead.

After the bank, Artie walked about a half mile to the very edge of the downtown area, past the U.S. embassy, which was surrounded by stone pillars and a row of bougainvilleas that were always in bloom. A half block away, an immaculate gravel path led to the tip of a jetty where the Hotel InterContinental, an extravagant glass-and-stucco mansion, sat gleaming in the sun, and to the right of the hotel was a pocket of surf reserved for gigantic cruise ships, themselves huge floating hotels, which arrived weekly filled with wealthy tourists from Europe, South America, and the United States. Off to the side was a tiny pier that received the smaller boats, and, in front of that, a bench, where Arthur Puckman, aka Alejandro Preston, took a seat and waited.

He watched gulls line up on the pilings and thought about how far he'd come. Since leaving home, he had changed his name and cut his ties. He'd secured his financial future in a way he'd been unable to for the thirty years, pulling himself out from under his father's thumb, and removing from his day-to-day life the extreme irritation of working next to a brother for whom everything—from finding love and friendship to selling elaborate security configurations to pawnbrokers—came easy. For the first time in his life, Arthur Puckman felt accomplished. Proud even. His face—thinner and slightly sunburned and peeling— looked different to him in the mirror. People like Beulah Johnson, Lydia O'Rourke, even the young lady at the barbecue took notice of him now. About himself, he would once have said he'd started believing his own bullshit, which everyone knows leads to preoccupation and dangerous mistakes.

When Jim first showed up at Regina Puckman's in South Philly, less than twenty-four hours after Gutierrez had gone down, he told Artie that many years ago he'd gone to MIT and that he and Chuck had once been close friends. Over the summer between Chuck's freshman and sophomore years, they argued over a woman and had a falling out. Jim said he heard about Gutierrez on the news as he was passing through town and felt the least he could do now was try to help Chuck and his family through the crisis. That was when Artie decided to tell him about the cash; the extravagant run of luck he'd had at the track. Jim told him his theory about capitalist reincarnation: how if you had enough resources, you could break free of entanglements and invent a new self. All you need is money, balls, and a willingness to act in ways nobody expects. Here, now, in Belize, Artie decided it was time for that new person to be born.

Manny brought his little skiff in near the restaurants that were most likely to pay him well for his catch. He tossed a nylon-coated rope onto a small dock and started wiping down his boat when he noticed the fat man waving. Manny was expecting him. The night before, Jim, the American, had told Manny and his brother that a man with a lot of cash would be contacting them about a ride. Jim had also told the brothers that the man with the money was not who he said he was—Alejandro Preston, a vacationing Cuban—but rather a representative of an American company who wanted to bribe local officials to allow extensive deforestation to advance their business interests. Manny carried a bucket with fish and headed toward the bench.

For Manny's brother, Carlos, the appearance of a corrupt American businessman had great potential. In Belize, the Mayans were a laboring class, and busting ass was simply what you did unless you were lucky enough to run a scam, win at gambling, or come across a wealthy benefactor. Although Jim hadn't been specific, the brothers were hoping Alejandro Preston would turn out to be the answer to their prayers.

"Jim said me you c-c-could set me up," Arthur Puckman said cautiously. The boy with the chocolate skin and the flat brown eyes nodded, as if he was either mildly retarded or was just barely able to understand.

"Manny Punta," the boy said, holding out his hand.

"Alejandro Preston," Artie said. "I need a ride to San Ignacio."

"When?" Manny asked.

"As soon as p-p-possible."

Manny smiled, showing a gold tooth. "Me and my brother, Carlos, we drive a lot of people out there. That's where our people are from.

What brings you to Belize?" Manny was shy and a little clumsy. He had buckteeth, which he made no effort to conceal.

"I had some success in b-b-business back home. I figure a man in m-m-my position ought to t-t-travel a little why he's still got his health." The two men started walking. They passed the InterContinental and headed down the road. In front of the American embassy, Artie tilted his fedora. "The road to San Ignacio," Artie said, haltingly, "is it s-s-safe?"

"Yes, sir," Manny told him. "Very safe, Mr. Alex."

By then it was almost noon, time for the shops to close. Mayans, Spaniards, Africans, and gringos scrutinized them. "Do you have a gun?" Artie asked next. Manny Punta took the question in stride. In countries like Honduras, Nicaragua, El Salvador, and Guatemala, police and underworld figures are often interchangeable. They go to school together. They date the same girls. They make money in the same ways. Traveling at night, you could count on being approached by con artists, banditos, and drug dealers.

"My brother does," Manny said. "He knew a driver who was robbed by the Guatemalans." He spit the word. Jim told them Mr. Preston would be cautious. He was carrying securities that needed to be deposited in a local bank. Jim said he represented an international group that had a scheme to break up the deal and save the Belizean rain forests. He promised the brothers a cash reward for getting the fat man there safely.

"I'll pay you a hundred dollars Belize," Artie proposed, sticking his chin out.

Manny kept walking. He hadn't said exactly how much, but Jim was promising the brothers a lot of money.

"Okay, two hundred," Artie said, thinking he needed to improve his offer. "I want to leave tomorrow. Can you pick m-me up in front of the Bank of Belize? Nine thirty?"

"Tomorrow's Baron Bliss Day," Manny said. "Banks are closed."

"Friday then."

"We have a blue van." The men shook hands. On his way back to the hotel, Artie passed the bank where every paper, every coin, every document of value representing his wealth, his security, and his freedom was tucked away. Jim was right. Despite the risks, he was better off keeping his money in a safe deposit box. This way, he could pick up and leave whenever he wanted. And there would be no computer records, no patterns, no Social Security numbers, nothing traceable. Soon, things would be perfect. Even with an occasional trip to Costa Rica for a medical checkup, Artie could live out his remaining days like a king. Unfortunately, though, he would have to carry his fortune with him to San Ignacio, which set him thinking about having a bag he could sling over his shoulder, something he could hold closer to his body than the blue valise he had long ago borrowed from his uncle Joe.

Along Main Street was a luggage shop that catered to wealthy cruise ship clients. It seemed wasteful to spend a lot of money on an item that would sit empty under a bed in San Ignacio, so Artie decided to venture a little bit out of town, hoping to find a bargain—something a native Belizean might buy—inexpensive, even a bit broken in. It was a beautiful day, uncommonly dry and breezy for late spring. He let himself wander, turning when he felt like it, stepping around children, piles of newspapers, trash and discarded containers of food, vacant yards, men playing dominoes on makeshift tables.

Soon, the streets began to turn uphill, and, a few times, he had to pause to catch his breath. He passed a landfill: a heap of stinking food and soiled paper, old discarded items, refrigerators, car parts, clothing and broken furniture, along with garbage in varying degrees of decomposition. He was surprised by how much these people, who had so little, threw away. A red wagon without wheels caught his eye and, beside that, a black object partially hidden by a wooden crate. At first, he thought it might be a dead bird or a garbage bag, but, as he moved closer, he saw a black bag, mud-stained, with two looping handles you could sling over your shoulder. He picked it up. A little scrubbing and it'd be perfect. He pictured himself loading his booty and carrying it into his new bank, then returning home and stepping out on the balcony of his new room overlooking the jungle, away from the scheming money changers and the drifters who set up cardboard houses and butane stoves to heat their meals. He lifted the bag with the very tips of his fingers. It was a miracle to Artie that Belize City hadn't erupted in plague.

The voice came from close behind. Artie reacted as he would have at home, clenching his butt and hunching his shoulders, while straightening in an effort to be on his way. "I'm talking to *you*, mon!" the man said. "Where you going in such a hurry?" Artie turned and saw an African man with dreadlocks tucked into a wool knit cap.

"I'm . . . I'm . . . I'm . . ." Artie stuttered.

The man stopped, his face inches from Artie's. He could hear him breathe. "Cat got yur tongue?" He grabbed the satchel. "What you doing wit an empty bag round yur shoulder?" Artie changed direction, but the man circled around, stepping in front of him again. "You want me to fill it wit ganja?"

"Leave me . . ." Artie said, spraying him with saliva.

"How about ya hire me to be yur guide?" the African said, putting his arm around Artie. "Get you home safe."

The truth was he could have used a guide. The streets up here weren't arranged in any particular order, and Artie had no idea where he was. Fewer people seemed to be walking around than when he had set off. Artie tried to push him away.

"Didn't you hear me?" the man said in Artie's face. Especially under duress, he was hard-pressed to complete a sentence, which further angered his attacker. When Artie began to wail, the African wrapped his arm around Artie's neck and pushed him toward a cement wall that ran alongside the sidewalk. Time slowed. Everything became fuzzy. Artie continued yelling until he felt a knife blade against his neck.

"No more Mr. Nice Guy," the African whispered, his face in close. "Shut up and give me yur money, fat mon. You can find yur own fucking way home." He took Arthur's arm and twisted it behind his back while pressing the blade against his throat. Artie's arm went rigid, then limp. He heard a crunching sound and felt a sharp pain in his shoulder. The part of his brain that controlled his voice, never much of an ally before, shut down completely now. "I . . . I . . . I . . . I . . . I . . . I," he stammered, jerking his other hand toward his pocket.

"Stupid mon," the African hissed.

When Artie awoke, he was on his back and his glasses were off. Intense nausea accompanied pain in his shoulder, his left arm, and his upper body. He was staring at a wind vane in the shape of a chicken that was mounted on a tiny blue house. A teenage girl holding her baby was leaning over him. His face was burning, his upper lip swollen, and his left arm limp by his side. He coughed and winced as he tried to roll over and stand. She leaned over and handed him his glasses. When he finally stood up, she held out a ten-dollar bill the African had dropped.

Arthur Puckman spent the rest of the afternoon in a hammock on the veranda of the Hotel Mopan, while Lydia O'Rourke, who'd fashioned a sling out of mosquito netting, brought him ice wrapped in a towel and codeine pills. He had one stiff drink after another, drifting in and out of consciousness, happy to be the focus of attention, happy to have learned his lesson about how dangerous Belize City could be, happy to be alive and to be receiving Lydia's kindness. At one point, when Lydia asked him what exactly he'd done in Cuba to be able to afford such a lengthy vacation, he babbled incoherently about the manufacturing business he once ran.

Pain woke him before dawn. With his good arm, he reached under the mattress but felt nothing. Then, with considerable effort, he pulled a beaded wire attached to the lamp. The room he was in was very similar to his own, except it was filled with books, wall hangings, and stuffed animals, including a very menacing-looking jaguar. He was wearing his boxers and the same shirt he'd worn the day before. His seersucker suit pants were draped over a chair, the belt still in its loops.

Artie touched his shoulder and winced. He could move his arm along a short arc, but the pain took his breath away. He remembered the mugging, which strengthened his resolve to leave Belize City. He took a codeine pill out of the jar Lydia had left him and swallowed it dry. Outside, a curtain of rain obscured an old car propped up on blocks. He was on the first floor of the hotel, most likely in Lydia's room. It was early in the day, perhaps just after dawn. Soon, the sun would come out and the taxi drivers would get into their cars, the electric wires would start hissing, and the first shift in Belize City—the security guards and hotel employees—would make their way from the hills downtown to work. After that, the money changers with their fanny packs and calculators would head toward the commercial district, passing the fruit stands and the tour guides and the street vendors, all of whom would start trolling for tourists and customers. One more day he had to endure before he would be leaving for good. One more day before he would enter the Bank of Belize with his black satchel, make small talk with Beulah Johnson and the security guard as if this day were like any other, except tomorrow he would take everything—paper, coin, and currency—out of his safety deposit box and carry it out with him.

Artie napped until late Thursday afternoon. He had dinner at the restaurant near the bay but was too distracted to enjoy his meal or the ministrations of his homely waitress. He was down to his last few codeine pills, which he decided to save for the ride. When he returned to the hotel, he got Javier to help him upstairs so he could pack. He loaded his dobb kit with dental floss, toothpaste, hemorrhoid cream, and Band-Aids and packed the blue valise with underwear, socks, shirts, and pants. The two rayon shirts he'd bought in Belize he stuffed in the black satchel, which he brushed off as best he could. Everything else he put in the trash. The night passed slowly. His shoulder hurt, and he was constipated.

In the morning, with some effort, he washed and dressed himself and then went downstairs. Maria had set a tray of muffins and juice against the wall, and Lydia emerged from the kitchen, smelling of cold cream and cigarettes. Artie explained that he intended to do some traveling over the next few weeks. He didn't mention San Ignacio, whether he intended to come back or when. When Lydia protested, he agreed to take along a roll of mosquito netting to use as long as his shoulder hurt him. "Take these, too," she said, handing him another vial of codeine pills. Maria fetched his bags, and the fat man hobbled down the steps. Despite the pain and stiffness in his body, he was feeling hopeful. For having escaped from his old life, for having survived yesterday's attack, for having proven himself braver and more resourceful than his father or Chuck had ever been, he felt large and expansive. This is what it must feel like, he thought, to be proud.

———

At 9:05 A.M., he entered the Bank of Belize and set the blue suitcase with his clothes on the linoleum floor. Pointing to the black satchel over his shoulder, he told Beulah Johnson that he would need some extra time. As they'd done every banking day for the past month, the two of them walked toward the tiny room. On this day, Artie lifted the lid to his safe deposit box before Mrs. Johnson could excuse herself, revealing wads of cash, mostly hundred-dollar bills, both U.S. and Belize, rolls of coins encased in plastic, various bonds and Treasuries paper clipped together in a legal-sized manila folder. It seemed important for him to show her—as a tiny child presents his body's output—to leave her with a visual of his vast wealth, his net worth, naked. Perhaps he wanted her to feel diminished when he emptied the box and terminated their relationship. Once she left, he began lining the bag with the contents of the box—every last stack of bills and securities—which he then covered with the rayon shirts before emerging from the room.

Despite the glimpse he'd offered her, Mrs. Johnson had no interest in what the fat man was doing. She never tried to guess her customers' whims or get involved in their business. She considered it bad taste to concern herself with the fortunes of the bank and inconceivable to imagine that one customer's withdrawal could have an effect on an institution such as hers. What she did notice that day was that Mr. Preston was in so much pain that he had difficulty moving. She offered to help him—an offer he accepted. Her last memory of him was looping the mosquito netting through the straps of the bag, so she could draw it tight against his body.

Manny looked fresh and relaxed behind the wheel of the van. He was wearing hiking shorts, thick wool socks, and a pair of battered old leather boots. On the seat next to him was a grease-stained paper bag and a thermos. Like most other large vehicles in the country, the van was probably bought cheap in the States and driven south from Galveston, through Mexico, into Belize. Artie made several attempts to lift himself up into the passenger seat before the back door slid open and a dark-skinned, stocky young man in his mid-thirties got out to help. "Carlos," the man said, sticking his hand out.

Carlos wore a pair of tan shorts and a white T-shirt with the words MAYAN EXPEDITIONS. He had jet black hair cut short and a careless grin, which could be construed as either glib or friendly. The change in temperature between the bank and outside caused Artie's glasses to fog up, so he didn't notice Carlos's hand. He put the blue valise on the seat beside him. "Why don't we throw this one in the back?" Carlos said, but he was unable to get the fat man to part with the satchel. Cars honked around them. Even before the tourists arrived, the streets of downtown Belize City were nearly impossible to navigate. Carlos finally managed to get Artie in by leaning against his hips and pushing with his shoulders. Old cars powered by rebuilt engines puttered along, their trunk lids tied down with rope. Motor scooters with helmetless riders and kids dragging fruit in wagons passed by them, some hauling large packages, others with headphones. Manny piloted the van forward, inches at a time. Artie jammed his good hand into his jacket pocket and unhinged the bottle, then swallowed a codeine pill.

As an economy, Belize is bush league. The finest luxury hotels have mildew in the lobbies. Mosquitoes swarm the eighteen-hole golf course where the half-dozen Belizean businessmen of any consequence meet to make deals. And the cinder-block fast-food shacks along the Western Highway look more like public restrooms than places you'd want to eat. For the most part, the road to San Ignacio has one purpose: to move Belizeans and Belizean goods back and forth between the ocean and the jungle.

After about an hour on the road they entered the town of Belmopan, a glorified little intersection that became the capital of Belize after Hurricane Hattie leveled most of Belize City in the sixties. It was a hot, humid, inhospitable little crotch of land nestled in the country, a place where, aside from bureaucrats forced to move for their jobs, only insects thrived. Carlos sat on the forward edge of the backseat talking nonstop in a patois that was unintelligible to Artie—a mixture of Spanish, Mayan, and English that blended with engine noise and the Spanish-speaking radio station Manny had tuned in. Thanks to the codeine, Artie was able to relax and ignore his guides, who bantered and laughed, waving and yelling to people who were walking by the side of the road. After a while, he closed his eyes.

Along stretches of unspoiled country, newly erected poles carried electricity into what was once jungle. Occasionally, a truck transporting animals or a school bus or a speedy little car passed them from the other direction, and the sun beat mercilessly on the van. Manny put his boot to the accelerator. They passed large fields with orange and palm trees tended by brown-skinned Mayans and groups of men sitting at tables in the shade playing cards and drinking cola. They passed gas stations, a church, a shack selling used tires with a sign that said MEKANIC and, underneath, WORLDS BEST HOT DOG. Carlos yelled to Artie from the backseat, "Where you from?"

"C-C-Cuba," Artie answered.

"Cuuuuuuuba, huh?" Carlos said, laughing. *"Cómo estas?"*

Artie didn't answer.

"Cómo estas?" Carlos repeated, leaning over the seat. Artie pressed his face against the doorjamb and said nothing. "Manny," Carlos yelled. "Is your friend mute?" Manny kept his eyes on the road. *"Cómo estas?"* Carlos yelled again, this time into Artie's ear, making a megaphone with his hands.

Artie looked at his driver.

"C'mon, Carlos," Manny said. "He stutters. He can't help it. Ain't that right, Mr. Alex?"

A truck barreled by from the opposite direction, and a blast of hot air filled the van. "What are you doing in Belize, Mr. Alex?" Carlos asked. He had a pretty good idea from what Jim had told them, but he thought he would have some fun.

"Vac-cation," Artie said.

"A Cuban who stutters in English!" Carlos said, laughing. "Have you seen the Blue Hole? Have you been to the zoo?"

Artie shook his head no.

"Why don't we take Mr. Alex to the zoo, Manny?" Carlos said, as if he'd suddenly hit on a fantastic idea. "We can show him the baboon sanctuary. I hear they have an ape named Fidel." Manny burst out laughing, blowing bits of saliva into the windshield.

"A-a-actually," Artie said, soaked with sweat now, "I would like to get settled in S-S-S-S-San Ignacio as soon as—"

"Or maybe we should take him for a hike in the jungle," Carlos yelled.

"He wants to get to San Ignacio before the banks close," Manny said.

Artie leaned back and inhaled earth and fertilizer and recent rainfall. It was his experience that the way to survive this kind of taunting was to ignore it. With his right arm, he rolled down his window and pushed his face into the hot breeze, and with his eyes half open, he counted electric poles, and, as he'd hoped, Carlos quit his harangue. A moment later, the van was filled with a smell, sharp and pungent. Artie turned as Carlos handed his brother a spliff, and Manny, with one hand on the wheel, narrowed his eyes and took several long hits.

At the Mopan, Artie had heard about strict new antidrug laws that Belize had passed to qualify for U.S. aid. Artie hugged the satchel tighter. What a disaster it would be if they were pulled over and searched, or if Manny got so high that he drove the van into a ditch. In his worst-case scenarios, he hadn't contemplated getting arrested.

Carlos pointed to a makeshift sign by the side of the road that said BAIT—5 KM, and something else in Spanish. This struck Manny as funny, and the two of them began laughing uncontrollably. The landscape was becoming lush, Eden-like. Manny started whistling—a kind of nursery rhyme that might have been a pop song. The wind created a kind of white noise, and the three of them fell silent until Carlos stuck his hand forward and pointed to something in the distance.

"Roadblock," he said, pointing. "Give me your passport." Carlos touched Artie's left shoulder, which made him wince.

Artie squinted. A teenager in a brown military uniform materialized in front of a Jeep that was blocking both lanes about five hundred feet ahead. As Manny pressed the brake, Artie looked around the cab, frantic. His passport was in his shirt pocket; woven in by mosquito netting Mrs. Johnson had tied around the satchel. "I ca-ca-ca-ca-ca-ca . . ." he sputtered.

"I'm not fucking around now," Carlos hissed, his mouth against Artie's ear. "Give me your fucking passport." From the backseat, he tried reaching into Artie's jacket.

Artie winced. Even if he'd wanted to give Carlos his passport, he couldn't have done so without untying the netting. "I ca-ca-ca-ca-ca . . ."

A uniformed man waved them over. "N-n-n-n-ooooo." Artie was wailing now, a combination of pain and fear. Carlos smacked him across the top of his head, knocking his hat and his glasses to the floor.

"Either shut up and let me get your passport out, or these guys will put us in jail!" Carlos said, dead serious now. The soldier made a gesture indicating the van should stop. Carlos leaned over the front seat holding his machete.

When Artie saw the blade, he started wiggling, like a man in a straightjacket. "Help! Help!" he cried out as they got nearer to the roadblock. "I'm being r-r-robbed!"

"Relax, Mr. Alex," Manny said. "They're looking for illegals. We just have to show ID."

But Artie was inconsolable. "They're going t-to kill me!" he insisted, leaning out the window.

As the van slowed, Carlos brought the blunt end of the machete down hard between Artie's head and his right shoulder so that, instantly, the fat man fell quiet and slumped forward. With the knife edge, Carlos slit the netting and pulled the satchel away from Artie's body, tossing it on the floor. For a second, Carlos fumbled in Artie's jacket for his papers, while Manny waved to the soldier. With his ass in the air, Carlos picked up Artie's fedora and used a towel from the backseat to prop up his head. As Manny brought the van to a stop, Carlos yanked the black bag up over the seat and tossed it behind him.

On the driver's side, Manny showed his ID. *"Cómo estás?"* he said. The guard looked inside. *"Turista,"* Manny said, smiling sheepishly and pointing to Artie. "We were supposed to go to the falls," Carlos added enthusiastically, "but our American friend had too much to drink." Carlos spoke in a jovial tone, one conspirator to another. The guard smiled. He couldn't have been more than eighteen. A truck piled high with fruit pulled up behind them, and the guard waved the blue van through. As they accelerated, Artie's head flopped forward toward the dashboard.

"Did you have to hit him so hard?" Manny said.

Carlos put his fingers to the fat man's neck. "Too much fat," he said, unable to find a pulse. There was a little bit of blood, sticky and warm, and a welt coming up on the back of his neck. "He's alive," Carlos said nervously.

They drove in silence. "Now what?" Manny asked.

A minute later, after unzipping the black satchel, Carlos was squealing like a kid. Mr. Alex, the English-speaking tourist from Cuba, was carrying more cash than the Belizean boys would see in their entire lifetimes.

Along the Western Highway, the Mennonites had cut dirt roads leading into their groves, some of which stretched for miles to the edge of the jungle. "Turn here," Carlos told his brother. From above, you would have seen a tiny blue dot crawling like an ant, followed by a cloud of dust. Manny cut their speed. The trail sloped, the dirt turned to grass, and then mud; Manny put the van in four-wheel drive. Carlos propped Artie up against the passenger door, adjusting the towel between his shoulder and his head. They rode in silence, the brothers lost in their own thoughts: Manny, afraid his brother may have killed a tourist; and Carlos, thinking he might never have to worry about money again.

At the end of the road was a trailhead that the tour guides used for especially adventurous groups who wanted to see Sepulcher Cave. Manny pulled into a clearing and cut the engine. Carlos slid the side door open and carried the black satchel to the trailhead. When he returned, Manny was standing by the passenger door, wringing his hands.

They worked in silence. Artie was so heavy it took the brothers almost ten minutes to drag him to the edge of the jungle. After a little while, the fat man's eyes fluttered, and he started moaning. What may have formed in his brain as expletives came out as a mess of consonants. He came to his senses slowly—first, taking in the trees above; then, focusing on Carlos and Manny standing; finally, seeing the black bag at the base of a tree. A look of horror crossed his face. "Take me to the American embassy!" he demanded.

Carlos laughed. "Mr. Alex wants to defect! He's unhappy with how Castro has treated him."

"I know my r-rights," Artie managed. "Your government would lock you up if they knew—"

"And what would our policemen do if they knew you what you were up to?" Carlos said, grinning.

"This is kidnapping. It's against the l-law!" Artie tried to stand, but he couldn't use his left arm to support his weight. "Thugs!" he spat, lunging for the satchel.

The brothers helped him up. "Aw, Mr. Alex," Manny said. "It's not that bad."

Carlos lifted the satchel. "Come, Mr. Alex. We're gonna take a little hike." Manny led, clearing the trail, whacking at roots and branches with his machete, while Carlos prodded Artie, who limped along, wincing. The flora was dense and the canopy made it feel like dusk, even though it was just after noon. Without his glasses, Artie stumbled forward, barely able to see, swallowing a codeine pill every now and again to dull the pain. When Artie stopped, Carlos crept up behind him and whispered, "The coral snake is brightly colored. He lives in soil, and has short fangs that sink into flesh and just hang there." Fighting fatigue, Artie soldiered on.

After about two hours, the terrain changed, and the long, narrow trunks gave way to saplings, reeds, and rock. The trail, which took more frequent turns, was easier to follow, particularly when the sun broke through. Many times, Artie paused—angry, exhausted, and dizzy—but Carlos kept him moving. During one of those stretches, they came to the crest of a hill and stopped. Off to their left, between two giant rocks, was a drop of about fifteen feet; at the bottom was a pool of water fed from a waterfall. Straight ahead, the canopy seemed to stretch forever. Manny laid the machete on the ground and set his backpack against a tree. Carlos took the canteen from his backpack, took a long swig, and then passed it to his brother.

An hour later, after a steep decline, the three men entered a deeply shaded grove. In the center of the clearing was a fire pit with a few partially burnt logs and a blackened can. About fifty feet away the trees ended and the ground gave way to a ravine. Carlos took the black satchel off his shoulder and spilled the contents on the ground. "Drink," he said to Artie, pointing to a creek. Artie lay down and pressed his face against the black soil, gulping, then splashing water on his neck and head. The sight of his money spread over the ground seemed to unhinge him. Carlos pointed a pistol at the base of a spindly tree. "Sit," he said.

"I'm a reasonable man, Mr. Alex." Carlos began lifting wads of currency from the bag, stacking them one beside another so that they stretched from Artie's knees to Manny's machete, four feet away. "And I'm prepared to make a deal with you. You help us, and we'll help you." Manny was mesmerized by the money. He'd never seen so much of it in one place. Carlos was drawing circles in the dirt. "There are laws against transporting stolen currency—"

"It isn't stolen," Artie said angrily.

Carlos smiled. "Cut the crap, Mr. Alex. We know you're not from Cuba, and we know you're not here on vacation. We're not stupid." He put the pistol under Artie's chin. Then he leaned in close and whispered, "Where's it from, man? Who's going to come looking for it?" Artie turned away.

Carlos spoke next to his brother. "You know what the problem is, Manny?" Carlos said. "Mr. Alex here still thinks of us as a couple of wetbacks for hire." He was staring directly into Artie's face. "Give me the machete," he said, extending his hand. Manny handed his brother the blade. "He needs to think of us now as partners. . . . Tie him up," he said.

Manny took the mosquito netting out of his pack and wrapped it around Artie's torso. With his foot, Carlos moved a stump to within inches of the tree.

"You can have h-half of it," Artie said. "I swear you c-can take half!" Carlos pushed his face up close to Artie's. "I w-won't tell a soul," Artie whimpered.

"That's better," Carlos said, watching Manny make a knot. "That's much better." Artie shook his head from side to side. "Noooooo."

"Besides sharing things," Carlos continued, "partners show their commitment in other ways." He had the same gleam in his eye that Artie recognized from kids on the playground—boys who grew up and got in trouble, who got sent away to reform school and jail, some of whom died violent deaths. Carlos took Artie's hand in his and spread his fingers on the stump. Then he put his hip against Artie's neck to prevent him from moving. A large bird fluttered from a stand of trees nearby and then the jungle grew quiet. There was a brief struggle, and then Artie made an owlish sound as Carlos brought the machete blade down, releasing flesh and bone—everything from the first knuckle of his index finger down. When he came to, his right arm was above his head, tethered to the tree, his fist wrapped in one of his spare shirts. Manny was kneeling beside him with a bottle of water. "Now we are partners, Mr. Alex," Carlos said. Artie looked up at his hand and passed out again.

When he finally woke, it was nighttime, and the sounds in the jungle were louder than city traffic. His entire torso, from his neck down to his belly, was burning and it felt as if his shoulder had slipped out of its socket. His hand was completely numb, except for the stump, which ached as though the finger was still attached and had been stabbed with a hot fork. A rivulet of blood had trickled down his arm and dried, crusty. Carlos was kneeling in front of a small fire that he tended with a stick. A thin streak of blood had sprayed across the securities that were stacked neatly in piles next to the cash. The sound of insects was everywhere. Manny was walking back from the creek.

Quietly, Artie began to sob. "Our f-f-father, who art in heaven . . ." His shirt was soaked with blood.

Carlos walked over to where he sat and cleared his throat. "The money, Mr. Alex. Whose is it?"

If he said nothing, Carlos would probably continue to torture him. If he told the truth—that the money was stolen and that only a paralyzed old man and a guy about to go to prison knew about it—Carlos would likely steal it all. He took a deep breath, fighting off nausea and pain, and said nothing. Above them, the canopy rustled. In the creek, frogs feasted on insects, and lizards the size of small rodents hunted along the banks. Nearby, cats prowled, and monkeys howled in the distance like hyenas. Dark green slowly became red before disappearing into black.

"I have a proposal for you, Mr. Alex." Carlos was speaking slowly now. "You need to listen carefully, because what you say will make a big difference in what happens. Understand?"

Artie nodded.

"We're going to keep the money." He nodded his head slowly. "All of it. There's nothing you can do. Finders keepers. It's the law of the fucking jungle." Artie was crying now. "We're going to use it to buy some land, a goat, some dogs, and maybe a few chickens. What do you think, Manny, will we get chickens?" Carlos paused, curious to see if the fat man had any fight left in him. "We'll move our mother up from Belize City and start a little business. Who knows?" Artie stared blankly at the leaves. "Here comes your part. Are you ready?"

Artie blinked, releasing a little flood of tears.

"If you agree to keep the secret—and that means telling nobody— not the boss of your company or Mr. Jim, even a whore, well, then we'll set you up like a brother with a house, a yard, a cook, even a woman if we can find one ugly enough." Manny, who was standing off to the side, laughed nervously.

"You'll have enough to live on, but you'll live our way, in our village, under our supervision. No communication with the outside." He let the words sink in. "If you can accept this and never speak of what happened here or of the money again, you can walk out in the morning with us. If you can't, or you say you can and then try to contact someone—anyone—we'll arrange an accident much more serious than this." Artie lay on the ground, his body shaking, his eyes open wide. Carlos paused. "The choice is yours."

For a few hours, Artie sat there, lashed to the tree. At one point, while the brothers slept, he started mumbling, then talking. He said he was only a mule carrying money to Belize for his older brother, who'd soon be coming to reclaim it, and that their chances of keeping the money and evading the people his brother would surely hire to find and save him were remote, at best.

At dawn, Carlos untied Artie and helped him up. He walked him to the lip of the ravine and turned him around. The three of them stood still for a long time. After a while, the howler monkeys quieted down, and the sun began to rise, filtering through the jungle canopy. Apparently, having thought the whole thing through to his satisfaction, Carlos lifted the pistol and held it against the back of Artie's head. There was a loud bark, an explosion of sparks, and Arthur Puckman collapsed into a gorge where, over the next few days, his remains were picked clean.

Frederick explained the hack to the newly formed Fenway Park Revolutionary Council, which consisted of Frederick, Chuck Puckman, and Lonnie Clark, a sad-looking photographer Frederick had met in California the summer before. Lonnie dropped out of UC Berkeley to follow a girl back east, but, unfortunately for Lonnie, as soon as they arrived, the girl took off to the cape with her high school boyfriend. Frederick suggested Lonnie crash in Brighton, which he did, decorating the rooms with prints of hippies in Golden Gate Park.

It was about three weeks before the Democratic National Convention and they were meeting behind an abandoned apartment building. "The Sox are playing the Tigers at home a week from Sunday," Frederick said, unloading pots and pans from a duffel bag. "It'll be broadcast nationally." He poured vinegar into a skillet. "You might remember this from grade school," Frederick said. "When you mix acetic acid and sodium bicarbonate, you get carbonic acid and sodium acetate. The acetate's stable. What wakes it up is the carbonic acid decomposing." As he said this, he added a large box of baking soda and several packages of food dye. The mixture gurgled and turned cherry red, then foamed yellow and orange. The three of them leaned over the stinking mess.

Lonnie broke the silence. "Nobody but the guy standing in it would notice this." Chuck tried not to laugh. On some level, he still believed Frederick was kidding. That he was all talk and bluster.

Two days later, in a booth near the back of a coffee shop in Inman Square, Frederick opened his composition book, which he'd filled with formulae and new sketches. Beside him in a shopping bag were chemistry textbooks. "What is there in abundance on a ball field?" Frederick asked.

"Baseballs," Lonnie answered.

Frederick shook his head. "What moves in a predictable path?" A white residue like lime formed around the edges of his mouth. "C'mon, man, think!"

"The ball?" Lonnie said, undaunted.

"Players?" Chuck guessed.

"Right. And what's the most abundant metal in the Earth's crust?" Frederick asked, looking at Chuck.

"Aluminum."

He slapped the table hard. "Bingo. The catalyst and the reaction!" Frederick had his arms behind his head, gloating as if he expected his friends to stand up and applaud. "Lay a little glycerin on top of aluminum and iron oxide, add some potassium permanganate, and, boom, like a fucking volcano."

"How you gonna get it on the field?" Chuck asked.

Frederick smiled. "We don't need a lot. I figure we can bury a couple grams somewhere." He turned his place mat over and sketched a diamond. In between second and third, he drew what looked like a penis with wavy lines inside. "The permanganate goes in a condom filled with water. On game day, I'll put the rubber in a trench and cover it with dirt. The later it gets—the more hits and walks there are, the more the bases load up, the more times teams change field—the more likely somebody'll puncture it with their cleats." He stabbed the paper with his pencil.

Chuck and Lonnie just stared at him, a mixture of skepticism and incomprehension. "The permanganate will leak, causing the iron oxide and aluminum to interact. Let's just hope the cameras are rolling." Frederick clapped his hands and grinned like a kid.

"What if it doesn't work?" Lonnie said.

"I'm not asking you to guess whether it'll work," Frederick hissed. Chuck liked the whole thing better when Frederick pitched it as a hack. From what he knew about thermite reactions, this could be a disaster. "All I need from you is a little help setting it up," Frederick said. "When the opening pitch gets thrown, mine'll be the only ass on the line." They sat there like that for a few seconds, nodding their heads.

"What's the point?" Lonnie said, breaking the silence.

"The point is the banner we're gonna open in center field." Apparently, neither Chuck nor Lonnie responded with the appropriate level of enthusiasm, because Frederick leaned forward and pulled them close. "A war is raging, my friends. Our brothers in Southeast Asia are doing what they can to stay alive." Chuck noticed a little quiver under Frederick's eye. "Lonnie, you're in charge of procurement; Chuck, you're in center field with me. Nobody says a word to anybody about this." Frederick slid the book back in his knapsack. "One more thing," he said, looking at Chuck. "Lorraine knows nothing. You understand?" He slipped out of the booth, past the cashier, and out the front door. On his way out, Chuck picked up the place mat and stuffed it in his pocket.

That week, the Red Sox went on an extended road trip. Frederick traveled, came back, and then went away again. Chuck repaired his relationship with the road manager of the Inter Galactic Messengers by placing a larger-than-average order. That summer, he was moving about twice as much weed as he had during the year. The temperature in Boston took what appeared to be a final leap. Chuck pretty much forgot about the Fenway hack until the Wednesday before game day, when Frederick and Lonnie showed up at his apartment in the middle of the night. Chuck put Creedence on the record player and got the bong gurgling. Underneath his glasses, Frederick's eyes were rimmed in black, as if he hadn't slept in days. He kept touching the corner of his mouth with his tongue, as if confirming the presence of something.

"Lonnie ran into some problems," Frederick said, as if he was talking about a kid who'd pissed himself. He opened his composition book and turned it so Chuck could see. His fingernails were bitten down to the quick, and his cuticles were caked with blood.

$$Mat's \ Needed$$
$$Fe - 50 \ grams$$
$$Al - 15 \ grams$$
$$KMnO_4 - 20 \ grams$$
$$glycerin - 3 \ milliliters$$
$$Rubber - X$$

Frederick explained that, for the past few days, Lonnie sat in a phone booth with the yellow pages and a stack of dimes, calling chemical supply companies, hoping to find one who'd sell to him. "They busted my balls, man," Lonnie said defensively. "Asked me a thousand fucking questions. What company are you from? What's your damn tax number?" He had a droopy, hangdog look to him.

Chuck had a sinking feeling about what was coming next. "This here's the MIT lab," Frederick said, pointing to a blank page. He drew a floor plan that showed aisles, a half dozen lab stations, and the supply closet. On the opposite page, he made a grid that was supposed to look like shelves. "Get yourself in there on Saturday night, put on a lab coat, set up at a table, light a Bunsen burner—do whatever you have to do to look natural. It's usually empty around then; there's no security to speak of. If you see anyone, don't talk or make eye contact, and don't do or say anything memorable or suspicious." Chuck remembered the teaching assistant describing Frederick and his expulsion from MIT.

"When nobody's watching, go over to the supply closet and fill these." Frederick took three metal film canisters out of his pocket and put them on Chuck's bed stand. "Take a bus to the subway and the subway to the bus station." By this time, Frederick was certain he was being followed by the Feds; he was always talking about scrubbing himself—a technique for losing a tail that involved crossing streets for no reason, doubling back, and taking shortcuts. "Lonnie, you be sitting under the Greyhound sign. When Chuck shows up, act like you don't know him. He'll put the knapsack on the chair next to you and leave. Don't look at each other. Don't talk to each other. You got that?"

Chuck nodded. The new plan was for Lonnie and Frederick to hold the banner and for Chuck to come to the park with a pad of paper and a pen and sit behind third base. Frederick wanted Chuck to chronicle the hack from up close, describing the reaction of the players, the umps, the managers, and the fans closest to the field as the ground curdled, smoke rose toward the sky, and the banner in center field unfurled. It was unclear to Chuck whether this was a bone that Frederick was tossing him, or whether he saw it as vital to the hack. Frederick promised he would publish Chuck's account in an underground newspaper called *The Mission,* which got wide readership in radical circles. Chuck lit a cigarette and leaned back in his chair.

He was unhappy with his new role. He preferred the original assignment. It was simple and safe and, because Frederick had asked her to paint the banner, it required him to have contact with Lorraine. Getting the chemicals made Chuck much more of an accomplice, which bothered him. If the hack went sour, he could find himself in big trouble. Worse, Frederick seemed impatient and reckless, and too much seemed to be riding on it now. What had seemed like a funny stunt involving the national pastime and a Boston shrine—Fenway Park—had turned serious. And like many leftists, Frederick seemed desperate, probably because at the beginning of the summer, he had promised a roomful of radical leaders he would draw thousands from his hometown to the Democratic National Convention. By late August, after the threats from Mayor Daley, even diehard radicals were backing out of going to Chicago.

To Chuck, the only good thing about the hack now was that Frederick was putting himself in harm's way. If it failed, he would get knocked down a few pegs, making him slightly more tolerable to be around. And if it failed catastrophically, or even succeeded in a big way, Frederick either would be too hot to hang around town anymore or would get busted, taking him out of Lorraine's and Chuck's lives for a little while and giving them room to have a real relationship. Chuck thought about these things, but said nothing.

By Saturday, the humidity intensified until it began to rain. Chuck felt sluggish, the beginnings of a cold. When the sun went down, he put on a rain slicker with a hood and left his apartment, doing as Frederick suggested, cutting through the back streets of Alston, catching the Green Line to BU and then taking a taxi to MIT. The building that housed the chemistry lab had a huge iron door that led into a cavernous lobby with wide-cut marble steps. Chuck took the stairs slowly, his hood up, his head down, holding the railing. At the top of the third landing, he entered a hallway with high ceilings and classroom doors with opaque glass panels and old-fashioned-looking numbers stenciled on them. He could hear music inside, but the door to the lab was locked. Relieved, he turned and started home.

Halfway down the steps, he hesitated. If the lab was indeed closed, it would appear that Frederick had miscalculated and Chuck would be excused for not accomplishing his mission. On the other hand, if whoever was inside had simply stepped out for a cigarette or a bite to eat and Chuck aborted, he would face Frederick's wrath. Chuck's throat tightened. Near the subway, he stopped and turned back.

This time the door to the lab opened into a room with a long corridor and several workstations separated by metal shelving jammed with textbooks, burners, beakers, and test tubes. Chuck lifted the clipboard off the wall and signed in as "Barry Goldwater." He felt a bead of sweat drip down his back as he removed his slicker and lifted a lab jacket from the laundry basket. The front desk, where a student usually sat, was empty. Chuck walked to the workstation closest to the supply closet, poured some water into a beaker, set the burner on low, and listened.

Beside the radio, there were no other sounds—no voices, no footsteps, no water running, no beakers clinking, no burners blazing. Chuck took the film canisters out of his knapsack and shoved them in the lab jacket. As Frederick had promised, the supply closet was unlocked. Taped to the inside of the door was a grid that mirrored the layout of shelves just as Frederick had drawn in his composition book.

Along each shelf were a dozen glass jars and bottles with chemical designations. A pencil dangled from a string, the idea being you deducted whatever you used so that someone in charge would reorder when necessary. The last date on the sheet was 4/26/68. Frederick was right about this, too—it was not a well-tended system.

Chuck reached for a jar on the top shelf labeled Al. As he did, a spigot opened behind him, and he heard the sound of water in a sink. Holding the canister with one hand, he tapped out the silvery powder. As he returned that jar and reached for the iron oxide, the spigot went off and he heard footsteps. He looked up into the closet and turned his head away, waiting. A woman passed, close enough that he could smell her shampoo. The door to the outside hallway opened and then closed. Quickly, Chuck tapped the jar of iron oxide against the canister, closed it, and then did the same with the permanganate. When he finished, he shut the closet door and hurried back to his workstation. While he busied himself emptying his beaker of boiling water, the door to the lab opened, and the girl returned. Again, he turned away. When she got back to her station, she turned the radio up.

Moving faster now, Chuck dropped his lab coat back in the basket and wrestled into his rain slicker. Outside, a tiny voice inside him said it wasn't too late—he could skip the drop and go drinking or, better yet, hitchhike to Connecticut for a few days. The rain had slowed to a drizzle, but it was colder now because the wind had picked up. He imagined being questioned by the dean of students, trying to come up with a plausible reason for being in the lab over a weekend before school started. That made him think of his father double-talking an army recruiter, sitting out the Korean War so he could chase women and set himself up in business.

Chuck walked the narrow path that ran along the river. His throat wasn't as raw as it had felt earlier, but he was shaking. When he got to the lawn where he'd first met Frederick and Lorraine, he crossed Memorial Drive. On the other side, he knelt, facing the retaining wall, pulled his hood up, and lit a joint.

When Chuck woke on game day, he tried to piece together his actions the night before. After getting high, he stood by the exit ramp of

Memorial Drive and caught a cab, forgetting Frederick's advice to scrub himself. If someone had been following him, they'd have seen a short, nervous-looking kid stagger into the bus terminal and rush toward a young man, who was so happy to see Chuck, he hugged him. From there, he walked thirteen blocks to a bar in Kenmore Square, where he spent several hours trying to convince a couple of locals to attend the Democratic National Convention, as if he, Chuck, and not Frederick, was a bigwig in the radical movement. Once home, as evidenced by the loose foil and the pipe paraphernalia on his bed stand, he'd smoked some of his best black hash before falling into a deep sleep. He swallowed a throat lozenge and lit a cigarette, setting the ashtray on his chest and looking at the clock. It was ten thirty A.M.

By now, Frederick would have buried the powder and the rubber. In a half hour, Lonnie would pick up the banner from Lorraine and head over to Fenway. Chuck's ticket was on a plastic milk crate. The hack was in motion. There was no stopping it. No turning back. What would happen next was out of his control.

Along Commonwealth Avenue, window air conditioners were grinding against the humidity. Heat seemed to sink into the asphalt and then radiate in waves, warping Chuck's view of cars and the apartment houses he passed. Chuck's throat was sore, and he felt put upon once again being Frederick's lackey, having to participate in this radical action so that Frederick could exaggerate his accomplishments as a revolutionary. Most of all, Chuck resented being Lorraine's unofficial lover, her back-door man.

When he got there, she was standing on the porch holding the painted white sheet like a game-show girl modeling a breakfront. She had on a red cotton shirt and a pair of shorts with the letters BC stenciled on the thigh. At the base of the steps, Lonnie was sitting on his bike, smiling. When Frederick commissioned her to create a banner for demonstrations leading up to Chicago, Lorraine and her friend Toby had sewn two sheets together and then painted a huge mountain packed with dirt and dotted with trees, using whatever arts-and-crafts supplies they could find. About two-thirds up, a thin line of cirrus clouds crossed the vista, and, still higher, there was a dark crust that resembled an asshole. At the apex, neon lava spilled out of the crater down the sides in red Day-Glo rivulets. Above that, in black spray-paint smoke, with silver glitter around it, she'd written in block letters the words PEACE ERUPTS NOW! A cluster of neighbors stood admiring it, until she and Toby folded it like a flag and then handed it to Lonnie.

After Lonnie left, Chuck and Lorraine walked down to Harvard Avenue, where they bought an assortment of Popsicles, slushy drinks, mixed nuts, and a quart of orange juice. Because Lorraine knew nothing of the hack, Chuck decided to blow off attending the game. How important was a written account of something the entire country would be watching? On their way back, Chuck stopped at a package store and bought a bottle of tequila. At home, Lorraine set up a fan so it blew on the couch, and Chuck turned on the game.

It was midday and already it was sweltering hot. Lorraine disappeared into the kitchen to get some ice. When she came back, she'd pulled her hair back and slipped off her shorts. Chuck took aluminum foil with a chunk of hash and a few clumps of weed from a bag in his pocket and broke it into pieces on a newspaper. Lorraine spiked their drinks pretty hard, and they got comfortable on the couch. After the announcers called out the Red Sox lineup, a troop of Brownies from Lowell sang the National Anthem. Lorraine reminisced about her time as a Girl Scout, then started in about the people she'd met and the policies she'd written that week. The Red Sox took the field.

"If you could have lived in any time in history," Chuck asked, eager to change the subject, "when would it be?" It was the kind of thing Lorraine liked talking about.

"The Middle Ages," she said without hesitation, "when Frederick and I first met."

He sipped his drink.

"Somewhere in northern Europe," she said next, dead serious. "We had different physical embodiments, of course. I was thin and frail, and he was tall and Nordic-looking. He had the same laugh," she said, as if she were remembering, "and a long red beard." Chuck shifted his attention between Lorraine and the game, quite buzzed now.

"How'd you meet?"

"He was a soldier, and I was a wet nurse tending one of our lord's daughters." She closed her eyes and breathed in, as if recalling the smell. "Thieves threatened our lord's livestock. We were young, maybe fourteen or fifteen, already betrothed to others." Betrothed, Chuck marveled. Who uses a word like that? The Detroit Tigers went three up, three down, into the bottom of the first inning. Once, stranded at the reservoir in a thunderstorm, Lorraine told Chuck that death was merely a transmutation of matter, not the crisis of consciousness people made it out to be. Several times that summer, Lorraine swore she'd lived before, perhaps many times. Chuck imagined Lorraine wrapped in animal pelts, hair unwashed, her face blackened, wearing an expression of wonder.

He wanted to ask her what caused déjà vu, precognitive awareness, memories of things that may not have actually happened, but he knew what she'd say: "Not everything is explainable by science." Besides, it's one thing when someone you love tells you they're in love with somebody else. You might still hold out a sliver of hope that someday something might change. But this cosmic connection asserted in one lifetime and born in the next, what do you do with that? Chuck wanted to tell her that Frederick was no revolutionary, just an ordinary sod, hooked on speed and expelled from college for truancy. Out of the corner of his eye, he watched the Red Sox leave the field, vaguely aware that a hack he was at least peripherally involved in might soon rock Fenway Park.

Someone in one of the bedrooms was playing music, and there was the smell of something cooking in the kitchen. The oscillating fan sliced the air in a slow annoying scrape. On television, an announcer in a blazer faced the camera while little figures in brown uniforms pushed wheelbarrows and dragged rakes along the top of the screen. The station cut to commercials again. A feeling of sadness came over Chuck. That afternoon—the last the two of them would spend together—he had a precognition of his own: No matter what he said or did, no matter how many times they fucked or hung out, Lorraine would always see herself connected to a man she had known for more than seven centuries. In the heat of the early afternoon, perhaps to console himself, he reached over and touched her hand.

She let her head fall in his lap, causing the newspaper and its contents to spill onto the floor. They came together slowly, clumsily—her hands moving to unbuckle his belt, him lifting her T-shirt and, as he did, sliding out of his shorts. Their lovemaking that day was urgent and confused—a tangle of limbs, torsos inverted and intertwined. Lorraine's sexuality—her appetite for pleasure, her interest in the moist and murky intersections of the human body—was such that she was able to focus on a tiny sensation for what seemed like hours. She took him in her mouth and then stopped, blew on his skin, and then took him in again. She let him probe her with his fingers until they were both wet. Chuck's desire spiraled until he felt the entire focus of his being shift from his head to his loins and back again. At the same time, his craving to disappear inside her was so strong it flooded him. With the television droning, Lorraine sitting on the couch, her legs open, Chuck pressed his arms against the sofa cushions and buried his face in her hair while, outside, a motorcycle engine cut out and footsteps sounded on the steps and Frederick Keane, Lorraine's knight in contemporary garb, threw open the screen door and stood, mouth agape, before bursting in.

In a masterstroke of bad timing, Frederick grabbed Chuck's shoulder at the exact moment he climaxed, causing him to freeze with his shoulders hunched, holding his breath. For a few seconds Chuck was unable to locate himself in space or time. When he came to, Lorraine had grabbed her T-shirt and panties and was scrambling toward her bedroom. Frederick tried to lift Chuck so he could knock him down again, but his rage was too much. With his foe cowering, Frederick looked around the room, grabbed the TV, lifted it, and smashed it against the floor. He picked up the coffee table, sending the drinks flying. Roaring, he moved around the walls, punching the photographs Lonnie had put up, leaving a red swirl of blood.

Chuck crawled into a corner of the living room, cutting his hand on a sliver of glass. He covered himself with a pillow while Frederick screamed insults that both paralyzed and astonished the naked man. "You're a coward! An asshole, an idiotic, wannabe radical, following me around all summer hoping something I say will plant itself in your head and wipe that blank expression from your face!" It was as long and personal an attack as Chuck had experienced, except by his father, who used to tear into Artie like this when they were kids. "You're her lapdog, man, wagging your tail every time she walks in the room." Chuck felt tiny and deflated in the same way he imagined his brother had felt all his life.

When Frederick finished with Chuck, he moved to Lorraine's bedroom door. Wood around the hinges splintered. Inside the room, Chuck heard her pushing something, maybe a chest of drawers, across the floor. When it became apparent that Frederick was going to break down the door, Chuck heard the chest move again and the sound of hardware— a lock unlatching. "Pack your things!" Frederick screamed at her. "Now!" The floorboards shook. From her room, there was the sound of a mirror or the glass in a picture frame shattering. As Chuck scrambled into his shorts, Frederick was carrying a half-closed suitcase and dragging Lorraine toward the door.

After having the palm of his hand stitched, Chuck retreated to his apartment, listening to music, siphoning smoky medication from his bong, eating old pizza from the box, and pacing. In one fell swoop, however fraudulent Frederick claimed they'd been, Chuck had lost his lover and his only friend. His days were a blur. A couple times, he wandered up to the house in Brighton. The couch in the living room had been hauled outside and replaced with the one from the porch, and Lorraine's room, including the bed and dresser, had been sublet to a young man. Nobody had seen or heard from Frederick or Lorraine. The last time, on his way home, Chuck nearly collided with Lonnie Clark. "I'm heading back to San Francisco," the photographer said.

"You wanna get a beer?" Chuck said, at once anxious and eager for details of the hack.

"Sure," Lonnie said. It'd been a strange couple days for him, too, and he felt like talking. "The night of the drop, I took the knapsack with the film canisters to that commune in Cambridge. I only saw him for a minute. There must have been a dozen of them laying around, hippies, some of them naked." Lonnie smiled and shook his head. "Frederick was wired, man. We went upstairs, and Frederick filled the rubber with water. The fucking thing turned purple. It looked like a big bruised dick."

Lonnie spent the night before the game in the Back Bay. "After I saw you at Lorraine's, I took the Green Line to Fenway and met Frederick inside the park. He'd gotten us each a ticket, four seats apart, in the first row of the center-field bleachers. He was nervous, man," Lonnie said, grinding out his cigarette. "Like a guy at his wedding."

Lonnie described the infield. "Even though it was hot and hazy that day, the field was crisp—sharp lines, burnt orange and white bases, puffy like pieces of cereal." A man read announcements into a microphone, his words cascading over one another in center field. Frederick held a pair of binoculars in front of his glasses, alternating staring at a patch of infield and scanning the stands behind third. "He dug a trench a few feet off away from second, using his wheelbarrow as a sight block. The whole thing took less than a minute." When they first met up, Frederick told Lonnie he was worried that chemicals had leached off in the film cans or that he'd covered the rubber with too much dirt. "Until the game started, he kept looking for you in his binoculars," Lonnie said. At one thirty-five P.M., about the time that Lorraine and Chuck were drinking tequila sunrises, the umpire yelled "Play ball."

Lonnie switched to the voice of a baseball announcer. "The Tigers and the Red Sox went three up, three down, in the first inning. In the top of the second, there was a single and a walk, but nobody got to second base. The Tigers walked the lead-off man and then retired the sides. In the third inning, it was the Red Sox—three up, three down. Between innings, you could see a little trail of smoke rising from near second base. It might have been Yastrzemski from left field or Petrocelli on his way in; or the rubber swelling from the heat; or maybe a pebble that punctured it. It looked like a campfire somebody'd pissed on."

Lonnie smiled. "A couple of curious Detroit players wandered over to see what had happened. The second-base ump waved to the guy behind the plate, who called over the head groundskeeper. The guys in the outfield tossed a ball around, the pitcher put his jacket on, and the guy in the on-deck circle went back to the dugout." He shook his head. "That was it, man. The crew brought out rakes and hoses, and they smoothed it out with the big brushes. There was no emergency, no announcement, no reaction from the crowd. I don't know what they did on TV, but a radio behind us kept playing commercials. I was waiting for Frederick to drop the banner, but he just held real still, with the binoculars in front of his face."

Lonnie reached into his camera bag and handed Chuck a series of eight-by-tens, beginning with an out-of-focus shot of people in the stands and ending with a groundskeeper dragging a broom across the reddish dirt. "By the time the game started again, Frederick had split. The Sox lost, the hack flopped, and somebody ripped off my bike. On top of that," he said sheepishly, "I left the fucking banner in the stadium." It was a bad day for the Fenway Park Revolutionary Council. What was supposed to have been a brilliant piece of revolutionary theater that would have catapulted Frederick to legendary status in the countercultural revolution was a dud, a nonevent. The hack went slack.

"Have you heard from him?" Chuck asked.

"They're at the Democratic Convention in Chicago," Lonnie said, rolling his eyes. "Me, I'm getting out of here. Back to California." They stepped out into the cool night air and shook hands. "I'll send you a postcard."

Chicago was a disaster. It was all over the news. Twelve thousand cops, five thousand guardsmen, and six thousand army troops with tear-gas grenades, nightsticks, and firearms beat and arrested a couple hundred unarmed longhairs, including Frederick and Lorraine. The Democratic Party rejected the peace platform and nominated Hubert Humphrey, a flap-jawed Minnesotan hand-picked by LBJ.

Maybe it was the cumulative effect of the assassinations—John and Robert Kennedy's, Martin Luther King's, Chaney's, Goodman's, and Schwerner's—the civil rights workers, and black leaders like Malcolm X and Medgar Evers. Maybe it was the bystanders who were beaten or lynched or shot to death for being the wrong color or in the wrong place at the wrong time. Maybe it was the lies and the made-up progress of our military in Southeast Asia. But it was at that moment the political ground of the sixties began a seismic shift. Men who'd secured deferments by staying in graduate school decided to get married. Drifters looked for jobs. Renters bought houses, taking out thirty-year mortgages. Slackers, those who'd been intentionally unemployed—living off the land, turning on, making music, and loving each other freely—quietly started careers or enrolled in graduate schools. Flower children became gardeners and advertising managers; Hell's Angels became felons; pacifists became introverts; and angry young women turned into radical feminists.

People like Frederick moved to communes, became bomb-wielding revolutionaries, or put on suits and ties and became professors or journalists. Few people realized it at the time, but the fall of 1968 pretty much marked the end of the sixties as an ideological era. Before it, people seemed hopeful, radiant, and energized. That summer, everything changed. In place of hope, children of the sixties began feeling dread. It was like the sun disappeared behind a wall of clouds. The Age of Aquarius—the days of free love and flower power that had started with fast food and the handsome president, sleek cars and color television, cures for crippling diseases and the exploration of outer space— morphed into something much darker.

Back in Philly, after an extraordinarily good year in the security guard business, Charlie Puckman Sr. surprised everyone who knew him by hiring his oldest son, Arthur. Just before Labor Day, Chuck reenrolled and settled into a dorm room at MIT—a plain-looking four-story building with mostly seniors. A few nights after he'd settled in, Chuck heard someone tapping on his door in the middle of the night.

Much to his surprise, it was Frederick Keane, looking like a half-tone version of himself. "It's bigger than we are," Frederick said, pushing his way in. "It's bigger than Fenway, bigger than Chicago." He paced the tiny room like a caged animal, walking to the window and back, licking his lips, wiping his nose on a shirt that smelled as if he'd been wearing it for days. The muscles of his jaw moved under his sideburns. "This Sunday's an open house over at the lab." He sounded out of breath. "Here's what I need." He rattled off the same chemicals Chuck had procured before. "Lorraine will come pick them up tomorrow night." He made no mention of what had happened two weeks earlier.

"Lorraine?" Chuck said, his heart racing. "Here?" There would be contact again. Discussion. Rapprochement. They would have a few hours together. Frederick stuck his right hand out, angled up for the freak handshake. It was ice cold.

The next day, Chuck washed the sheets on his twin bed, stuffed the rest of his laundry in a bag, and replaced the harsh white bulb in his study lamp with a red one. Then, just as Frederick had asked, he followed a group of students into the lab and set himself up at a station. When everyone had either gone or gotten involved in experiments, he went over to the supply closet and quickly withdrew the same three containers. Fifty grams my ass, he thought, dropping them in his pack. I'll give him the fucking jars.

After dinner, he rehearsed what he would tell her. "Frederick didn't quit. He was thrown out of MIT for stealing. He's a speed freak. He doesn't care about you or anybody." Chuck passed the early part of the evening smoking little bowls of hash and reading magazines. A dozen times, he made his way down the hall to make sure the elevator was working. At midnight, he opened his door a crack and studied the light pattern that spilled on the floor. A half dozen times, someone other than Lorraine walked in its path.

Chuck woke to the sound of glass breaking and footsteps, heavy and hurried. The dial on his clock showed five o'clock. His door was still open. She was very late. "Chuck," a voice whispered. He strained to see. The door opened slightly. "You got the shit?" It was Frederick. Something had gone wrong again. Chuck reached for the lamp. "Don't touch it." Frederick whispered again. His glasses reflected light from outside.

"Where's Lorraine?" Chuck said. He wanted to say no, he hadn't gotten the chemicals—to tell him that he hadn't even bothered to try—but by then, Frederick had grabbed the knapsack and turned it upside down on his desk. "Where is she?" Chuck said weakly. It came out as a plea.

"I was just playing with you, man." Frederick took the jars from Chuck's knapsack and stuffed them in his. "She told me to tell you she never cared about you," he said, standing over the bed. Then he was gone. Chuck listened to the sound of glass crunching as Frederick made his way down the hall.

———

Three weeks later, in early November, a postcard arrived with an Ansel Adams photograph of the Rocky Mountains, lush in detail at the low elevations, snowy and crisp at the top. It was postmarked Boulder, Colorado. On the back was written "N.Y. Times, Oct. 23, pg. 3." Chuck walked along Memorial Drive, past the bushes where he had first seen Lorraine stretching. That would be Lonnie, he thought, lucky to be away from all this.

In the library, Chuck sat among students and professors reading back issues of foreign newspapers, magazines, and technical journals. He found the October 23 issue of the *Times*. The front page had articles about President Nixon, floods in India, and a giant drug bust on the border of Texas and Mexico. On page 3 was a thin column.

UPI Oneonta, N.Y. An unusual explosion rocked an area in front of a Selective Service Induction Center in upstate New York yesterday, killing a teenage boy and severely burning three others. Witnesses reported seeing a young man carrying a brown box approach the building, which had been picketed several weeks ago by antiwar demonstrators.

Asher Worman, owner of the Five Star Deli, said he heard an explosion before seeing a plume of fire extending several stories into the air. Waves of heat melted parking meters and blew out plate glass in nearby commercial establishments.

"It was like a volcano," Worman said. The boy, who was a tenth-grade student at White Pine High School, had been a part-time deliveryman for the deli for only six days.

While authorities speculate that antiwar demonstrators were behind it, they were baffled by the type of bomb and the severity of the blast. The three survivors suffered severe third-degree burns and are in critical condition at Graduate Mercy Hospital. No other injuries or structural damage was reported.

Suddenly, everything changed. In an instant, Chuck felt less like an MIT student and more like a criminal. Any currency of cool he'd earned hanging around Frederick was gone. It seemed as if his classes were being conducted in a foreign language. Even mathematics was impenetrable. He reviewed his visits to the lab to be sure he hadn't left anything incriminating behind. He considered the possibility that Lonnie, now halfway across the country, might somehow implicate himself and Chuck in the Fenway hack. He was struck by the audacity of Frederick's action. If the law were to catch up with him, Frederick would be fucked. Over the next several days, Chuck's mind scaled a ladder that teetered before collapsing into paranoiac gloom. His instinct was to leave Boston immediately—to disappear—yet to do so would expose him to the draft. He needed cash, and to get cash, he needed to do a big deal.

There was a period of about a week that fall when Chuck Puckman sat in his dorm room, day and night, paralyzed with fear—listening with anticipation for footsteps signaling his imminent arrest or a phone call from the road manager of the Inter Galactic Messengers. The call came first. It turned out that the Messengers were having a little crisis of their own. Chuck's friend Augie explained that the lease on the house in East Windsor would be up soon, and the band was hoping to buy an old Victorian in Hartford, for which they needed a large down payment by Christmas. A shipment of weed was expected from Colombia in a few weeks. In code, the two of them arranged for Chuck to buy ten kilos for a small deposit up front. If he paid for it in full before then, there would be no interest. If he missed the deadline—even by one day—he would owe them double. Chuck made his calculations. If he broke it up into quarters and sold them to distributors, he would have the money by December, which meant he could be in Canada or Key West by Christmas.

Sampling a big buy is an art. You want to taste enough to know you're getting good stuff, without getting wasted. There were three of them in the room, including Augie and Frederick's nemesis, the road manager. Chuck took a pinch from each bag and laid them in little piles on the glass table. For the first hit—the one that dulls the taste buds—he took out a tiny stone pipe, brand new, and pressed a shred of leaf against the screen. Tilting the lighter, he created a second of suction and then took a small furry wisp of smoke into his mouth. Quickly, he blew it out. Twice more he did this from the other bags before indicating his approval. Heads bobbed on shoulders, and there were forced smiles and handshakes. Chuck set his deposit, ten crisp twenty-dollar bills, on the table. Then he opened a canvas suitcase with two leather straps and laid the bags inside. Downstairs, Chuck stopped to say good-bye to a few of the girls he recognized from prior visits. If things went as planned, he would never see them again.

On the ride home, Chuck imagined carrying his suitcase up the staircase to his dorm and double-locking his door. His routine was the same: After stuffing a towel under the door, he would light incense and open the bags one at a time over newspaper, setting the clumps on his laboratory scale and breaking them apart. He was thinking about how to accommodate this quantity quickly when the little car he'd borrowed for the day sputtered and then stalled fifteen miles west of Worcester. For a few minutes, he sat there, his forehead pressed against the steering wheel. How stupid to run out of gas carrying so much dope.

Traffic whizzed by in both directions. To his right, a thick stand of maple trees quivered with the remnants of leaves: red, yellow, orange, and gold. His problem was the smell. If he left the weed in the trunk, a state trooper might stop and inspect the vehicle. If he took the suitcase with him, he would be dependent on somebody cool giving him a ride. He cursed Frederick for having set these events in motion. A mile earlier, maybe more, he'd passed an exit. He decided to stash the suitcase in the woods while he hitchhiked back for gas. It was risky, but there were no other good alternatives.

Forty paces in, he found a maple tree whose trunk split six feet off the ground and buried the bag underneath some leaves. He tried to memorize the spot using a crude form of triangulation. It took less than thirty minutes to hitch a ride to the previous exit. At a Texaco station, he bought a five-gallon container of gas and caught a ride from the owner back to his car. After retrieving the suitcase from the woods, Chuck experienced a moment of relief so strong it resembled euphoria, and after a week of unremitting worry after hearing about Oneonta, that feeling extended for the rest of the ride.

On the outskirts of Boston, he exited the Mass Pike and drove into Cambridge. He found a parking place near an empty lot and walked about seven blocks to his dorm room, carrying the canvas suitcase up the stairs carefully, as if it were a bomb. He turned his room key, opened the door, let the bag gently down onto the floor, shut the door behind him, leaned back, and closed his eyes. Before he opened them, he knew something was wrong. The room was close and fresh with the smell of sweat and cigarettes.

"Hello, Charles," a gravely voice said. "My name's D'Mitri, and this here's Special Agent Russell. We're with the FBI."

Saturday, March 14, 2000

"From the get-go, everybody suspected Weather Underground." While Special Agent John Russell drove, Eric Dodson riffled through a stack of memos, photographs, transcripts, and notations testifying to the absence of Keane. "In the fall of 1968, you had radical factions blowing up statues and sending letters of attribution to the papers—pipe bombs, cluster bombs, antipersonnel, carpet bombs, Vietnam vets fucking around with napalm, frag bombs, phosphorous and defoliants, you had bombs that sucked the air out of buildings, bombs that suffocated people, bombs that simulated earthquakes, bombs that caused buildings to cave in. Still, something about Oneonta was different." At a traffic light, Russell swallowed a pill, his hands shaking.

"Different," Eric Dodson said, nodding. "How?"

"Like a fucking Salvador Dali painting, that's how," Russell answered. "It melted a mailbox. It vaporized a street sign. It liquefied a kid and peeled flesh off a couple bystanders. Guys who'd been working domestic security for years had never seen anything like it."

"Did you see it?"

"Didn't need to. I talked to the bomb squad," Russell said confidently. "Off-the-shelf stuff—iron oxide, permanganate, aluminum."

Russell took a sip of water. "Used in a combination that hadn't been seen before in the radical movement."

"And the target?"

"The Selective Service Building in Oneonta."

"Why the kid?"

"Mistake," Russell said. "We talked to his mother, his teachers, his friends. He was sixteen years old. No political leanings, no friends in the movement, nothing to protest except his curfew. He was in the wrong place at the wrong time."

"And the others?"

"Same deal. A high school teacher, a housewife, and a barber. Three people with nothing in common—no connection to anything—burned over fifty percent of their bodies—hair, skin, cartilage." Russell looked at his watch. In ten minutes, they'd be at the Nadias', in time to see the girl coming in from last night or going out for the day.

"Why was he holding the bomb?"

"Why do you think?"

"You said the kid had already made his deliveries for the day."

Ordinarily, Russell would have shown a young agent some encouragement. Asking questions, thinking out loud, making leaps, testing hypotheses, this was the job of an apprentice in every field, particularly law enforcement. The real trouble was, after thirty years, Russell didn't know. "In a little while, Septa starts running," he said, changing the subject again. We should keep watching her."

"How'd you know it was Keane?" Dodson asked.

John Russell kept his eyes on the road. "The Oneonta police called the crime scene unit, who called the bomb techs, who took one look at the crater in the sidewalk and called the Bureau." There were a half dozen faded Polaroids stapled to a manila backing. In one, a uniformed cop stood beside a gaping hole where sidewalk should have been. In another, onlookers behind yellow tape stared into the void, perhaps imagining the molecules of a teenage boy. "It was big news for a college town," Russell said, heading east on Street Road. "There'd been protests against the Vietnam War, and a few arrests, but no violence. These kids were into drinking beer, watching stock car racing, and riding snowmobiles. Nobody even burned their draft cards."

"It says here that the Volcano Bomber investigation was part of something called Weatherfug out of Chicago." Dodson was looking at a section of the file that detailed the Oneonta bombing incident.

Russell stuck a toothpick in his mouth. "There was the usual jurisdictional bullshit," he said sideways. "The FBI is a paramilitary structure. Back then, there was a special agent in charge of each office, and an assistant and supervisors who directed squads that specialized in three basic areas—violent crime, domestic security, and bank fraud. This was right after the Democratic Convention," Russell said. "Our undercover agents were telling us that the radical groups were in the process of spinning off military units. The police in Oneonta were happy to turn the whole thing over to us."

It was close to six A.M. and the sun had just crested over the horizon. Russell pulled out a pair of silver sunglasses. "The bomb squad isolated two chemicals that combined to produce what's known as a thermite reaction." He looked over at Dodson. "It's unusual. Aluminum extracts oxygen from the iron oxide and forms aluminum oxide, which combines with the iron oxide and releases heat. Lots of it. Enough to weld iron underwater or to fire booster rockets."

"Jesus," Dodson said.

"Our agents interviewed guys at Monsanto, chemistry professors up at the State University, personnel managers at the metals factories, the out-of-state firms that build the big tunnels."

"NASA?" Dodson said.

"Everybody there has clearance," Russell said. "You gotta remember, this is 1968. Radicals didn't work straight jobs."

"So what happened?" Dodson asked, his frustration evident.

"The Bureau pressed its informants, but after the Democratic Convention, most of the heavy hitters were either laying low, at emergency meetings, or locked up awaiting trial. The New York City office thought it was a whacko—some ex-con, or vet—who went over the edge."

"Mind pulling over?" Dodson said, as they approached a 7-Eleven.

Russell turned into the parking lot and let the car idle. "Try to remember this is October 1968," he said, before the young agent could let himself out. "I wasn't much older than you are now." Dodson was holding on to the door handle, his head facing Russell, his body turned away. "Working the Boston office. We got an Airtel from Chicago. They had no leads. So we asked around—students, boyfriends and girlfriends of known radicals, drifters. We got nothing."

"I'll just be a second," Dodson said, opening the car door. He had to piss. A bread truck was parked on the side of the store, and a guy with a kidney belt was unloading plastic crates. Maybe over the summer, Russell would volunteer to help crack cold cases. No way he was going to spend his sunset years delivering pizza or feeding pigeons in Fairmont Park. Dodson came back with a couple of egg sandwiches and two coffees. He set the cardboard tray between the two of them and pulled a wad of napkins out of his shirt pocket.

Russell shook his head. "Coffee on a stakeout?" Dodson ignored him. Russell backed the car up and then pulled into traffic. "I knew this cop who hung around Fenway Park. Big baseball fan. Turns out, there was a Sunday game in August when an area between second and third base started smoking. It was no big deal, but the game was televised and the owner was pissed." Dodson took a bite out of his sandwich. "The head groundskeeper wanted to make it seem like it'd been some kind of accident—a cigarette butt or something smoldering in the dirt—but Mr. Yawkey insisted the cops check it out."

Russell found a parking space at the end of Medley about six houses from the Nadias'. He rolled down his window and tapped the mirror with his index finger so he could see the sidewalk in both directions, angled the car for a quick exit, and turned the ignition off. He blinked several times, as was his habit, until he saw the street with fresh eyes. A slow-moving van threw shopping circulars onto the lawns. A storm door slammed shut. From behind them, a dog started barking and then stopped.

"At this point, the baseball season was just about over," Russell continued. "Most of the grounds crew was gone. The cops talked to a few old-timers, but nobody'd noticed anything suspicious. There was this one guy, though—a wetback. He emptied the wheelbarrows that day. Remembered a metallic smell. I had the Dumpster scraped."

"You gonna eat that?" Dodson interrupted, pointing to the other sandwich.

John Russell squinted at the younger man. "Maybe."

Dodson was bored. So far, with the exception of the story of Stardust's New Year's Eve adventure, everything the old man had told him about the Volcano Bomber was in the file. Dodson was beginning to think that the old man's better days were behind him, and that maybe he was tracking the Nadia girl out of some kind of obsession. As for what happened Friday, the girl had probably skipped work because she could. With her mother's pension in the bank and the prospect of selling the house, why *would* an attractive thirty-year-old woman care about some Joe job? Dodson told his ASAC as much yesterday. "For his tracking skills alone," his boss replied, "you should spend a day or two with John Russell." Still, as far as the young agent was concerned, he was wasting another precious weekend in Philadelphia, one of only a few so far when he'd had a chance to make social connections.

After that, the agents fell silent for a while. Dodson whistled and tapped his fingers against the dashboard; Russell picked his teeth and filed his nails. Just before ten, Dodson stated the obvious. "Keane's been underground for over thirty years now, longer than any other radical fugitive from the sixties."

"You saying you think I fucked up?" Russell said.

"No, yeah, I mean, no." Dodson rolled his eyes. "It's just . . ."

Russell stared at him, smiling.

"I mean, how's he been so . . . elusive?"

Special Agent John Russell put his arm behind his head. "You want to know what makes a good fugitive, don't you?" Russell took a deep breath in and blew out. "Well, that's a damn good question, and I'm going to answer it if you promise not to tell anyone. Okay?" He looked in the rearview mirror and smoothed his hair. "The best fugitives, Agent Dodson, are the ones who master the art of not . . . getting . . . caught."

Dodson flinched. "So how come the guy who's supposed to be such a great agent couldn't find him?" He said it quietly.

"*Becoming* a fugitive isn't that difficult," Russell said quickly. "Anybody smart can find the name of somebody his age who died, write the Bureau of Vital Statistics for a copy of the birth certificate, and get himself a Social Security number, a driver's license, a bullshit job, some credit. It's *staying* a fugitive that's tough—cutting yourself off from your family and friends, building a new life, finding new things to care about, blending in. That's what Fergus Keane has done really well.

"Think about it," Russell said. "The Unabomber writes a letter that his brother recognizes. Serial killers are like addicts. Revolutionaries get impatient. But Keane is an anarchist, and in anarchy, there are no patterns, no precedents. Nothing needs to make sense. You want to know how come I haven't found him, Agent Dodson? I'll tell you. Either Keane's dead, or he's a better fugitive than I am an agent."

They weren't getting anywhere, and they both knew it. The chances of Stardust Nadia walking down the street arm in arm with Fergus Keane this afternoon were so low it was ridiculous. More likely, Dodson was involved in some kind of FBI hazing ritual. The young agent let himself out of the car.

It had started to rain lightly. John Russell took out the racing form. In ninety days, this case and all the bullshit he'd put up with for thirty-two years at the Bureau would be somebody else's problem. Somebody on the street turned their downstairs lights off. Two houses down, shades came up. Russell put on his reading glasses and circled his bets. There was a time, Russell thought, leaning back, a man's car was his castle. A place you could be alone. You could do your job without being interrupted by cell phones. He considered himself a damn good agent. He didn't bellyache in public or write ambiguous reports that covered his own ass, and he could follow a trail, ferreting out the scumbags as well if not better than anybody. His only problem was getting along with people. And in the FBI, if you couldn't develop "assets," you didn't get promoted.

Dodson returned to the car.

"What you learn about surveillance over thirty years," Russell said, calmer now, almost apologetic, "is that for the most part, nothing happens. An agent who's jacked up or haunted by something, or is driven to make the world a better place, lasts about two weeks. Guys looking for quick answers fuck things up. They start trying cases in their heads. They miss subtleties, and they overreact when it's time to move." You kids are academy-trained, but you need time in the field to know your ass from your elbow.

"A good agent sees patterns," Russell said. "Somebody lingers by the mailbox too long or looks at their watch a lot. They start missing work, or coming in late on weeknights." Russell started the car. "Listen," he said. "Nobody's seen Keane in over thirty years. He didn't show up at his mother's funeral. He's never visited his father's grave, his old lady, or his little girl. Whether he's even alive is anybody's guess. Buy me a bourbon, and I'll connect the dots for you as best I can."

They drove slowly toward the boulevard. "Oneonta's a small town," Russell said, more relaxed now. "We interviewed people who were downtown that day. Four blocks from where it blew, a woman saw the boy walk out of an office building, cross the street, and enter an alley. He was wearing a short-sleeve shirt. Shorts. Sandals. There was nothing in his hands—no boxes, no bags, no nothing." Russell switched from the center to the right-hand lane. "Five minutes later, the deli owner saw the kid holding a package—brown, about the size of a shoebox. We don't know if he was taking a shortcut or meeting somebody. All we know is when he crossed the street—boom. A little piece of downtown Oneonta disappeared. The next day, the Selective Service headquarters in Washington, D.C., gets a letter." He pointed to the file on the seat between them. "Peace Erupts Now."

Russell turned right on Broad Street and then made a U-turn, snagging a parking space right in front of the bar. "I was pretty green at the time," Russell continued, "but when I heard this, I remembered something my friend Reilly—the cop in Boston—told me." In the daylight, the Stinger had a kind of southern, downhome diner feel—a blackboard with the names of sandwiches scribbled across it and a bunch of ketchup dispensers on a tray near the waitress station. Inside, Russell continued.

"The day after the incident at Fenway Park, they found a banner: two sheets, sewn together and covered with acrylic paint. It was a volcano, crudely drawn, but recognizable. Underneath was the message 'Peace Erupts Now.' Somebody found it in the centerfield bleachers."

Eric Dodson motioned to the waitress. This, too, all of it, was in the file.

"When we called the Chicago office, the investigation shifted into high gear. Agents started collecting records of one-time purchases of aluminum and iron oxide by private individuals, industrial-welding contractors, even high school and college labs in the preceding months. There were only a dozen weld shops in New England that would have had anything to do with exothermic reactions, and we visited them all, asking about irregularities in workforce, workers who'd quit, customers with seditious tendencies, and chemicals that might have mysteriously disappeared from their inventories. Nobody'd been ripped off. None of them had fired any employees.

"Out of a couple hundred high school and college labs, only about sixty were large enough to have these three chemicals in sufficient quantities, and, of those, only a handful allowed students access. For the most part, students told teachers when they were ready to conduct experiments, and teachers gave them what they needed. Of all the labs I talked to, only a couple thought it possible their labs could've been ripped off. When I asked about radicals, I got nothing, except from this one graduate student at MIT who said he thought it would be worth our while to come over for a visit."

"So he gave you Keane?"

"Not exactly." A waitress approached and asked them what they wanted. "He told us there was a guy who'd left school the year before under questionable circumstances. The graduate student didn't remember the guy's name, but he put us onto an undergrad who'd been asking about him a few months earlier." The waitress brought them drinks. Dodson narrowed his eyes. There was nothing about this in the file.

"What was his name?"

"I don't remember. The Chicago office was under pressure from D.C. Nobody had claimed responsibility for Oneonta, and Hoover was having a fit. My boss—a guy named Lou D'Mitri and I—we decided to pay this kid a visit." Russell took a sip of bourbon and closed his eyes. "We let ourselves into his room, which was a mess—balled-up blanket, stained mattress, standard-issue desk and chair, piles of dirty clothes all over. Under the bed were some porn magazines, a couple of pipes, some rolling papers, and a laboratory scale.

"D'Mitri's's theory was that everybody has a secret—some blemish or indiscretion, an embarrassment. It doesn't have to be illegal. Our job is to guess and then mention it, stand next to it or refer to it obliquely, and then threaten to reveal it. The kid came in a couple hours later, hauling a suitcase. I started questioning him. " 'Did you ever know a guy who went to school here? A big talker, radical, may have stolen shit from the lab?' At first, he said nothing. 'Never heard of the guy.' I kept pressing him, while D'Mitri just stared at the suitcase, which was getting pretty fragrant." Russell smiled. "Some guys'll piss themselves if you get the pressure just right. After a while, the kid couldn't even see straight." Russell started giggling. "It was the three of us in this tiny little room." Russell was talking in falsetto now. "It was shameful!" He put his palms down on the table and let his shoulders heave. He pulled his handkerchief out and put it to his face.

"What happened?"

John Russell wiped the tears from his eyes and emptied his drink. "The kid gave us a physical description: twenty-three or twenty-four years old, about six feet, reddish brown hair, mustache, freckles, glasses. The funny thing is," Russell said, turning serious, "we didn't really need it. We already had a list of Fenway employees we were in the process of crossing with kids that dropped out of MIT.

"The registrar had something like six students named Fred or Frederick enrolled during the four prior academic years. Four were in good standing; and two had graduated. There was nobody named Frederick on the Red Sox payroll, but the guy who fit the description had worked the day of the incident. Fergus was his name. Fergus Keane. The address on his W-2 was a house in Worcester.

"We went out there one day, D'Mitri and me. In those days, we wore the dark suits and dress shoes. When his mother came to the door, she thought we were undertakers. Mom said she hadn't seen her boy in months. We tested the chemicals we found in barrels in the backyard, but they turned out to be motor oil and transmission fluid. A couple of us watched the house for a few days and talked to the neighbors. Fergus was a smart kid who didn't have much of a childhood. His dad ran booze down from Canada—part of Joseph Kennedy's operation. The old man became pretty fond of the stuff himself. One night, Fergus came home and heard his mother wailing. Turns out mom and dad were going at it pretty good. Rough sex or something. I don't know. Whatever it was he saw, Fergus took off."

"Within a week, the U.S. attorney issued a warrant for Keane's arrest. Keane's high school picture was copied, distributed, and posted in police stations, FBI branches, and U.S. Post Offices from Boston to L.A. By late November, he was on the most-wanted list, which is when I heard from the MIT kid again. He said he'd seen Keane in Harvard Yard with some people who were selling copies of *The Mission,* an underground magazine with anarchistic leanings published by a commune in North Cambridge. He had the feeling Keane and his girl were crashing there.

"We knew about the Highest Choice, a commune where drug addicts, drifters, and dropouts loyal to a self-styled guru Leland Medvec lived. The place had marathon acid parties, group sex, and long rap sessions where people sat in a circle, picking away at each other's faults until Medvec interceded, usually by making a speech and then suggesting that to demonstrate their liberation, somebody's girlfriend come upstairs and fuck him.

"We had an informant at the time—a nursing student named Anna—with long brown hair and granny glasses." Russell's eyes sparkled. He was in his element now. "We had her warm up to a couple of the guys out there, and she wound up getting pretty close to Medvec. When she found out they were expecting Keane and his old lady to show up soon, we started watching the place.

"It was a Monday night—late November 1968. Anna called just before midnight. She said Keane and his girl had just gotten back from a road trip and they were really wired. Somebody gave them a couple of reds, and Anna guessed they'd be asleep within the hour. We told her to clear out. When she left the house, Keane was babbling like a baby. One hour before dawn, we had sodium lights up, agents all over the place, and both ends of the street sealed off. It would've been suicide for them to fight."

Russell took a sip of his drink and grimaced. "When we got inside, the house was a shithole. We searched it for four hours, looking in closets, crawl spaces, tunnels, and trapdoors. There was all kinds of drug paraphernalia, pornography, and seditious materials, but no weapons and no explosives. We rounded up sixteen people that morning, including Lorraine Nadia, Keane's girlfriend. But Keane was gone."

Eric Dodson considered the possibilities. "Scribbled on meth, somebody can stay awake seventy-two, ninety-six hours straight. It sucks the nutrients out at a metabolically accelerated rate," he said.

"What are you talking about?" Russell asked.

"I'm just saying, some people think they're invincible; others get paranoid. If you're a fugitive, paranoia can work for you."

Russell leaned back against the booth and closed his eyes. "Medvec found a liberal lawyer from Harvard to defend them. Lorraine claimed she knew nothing about Fenway or Oneonta. We wanted to hold her, but she was pregnant. Eventually, Medvec's lawyer got the prosecutor to back off."

"That's it?" Dodson said. "That's the closest we've come in thirty years?"

Russell was exhausted. Between the radiation treatments and work, he didn't have the stamina he used to have. "A couple weeks later we found an old school bus with stripper from a hair dye kit and some cigarette butts with Keane's prints on them. In the spring, police picked up a guy in New Orleans who said he'd met Keane washing dishes, but by the time we showed up, he was gone." Russell's face was sagging. "Since then, we've watched his kin; we've tried to send messages to him through other radicals; we've even tried baiting him over the Internet, but the trail went cold."

"Ever doubt he did it?" Dodson asked quietly. If there was going to be a moment when John Russell let his guard down, this was it.

Russell shook his head, and reached into his shirt pocket. "Nah," he said softly. "A few days after Keane disappeared, somebody sent me this." Carefully, Russell unfolded a withered piece of paper, folded over many times. It was a place mat—the one from the diner—with Frederick's scribblings.

Dodson put some money down on the table and followed the older agent outside. Russell took a seat behind the wheel and rolled down his window. As he did, his eyelids fluttered, and he took air in through his nose. It was late afternoon, dusk. A streetlight spilled through the windshield, casting a shadow over his face. "I've had my successes, Agent Dodson," Russell said. "A couple citations, a promotion or two. You could say I've had a pretty good run." Russell's shoulders slumped against the upholstery. There was a long silence. "Why don't you watch the house yourself tomorrow? Can call me if you need to."

Eric Dodson laid his jacket on a table in the foyer and opened the refrigerator. He took out a stack of deli meats, cheese, and three different kinds of mustards and set them on a large serving plate—the only dish he owned. With a bread knife, he slathered mustard on the meat and wrapped it in a piece of cheese. Still standing, he opened the Keane file to a page he'd marked and began reading.

In 1971, a farmer in Indiana hired a kid from the east who took off with a hundred bucks in cash, his 1963 red Rambler, and his eldest daughter. There was a photograph of the guy bending over—long, reddish brown hair, glasses, handlebar mustache, his face partially visible. It may or may not have been Keane. The car showed up clean of prints in Denver.

In the mid-seventies, there were Keane sightings at truck stops, state parks, and in small towns from Northern California to Maine. People said they'd seen him doing everything from splitting wood outside a ranger station to counting change in a tollbooth, which of course no fugitive would do. In early 1980, the U.S. prosecutor in Rochester charged Fergus Keane with the Oneonta bombing.

Dodson made himself another lunch meat roll and riffled through the rest of the file. In thirty years, there'd been nine case agents, two reenactments of the Oneonta bombing on *America's Most Wanted,* dozens of bulletins dispatching cops and marshals to remote locations where special agents had received tips or hunches that Keane was about to come forward for an event; everything from Frederick's mother's funeral to the big moments in Lorraine Nadia's daughter's life. Every once in a while, a U.S. attorney somewhere would hear from some lawyer asking what would happen if his client, a radical from the sixties, surrendered, but it was never Keane, or, if it was, he never materialized. Dodson put a piece of Lebanon bologna and a chunk of Italian table cheese in his mouth.

By the time Russell got home, it was raining hard. His throat felt like someone lit a wad of paper and shoved it in there, and his head hurt. Over the course of a career, a law enforcement officer becomes identified with a case by the amount of time he puts into it, the progress he makes, how badly he screws it up, or, in some cases, the notoriety it gets. Some agents develop specialized knowledge or skills—the former art student who breaks up a counterfeiting ring, the Italian kid who goes undercover in the Mob, the former CPA who traps an embezzler.

The Volcano Bomber was John Russell's baby. It spanned his career. It facilitated his learning things that became his specialty—explosives, sixties' radicalism, and fugitive behavior. Unfortunately, with the exception of his linking the Fenway prank and the Oneonta explosions by the ingredients of the bomb—no small accomplishment—Russell had little else to show for himself as he neared retirement. Maybe it was the same for men in corporations, he thought, putting a lozenge in his mouth. All these years, he'd kept his nose clean. There may not have been many promotions, but there weren't any scandals either, something pretty rare in this day and age. He poured himself another bourbon and turned the radio on low.

Summer 1974

It was slow at the bank, which meant Lorraine Nadia was contacting delinquent safe deposit box holders, a task she despised, when a coworker slid a postcard across her desk. On one side was a picture of Niagara Falls. On the other, a long-distance phone number and 8PM written in block letters. The man who answered had a high-pitched voice and talked like a sports announcer. He told Lorraine that a certain individual would like to see her and gave her directions to a turnoff near the Scranton exit of the Pennsylvania Turnpike.

Lorraine left work early on Friday, stopped home, threw some clothes and toiletries in one bag—toys and coloring books into another—and picked her daughter up from day care. To be sure she wasn't being followed, she took a circuitous route north—309 North to the Northeast Extension to Route 6 East to a turnoff near Steene, where she pulled over, rolled down the windows, and let the smell of hay and horseshit soak into her clothes. About an hour after sunset, a woman with long black hair in a pickup truck pulled alongside her and waved, indicating Lorraine should follow. Ten minutes later, the pickup turned onto a dirt road.

After the raid on the Highest Choice Commune, Frederick disappeared. It had been the plan all along. He would hitchhike to the cape or take a bus to Ann Arbor or Providence—it didn't matter—as long as he avoided his old haunts and didn't contact anybody from his past for a while. Lorraine would return to Philadelphia. She had expected this even before the incident in Oneonta. Remembering this, she shuddered.

The truck stopped, and an Asian woman got out, thin and attractive, with a deep summer tan. "Joan," she said, sticking her hand out. "Keep your hands where they can see them and answer their questions, however ridiculous. These people have no sense of humor." Lorraine hooked the bag with their clothes around her shoulder and lifted her daughter, who was asleep. The white clapboard house was dark, almost deserted-looking, except for a dim light on the first-floor porch.

"Nobody said there'd be a fucking kid," a man said, shining a light in her face. Behind him, a group of people began a discussion about whether Lorraine should be allowed in the house with a child. It was typical communal bullshit, Lorraine thought—uptight utopians having an argument that could last all night long.

"I don't see a problem," somebody said. He sounded nasal, like the man she'd talked to on the phone. "You guys want to raise the next generation right, don't you?"

Lorraine listened to the crickets and slowed her breathing to match the girls. She'd expected something like this, and she wasn't worried. If necessary, she and her daughter would get a motel room in Scranton and wait for Frederick to contact them. The one the others called Alan stepped forward. He was short and twitchy, with a mustache and aviator glasses. He had a flashlight in one hand and a large silver pistol in the other.

"She's just a child," Lorraine said quietly.

Alan eyed Lorraine up and down, closer than was comfortable. "She's already seen too much," he answered.

A woman with a rifle came up behind him and whispered something. Alan continued staring at Lorraine as if he was trying to make a decision. "Take them upstairs, Pearl," he said, finally.

The house looked as if it had been empty for a long time. There was no TV, no stereo, no books on shelves, no lamps, no carpet, no wall hangings. What looked like old newspapers and empty food wrappers were scattered across the floor, and a stuffed chair and two couches were pushed against the windows. Beside the steps were several boxes filled with bullets and an array of pistols; there were automatic weapons leaning against the banister. Lorraine noticed a faint odor of mildew, rotting particleboard, and body odor.

The girl they called Pearl was wearing a curly red wig that looked like a shag rug and a man's dress shirt. Under her dark eyes were two groupings of perfectly round red freckles that could've been painted on. Her arms were rail thin, but muscular. Although she appeared to be five or six months pregnant, she had a starved look about her, and she reminded Lorraine of a cat trapped in a tree. Pearl led them to a bedroom that was empty except for an old mattress that had been pushed up against the wall, then stood in the doorway and watched as Lorraine took the girl's shoes off and started preparing her for bed.

Lorraine must have fallen asleep herself, because the next thing she knew, Pearl had disappeared and Lorraine could hear grunting and shuffling from downstairs. She tiptoed to the top of the landing. "Who'll drive her?" a woman said angrily. "As soon as possible," Alan said. Somebody said something about finishing a book. "We need to deliver it to someone we trust." It sounded like the woman who'd been holding the rifle. Then, out of nowhere, someone started upstairs.

Lorraine dropped to her butt and slid along the wall like a crab, hoping the floor joists would absorb her weight. Quickly, she turned the corner of the bedroom and slid onto the mattress beside her daughter, who exhaled sleepily. A second later, she saw Pearl standing in the doorway, her wig off, her brown hair tied back, wearing a T-shirt and no longer pregnant. She had thin, birdlike features and pale skin, and she looked familiar. Hollow eyes, a gash of a mouth, pencil-thin eyebrows— it was a face Lorraine had seen thousands of times—in newspapers, on magazine covers, and in television specials. Pearl, aka Patty Hearst, the FBI's most-wanted radical, was here in Pennsylvania with the remaining members of the Symbionese Liberation Army.

Patty tossed her a blanket. "It's for the girl," she said.

———

The next morning, Lorraine was awakened by the sound of a truck and a guy yelling "Northeast Propane." She scrambled to a window in the front of the house. The driver looked to be in his thirties, short brown hair, flannel hunting shirt, beer belly.

"What do you want?" Alan said from downstairs.

The man squinted. "I delivered to you guys earlier this summer." Lorraine heard footsteps.

"I don't care what you did when. Get back in the truck."

The driver smiled, uncertain whether he was being teased.

"Be cool, Alan," someone said. Lorraine heard someone giggle and then metal clicking and sliding.

"It gets pretty cold up here some winters," he said warily.

"Fuck off, man," Alan said.

"Whatever you say, boss." The driver put his hands out in front of him and started climbing back in his cab.

Lorraine woke her daughter and carried her downstairs. Out back, behind the house, a pond with lily pads glistened in the slanted morning sun, and behind that, a large white windmill spun lazily in the breeze. The three Symbionese Liberation Army soldiers carried their weapons through the kitchen. With the others watching from inside, Alan led his comrades in push-ups, jumping jacks, and sprints, and then Patty set up beer cans for target practice. The man Lorraine had talked to on the phone, Jack, walked into the kitchen, his hair sprouting in all directions. He took a large cardboard box out of the refrigerator and lifted a stiff slice of pizza. "They don't eat pizza, you know," he said. "Too bourgeois." Behind him, a tall woman named Mikki said something about going into town to get groceries. Lorraine asked Jack when he thought Frederick would arrive. "You mean Jim, sweetie," he said, correcting her. "This is the underground. The trains don't run on schedules, and we don't use people's real names." He had a nervous tic that made him look like he was flinching for no reason.

When they finished training, Alan announced that Joan, Jack, Judy, and Mikki would accompany him downtown to get hardware and supplies while Patty, Lorraine, and the girl stayed behind. "Gimme your keys," Alan said to Lorraine. "You can wander the grounds. Just don't talk to anybody." And for the next few hours, the three of them played tag on the trails, picked blueberries, threw pebbles at the windmill, and skinny-dipped in the pond. When the rest of them returned, they all had lunch and, after that, relaxed while Alan and Judy interviewed Patty out on the porch.

The book they were working on was to be a compendium of SLA military history and a political manifesto, loosely modeled after *Prairie Fire,* the Weather Underground's primer, except it would include reflections by the now-famous urban guerrillas. "They just want a recording so they don't get nailed for kidnapping her," Joan whispered to Lorraine. "Even though they write out the answers in advance, Pearl wanders. When she drifts from the party line, they turn off the tape machine. They've wasted dozens of hours, and they still haven't gotten what they want."

Over the next couple hours, Lorraine listened as Patty Hearst, media heiress, described her transformation into Tania, urban guerrilla. By her account, Cinque, the leader of the SLA, simply let her true personality appear the way a photograph develops in the darkroom. Patty made it sound as though Tania was her real identity and Patty was a rich, naïve, selfish little girl who'd been brainwashed by her upbringing.

"How do you feel about your parents?" Judy asked.

"They have no regard for me, and I have none for them," Patty said in monotone. "There is no doubt in my mind that if the Feds were lucky enough to find me, I would get it," she said softly. "They have no intention of letting me live."

For Lorraine, who sat braiding her daughter's hair in the other room, it was like watching a sci-fi movie where enemy combatants infiltrate someone's mind, forcing her words, her body, her entire being, to take up arms against friends and family. If Stardust hadn't become restless, Lorraine would've sat there and listened to America's most-wanted fugitive ramble all day.

While Alan, Judy, and Patty talked on the porch, Lorraine led her little girl out the back door and around front toward the Duster. She was thinking how odd it was that people still talked this way—railing against their parents and the Establishment—and about how she, too, was once preoccupied in this way. She remembered Frederick on their last night together in Cambridge. It'd been days since he'd had a good night's sleep, and he was talking in circles. Haunted by Oneonta and his ineffectiveness in the movement, Frederick had been visited with ulcers and agonizing toothaches, in addition to chronic back pain, insomnia, and impotence that had hobbled him for years. What ailed him may have saved him, she thought. If he hadn't been addicted to crystal meth, he might've been in the house when the Feds came. Lorraine lifted the bag of toys from the backseat and led her daughter to the porch.

As she mounted the steps, Judy crouched down and Patty rolled over onto her stomach, their nostrils flaring and their eyes glowing, peering down the barrels of their guns. "Drop it!" Alan screamed, pressing his pistol against Stardust's forehead. Stardust held still, holding her breath, her eyes wide open, her mouth a perfect O. Nobody breathed. Before anyone could move again, Judy grabbed the bag from Lorraine and turned it upside down, spilling crayons, coloring books, and magazines with word games onto the rickety floorboards.

"You should be more careful," Judy said, exhaling.

Lorraine and Stardust spent the rest of the afternoon upstairs reading, coloring, and trying to restore their breathing to normal. As the sun set, the soldiers drilled and then ate dinner downstairs. The atmosphere was even edgier than it had been earlier in the day. Just after eight o'clock, Judy heard a car wheezing in the distance. Wariness had turned to weariness, and with a mixture of embarrassment and tension, the others watched Alan extinguish the single bulb on the porch, while Patty and Judy loaded their weapons and took their positions.

Lorraine crouched behind a window upstairs, watching as a pair of headlights crept slowly toward the house. When it was about a hundred feet away, the lights went off, and they heard the door open and close. Lorraine held her breath. After what felt like forever, a man's voice, low and relaxed, called out, "Anybody home?"

From inside, a flashlight panned the yard, highlighting a lean figure with his arm shielding his eyes. There must have been some discussion, because a few seconds later, Jack was dispatched to greet him. "Jimbo, it's me, Jack." The two men embraced, slapping each other vigorously.

Lorraine hurried down the steps as Alan, Judy, and Pearl put their weapons down.

The first thing Frederick said, dropping his duffel by the front door, was, "Who did the decorating here?" His New England accent had faded and he was wearing jeans, cowboy boots, and squarish tinted glasses. His upper lip, which had always been covered in a mustache, looked puffy without one, and his hair was shorter than Lorraine had ever seen it, except when he'd been swimming or had just gotten out of the shower. He was lean and sinewy, and his hands were coarse and tan. Gone was the smirk. Handsome and settled even, in a plain-looking midwestern prairie kind of way, Frederick looked smaller than Lorraine remembered him. Mikki, Jack's wife, stepped forward and gave him a hug.

"Here's the deal," Alan announced so that everyone could hear him. "Judy and I will be making our own travel arrangements. You're responsible for Pearl—"

"Hold on a minute," Frederick interrupted, speaking to Jack. "The car ain't much, but it's mine for the next two weeks. The registration's clean, and I took the backseats out, which is where she'll ride, *if* she rides with me." Then he turned to Alan. "We leave when I say we leave. We travel a route I decide. Two weeks, give or take, and I'll deliver her to the Bay Area, to a spot of my choosing. After that, I'm gone. You dig?"

"Fuck that. You're here as my guest," Alan said, all eyes on him now. "You go when I say you go." Although he was several inches shorter than Frederick, he stuck his chin in Frederick's chest.

"Let's be very clear about this," Frederick said. He was grinning, and his eyes seemed lit from behind. "I'm here because I volunteered to drive the girl home. I'm not interested in you, your plans, or your cause, which, as far as I can see, isn't really a cause at all."

"Our comrades didn't go down in a hail of fire to have their names dragged—"

"All you jerk offs did was shoot a school superintendent and rob a couple of banks."

"Death to the Fascist Insect That Prays on the People!" Alan stiffened in salute.

Jack held up his hand. "Wait a minute, guys. We're all on the same side here. . . ."

At this point, Judy, who'd been watching them closely, spoke. "It's okay, man," she said, touching Alan's arm. "Jim doesn't have to agree with our positions to drive Pearl home." Neither Judy nor Joan could take her eyes off Frederick. It was as if they hadn't seen a man in months. Patty was watching Stardust, who was on the landing in front of her mother, rubbing her eyes.

"Okay if I put the girl to bed?" Patty asked Lorraine, who nodded. Alan made a dismissive gesture.

"I'm ready for some rest, too," Frederick said. Judy and Joan both stepped forward, but Joan got there first. Frederick hoisted his duffel. "I'll see y'all later," he said, nodding to Jack.

Lorraine needed some air. With Alan's permission, she let herself out the front door and circled the house, looking up at the moon, the peeling paint, the bare bulbs that hung in the second-floor hallway. The smell of pine trees and the sounds of night reminded her of summers in Boston. After almost seven years, Lorraine knew that if Frederick were ever to contact her again, it would be like this—hastily arranged, edgy, and remote—way outside her comfort zone. When she thought about him now, it wasn't all charged conversations and the courage of your convictions. Lorraine's love for Frederick had been desperate and ground-less, fierce in the way you could be loyal to a concept. Imagining herself with him now brought on a feeling of weariness, of perpetual tran-sience, of never having or wanting things beyond what she could earn in a week or carry on her back—the kind of life that was wholly unsuit-able for a child.

After a few minutes, she let herself back in the house and quietly climbed the steps, pausing outside the bedroom when she heard her daughter say, "Make something up."

"Okay," Patty said. Lorraine slipped into the bedroom, where Patty and her daughter were lying side by side. "But you have to promise not to tell anyone, especially Teko and Yolanda, the people with the guns." Lorraine took a crayon and opened one of Stardust's coloring books. As Patty spoke, Lorraine transcribed.

"Once upon a time, a long, long time ago, many years before you were born, a man traveled across the kingdom and discovered gold. He traded gold for other riches, and soon he became the most powerful man in the land."

"Like a king?"

"Yes," Patty said, "like a king. Then the man found a pretty wife, who dreamed of having a son richer and more powerful than anybody in the world. And when their little boy was born, the mother taught him the ways of the world and filled his mind with stories about faraway lands and beautiful treasures. The boy was young and curious and brave and adventurous."

"Not like the man downstairs?" Stardust said.

"Not like him at all," Patty said. Except for the setting, she might have been a babysitter reading to a child. "Before long, the boy was old enough to leave his parents' house and go to college. When he came back, he found a young princess to marry."

"How do you get to be a princess?"

"I don't know," Patty said, pausing, "but they had five little boys, one after another. Can you imagine that?"

"I hate boys," Stardust said.

There was a long silence, as if Patty was considering Stardust's position seriously. "What the young man wanted most was attention, and so, with his father's help, he started a newspaper. At first, the stories were accurate, but soon he realized that people wanted to read things that were exciting, so he started exaggerating them, even making some up. The wilder the stories, the more newspapers people bought and the richer he became. He was so successful that, after a while, a pretty movie star became his girlfriend."

"He had a girlfriend and a wife?"

"One day, he decided he was going to build a castle out of marble and stone and fill it with paintings and statues. No expense was spared, and when it was done, he and his girlfriend had incredible parties with movie stars and foreign dignitaries." There was a long pause, and it sounded as if Stardust was shifting position. Lorraine could see them both clearly now in the moonlight, lying side by side. If Patty was aware of her presence, she didn't show it. "Even though he was the richest and most powerful man in the world," she continued, "he was very sad."

"How come?" Stardust asked sleepily.

"I'm not really sure, but I think it was because as soon as he had one idea, he came up with another one that he liked better. And the more he accomplished, the more he regretted not doing. Nothing was enough. He hated getting old. He didn't want to die."

"Me neither," Stardust said.

"Nobody does," Patty said softly. "And by the time he did, he was a jealous, grumpy old man."

"Did the princess live happily ever after?"

"No," Patty said. "She died, too."

"That's a sad story," Stardust said.

Patty rolled over and knelt beside the bed, staring for a long time at Stardust. Lorraine set the crayon and coloring book down and shut her eyes. After a while, Patty sighed, long and mournful, then leaned over and gave the girl a kiss. "Good night," she said softly. Then she brushed past Lorraine and she disappeared.

The door to the bedroom was open. Joan had her shirt off and she was leaning over Frederick, who was lying on his back with his hands behind his head. Moonlight fell across her shoulders, which were smooth and brown. She said something that caused them both to laugh. Lorraine was in the bathroom directly across from them, the faucet on, leaning over the sink, splashing water on her face. When she turned around, Frederick called to her. "Lorrie, c'm here."

Joan crossed her arms. "Looks like you're doing well, Jim," Lorraine said, smiling.

"If you think this is what life on the run is like, you're wrong." He was smiling, too. "How long have you been stuck with these lunatics?" It was unclear whether he was talking to Joan or Lorraine.

Joan answered. "All summer. My boyfriend's in the slammer. Jack and Mikki invited me out last spring, but these people are nuts with their push-ups and jumping jacks and cleaning their weapons like there's gonna be a revolution out here any minute." Lorraine liked Joan. She was real.

"Lorrie," Frederick said, patting the bed. "Sit down." Joan stood up, her small breasts brown from sunbathing. "Talk to me," Frederick said. "Tell me everything." Joan put her shirt on and said she was going downstairs.

"I need to listen for Stardust," Lorraine said, sitting on the edge of the mattress.

"Cathy and Hash told me you were still in Philly," he said.

She felt her pulse quicken. "That fucker almost killed us!"

"He's an asshole," Frederick said quietly. A cloud passed in front of the moon, darkening the room. Six years of separation settled over them. Downstairs, a woman laughed, a tight little peal, and somebody dropped something heavy. Lorraine's fingers moved down his cheek, tracing him. She remembered nights trying to wake his passion—Walden Pond, Cambridge, Chicago. Sounds rose from inside her, muffled. "It's been a long time," she said.

"So tell me," Frederick said softly. Lorraine closed her eyes.

"Tell you what?" Everything about him was familiar—his smell, the feel of his skin, her hunger for him, which always went unsatisfied. Letting her finger enter his mouth, he surrounded it with his lips, pulling in as she pulled it out, barely accommodating, but not resisting.

"You married yet?"

She let her face drop against his neck; the rest of her weight pressed against his torso. "Nope."

He let his head fall back. She leaned in. He pulled away. It was the game they'd always played. She moved her hand down his chest to his torso, and down lower until he pushed it away. The one with no ending.

"How about Puckman?" His upper lip curled. "The little fucker."

She shook her head. After Frederick, Lorraine had a succession of lovers, who, deep down, were unaccustomed to getting what they needed; who, for whatever reasons, were invested in feeling undeserving and ashamed; and whose frailty seemed designed to elicit nurturing. Men who felt trapped or weighed down with grief, who relied on women to feel their feelings. She slid her cheek down until it rested on his belly and began humming an old song, a jazz standard, a melody that seemed to her as if it could have gone back to the beginning of time—something her father may have played on the saxophone, or her mother may have sung to her late at night.

From far away, he let his fingers rest on her neck, the side of her face, her hair. She held her face just above him, touching his belly with her breath. He was still as stone. " 'I'm a little lamb who's lost in the wood . . . I know I could . . . always be good . . . to someone who'll watch over me.' " She held that position for a long time, feeling him resist, react, and then resist again, this moment as much a part of their story as any other.

"Weren't you two together?" Frederick asked, his voice higher now, constricted. "After the kid?"

"He's never even *met* her."

"He coulda made you an honest woman."

"It's not the same thing, Frederick," Lorraine said. "What your father did to your mother. That isn't love. It's not what has to happen between a man and a woman."

When Frederick spoke again, his voice seemed to come from an entirely different part of his body. "Fuck these people," he said suddenly, motioning toward the door. "I don't know whether they lucked into her or somebody powerful is calling the plays from the sidelines." He rolled over and sat up. "Either way, it's a fucking waste to have Patty Hearst and not know what to do with her." The noise from downstairs had stopped, and the sound of crickets filled the room.

"What are you doing here, Frederick?" Lorraine said softly.

"They want me to drive her back to California." Frederick stood up and walked to the window. "So they can rob banks. It's a fucking waste."

"Frederick?"

"She should be in a safe place, and they should be issuing communiqués that'll really shake things up."

"Why did you send for me?"

"Calling for economic sanctions against big corporations—massive boycotts and picket lines, that kind of thing." From behind, Lorraine noticed his hairline, the skin behind his ears, which sagged, and the slope of his shoulders.

"Do you ever think about coming in?" Lorraine asked, touching his arm.

"Nah," he said, looking into the dark. She could see his reflection in the window. "Out here, I'm king." He closed his eyes. "They'd lock me up and throw away the key." For a moment, Lorraine thought she saw him wince, as if he was going to cry. "Lorraine." He spoke through clenched teeth. "Maybe we could do this thing together. Nobody'd be looking for a straight couple driving cross-country. We could set her up someplace and make tapes. You could get them delivered, do the shopping. . . ."

"Frederick," Lorraine said. "You chose this life as much as I chose mine. Don't ask me this. Don't ask me to give up my little girl's safety—"

"It's not just about giving up, Lorraine." He got up and walked to the window. "It's about getting something, too." He put his hands on his hips.

"Don't," she said, bracing herself.

"You don't have to feel like you ran away, Lorraine."

"Fuck you, Frederick. *You* ran away. I had a child—a living, breathing human being with moods and desires and a future that is completely dependent on me. Did you even see her, Frederick? Did you notice how beautiful she is? Would you like me to bring her along? Pull her out of school? Hide her from kids her own age?"

"What happened to you, Lorrie?" he said, shaking his head.

"Life happened to me." Lorraine had a feeling that every moment, something vital was passing between her daughter and her—a medicine that had to run its course for it to be effective—to interrupt it now for a cause or a man was unthinkable.

"How can you just forget?"

Lorraine reached for his hands. "That's the problem, Frederick. We remember things that no longer serve us. What you saw between your father and your mother. Oneonta. What the two of us had." She drew herself up on her toes and kissed him on the back of his neck. Then she slipped into the room filled with the fragrance of her little girl.

———

When she woke Sunday, the farmhouse was wrapped in a gauzy shroud. Out back, the soldiers were drilling. Lorraine gathered their clothes and Stardust's toys and stuffed them in a bag. She folded the papers with the story into a tiny square and put it in her pocket. From the front window, Lorraine confirmed that her car was parked where she'd left it—at an angle facing the house. Quietly, she woke her daughter, walked her to the bathroom, and then led her downstairs into the kitchen. Joan was scraping the bottom of a jar of instant coffee.

"How come you stay?" Lorraine asked. Joan shrugged. A saucepan with water had started to boil. "Where am I gonna go?"

"When's the last time you saw your boyfriend?"

"I don't know. A year, maybe more. I don't even know if we're on anymore." Joan offered Stardust a bowl of cereal. I see other guys now and then." And then, remembering, "What about you and Jim? Are you together?"

"A long time ago," Lorraine said. They looked out the window at Alan and Judy, who were crouching behind a tree.

Joan ran her fingers along the countertop. "Well, I hope I didn't—"

"No, no," Lorraine said quickly. "He's all yours. I mean, you can't be in two worlds at the same time, can you?" They laughed. Joan held her hair back while she sipped her coffee.

About an hour later, while Alan was in the shower and Judy and Patty were out back cleaning their weapons, Joan tiptoed into the bathroom, removed a wad of keys from Alan's jeans, separating the ring with the First Philadelphia Bank insignia on it, and tossed it to Lorraine, who'd already put Stardust and their bags in the front seat. The Duster wheezed and sputtered, and then started. Lorraine brought it around in a turn that barely missed the corner of the front porch, pulling Stardust in close and accelerating through a patch of hip-high weeds. As she did, she looked in the rearview mirror and saw Alan on the porch waving his pistol, trying to hold a bath towel around his waist. He got off at least one shot, maybe two—neither of which hit—most likely, thanks to Frederick, whose arm came down from behind, knocking the pistol to the ground.

Friday Morning, March 13, 2000

It was just after midnight by the time he made his way from Ivy's backyard to the boulevard and traffic had thinned to an occasional whooshing sound on either side of the median. The big-box retail stores, so garish when lit, seemed lifeless and unwelcoming. Each time a car passed, Chuck felt the air sucked from around his body, drawing him closer to the road. In that split second between future and past, the negative pressure of now, he imagined his legs crumbling beneath him. To do it right, he would need to judge the speed of approaching headlights and calculate his timing against the reflexes of the driver. One, two, three . . . drop, then roll. It was a simple enough maneuver. There would be a split second of noise, perhaps an explosion of pain, and then nothingness—no returning to Rahim without Ivy, no sentencing hearing Monday, and no trying to survive in a six-by-nine-foot cell with human beings who'd been reduced to animals. Unless he miscalculated.

In certain cities, especially in the Northeast, when you've exhausted your family, baffled your physician, when you have no money for a hotel and the emergency rooms are tired of seeing your sorry ass, when you're sick without symptoms, without job, without spouse, without steady routine or religion, and you want to find a safe place in the middle of the night, you go to a diner. Chuck found an empty booth and sat down. A waitress with teased hair wiped the table with a sopping rag. At the counter, a tall man wearing calf-high boots drummed his fingers on a black motorcycle helmet and stared into the refrigerator case. Chuck took out a pack of Benson & Hedges. As the waitress approached, he was reading a place mat that advertised local businesses no diner customer was likely to patronize—a scrap-metal yard, a shop that rebuilt transmissions, a physical therapist who comes to your home. The clock over the door read twelve forty. It was too late to catch a train home, and a taxi would have cost him at least twenty, maybe twenty-five bucks. An almost unrecognizable version of a Bee Gees song leaked from speakers overhead.

"There's no smoking in this section," she said, pointing to a small sign on the cash register.

"Cranberry juice," Chuck said. "And a glass with ice." Rail-thin, with blonde hair that looked like wire, she wore a plastic pin that said PENNY in red letters on white background. There was a small gap between her front teeth. She returned, sliding an ashtray across the table. Something that might have been compassion crossed her face. You learn a lot about humanity serving people all night for two bucks an hour plus tips.

Chuck put a napkin on his saucer and finished his cigarette. The guy at the counter walked bowlegged to the door. From his back pocket, Chuck took the pint bottle out. A minute later, Penny returned with a glass filled with ice. "You got kids?" Chuck asked.

She nodded.

"Reason being, I got these fish." He lit another cigarette. Penny shifted onto one foot, as if she was going to stand there awhile. Chuck took the bottle out and offered it to her. She shook her head. "It's no big deal. You feed 'em in the morning, you stare at 'em during the day if you want . . . only have to clean the tank every once in a while. . . ." Chuck's voice trailed off.

"How come you don't want 'em?" Penny asked.

"I'm going away. Got some business to take care of." She noticed the lines in Chuck's face, the splotches of red on his hands, his eyes rimmed in red, and the skin underneath, dark and wrinkled. A couple of teenagers entered, eyes glazed, zombies. Penny followed them to a booth in the back with menus. An orchestral version of "Yellow Submarine" oozed from the ceiling tiles. Chuck poured. More patrons came and went—an older couple unable to sleep, a couple of cops with radios crackling on their lapels. Chuck thought about his predicament—the sentencing hearing, his estrangement from his daughter, his brother's disappearance with the family jewels.

Put the past behind you, his father used to say. No matter what you've done, forget about it. Move on. It's pointless and painful to try to true up what happened with what should have been. In time, your feelings fade, and whatever you felt guilty about gets replaced by what you do next. At the other end of the counter, Penny ran water through the coffeemaker. Though he thought about Lorraine on occasion, Chuck had never contacted her. Her disappearance from his life after that afternoon in Brighton was so complete and his transgression against Frederick so egregious, he followed his father's advice to the letter, forgetting about his foray into the counterculture, blotting out his failed attempt at college, obliterating memories of his first love. Until he read Lorraine's obituary, he'd forgotten about the child.

"Ya ever hear of the Volcano Bomber?" Chuck asked the waitress after she'd set the teenagers up with menus and drinks. Penny was standing at the end of the counter waiting for them to decide what to order. In the kitchen, the chef had turned his own radio up. Chuck looked up at the clock over the door to the kitchen. It was just past one.

"Can't say that I have," she said, walking toward him, filling the condiment jars.

"Yeah, well, like they say, if you can remember the sixties," Chuck said, "you weren't there." He mixed himself another drink, blew out a cloud of smoke, and squinted. "We had a thing for the same girl," he said, and then winced. "He was a radical. The real thing. He knew how to make bombs." Chuck narrowed his eyes. The muscles around his jaw twitched. It occurred to him that, until then, he hadn't spoken to anybody—even Rahim—about Frederick and Lorraine. "We had a thing for the same girl," he said again. For some reason, he pictured Gutierrez standing next to a mailbox holding a brown box.

After the kids left, Penny sat on a stool across from Chuck and, for the next several hours, his back up against the window, his feet dangling over the seat, Chuck told her everything—the Fenway Park fizzle, the scene at Lorraine's the blast in Oneonta, his near bust, and the relief he felt steering the FBI to the commune in exchange for his own freedom. It felt good to unburden himself—uncommonly good—better almost than any buzz he'd put on since the accident. "I double-crossed him," he said finally. "And he's been a fugitive ever since."

"What happened to Lorraine?"

"She was killed in some kind of mountain-climbing accident." Outside, tiny flecks of snow appeared under the parking lights.

"And the kid?"

"What kid?"

"You said she was pregnant."

"It was a girl," he said wistfully.

Penny walked to the cash register and reached underneath. "Interesting," she said. "Like a soap opera." She handed him a telephone book.

Chuck already had a vague idea in what section of the city Lorraine had lived, thanks to many hours he'd spent online since starting Softpawn. Just after four A.M., he made note of the address, pulled his jacket tight around his neck, and gave Penny a peck on the cheek. By then, the cars that remained in the parking lot were covered with a thin coating of white, which made them look pristine. After a while, he flagged down a cab, which followed a delivery truck on the boulevard, past the Nabisco plant that made everyone sentimental with the smell of shortening and vanilla. By the time they got to Street Road, the snow had turned to rain.

"Here's fine," Chuck said, in front of a 7-Eleven. He shuffled out, looking clownish in the plaid jacket, sneakers, and Mariner's cap Penny had given him. Inside, Chuck took a ham sandwich from the warmer, a package of vanilla wafers, and a bottle of Arizona iced tea. At the cash register, he bought a soft pack of Benson & Hedges and the Friday *Inquirer* and handed the clerk a ten spot. The radio was playing the reggae song about redemption.

The houses on Medley Street were functional, drab, well-maintained brick twins, like those inhabited by many hardworking Philadelphians carrying too much debt to be concerned with aesthetics. Inexpensive cars were parked tight against both sides of the street. As Chuck rounded the corner, second-floor lights were switching on. Soon, people would be showering, brewing coffee, and rushing off to work, ordinary people leading ordinary lives. For the second time in twelve hours, Chuck scanned mailboxes for an address.

Number 1456 was easy to find: It had a FOR SALE sign planted on the front lawn. Next door, an overweight woman in a terry-cloth robe hobbled down the driveway to pick up her paper. A man in a maintenance uniform walked to his car. From behind an SUV, Chuck tucked his newspaper under his arm, unwrapped his sandwich, and waited. At six thirty, the light in the Nadia house switched on. A scrim of daylight appeared over a row of houses toward the east. Just before seven, Lorraine's front door opened.

Stardust Nadia was wearing a blue skirt, light stockings, and a waist-length jacket that opened as she locked the door behind her. Her hair, still wet, was much shorter than her mother's. She was carrying a small handbag. The resemblance was striking—her stride, the way her hips swayed, her hands, the little twist of her neck to shake the hair out of her face. Chuck knelt between two cars, pretending to tie his shoes. He struggled to think of something to say before she got in her car and drove off. Fortunately for him, she kept walking.

As the sun climbed over the row houses, Chuck followed Stardust precisely as he had followed Lorraine on the campus of Boston College. Down Medley to Appleberry, left at the corner, and then left again. He paused under a bridge and watched her skitter up the steps two at a time as the train arrived. The conductor called, "All aboard," just as Chuck hit the platform. With what remaining strength he had, he pulled himself into the second car as it began to move. Inside, he doubled over. It took him a long time to catch his breath.

Monday, March 16, 2000

"I get it," Stardust said, sitting up. "I'm here because you have no one else." It was dark. She could sense Chuck in the room with her, smoking.

"No." He was near the door.

"I'm here because you're scared and you can't think of anyone besides my mother to call, and now she's gone." It was the end of the third day, or perhaps the beginning of the fourth—longer than she'd ever dreamed she could spend with a man who might be her father and still not be sure. He'd talked exhaustively about the past, yet he'd revealed nothing of himself. So she was trying to provoke him.

"No," he said, louder.

"I'm here because—"

"Stop!" Chuck was thinking about the agents in his dorm room, the little particles of smoke and dust suspended in the stale air. "It's much more complicated than that."

"What could be more complicated than this?" Stardust said, opening her arms to include the two of them, the tiny windowless rooms, the not-quite-converted factory. The weekend had been more like a history lesson than a reunion.

"After the raid on Higher Purpose, I meant to square things up with your mother. To help her out if I could." He sounded petulant. He'd betrayed Frederick and Lorraine just as Artie had betrayed him. They hadn't meant for the boy in Oneonta to be holding the package when it went off, any more than he'd intended for Gutierrez to be in the tank that day. "You do certain things," he said, "then everything around you turns to shit. . . ." It wasn't a confession. It wasn't an apology. "I gave him up. I made a deal for myself. I sold him out. I gave the FBI Frederick's name. I told them where to find him." Stardust saw him wince when his cigarette glowed. "The truth is, I wanted them to get caught."

So you betrayed somebody, Stardust wanted to say. Big fucking deal. You wouldn't be the first person in the world. But she didn't. She held her tongue. A strange, familiar feeling rose up in her chest.

"All my life, I've done what's best for me," Chuck said. "Everything you see around you—everything I have—I got off somebody else's back."

To Stardust, betrayal and contrition were ancient and animal drives, like fucking or hunting, neither evil nor righteous. You do the things you do, and you get over them. Plain and simple. She imagined the sun outside rising, commuters on the early-morning trains. From the other room, she smelled bacon, something spicy, coffee maybe, with cinnamon. "Why didn't you come for me?" she asked.

For this, Chuck Puckman had no answer—just an ache in the pit of his stomach and a slightly sickening feeling that would crystallize much later in thought—after he'd had hours upon hours to reflect. The weekend had imposed a kind of wakefulness on him that was more painful than anything he'd ever experienced. It was then, only hours before his sentencing hearing, in the dim light and the moist, close air that he began to acknowledge his responsibility for separating a young woman from her father. "I'm sorry," he said, unable to swallow.

There was the sound of clothes rustling, and then the door opened. Stardust watched his silhouette appear and disappear against the light in the hallway. From the bathroom, she heard a roiling, choking sound that seemed to come from the bottom of the ocean. A toilet flushed. Stardust let her head fall back against the pillow. It flushed again. She found the lamp switch and put her clothes on. Then she made her way down the hall into the kitchen, where she poured herself coffee.

A half hour later, when Chuck emerged, his face was clean-shaven, and his hair was slicked back. For a long time, he stood beside the fish tank, tapping cylinders against the glass, watching the fish swim up, one species at a time. He was wearing dress slacks and a clean shirt, and, in the light of the tank, Stardust saw a soul-less man, not unlike the lawyers she rode the elevators with every day. In the kitchen, Rahim wiped down the surfaces with a towel, scouring the toaster oven, the refrigerator door, then the oven top; glancing nervously at the two of them. "Technology is destroying our quality of life," he said randomly, as Ovella began serving breakfast.

Stardust put a spoonful of sugar into her coffee. Chuck walked in from the living room, holding up a bright orange cylinder. "Twice a day," he said to Rahim, jiggling the plankton.

"Take the gross national product," Rahim said. "What economists would like us to believe is a numerical representation of the value of all goods and services manufactured and performed in the U.S." Rahim looked at Chuck for some kind of acknowledgment, but he was just staring into space. Ovella passed around a plate with bread and muffins. Rahim continued. "Most people cite the rise in GNP as evidence that technology and free-market capitalism are improving quality of life. But it's a fallacy. Sure, people suffer from violence, disease, and social ills, but on the whole, they say, our standard of living is higher than it's ever been. Well, that may be, but our quality of living sucks, and we can prove it. If you were to measure GNP with all the waste taken out—if you added up the cost of things people buy that get lost or that don't get used . . ."

Rahim was agitated now. His neck extended forward over his breakfast plate, and they could see little beads of sweat above his mustache. "Religious relics, bookmarks, lawn chairs, pressure cookers, electric toothbrushes, back scratchers, gift subscriptions, dictionaries, diet food, not to mention doubles of things people buy, forgetting what they already own—clothes that sit in closets, stuff that gets sold on Softpawn, everything that's returned to manufacturers, dumped in landfills, or dumped in foreign markets—along with what people buy, but later admit they didn't enjoy—bad movies, lousy books, shitty meals, impossible self-help regimens, failed medical procedures, outfits that look better in the store windows than they do on our bodies, well, shit! Our gross national product is shrinking! Our mental metabolism is so fucked-up, we don't even notice this!" He was on his feet now, pacing.

Stardust had an urge to laugh. It wasn't just the tension around Chuck's sentencing, or hearing a bone-thin ghetto guy make a speech about macroeconomics. It was the incongruity of everything.

Ovella got up and put Coltrane on. Rahim returned to his seat, dejected. The four of them poked at their food. For a long time, nobody said anything. When they finished, Rahim started clearing the dishes.

"Whatever happens . . ." Ovella started, but Chuck held up his hand.

In the bathroom, Stardust applied makeup, covering the bump on her forehead. A cloud of moisture hung in the air, and she smelled shaving cream and hair tonic. Chuck's towel was balled up on the floor, as if he'd be home soon. In the bedroom, she folded the sweatpants and sweatshirt she'd worn all weekend and then slipped into her skirt.

"Taxi's here," Ovella called from the other room.

Stardust took a last look around, which is when she noticed the picture. The frizzy-black-haired boy with the beard and the unfocused expression and the loopy grin was Chuck. Frederick, taller by almost a head, was holding a beer and looking directly into the lens, a menacing expression behind his glasses. Lorraine was almost outside the frame, staring away, ever hopeful and distracted. Stardust flipped it over and pried the little prongs back, then slipped the photo in her purse beside the flashlight, toothbrush, and panties.

In the cab, Chuck emptied a prescription bottle into his hand, leaned his head back, and swallowed. Stardust looked at him carefully. It was the first time she'd seen him in daylight since the walk from the train; his face seemed translucent and his body even smaller than before. She imagined him younger—his hair black, his lips full and moist, his nose and eyebrows less prominent, the skin around his eyes and mouth tighter and much smoother.

Stardust Nadia had been born in June 1969, the summer of love— Shelly, until a few months after Woodstock and the Joni Mitchell song from which she was renamed. Now, thirty years later, wrestling with the issue of paternity, less than an hour before Chuck would be lifted by the talons of justice and locked up, far from where he could provide answers she was unwilling and unable to let it go. This was her shot. The cab turned south on Broad Street. In the distance, they could see William Penn on top of City Hall. "Maybe your mother was right," he said finally. "Maybe we keep coming back after we die until we get it right." He wasn't ready for this either.

"I wish *my* generation had something to push up against," Stardust said softly. The western entrance of City Hall was surrounded by city workers picketing. Sunlight bounced off the scaffolding. A pigeon arched toward them and descended, landing on a trash can. The driver turned off the meter and looked in his rearview mirror. Commuters were streaming out of Suburban Station, umbrellas and newspapers tucked under their arms, an occasional gust of smoke wafting toward them from vents in the sidewalk. Chuck pulled a manila envelope from his shopping bag.

"In case something happens," he said, staring straight ahead. "This is the deed to the factory. Let Softpawn run. Rahim knows what to do. It'll pay the bills. It'll keep people working." He asked the driver if he could borrow a pen, then scribbled the name "Eddie Palmieri" on the outside of the envelope. "If you have questions, call Eddie. He knows where most of the skeletons are." Chuck slid a twenty through the Plexiglas partition and opened the side door. For the second time in four days, Stardust Nadia followed him of her own volition.

There are detailed descriptions of every car, every pier, every office building, and every military statue blown up in the late sixties and early seventies, yet there's very little about the Volcano bombings and almost nothing about Frederick Fergus Keane. You get no hits on the search engines, no archived news stories or files from the Freedom of Information Act, no pictures from his high school yearbook. In the written and recorded history of the SLA, including seven audiotapes the group made and delivered to San Francisco radio stations, there's no mention of an eighth tape or its transcription—the one Lorraine claimed to have received in the mail just after she returned from Honesdale. It's as if Fergus Keane didn't exist and the Volcano bombings never happened.

For a long time, I tried imagining his life. Did he blend into the heartland or drift back to New England? Did he settle down or continue as a provocateur? There are so few data points—born in Worcester, Massachusetts, in 1943, attended MIT in 1966 and perhaps early 1967, disappeared the morning of November 12, 1968. I spent several months at the main branch of the Philadelphia Public Library researching the sixties. I visited thrift stores, collecting record albums, vintage clothing, and knickknacks from that era. In the dining room of my mother's cottage, I posted a ten-foot section of blank newsprint, to which I attached photographs and posters, bumper stickers, and copies of newspaper headlines in the approximate order in which they had occurred. I went to New York City. In Columbia's archives, I found articles, interviews, and books about the SLA. I listened to the recorded voices of Don DeFreeze, aka Cinque M'Tume, of Bill and Emily Harris, Alan and Judy from Honesdale, Patty and the others—long, tedious declarations of class war, demanding the redistribution of wealth and the dissolution of white society—comically overwrought by today's standards. With the help of Patty's agent, I got copies of her numerous television appearances, which I watched several times to try to determine my friend's state of mind when she was released.

This much I do know: Frederick's manifesto differs markedly from anything attributed to the SLA. It is not, like so much of the sixties rhetoric, naïve or dated. There's no passing the microphone around. No amplified outrage. No evidence of groupthink. It's one man's voice, and the speaker is cynical, self-aware, with faint traces of what could be described as a working-class New England accent. And although it refers specifically to the SLA, it takes a much broader view of society than any of the other missives from that time. A professor from Berkeley I talked to says it is as cogent and authentic an attempt to square up Marxism and modern times as he's heard, its title alone worthy of a spirited debate about free speech and the impact of media ownership in the hands of giant corporate conglomerates. And yet if there is such a thing as Frederick's manifesto, there is no evidence of it either in the public record or in government files I was able to get released under the Freedom of Information Act. There is nothing but the typed letter Lorraine received from Salt Lake City, Utah, postmarked August 1975, and a beat-up cassette tape I found in the box she gave me.

CAPITOCRACY

You'd have to be an idiot not to notice how the companies that sponsor radio and television shows influence content. You think the news is objective? You think there's such a thing as free speech? You think we have freedom of the press? Think again. People in this country have been lulled into a voting and consuming stupor.

Our economic system needs consumers to consume. In the twenties, William Randolph Hearst transformed journalism into hucksterism. The media's the army the ruling classes use to exert control over society.

Democracy's been trumped by capitalism. Choked out like a weed. Company owners and politicians use the media to bully and brainwash people into buying products and voting for policies that keep the system going.

Last year, using a made-up revolutionary group called the Symbionese Liberation Army, the government annihilated two movements that were threats to American society—radicalism and black militancy.

Using techniques they learned during the Korean War, the CIA got a black ex-con to brainwash and coerce a group of middle-class white kids into wreaking havoc. Over a twelve-month period, these idiots murdered a black superintendent of schools, kidnapped media heiress Patty Hearst, and robbed banks, all in the name of the radical left.

Public opinion is swinging to the right. The government got what it wanted, and old man Hearst got what he deserved!

For a while, I was obsessed. I hired a lab to do electron dispersion spectroscopy, which confirmed it to be standard issue paper, prepared on a Smith Corona portable electric, exactly the kind manufactured from the mid-sixties to the late seventies. I examined the rhetoric, studied the syntax, broke down the sentences, hoping to find a writing sample from Frederick's high school days. I even engaged a company that specialized in forensic audio enhancement, hoping to identify background sounds and to pinpoint the accent of the speaker on the tape.

But the more time I spent thinking about it, the less interested I became in the actual transmission and the more intrigued I was by the content. The concept of capitocracy, Frederick's term for the fusion of our economic system with our form of government, and his manifesto, seem powerfully prescient. "Who owns the means of bewilderment," my professor friend says, "owns our country."

As to whether or not the government released a small but virulent dose of radicalism to inoculate the country from an all-out revolution seems like conspiracy theory that may never be proved or disproved. Still, it's hard to ignore what Frederick asserted—that the fall of the Symbionese Liberation Army coincided with the disintegration of the black militancy and youth movements of the sixties.

In August 1975, a year after Honesdale, Patty Hearst was arrested with Wendy Yoshimura, the Asian girl Lorraine called Joan. The trial was a circus and Patty's defense abysmal. Despite being kidnapped and tortured, Patty was convicted of bank robbery and sentenced to seven years in federal prison. This is what happens, the local Hearst paper editorialized, when children rise up against their parents, when blacks take up arms against whites, and when liberalism prevails over conservative values.

Old news stories drop like meat through a barbecue grill. Chuck Puckman's sentencing drew no reporters, no sketch artists, and nobody taking pictures of the blonde by his side. Though she didn't know for sure at the time, Stardust Nadia suspected, and therefore testified, that she was indeed Chuck Puckman's daughter, who, until that weekend, had never met her father. Owing to the tragic and recent loss of Stardust's mother, Wilkie Crackford argued Chuck's sentence should be de minimis.

The last time I saw Lorraine was a week before her trip. She still had some things she needed to buy, so we met near an outfitter in Suburban Square. Over corn soup and quesadillas, she told me she was eager to test herself against the elements, and I believed her. There was nothing morbid or ominous about it—no hint that she might not return—other than that what we were working on would be the basis of her memoir. If anything, there was a kind of settledness or resolve that she may not have possessed the first few times we met.

I remember a particular moment with Lorraine. It was a Sunday afternoon—my favorite time of the week—when everybody is momentarily aligned in the absence of ambition. Lorraine had been talking for almost an hour: about Frederick's frame of mind after the Fenway hack, the disastrous turnout at the Democratic National Convention, how their VW kept breaking down on the way back from Chicago, and how the guy driving it kept hitting on her while Frederick fooled around under the hood. She remembered getting back to Cambridge, Frederick hell-bent on making his mark on the movement. He'd decided on a target in upstate New York. When Frederick insisted on using Chuck to gather the chemicals, Lorraine objected. She said she had a really bad feeling.

"Betrayal is a form of completion," she told me, describing the night of the raid on the Higher Purpose Commune. "Death within life is a central theme of the Tarot. When you draw certain cards, you have the opportunity—the obligation actually—to re-create yourself. As long as you do, you keep on living. When you stop and wind up just skating along, you lose your personal power and you might as well be dead."

Stardust never went back to the reception desk at Drinker & Sledge. After Chuck was sentenced, she sold the house on Medley Street, collected Lorraine's pension, and moved to a furnished apartment in the art museum area. Within a few weeks, she got back in touch with Rahim and Ovella, and, that spring, the three of them refurbished the little apartment above the factory. In May, while sifting through receipts, mail, and old phone messages, she came across my name and remembered the inscription I'd written on the inside cover of What Mattered Most. *We met on a weekday morning in the back of the Reading Terminal Market. In her khaki skirt, vintage suede jacket, and a baseball cap, she looked like a distracted, impatient, slightly edgier version of her mother. At that time, I really didn't know what, if anything, I was going to do with what Lorraine had told me.*

As soon as we sat down she told me. "My mother passed away over Christmas." She put my book on the table and folded her hands. "I want to know everything." Though she was matter-of-fact about it,

I could see how much she hurt. I told her about our meeting at Borders and Lorraine's interest in Patty Hearst, about whom Stardust knew very little. I outlined the story of the Volcano Bomber and tossed about some conspiracy theories and then excused myself to pick up my niece after school.

Until then, I'd been sitting around the cottage in Merion wondering what to do next. Until then, I'd considered Lorraine a quirky, colorful character, but my interest in her had been casual. I'd felt more disappointed than anything—discouraged that I'd wasted six months of my life on a project that would go nowhere. But late that night, looking through the boxes, I pictured Stardust, walking around the house by herself, and I felt sad thinking that Lorraine's life was like so many other peoples' from the sixties—dramatic, idealistic, passionate, and romantic even, but ultimately incomplete—no big revelations, no payoff, no catharsis, no intimation of meaning or symmetry that one hopes to have at the end.

Over the next few months, I invited Stardust out to visit as often as she wanted. She listened to her mother's voice on the tapes. She pored over photographs and mementos that Lorraine left me and tried to match them with events she researched about the sixties, about radicalism, about protests against the war in Vietnam, about the race riots, and about Boston in the late 1960s. She became fascinated by Patty Hearst and the SLA, studying psychological materials available on the Stockholm syndrome. Together, we visited a professor at Penn who specialized in kidnappings and hostage psychology, and Stardust argued, quite eloquently I thought, that everyone, to some extent, was brainwashed by their culture. Gradually, she opened up, and, about a month after we met, she told me Chuck's version of the events in 1968 and what became of his life after fleeing Boston, which is when it occurred to me that the repercussions of the Volcano bombings—indeed, the real legacy of the radical movement—weren't really being felt until now. In a general way, the same things that happened to Chuck Puckman, Lorraine Nadia, and Frederick Keane happened to thousands of other young people who came of age during those years. My interest became an obsession, so when Stardust invited me to meet Rahim and Ovella and to see what they were doing at the factory, I accepted.

I would like to believe that parents are an irreducible fraction and that, underneath their rage, all children hold a reservoir of forgiveness. Few of us are fortunate enough to hear a parent explain what ignited them and made them feel alive. Most of us are left to puzzle out the meaning of our parents' and our own lives from their lifestyles, the things they say, or, in rare cases, the things they accomplish. Stardust Nadia looked long and hard at the photograph she took from Chuck's room and made several decisions.

She let Rahim continue to run Softpawn, which produced a steady revenue stream and employed several of the neighbors and former employees. Together with Ovella, who'd long felt that what the neighborhood really needed was a day care center, she converted the little office of Puckman Security into a playroom, installing a rubberized floor and a big-screen television with a VCR—a place where young women could leave their small children while they worked. Stardust believed that workers who'd formerly operated punch presses and assembled security guards needed new job skills in order to be employable in the future, and, with Rahim's help, she refashioned the area of the factory where Gutierrez succumbed to trichloroethylene fumes to a job-retraining lab. While Chuck served his sentence, the old Puckman factory became busy again—with Rahim entering data to Softpawn; infants and toddlers watching videos and napping; and a half dozen men in their forties and fifties learning to repair copiers and computers, read blueprints, and program computer numeric-controlled equipment.

I remember vividly the moment I decided to tell this story. It was early fall, a delightful time in Philadelphia. We were sitting in a used bookstore in the Italian Market, a few blocks from where the Puckman boys grew up. Stardust had put on some weight and had let her natural hair color grow in. The lines in her face had softened, and there was a receptiveness there that I construed as good humor. She was wearing jeans and a beige cashmere sweater. She looked well rested.

"My mother didn't seek you out for nothing," Stardust told me over coffee. "She wanted you to write this."

———

Eddie Palmieri wouldn't talk, but Wilkie Crackford was a font of information. Lawyers, like writers, are parasites. The best ones are profoundly uninteresting, sucking whatever life experience they can from their clients. Crackford gave me most of the details about the EPA investigation and the charges facing the Puckmans, including many that should probably have remained confidential. In Wilkie Crackford's opinion, Chuck's sentence—thirty months—was a masterpiece of legal strategy.

I found John Russell completely by accident. A writer friend of mine was doing a piece about retired detectives who solved cold cases using psychological profiling and technology. The two of us were having beers with a forensic sculptor who was bragging that the FBI commissioned him to reconstruct victims of crimes from faded photographs and decomposed skulls. As my friend and I were leaving his studio—a gallery of body parts and grisly photographs—I noticed two busts, side by side, one of which looked remarkably like Frederick Keane. The sculptor put me in touch with his FBI contact, Eric Dodson, who, after clearing me with the FBI media department, told me to call retired Special Agent John Russell.

Russell had been relieved of duty for about six months by then, and he was so sick, our chats didn't last very long. He told me what he'd told Dodson—how he'd identified and then tracked Keane to the Midwest before losing him, but he professed no awareness of Frederick's involvement with the SLA or Patty Hearst, the manifesto, or the safe house in Honesdale in the summer of 1974. It could have been his rapidly deteriorating health, or an old G-man being tight-lipped, but Russell didn't seem the least bit curious about Chuck Puckman, even after I told him what I'd learned from Stardust. When I mentioned Chuck's current predicament and his brother Arthur's disappearance, Russell referred me to a retired IRS agent who specialized in international money laundering, tracking U.S. Savings Bonds and Treasuries redeemed in foreign banking centers. A few days before Special Agent John Russell passed away, his friend faxed me a list of suspicious transactions they were looking into, including a flurry of securities that were presented for redemption at a tiny little bank in the town of San Ignacio, Belize.

In early September, I rode one of those yellow school buses out the Western Highway from Belize City to San Ignacio, a dusty little town of crooked streets jammed with barefoot vendors, locals, and ecotourists. I said I was a reporter for Outside Magazine *doing a story on jungle adventures. It took the owner of the Internet café a couple days to find me a guide who, for a hundred dollars U.S., agreed to show me around. As we rode back up the Mopan River at the end of a long day of sightseeing, I asked if he knew anything about an American who showed up in Belize with a lot of cash. His face lit up. "Everybody knows about Mr. Alex," he said.*

When they emerged from the jungle, Carlos spent fifteen thousand dollars in about ten days, paying off his debts, selling the van and buying himself a 1975 Mercury Cougar with leopard-skin seat covers. He put deposits on three adjacent lots—one for his mother, one for his young wife, and one for his girlfriend—and bought a few suits, a pair of field glasses, and a new generator, but it turned out to be a lot harder to cash securities in Belize than he'd expected.

"The brothers were very happy when Mr. Jim first showed up," the guide said, paddling. "Mr. Jim told them they'd do much better at the banks in Guatemala. Two days later, they found Carlos in Tikal, hanging upside down, his belly slit. Manny stuck around for a few weeks and then disappeared. He had the shits, waiting for the fat man's brother. Nobody's seen Mr. Jim or any of the money since."

I visited Chuck a dozen or so times over the next twenty-four months in a minimum-security prison in rural western Pennsylvania, about eight hours' drive from Merion. Each time I went, I stayed at a Motel 6, busying myself the night before, reading about white-collar crime, preparing questions, and transcribing notes. The facility was a cluster of sandstone and stucco buildings, a cross between an industrial park and a summer camp, that looked as if it had been dropped into a patch between rolling hills. There were no barbed-wire fences, nothing to keep the inmates from wandering off. After the requisite background checks, pat downs, and bureaucratic delays, I was led inside what looked like one of those old-fashioned sanitariums, the kind that existed in the United States before President Reagan decided to let crazy people fend for themselves on the streets.

Chuck and I met on Saturdays in a huge common area among the families of other men who'd either flown to Pittsburgh or driven for a long time to see their husbands, sons, or daddies—accountants, embezzlers, stockbrokers, and low-level drug dealers—dressed in khakis or jeans, T-shirts, and sneakers. We sat in fake living rooms filled with what looked like rented furniture. The prisoners were educated and cagey, full of contrition and hope—the kind of people you'd see at a country club—except they were dressed down and their skin was loose from having lost weight.

In a federal prison camp, inmates have certain privileges unavailable to those in the dog-eat-dog world. One of them is the ability to cultivate friendships with other men. Another is time to reflect. Chuck had a buzz cut and a white beard he kept trim, and he looked fit and relaxed. When I told him what Lorraine had said about Frederick's impotence, he was stunned. Until then, he'd believed that Stardust's testimony on his behalf was an act of kindness—not quite perjury, but not substantiated, either. He'd never really adjusted to fatherhood the first time, so having another daughter from whom he was estranged, at least initially, was too heavy a burden for him to bear. It's hard to know what goes through a man's mind when he learns something like this. As for inviting Stardust to visit, he shook his head and said, "Not yet."

His roommate was a seventy-year-old confidence man, in for the third time. Jerry Cosy, a wiry guy with a big nose and a two-hundred-and-fifty-watt smile, had a habit of making aggressive predictions about the businesses he brokered, which induced buyers and sellers to make deals that invariably fell apart. The problem, according to Jerry, was that in his most recent transaction, instead of trying to rectify matters, the buyer brought the matter to the attention of the SEC, who'd investigated Cosy and his partners and found them guilty of fraud. When *he got out this time, Jerry Cosy was preparing to enter a completely new business based on a concept he called aggregation.*

"Separately, things have no meaning," he told Chuck late at night. "Events appear random. We feel isolated. We take things for granted. But when you aggregate them, you see their impact in a new way. Things you wouldn't normally associate with one another appear linked—climate and regime changes, fundamentalism and sexual deviance, depression and materialism."

"As you get older, you need a project without an ending. When this thing is over, when you get out, give me a call. You have a factory and some cheap, dependable labor. With a few computers, we can set up an operation—clipping stories from the news, entering data, and identifying trends. We could publish our findings. Send out one of those high-priced newsletters. Make a fortune."

Unlike people who enter prison from the bottom rungs of society—beaten and scared, penniless and addicted, men who read the Koran and accept Allah in a sudden gesture of hope—the changes that occurred in Chuck were slow. The main reason was that, compared to what he'd feared would happen to him, the experience wasn't too bad. He had a place to sleep, he got three squares, and he was never in any personal danger. Sure, somebody told him when to get up, when to eat, when to exercise, and when it was lights out, which might have been a constant reminder of his transgressions, but everyone around him had fucked up. Humiliation was optional.

By early fall, Chuck's thinking, influenced by Jerry Cosy's ideas about aggregation, had advanced to a philosophical muddle, the kind a couple of sensitive teenagers might find themselves grappling with before collapsing with giddiness or exhaustion. It was as if introspectiveness, useless to his father's generation, had suddenly overcome Chuck Puckman, thirty-five years after it had blossomed in his peers.

By our third meeting, Chuck was clear of his dependence on alcohol and various medications and was applying a familiar logic to his predicament. He told me his life to date had been meaningless—at best, an instinctual shuffle—rather like his tropical fish swimming to the surface for food before returning to the depths of their tank to absently poke about for any little scraps that had fallen to the bottom. He knew that times when something should have stirred inside him, he felt nothing, but that understanding, in and of itself, was not the same as the experience of emotion. He had developed various theories for this. One in particular I remember him telling me was that everything lives side by side within us—irritability and calm, virtue and vanity, good and evil, piousness and lust, love and hatred—and that one of the costs of rationality is that one urge cancels another.

"The problem," he said, "is that we want to love ourselves, yet we're fundamentally unlovable, so we convert our disappointment into aggression toward other people, usually the ones we love." At the time, I wondered whether this was a revelation—the identification of the cause for our primordial ambivalence—or some kind of rationale for what Artie had done, and for how far Chuck had fallen. Near the end of his sentence, Chuck had accepted aggregation as if it was a kind of belief system, and he began applying it in a more personal way.

The last time I saw him, he told me he believed if he could roll up the events of his life—the things he'd said and done; the way he lived and loved, or didn't love—they would form some pattern, or significance, he just didn't know what. This realization appeared as a light someone had switched on inside his head, visible as a glow behind his gray eyes. It manifested itself in plans he made with Jerry Cosy, in conversations he had with Rahim and me, and in letters he began writing to Stardust, which chronicled his deeds and misdeeds in different-colored ink—a map of the inner workings of his mind— connecting Gutierrez with the boy in Oneonta, the civil rights movement with the EPA and OSHA, and his brother, Arthur, with Frederick. It was as though, in the solitude of his cell, Chuck embraced aggregation as a metric for spirituality, a blend of commerce and karma, carefully calculated to balance like an equation, more like a diet than a religion, except for the relief it appeared to provide him as he served his time. I stopped visiting him when I had enough to tell this story and because of my hesitancy to tell him what I am about to reveal.

In January 1999, as Ramon Gutierrez was being wheeled from the Puckman factory, a dozen young radicals sat on a disguised fishing trawler listening to environmental news releases and plotting upcoming actions. Over the years, to an ever-dwindling audience, members of the ecoterrorist revolutionary splinter group Greenspace pierced the hulls of tuna fishing boats, sabotaged corporations they believed polluted the oceans and rivers by appropriating the airwaves, destroying and subverting press releases, maligning government agencies, and jamming cultural and political messages using a combination of computer hacking, art, mischief, and guerrilla semiotics. When the Gutierrez–Puckman Security story broke, Fergus Keane, commander emeritus, decided to enter the United States and travel to Philadelphia to look for his old nemesis.

Late Sunday night, Frederick wandered into one of a half-dozen bars in Kensington where Coleman Porter was celebrating his good fortune by playing Artie's videotaped confession. It was Frederick Keane who showed up in Regina Puckman's house the night Artie disappeared, Frederick Keane who inspired and arranged Artie's escape, and Frederick Keane, aka Mr. Jim, who left Guatemala with the Puckman fortune.

It's anybody's guess where he is now. Maybe, for the first time in almost thirty-five years, he listens for waves lapping against his houseboat instead of jolting awake at the sound of car doors, police sirens, or dogs barking. Perhaps he visits his fortune the way Artie did rather than sleeping with a pistol under his pillow. I doubt he worries about setting up his perimeter, establishing aliases and elaborate warning systems, or keeping hunters like Eric Dodson at bay. Frederick's bank might be a cave in the jungle, a safe deposit box in Luxembourg, or a computer terminal in an Internet café somewhere. Where he is now, it could be early morning or the middle of the night. I imagine him swimming, water skiing, spear fishing, playing pool, napping, riding a four-wheeler, unhooking the nylon cable connecting the trap to the boat and winding it in a circular motion, elbow to hand, elbow to hand, warm seawater splashing over the polished rail.

Acknowledgments

I would like to thank Bob Miller and Molly Russakoff for their careful reading and honest input over the course of several drafts; Deb Abrahamson and Sarah Silver for their meticulous edits; Liam Rector and the staff and faculty at the Bennington Writing Seminars for lighting the footpath; Dan Halpern, Amanda Urban, Adam Shapiro, Fondue Mike Siegel, Sabra Hammond, Dan Booth-Cohen, Frank Doyle, Willie Reagan, Richard Scher, Ted Simon, Phil Tankle, and Seth Weber for their help; my parents, Janet and Bob, and my children, Scott, Sarah, Bec, and Jenna, for their love and support; and especially my wife, Anne Wainer, for inhabiting this imaginary world with me.